C000175722

WATER'S EDGE

T J SHEPHERD

ORCHARD
PUBLISHING

Copyright © 2019 by T J Shepherd

All rights reserved.

No part of this book may be reproduced in any form or by any electronic
or mechanical means, including information storage and retrieval systems,
without written permission from the author, except for the use of brief
quotations in a book review.

The rights of T J Shepherd to be identified as the author of this work have
been asserted in accordance with the Copyright, Designs and Patents Act
1988.

This is a work of fiction. All characters in this publication are fictitious and
any resemblance to real persons, living or dead, is purely coincidental.

A CIP catalogue record for this book is available from the British Library.

ISBN 978-1-7392761–0-2 (Pb)

ISBN 978-1-7392761-1-9 (e-book)

Website www.orchardpublishingconsultancy.com

Email info@orchardpublishingconsultancy.com

❀ Created with Vellum

For Anne Fine who read the draft and provided invaluable help,
advice and encouragement

CONTENTS

1

THE FIRST DAY - PART ONE

David held the ferry rail. Thin ridges of muscle stood out on his forearm as he gripped the white painted metal. His stomach tensed with anticipation and foreboding. Instinctively, his other hand clutched at the bag that held the map connecting him with his first visit thirty years earlier. He had made the decision to return in a quest to salvage whatever remained from the wreck of his life, to recover from the depths those few valuables that still survived. It was a desperate attempt but there seemed to be little else that he could do. He had exhausted more conventional methods.

Vibration pulsated through him from the rail and deck, adding to the feeling of nervous excitement. The clumsy vessel carried him forward over the flat waters of the Venetian lagoon. Gulls wheeled, welcoming, overhead, their resonant cries piping his arrival. Sunlight fragmented and flew from the gleaming sheet of broken mirrors that floated on the dark water. Its silver fire forced him to narrow his eyes, the sky and the water merged, and he floated through

a strange blue blinding space. In this blue haze the contentment of a child spread through his body.

He turned his eyes across into the darkness between the
decks. As they adjusted, he was able to observe some of the
other passengers. An impeccably dressed Italian family sat
immediately in front of him. He looked down at the
daughter who wore coiled metal snakes hanging from her
ears, their ruby eyes glowing darkly in the sun, bodies
springing with every movement of her head. A group of
middle-aged American women in aggressive trousers stood
looking out over the opposite rail with video cameras held
ready. Next to them, two German couples, apparently
looking around for their children to join them as they
looked out across the water for a first glimpse of Venice.

To his right was an English family. The girl, about nine,
and the boy, a little younger, were vying for occupation of
the larger part of the seat, pushing at each other whilst
looking the other way, elbows jabbing into ribs. Their father
was trying to read to them from a guide book, ignoring, or
oblivious of, the fact that neither of them was listening. The
mother rummaged desperately in a large bag of fizzy drinks
and crisps, passing them upwards without looking at which
hand was taking them.

Suddenly the girl stood up, forgetting the struggle for
territory, and pointed past David along the side of the boat.

'Look! Look at that bird. It's got the bread look; it took it!'
She ran to the rail.

'I want some Mummy; I want to do it!'

David saw what had caught her attention. A young boy
with a brown paper bag was holding pieces of bread out
through the rails. Everyone watched as gulls swooped with
pinpoint accuracy to take it. Sometimes a bird would drop

the bread, and another would dive and recover it in mid-air. David watched transfixed by the animated patterns of their flight. Suddenly a large gull swerved from its course caught by a wind shift and its wing almost brushed his face as it wheeled away with its trophy. He recoiled, gripped by an involuntary panic.

Winged things beat their way out from the cage of suppressed memory. He held his breath to keep them down, rob them of the air to fly. He strained in the darkness to close the walls of his mind and shut off their escape. They must not get free. A violent crack sounded somewhere within. The wings pierced through him and he wanted to scream but quickly covered his face with his hands and in the darkness the wings broke free in his head.

The training seminar forced itself through into his consciousness. He had been standing in front of two hundred delegates. The projectors, computer terminals, music for the launch of the new product had been prepared. All he had to do was stand and deliver the training lecture whilst the audio-visuals moved slickly from one effect and demonstration to another. It should have been easy; it was a part of the job that he usually enjoyed, the closest he came to using his acting skills.

He brought the first slide up on the screen.

'THE MARKET - WHERE ARE WE NOW?'

He was aware that his voice had begun to talk but he felt strangely detached, listening to himself. Slides changed.

'THE WAY FORWARD - DESIGN FOR THE FUTURE'

He heard himself speaking about sectors, the next wave, future proofed solutions; it was no longer under his control but that of the automaton delivering the presentation. Panic made him begin to struggle back, to re-occupy the body that stood there.

As bodily sensations returned, he felt sweat running cold over his skin; however hard he breathed he still seemed short of oxygen. Suffocation lead to panic and his mind raced so he could not hold it on the subject of the talk. Voices carried on frantic conversations in his head and he tried to drive them out. They distorted and pulsated. He told them to go, at first to himself but they laughed and jeered. His mouth was giving the talk, but the voices would not go.

Then he began speaking to them quietly, just between sentences when he thought the audience wouldn't notice but it made no difference; they ignored him. He had to make them go. They would not listen, so he shouted, and they came at him with wings and claws; he had to defend himself. He beat them off with his hands; he tried to grasp them and wrench them from his brain, dashing them down before him and trying to grind them into submission. A searing, slicing sensation of tearing claws and the stabbing of beaks ripped at his flailing hands. The desk in front of him grew red. The voices rolled forward triumphantly, echoing and surging, a great wave of vibrating sound reverberating in the dark space of his skull.

The images and noise were now like the recollections of a dream. He had to piece together what happened next from talking to other people who had witnessed it. There had been shock, embarrassment and even tears. He was led from the stand by Rachel his P.A. who, though resourceful as ever, had been quite traumatised by the event. A bewildered first-aider was called up from the floor. David's hands were dripping with blood where he had smashed a water glass, crushing it into the desk with his bare hands as he tried to destroy the winged invaders.

A coffee break had been declared early. The PowerPoint presentation was hurried through by an area-manager. No-one paid it much attention and there were noticeable empty chairs. In the meantime, he waited in a seminar room with Rachel and a cup of tea, whilst an ambulance was called. The paramedics checked his wrists and hands for glass and dressed the wounds.

'You'll be fine. We just need to get a doctor to look at this and see if you need to be stitched up.'

They continued talking reassuringly and took him to hospital where a doctor sedated him.

He spent two nights in hospital where he was given a thorough medical check-up and visited by a psychiatrist. It was stress, overwork and various un-named, unresolved personality problems or disorders. He was given an appointment, a packet of anti-depressants and sent home. An appointment would be made to discuss therapy or some kind of counselling but now he needed rest. His hands hurt and the dressings were a nuisance, but they healed quickly. If only the mind were so resilient.

The company had put on a show of being understanding and told him to take a break, an extended holiday perhaps, but he was under no illusion what a breakdown meant in a sales career. It was like being injured in the police. He would be offered something undemanding, a desk job, but really he was finished. His wife, Thelma, had been distant but not hostile as if she recognised that perhaps, in his different world, something was happening that she did not understand.

He had tried to explain that he felt he had buried his

talent, 'that one Talent which is death to hide' and was doomed to be cast into outer darkness leaving no trace of what should have been his destiny. On rare occasions, when silence became too oppressive, he spoke nervously of the pointlessness of his work and the ultimate irrelevance of the all- important sales figures, the feeling that his life was sliding by without any trace while he commuted to the city. Thelma dismissed it all as middle-aged neurosis, male menopause, unrealistic expectations and a generally unbalanced view of life.

It was this dismissal of anything beyond the material and the practical that caused their worst disagreements, that and the lack of anything even approaching a satisfactory physical and emotional relationship. She had been slim when they married but now she was thin as if her body as well as her feelings had dried up. He recalled vividly Thelma screaming at him in a particularly bitter row.

'It's your bloody mother's fault, it's all her fault, you're not special she just made you feel that way. She treated you as if you're special and now you think you're some kind of frustrated genius; well don't expect me to do the same! You wouldn't be like this if she hadn't given you this ridiculous sense of self-importance; you'd be happy not on the verge of a breakdown. Why can't you see it? Why can't you enjoy what you've got?'

'Well at least she was human.' he had shouted back. 'She was warm and had feelings, she knew what love was, she didn't have eyes like ice. Even her memory after twenty years is warmer than anything about you. And so what if she made me feel special, that's what a mother is supposed to do but of course you wouldn't know about that!'

As soon as he had said it, he regretted it. It wasn't fair. At the time of their marriage he had wanted someone who would not lean on him, someone who would be independent and help him to achieve a comfortable level of material prosperity. They worked well together, as a team, got things done. It was an enjoyable companionship without the threatened loss of identity that had accompanied previous intense emotional relationships and it gave him a home again. She did not want children which at the time seemed ideal. He could not complain that he had not got what he wanted, just that he had not seen clearly enough through what he wanted to what he needed.

As his fury subsided, he admitted to himself that her argument sounded reasonable, very logical. He had even tried to accept the idea but could not let go of his sense of destiny and the feeling that if only he could bring himself back to that destiny all would be well. He was only failing because he was shut off from the inner powers of his true self.

He had thought about divorce many times and knew that she had too. It would be easy with no children to consider but when he contemplated it, he saw a dark gulf, a tearing away of all that he now recognised as home, family and security. His mother had gone, taken into the darkness by cancer when he was twenty-one, and he could not face tearing up a second home.

Now, even his material success had collapsed, brought down by the fatally weakened struts of mental and emotional stamina that had supported the towering folly for so long. Two months of drugs and rest had not brought him to the point where he could even begin to contemplate a return to the high-pressure sales environment.

The anticipated appointment arrived in the post,

inviting him to visit a consultant psychiatrist with the aim of 'identifying the most appropriate way forward'. He phoned to confirm it. The initial exploratory session would be with Dr Susan Gray.

Two weeks later he drove into the car park of an anonymous brick building, late Victorian on the outside and Health Service plastic inside. The mind was not covered by health insurance. He went to the reception desk, enclosed like a post office, and said his name. The woman behind the screen looked down and crossed his name from a list.

'Just wait over there, please.'

He walked to the arrangement of chairs and looked over the dog-eared magazines on the table. There was nothing even remotely readable, not even a car magazine.

He waited, growing anxious about who might come in through the doors. He did not want to be seen there, exposing an inability to cope with the basics of life. It could not be the inconsequential kind of banter over minor ailments that one might have in the G.P.'s waiting room. One's sanity or otherwise was hardly a suitable topic of casual conversation.

He wished he had not left additional time to find the place. He checked his watch again. Two minutes since the last time, eight minutes left. He began reading the posters on the wall explaining the normality of stress and depression, the statistics that showed almost everyone was likely to suffer from it at some time or other. He tried to find this comforting.

Suddenly the doors to the waiting room from the consulting rooms, and whatever else lurked in the building, were flung violently open and a man in his thirties, muttering and casting his eyes wildly around appeared in the middle of the waiting room. David expected alarms to sound and the doors to lock automatically but nothing happened. The man fought through the empty space of the room, as though struggling to overcome whatever demons opposed and threatened him. He walked towards the main door as though striding through water. Again, nothing happened, no-one appeared with strait-jacket or hypodermic. He vanished into the car park. David wondered whether he should inform someone, the receptionist seeming not to have noticed, but after a short while beyond the door, in the sunlight, the haunted warrior against demons returned, victorious by his newly calm demeanour. He walked quietly to the double swing doors, pressed the button that released the lock and disappeared back into the shadowed space from whence he came.

David felt his own existence in such a place to be a fraud. He was not mad, just found the pressures of life as a sales director too much. He was wasting a psychiatrist's time that should be spent on the truly demented, those who lived in a perpetual world of dark unreality. He was about to get up, mumble apologies and leave when the doors opened again and a slightly built, brisk, short haired but not unattractive woman in her thirties appeared. She smiled reassuringly.

'David Green?'

'Ah, yes.'

'Susan Gray. Just come through, would you.'

The consulting room had soft, comfortable furniture and she gestured to him to sit. She sat to one side and in front of him, roughly in the position he had taught sales reps to sit by a customer's desk. Not opposing, not too familiar. She studied the notes from his G.P. and then took out a clip board and attached a form to it.

'Right, we'll just go through some background. Is that O.K.?'

David found himself feeling ever more sane, and ever more a fraud.

She began with facts: name, address, that kind of thing and then moved on to his childhood.

'Were you a close family?'

'Well, yes, I suppose so, that is, I was close to my mother.'

'And now?'

'She died when I was twenty-one.'

She looked up as if inviting him to say more. He struggled to bring his mind into some kind of life but by the time he was on the verge of speaking she said,

'And your father?'

'We, well we got on well until the usual teenage rows and then, I suppose it never really recovered. I mean we got on O.K. but there was a distance despite all the things we had in common.'

She looked up, straight into his eyes.

He felt himself getting tense, anxious. He couldn't sum up the complexity of such relationships in the space on a form. She should know that.

'Music mainly, he was a musician.'

She looked down again and wrote.

'And you're married?'

'Yes.'

Again, she looked up. She seemed to have expected more. He wasn't being intentionally difficult, but his mind felt as though it had set like concrete.

'How long have you been married for?'

'Eighteen years.'

This time he tried hard to say more but nothing came.

What could he say after all? Eighteen years of going to work, professional advancement, setting and achieving targets and meeting deadlines. Eighteen years of weekends attending to the trivial demands of house and garden, occasionally sitting back in the garden with a glass of wine, watching the sun glint from the pond and feeling content and happy, before asking himself why this was not enough. They had good holidays and respected each other's different interests so long as they did not grow too insistent or threaten the stability of everyday life. What demonic urge was it that drove him, amongst all this material comfort and domestic stability, to such a state of collapse that lead to his being here, failing to answer the simplest of questions?

'Children?'

The type of simple, straight forward questions that could be worked out from a CV or an application form. Yet why did they make him so uncomfortable? Either it was because he suspected they were being used to slide past his defences or because they were the very areas of his life that avoided thinking about.

'No.'

'How do you feel about that?'

'It was a sensible decision at the time. Now I'm not so sure.'

'And your wife, how does she feel?'

'I... I think... I don't really... I mean, being honest, we don't actually talk about it but I think she is happy as it is. With her career I mean.'

Had Dr Susan Gray been peeling back the layered veils of his deepest dreams and complexes he could not have felt more uncomfortable, or more exposed. The questions continued until the spaces on the form were used up and she said, 'Is there anything else you would like to ask?'

This was the question he expected candidates to prepare for at a job interview, the key one that made the difference. Answer 'No' or 'How many days holiday will I get?' and they could forget the job. But here, now? What was there he could say that would drive to the centre of his predicament?

What could he ask perched on a thin armchair peering into an abyss forty-six years deep, through furnaces of sealed emotion and lost inspiration? How could she help him interpret letters revealed by fire, corroded onto white hot metal and hidden in the crater's depths or leaping images of soul-searing film created from the rolling smoke and incandescent rocks that exploded into star shot fire trails before the unstoppable roar of breath blowing from the bellows of life? What could he say as he lifted his eyes away from the abyss to encounter desert horizons rendered lifeless by the unquenchable heat of the sun, every possibility of loam burned into dry sand, every drop of imagination's water evaporated and his being crumbling into a handful of dust? What was the question he could ask that would convey all this?

There was a pause: he had to speak and said,

'Where do we go from here?'

'Well, I'm not sure that psychotherapy would be appropriate in your case and anyway there is a long waiting list. I can recommend you for a series of ten counselling sessions if you feel that is what you would like to do. At the end you can come and see me and discuss it.'

How far into the abyss would he descend in ten sessions with his counsellor sitting on his shoulder? Would they release the fires and breath the sulphurous fumes together or would he be taught to paint flowers over the dead land and make water meadows from its stony rubbish? On the other hand, what would he do if he closed off this possibility, if he did nothing?

'Yes, I think that would be a good idea. When would they start?'

'Well, you're lucky you can go during the day but there might still be a wait of a month or two. They'll phone you. Is that O.K.?'

She could have been selling with her constant seeking of agreement.

'Yes, fine.'

A discrete glance at her watch and then,

'Right, well, I'll see you again in a little while. Continue to see your G.P. for the medication. I'll show you out.'

They stood and walked. She left him at the door from which the tormented soul had emerged earlier with drawn sword against hobgoblins and foul fiends. David shook hands and fumbled in his pocket for his car keys. If that was to be the limit of what was available from medical and psychiatric science, he would need to take steps towards his own solution.

He settled into the familiar and comforting environment of his car. The supportive leather seats held him; the precise clarity of the dashboard waited to give him all necessary information. He turned the key and the tachometer told him that the engine was ticking over at 750 rpm exactly. He pressed play on the CD and a Bach fugue calmed and restored order to his mind. The climate control ensured that the inside was held at nineteen degrees precisely. It was a place where he was in control. He could determine the music, the temperature, speed, direction and the destination.

Over the next few days he began to formulate a plan of sorts. If he had been wandering lost in a desert, then to find his way again he must revisit the time when he had last felt his life to be on course, integrated, whole. To rely on memory was to risk the retelling of his life by the spirits of shifting sand; tales told to explain, to justify the choices made over disappearing paths and through dunes that rose and fell in the capricious wind; paths followed in pursuit of mirages rising from memory and taking new forms with every repeated visit. His only primary source in this histor-ical investigation was the poetry he had written as a teenager when he had strained every channel of perception to draw down images and transmute them into words.

He trod carefully along the rafters in the loft and leaned to reach a heavy, metal-banded trunk set against the wall. The lid was sprinkled with fine white dust fallen from the mortar between the bricks of the chimney. It had been untouched and unmoved since they arrived in Wimbledon seventeen years ago. David stooped to avoid knocking his head and, leaving ghostly fingerprints in the dust, cautiously lifted the metal catches. Why cautious? He had a feeling that anything could be released once the seal was broken and the lid was lifted: pandaemonium, all the ills of the world flying on leathery wings. He stepped back involun-tarily and hit his head hard on the rafters. The threatening wings again. He had thought that perhaps they would be satisfied with bringing him to this desperate state but still they waited to ambush him. Annoyed by the numbing blow, he moved forward and flung open the trunk.

Inside, the grave goods of his former life lay emptied of significance, thinned of life, ready to disintegrate and pass through into darkness. Exposed to light and his gaze he watched them draw in life from his consciousness. As life filtered through them, they began to reflect back energy stir-ring intimations of memory sealed below strata and substrata of existence. He stooped and lay his hand on them, testing their solidity, their strange suspended continuance, locked away from the world of change.

He picked his way through the notebooks, boxed photographs and several unsold copies of a book of poems published the year after he left university. He needed to dig deeper, farther back than that. Near the bottom he found a cardboard box and slid it out. Inside was a map of Venice bound to a small notebook with a piece of ribbon. He took them out and sat perched against a rafter, turning to allow the light to fall on them. He untied the ribbon and flicked through the notebook – dates:

'5th August 1966 Three Islands trip. Murano. Bought glass cat for Jane, Mum bought a vase. Later went to Torcello, gold mosaic of Last Judgement. Made Mum laugh about it when Dad was off taking photos. Had pasta in café by canal. One day I'll bring Jane.'

Thirty years had passed, and the handwriting was only partly familiar, related to his but not the same. He closed the book and carefully unfolded the map as though it were an ancient manuscript. Along the edge was another handwriting, cursive, artistic, his mother's: 'Tintoretto – Scuola Grande di San Rocco' and an asterisk. A corresponding asterisk had been drawn carefully on the map behind I Frari. He felt her warmth, and her concern about things that grew into an ever-present anxiety. If only she could have overcome that vague and nameless fear, she would have had so much more enjoyment from their time together; a time so cruelly and painfully shortened. He closed his eyes. Tears were rising somewhere within. He tried to see her face, the face that had been the centre of his life when he was a child, but his mind stayed obstinately blank. The memories of his childhood were there, somewhere, but sealed behind a barrier created by their separation.

He folded the map and tied it to the notebook again. In the bottom of the cardboard box were two notebooks, one labelled 'Poems 1964 – 1967' and beneath that another, spiral bound, dated 1968 – 1972. He replaced the map and Venice notebook in the box and then made his way back to the trunk to close its lid. Enough of the past's demons had been released. As he shuffled to the loft trap door, he clutched the cardboard box to himself. When he reached the bottom, he noticed that the edges of the box had left bright red indented lines on his hand.

For the second time that year, Venice had come to his attention. In January, he had heard the news of the fire at La Fenice. Now, the destruction of that symbol of the art, the culture, the imagining soul of Venice, returned and joined with his own destruction. He had seen pictures of its burned-out shell, the twisted beams and jagged, charred remains of a place where rich and powerful dreams had once been brought to life. Now he saw it as a corollary of the death of his own inner being and the forces of imagination that once fed it. The future of La Fenice was still unknown but its name promised that it would rise from the ashes. Could he too rise again, invoke the phoenix?

The map from the loft was spread on the large, stripped pine table when Thelma arrived home from work. He called, 'Hello! I'm in the dining room' but she went straight past to the fridge.

'God, I need a drink. It's been a hell of a day.'

He had started folding the map and was about to go to the kitchen when she appeared in the doorway.

'What are you doing?'

'Oh, it's a map.'

'I can see that.'

'Venice, an old one from the trunk in the loft.'

She glanced at it as she sat down. His eyes flicked quickly to his mother's writing and he hoped she wouldn't notice it.

'What do you want that for?'

It had been careless of him to still be looking at it. He had not wanted to say anything about it. He did not know how to explain it, wanted to keep it hidden inside to gather more strength, his secret source of new life. Looking at the map had given him the germ of an idea, the beginning of a plan. A quest.

'I just thought I'd look through some things, in the loft.'

'There's a lot of rubbish up there, we're going to have to have a clear out soon.'

'I'm feeling cooped up here every day. I know there's the common and I've got my books and everything, but I need a change.'

He felt guilty when she was working so hard and all he had to do was read and walk on Wimbledon Common, but he would have to bring it up somehow. There was a pause before she said,

'Yes, I think we both do. I was talking to Caroline today. We went through my diary and I think I can get a week at the end of the month.'

He calculated quickly, not having expected a positive response never mind one as quick as this.

'What do you think about Venice?'

'Oh, that's your sort of thing. What am I going to do? I want to relax on the beach or a cruise.'

This was not in the spirit of a quest, a mission. He would need time alone, following the clues left in his psyche by his former visit to Venice, if this project were to have any chance of working the transformation that he sought.

'We could go back to where I went with my parents when I was sixteen. That's a fantastic beach and it's only a short ferry ride into Venice. I could spend time there while you relax.'

It was going well so far, and he decided to pursue it.

'I could even go out first, for a week; I could get the sight-seeing out of my system and then we could spend most of the time on the beach.'

'You should be resting too.'

'I would be.'

'Well, we could. See if you can get some information. I've been worried about you moping about at home. I'll check the diary again tomorrow and let you know which day I can fly out.'

It had been easier than he could have possibly hoped. Thelma rang with the dates and he went straight onto the internet and booked a hotel near Cavallino on the Jesolo peninsula, a ferry from Dover to Calais for himself and a flight for Thelma. He would rely on finding a Gasthof on the way down, somewhere around Stuttgart.

Thelma was surprised but not displeased when she found he had acted with uncharacteristic swiftness.

'I thought you'd book a package. Why drive all that way when you could sit back and relax in a plane. It's not as if we need the car when we get there.'

'I'd just rather drive; it seems more of an adventure.'

Thelma looked with the strange mixture of hurt and incomprehension that so often appeared on her face when he was not explaining something that he felt she wouldn't understand.

'You'd get more time there if you flew. You're supposed to be resting you know.'

There was no rational explanation. It added to the sense of its being a quest: to set off from home under one's own steam, cross the channel by ferry and drive across the flat Belgian plain to the rolling vine covered hills of the Rhine valley. It was a pilgrimage, travelling to the Black Forest and then out across Bavaria to Austria and the Alps. To miss out this experience would reduce the otherness of Venice. Goethe, Byron and Wagner had travelled through the alps by horse-drawn coach. The Rhine, the forest, the mountains, were essential precursors of Italy, each adding their own set of images. In fact, he regretted that he could not spend longer in each of them on the way. He tried another explanation.

'You know I enjoy driving. The BMW doesn't get a chance to show what it can do here. And it was the route we used to take when we went to Italy or Austria on family holidays as a child. I just want to revisit it, bring it back.'

'Be careful you don't do too much of this 'bringing things back', you don't want to be ill again.'

Return as a dog to its vomit – is that what he was doing? Was it just morbid introspection or a journey of self and discovery?

'I can take most of your stuff with me, so you won't have too much to carry. And meet you at the other end,' he added. It was probably this that finally persuaded her that there was some practical benefit in his plan.

Next day he walked out onto the common. The sun was hot, and the grass smelt strong and sweet. He sat at the top of a hill under a group of scots pines and opened the 1964 – 67 notebook. Like the diary, the poems were written in a hand that was not quite his. The poems that once distilled the essence of his life were now quiet and strangely distant. The rich metaphors, conjured from the darkness at three in the morning, were glazed over and reluctant to give up their encased emotions. They formed a vision of life created from a central perception of all his sensory, emotional and imaginative experience; his own being before the claws of compromise, commerce and cowardice had slashed into his persona, tugging and tearing until it was an unrecognisable parody of himself.

And it was that parody of himself that went each day into the concrete and glass office block to put more and more effort into selling software solutions to other people's problems. He was selling his time, selling his life for something that meant nothing to him, had no significance beyond the payment he received at the end of each month, handing over the irreplaceable life his mother had given him, the infinite complexity of growing and learning nurtured by her and taught by the experiences of nature that she led him to, betraying her love by living a shallow life devoid of meaning.

If he could solve other people's problems with software, could he not at least begin to solve his own? Establish the situation, define the problem, explore what will happen if it isn't solved and then offer a solution. 'Design for the Future.' He gave a brief shudder at the recollection of the seminar. He would apply the same process to his own problem but here he would have to design, write and install his own code. Find a way back, within, re-program: that was why he had to go to Venice.

The cries of the gulls filtered through to join his rising memories. Circling high over the cliffs they had watched his departure from Dover, calling to each other the news of his leaving. Gulls that had once been the voice of the sea for his childhood, now carried a threatening note of all the wings that had beaten out of darkness to destroy the last threads of his sanity.

Gulls' cries in his consciousness were joined by the sensation of the lagoon's warm breeze passing over his skin. His eyes took in again the blue water made brilliant by the sun. He swayed and his desperate grip on the ferry rail left his knuckles as white as the flaking paint. He breathed steadily and felt the blood and warmth return.

He forced himself to watch the gulls for a little longer, to try to exorcise this new aversion to winged things. If he were to fulfil his task then he could not keep his mind sealed shut, he had to allow the images to come out, however frightening.

David followed the gulls' flight until he felt the tension begin to disappear and then allowed his eyes to move across into the shadows between decks. His attention was caught by sunlight shining on the creamy white dress and blonde hair of a girl who was talking animatedly. She stood with a small group of friends leaning on the hand-rail. He felt a sudden irrational jolt of recognition. She was engrossed in her conversation and so he allowed himself to stare, trying to work out where he had seen her before. He tried to make out what she was saying but the breeze and the engine noise blurred the words. There was something about the way her hair was plaited and coiled and her light, floating, creamy white dress that was reminiscent of a Renaissance painting: Botticelli perhaps. Beyond this association, however, there was something else, something about her that seemed strongly familiar. Where had he seen her? A colleague's daughter at a company gathering, or maybe a girl at the local supermarket checkout? He was sure that was not it; she was significant for him in some way but he could not think how.

He turned to her friends for clues. The youth who appeared to be with her was athletic and strong chinned, with fair hair. The other girl was dark haired and attractive in a less striking way. She was talking quietly to a boy with a softer rounder face and large brown eyes, not unlike himself at the same age. Their confidence, the sense of new life ever expanding in its potentialities excluded him. He felt his age fall like a veil between them. To them it would seem impossible that this new opening of life through the gate of adolescence would also pass away, like childhood, and all things become darker.

The ferry began to turn away from the low strand of the Lido. It was too late to turn back. Nervous foreboding began to get the upper hand over excited anticipation. He was fated now to confront that which had been part of his inner mythology since he was sixteen. Then it had flowed freely into the rich patterns and emotional intensity of his unfettered mind that swirled and eddied with currents of new life, a bottomless pool swimming with teeming images. Now he was being taken by the ferry to face it, with the implicit challenge to tear open and free his mind again, or to face the unbearable sensation of seeing the city that formed an icon of his soul's youth and feel it crumble as dry dust in the desert of his heart.

Suddenly, people were moving across the deck to the right hand-rail; cameras were being pulled from pockets and handbags. David looked past them. Across the rippled blue-green glaze was the archetype of all Venetian scenes. Familiar from so many photographs, paintings, films; from when he saw it last, thirty years ago; from the countless times he had brought the images of that visit back into his mind: it seemed strange and unreal to see it there outside himself. But there it was. The tall, heavy tower of the Campanile, brick red, rose through white to a white edged sea-green spire. The heavy but delicately patterned Doges' palace rested on fine pillared arches as intricate as lace. The two columns at the entrance to the Piazzetta formed a gateway to the lattice work maze of water and narrow alley, canal and calle, that made up the inner world of Venice.

How should he react? There it was and he felt a strange numbness and yet at the same time a feeling that the reality was connecting somewhere deep within his psyche, a meeting occurring beyond his sight, beneath his awareness so that he could only stand and stare and allow whatever was to change within his mind, to change away from all control of thought. The image that possessed him was meeting its original and whether the outcome would be a deeper descent into insanity, the final dissolution of the mental landscape that sustained him, or inspiration to create a new beginning, he was powerless to influence or prevent it.

The ferry turned in towards the pier on the Riva degli Schiavoni; people were getting up from their seats. The perfectly dressed Italian family with the beautiful daughter, whose coiled snake earrings nodded gently against the white skin of her neck, rose. The American women talked loudly and watched the scene through video cameras. There was a lurch, much shouting and a groaning grating noise as they hit the clumps of dark heavy posts leaning in towards each other to protect the quay. Everyone was talking. The excitement was infectious and as David joined the crush to disembark, he caught a fleeting glimpse of the dress of the Renaissance girl before she disappeared into the dark of the lower deck. The uncomfortable feeling of inexplicable recognition came over him again and he was reluctant to let her go from his sight.

The asphalt and concrete landing stage floated, moving beneath his feet: a mid-point between water and land. In the metal shelter, crowds waiting to board the ferry, pushed up against the glass like avenging furies. David shuddered as he felt them straining towards him, eager to prevent his attempt at salvation. He allowed himself to be carried forward by the crowd surging forward towards dry land.

2

THE FIRST DAY - PART TWO

At last his feet touched the islands of Venice. Across his mind floated the idea that he should make some dramatic gesture, an outward and visible sign such as kissing the ground or embracing the stones. Instead he stood by a stall selling sunglasses, gondolier hats and slivers of coconut from small fountains of water and simply stared.

He realised that he had not thought out what he was going to do. The circumstances that led up to the holiday, the rushed preparations, the drive down had not left time for detailed planning. He had thought of the visit in terms of a spiritual odyssey, an attempt to heal his frayed and bleeding soul by revisiting sensations last felt when his being seemed whole, driven by a great imaginative fecundity, his mind a sunburst of ideas. With desperate faith he clung to the belief that this was not just a part of adolescence, doomed slowly to fade, thinning to nothing as the years drove inexorably on, but a state within him that he could revisit if he sought it determinedly enough.

He decided to simply immerse himself in Venice, allow

it to seep through into his soul and take what followed. If he were to enter this city to unlock the secrets of his own past, then he should enter through the great columns on the Piazzetta, marking the gateway to the Imperial city that held within its own past the secrets of the great civilisations of East and West. He ascended the flat, shallow, yet steep steps of his first bridge. Each footstep sank through time, the intervening years, reopening the sensations of that first visit. He paused on the bridge looking up the canal, in towards the centre of Venice. It was like looking into an Elizabethan maze garden, seeing far enough to be tantalised but then, with a change of direction all was hidden: the way to the heart remained a mystery. Fleeting shreds of shape and colour flashed near his consciousness, emotions, harmonics vibrating through him over the simple sound of stones, his mother's warmth, laughter. He strained to draw out anything that could be called a coherent memory, but it was like digging in sand.

Under the bridge came a flat barge-like boat piled high with Coca-Cola and Seven-Up, burbling slowly along the water into the hidden labyrinth. He felt much in common with that barge, weighed down by layer upon layer of crude alien experience accumulated through a life spent grubbing for money and devoid of creative force. He had drifted into computer sales and to his surprise was successful at it. He moved up through the ranks of management and was now sales director. The intended acting career had come to nothing and, after publishing a few poems and short stories, he stopped writing. Now he saw his past as a wide wasteland of experience, a dry expanse; experience as absurd and out of place as the cans, superficial and flashy, contrasting utterly with the intricate mystery of the ancient stones with which at sixteen he knew such harmony.

Onward over the next bridge, a quick look right and there through the mass of tourists he saw the Bridge of Sighs. Two eyes closed by four eight petalled stars looked back concealing, behind their fixed gaze, the one-way path into darkness, his darkness. Palace to dungeon, a shiver of recognition, a malevolent shadow. He was here to escape, to climb free along the leads and yet, the dungeon was familiar, safe. To escape was to face the unknown and lose the comfort of his present life; to be a prisoner like Byron's Prisoner of Chillon, the spiders and the mice playing in the moonlight of his everyday life were his friends; to them it was not a prison but their home. The ending ran in his mind:

> *'My very chains and I grew friends*
> *So much a long communion tends*
> *To make us what we are: --even I*
> *Regained my freedom with a sigh.'*

Yes, he had become so much a part of the world he despised, and it had become so much a part of him, that breaking free would be as painful, more painful even, than remaining a prisoner in darkness. All the comfortable palliatives, his job and the money it brought with it, his wife and home, all were on the line now. The price of freedom might be everything he had. As this grim parallel with his life sank through him, he closed out the penetrating stare of the bridge and moved on with a new sense of the seriousness of his quest.

The tourist crowd flowed from the Riva degli Schiavoni around the corner of the palace and into the Piazza as if it were a shopping centre or supermarket, looking for the latest advertised attraction on the shelves. Surely entering a place of such history, such power over the great throughout the centuries, demanded more thought, more ceremony than this.

David walked to where the gondola prows rose and fell, nodding on every ripple, rearing and plunging when the wake of a water taxi rushed through them to the edge of the square. He moved forward more determinedly, then stopped and turned looking up towards St Mark's. The two great Byzantine, granite columns rose before him, a Greek with a reptilian monster on the left and a Chimaera, now the lion of St Mark, on the right. He needed to make some symbolic act to help him leave behind the tyranny of years that divided him from the person he knew he had once been.

He focused his mind and visualised the last thirty years as a parched, cracked and arid desert. He had to leave the desert, with all its familiarity and dare to allow the water to flow in again. David breathed deeply and tried to see the water pouring through runnels in the sand, a rising tide to bring the desert to life.

He walked forward and around him images rose and fell, swirling away on each side. The sea rose, forming eddying currents around him. The great columns loomed, as if from a sunken temple in the Adriatic. The sounds of the square faded, and the rushing of water took their place. The weight of water increased, and it became harder and harder to push each leg forward. The sun fell in rippling colours all around, the golden light centred on the surface of the water above. His legs strained; each step harder than the last. His feet descended ever more slowly onto the flagstones until he stood between the pillars. All weight ceased. The sea around evaporated in an instant. The skin burning heat of the sun, its light brilliant again in the clear air rushed back. The coloured lights hardened into the stones of the Doges' palace and St Mark's on the right and into the heavy Romanesque arches, arcades, and balustrades of the Libraria Vecchia on the left.

Voices filled the air and crocodiles of tourists led by effigies of Micky Mouse or outrageously coloured parasols, criss-crossed the square. On the left a chamber orchestra surrounded by tables and chairs played classical pops. He was through the gateway; he had entered the city.

She had not changed; it was as though the intervening years had not happened here. He had gone away, passed through long years of change, journeyed through dark forests, walked on hills and crawled across deserts of mindless, meaningless work. His vision, perception, consciousness had altered. Now he had returned to the place that he had felt, from the first time he saw it at sixteen, mirrored his psyche, epitomised that state of being that he now sought and from which he had journeyed so far. Here those years of change had not existed, and he felt himself a time traveller, a being looking through a window cut off by his own experience from Venice present and his own past. He was walled-in by a dry wall.

A sense of helplessness flowed through him. Futile thoughts turned and circled waiting to descend on his failure: he should not have come; never go back; the whole idea was foolishness; how could it ever have seemed a possibility; how could he ever have hoped to rediscover his youth by visiting a city, even Venice? It sounded like a cliché; it was a cliché; the last refuge from an intolerable present and a hopeless future, but it was all he had.

He had braced himself for the possibility that Venice might have changed but was not ready for the full impact of his own change. A new being had crept through his mind and his body obliterating his soul in its journey to be born and he had not noticed it happening. Where all things were changing, he could not see it but, here where centuries take the place of years, he saw himself against a cloth of stillness and did not know what he saw.

He looked towards the clock tower with its winged lion and hammer wielding moors and his eyes focused on the lapis lazuli face of the clock. It was marked out by twenty-four Roman numerals. The Sun and the Moon floated on its surface, the twelve signs of the Zodiac around its edge, time moving in the Universe. He considered its turning; perhaps it marked out years rather than days, Venice floating on the blue pool of the clock face. Or did the hand just turn idly beneath the city whilst time itself stood still, the clock marking out the same day over and over again.

David sat down against the stone of an archway. In adolescence he had lived in a world where his mind rode on images free-floating between his consciousness and what-ever depths of invisible reality lay within. The images seemed to offer a way through to the eternal where perhaps his salvation lay. He had turned such experiences into a reli-gion. Religion told its eternal truths in myth and his was a religion in which myths created themselves and lived before his eyes. It was his secret, his sustaining reassurance that he was in touch with another reality not apprehended by the mass of humanity but only by a small chosen band of poets and philosophers to which he had felt he belonged. He had embraced the company of Wordsworth in his personal and immediate experience of that mystical oneness with the universe, Shelley for the rushing of the spiritual wind, Lawrence for the richness of earth and sex transmuted into the power of the soul and Nietzsche for the vision of dancing exultant on high mountain peaks.

It seemed, it was, so long ago, in an alien world before

work, before money, before marriage: before the wall. Was it just the hormone induced madness of adolescence or was it a vision of truth before he fell from the tightrope into the market-place? Had he grown older and wiser as well as colder and more cynical or had he seen then a glimpse of reality before turning away to take the easier but ultimately empty way of the world?

Now a crisis within had forced him to return, to follow the thin thread back through the dark, winding and dangerous maze and attempt to begin again.

He shifted his position. The stone pillar was digging uncomfortably into his back. He became aware of an ice cream being waved across his face by a child with its back to him. Ice-cream, accompaniment to childhood parties, sea-side holidays, summer visits to great houses and gardens, symbol of all things of pleasure. The child was completely oblivious to his presence.

'I don't like it.'

'It's what you had last time.'

'It's not, that didn't have bits in.'

'That's fruit.'

'I don't like bits.'

'They're bits of fruit.'

'I don't care.'

'Don't talk to me like that.'

The ice cream fell to the ground like a giant pigeon dropping, the cone remaining in the child's hand.

'You did that on purpose.'

'I didn't.'

'You're not getting another.'

The cone and a howl of misery and thwarted will went out into the air. The howl was absorbed by the general hubbub, but the cone landed on a moving carpet of feeding pigeons which lifted abruptly into the air and swooped noisily towards him raising a ragged wind against his face as it veered away from the stone columns.

His head pulled back with involuntary speed from the new flight of winged things. A dull, resonant explosion of darkness wiped the scene from his consciousness. As it returned, he realized he had hit the back of his head against the stone pillar. He sat allowing the scene to settle before him. The noise, crush and bustle of an infinite diversity of people moved in a chaotic dance before him, caught in its own energy being carried in every direction like the circling of thoughts when sleep would not come. This was the court-yard where many people's experience of Venice stopped, this and the well-marked, well-worn routes to the Rialto and the Accademia. He watched and the sound took on a distant resonance. The noise of voices in many languages babbled across the background of his mind. It often happened, like a recording, no one voice or noise catching his attention but giving him the sensation of being set apart, watching a film with sound effects played behind it. He carefully stretched his legs, leaned away from the pillar and stood. Then he walked until the crowd and the sound opened out into the broad space of the great square of St Marks.

The crowds were intent on the sights of Venice. The Rialto for trade, the Accademia for culture, St Mark's Square for society and the Basilica San Marco for organised religion. All this but most of Venice left untouched, a further maze beyond: the Venice that traced the patterns of his imagination, formed or given images when he was sixteen; bridges set at odd angles against covered fondamenti by narrow canals that turned abruptly out of sight; the paths over bridges disappearing under tall red earth walls into dark passageways before emerging into a small square, or campo, each with a small church and tables for talking and drinking.

That was the Venice that he had come for but first he needed to pause and take in the outer Venice. Too sudden an intrusion into the inner world and she would shrink away and not allow him to share her secrets. Too coarse an entry before renewing his acquaintance with her would prevent the heart of her flowing inner being from unfolding.

He headed for the tables in the square outside the dark arcaded entrances of Florian's. Another small band: accordion, piano, violin and bass, was playing 'La Donna Mobile'.

'Buon giorno signore.'

'Buon giorno. Che cosa prende?'

'Prendo cappuccino, per favore.'

'Va bene.'

Having ordered, he sat back and taking a deep breath relaxed into the none too comfortable chair to give himself up to watching social Venice.

'D' you mind if we join you?' The request seeped slowly into his reverie and announced itself as something of an emergency. The natural and seamless pattern of the experience of Venice unfolding in a single image was interrupted, broken at a stroke. It folded in on him as if a cord had been cut, or a bubble burst. He looked round and saw a large middle-aged American in a brightly coloured shirt with two ostentatiously large cameras around his neck. His wife wore trousers with a pattern so aggressive it was hard to believe that it was based on flowers. This could, he thought, be unpleasant.

'We're from New York City, it's our first time in Venice. This is just great. Where are you from?'

David had mentally decided to say nothing, to stay cut off but could not help himself replying, 'London'.

'There is absolutely nothing like this anywhere it's just awesome. Have you been here before?'

The American was not an easy person to ignore and his open uninhibited manner began to break through David's resolve.

'A long time ago.'

'You on your own? We could do with someone who knows the way around. Let me get you a coffee.'

'No, it's all right I've already ordered one.'

The American and his wife sat down at David's table signalling that there was no escape for him.

'Hey waiter, can we have two coffees, did you say you were on your own?'

'George, maybe he doesn't.......'

'Yes, my wife's coming on later.'

David did not add that it would be a week later.

'Look, we don't know where we're going or what we're doing. We've left our party so we can see Venice on our own but if you've some advice, that'd be welcome.'

His wife tried to break in again to halt the flow of George's overpowering friendliness but to no avail.

'I thought I'd got a map here. Honey have you got that map? No? Well we must have just left it back at the hotel. I'm George Wagner by the way and this is my wife Hilda. Hey, are you sure you haven't got that map?'

Wagner was pronounced like wagoner.

'I told you to bring it, dear. I don't suppose you've got a map there have you?'

This she directed at David, as much he felt to escape the unremitting questioning of her husband as out of any desire for a map.

He instinctively felt in his bag and brought out his map of Venice. At least she had shown some consideration and now the mood was broken it wouldn't hurt to help them out. They had just spread the map out on the table when the waiter brought the coffees and George insisted on paying.

'We want to see the Doges' Palace and the Rialto first and then tomorrow we can wander about a bit and get the feel of the place.'

David pointed out the Doges' Palace to them and indicated where the entrance was and then showed them the Rialto on the map.

'Do you know where the Mocenigo palace is?'

David's mind went dark and flustered by this he began studying the map again. It was not on the list of palaces on the flap as far as he could see and yet the name seemed familiar, strongly so. Perhaps they had got something wrong and it was in another place, Florence perhaps. He had not really done much homework on Venice except from memory.

'It's not marked on here.'

'It must be. It's where Lord Byron stayed.'

David looked up quickly, rapidly reviewing his assessment of George Wagner. He had obviously been rash in his stereotypical conclusions.

'George is very interested in Lord Byron, aren't you dear?'

'I certainly am, and I'd like to see where he stayed. Hey, look, it says Mocenigo here,' he pointed out the Calle Mocenigo on the map. 'It could be there. We'll make a trip there later, maybe the gondolier'll know.'

David felt he had failed rather badly but had become interested now.

'I thought the name was familiar, I couldn't place it. They interest me too, Byron and the other Romantics, I think he kept a giraffe there or something.' He found himself rushing his words.

'He sure did, and,' here George leaned forward conspiratorially, 'La Fornarina. What a woman eh?'

His wife looked indulgently at him and said,

'George buys every book he can find on Lord Byron; he's got practically a whole library.'

Before David could reply, George broke in again.

'Fancy you being interested in Byron. I'd love to have a chance to talk it over with someone else who's interested. I've brought an edition with me you'd like to see. Why don't we all meet up at the hotel tonight for drinks? We're at the Bauer Grunwald. Have you got the address honey?'

'I've got one of these cards.'

'Just ask for me, they'll know who you mean.'

George Wagner was now standing up and had accosted an innocent bystander.

'Hey look come on let's get a picture here, excuse me..., can you take a picture?' He pressed the camera firmly into the man's hands, 'OK smile everyone.'

He was certainly used to making things happen. They continued enthusing about what they had seen of Europe. They were really very likable, and their enthusiasm and energy had drawn David further and further out of the contemplative frame of mind he had felt necessary for pilgrimage and self-discovery. At last they had finished their coffee, and the eruption of flowing words began to slow.

'Well we're off to see the Doges' palace now. Don't you forget, you and your wife tonight. Just turn up.'

David watched them walking away, looking upwards, looking around, so different from the self-absorbed, dream-watching state in which he himself had arrived. He allowed his mind to work the implications of this. If he were to revisit his former self, was he going in entirely the wrong direction? Should he be more like them? Thirty years ago, he too had arrived looking upwards and around not down-wards and inwards and if he wanted the magic to work again should he do the same now rather than raking in the foul rag-and-bone shop within. He could, after all do that at home.

There was a paradox here, he reflected. Was it not the case that all other internal revolutions had occurred when he was most absorbed with something or someone outside himself and, what was more, had happened without his being conscious of it at the time? Perhaps internal revolutions could only take place when the consciousness was otherwise engaged and then become apparent later.

A hot green day on Wimbledon Common, many years ago. He sat on his favourite seat under the pines, looking down over the tops of trees to Richmond Park in the distance. He had written then that no matter how rich an experience, its richness and power only revealed themselves in recollection; that the conscious mind could only experience the surface skin, or at best the melody, whilst the depths that lay beneath, the counterpoint, the harmony that would transform the soul and rewrite the past, remained unknown.

The Wagners had gone and he felt washed up like a sea creature on a hard, unyielding shore. He felt drained and tired. He watched dispassionately as thoughts paraded before his consciousness. What should he do next? It was no good trying to look at Venice as the Wagners did, nor to seek again the impact of that first visit. There was no point in pretending that it was new again; a whole section of his inner world was built on a map and an image that seemed to mirror it. All that could be done was to let it take its course, allow the outer Venice to meet the inner, healing his fractured psyche, flowing in to fill and enliven the cracked and parched earth of his soul eventually perhaps even allowing his gondola to float and rock gently forward through the mysteries of the maze.

Consciousness slipped away from his tired mind and he arrived in a deep reverie, a communion of present with the dark waters of his inner self. Stone shimmered into water and water into stone and he found himself sliding down deep underworld rivers, briefly glimpsing black, tooth headed gondolas and dipping marble steps that disappeared under the flow of dark water like the steps that launched Odysseus and Achilles onto the wine-dark Aegean.

He returned sufficiently to be aware that his tiredness felt less empty, still devoid of purpose and direction but no longer barren; a feeling like the aftermath of illness before the restlessness of health returns. He sat back and again gave himself up to the present, soaking in the sun and absorbing a timeless and motionless contentment. This timeless floating held him. It was as if he slept.

Again, he returned and this time his senses stirred. Music gradually replaced the silence. Long shadowed rows of arcades reappeared. Pigeons and tourists filled the great space of the square. He felt the slats of the seat pressing into his back and legs. Slowly, he moved his arms watching them return to life. He watched his hand perform the intricate and instinctive task of picking up his sunglasses from the table. He watched his legs move and the angles straighten as his feet bore down on the stones. He paused and then walked.

From the burning square with its wide-open sound of voices spanning the space between its arcaded sides, he slid into the cool grey darkness of arched stone, the Sotto San Geminian where the square runs away at the lowly end, far from the golden light of the Basilica. The blinding, over-whelming experience of landing in this turbulent and sacred city, of passing through the pillars into the centre of his inner landscape had sharpened and sensitised his perception and his nerves. He felt as though the slightest pressure on his senses would cause him to be tossed and flung far into chaotic darkness. The cold, solid, stones with their breath damp in his nostrils and their weight the foundation of the city's timelessness encircled him in shadow and climbed above him like a vault. The darkness lessened as his eyes adjusted. He put out his hand and placed the palm flat against the stone. The flesh moulded itself to the cool roughened surface. The heavy sensation of permanence and stability calmed and reassured him. His arm began to ache and he lowered his hand. He looked around and saw that to one side, through a small archway of its own, a steep flight of steps rose away out of sight as if from an underground tomb.

He shivered slightly at the sudden chill and felt strangely naked now the sun no longer poured its heat through him. It was like entering a church and experiencing the vulnerability of remembering too late that shorts and bare arms were not acceptable. Behind him was the light, around him was the dark pylon made from heavy grey blocks of unyielding granite and before him was a labyrinth of sensation and emotion shaded and illuminated by a living map of water and stone. It was a map whose patterns charted, in the flow of ever-changing reflections and the still forms of marble and brick that determine their course, the hidden depths of consciousness that remain unchanged across the centuries. Behind him was the attraction of the brilliantly clear sun, the tourists scattered brightly coloured as a fairground across the space of the square, before him was the dark uncertain mystery of the maze. He passed through the gateway.

Beyond the arch the unchanging stones played temporary host to gilt edged glass windows filled with fashion displaying impeccable but ephemeral style. These were modern merchants trading with the new sea-born visitors as frantically and as effectively as they ever did in the days of the Venetian empire. Generations formed a flickering and changing play of light over the face of the stones; the ripple of water on rock, the light that had flickered in a long unchanging present since that first visit at sixteen.

He had missed Jane desperately. It was the first time they had parted since their relationship had begun. Before he left, they had kissed, each trying to melt into the other in the darkness. She undid her mac and pressed her body against him through her thin summer dress. Mouths wet as they tried to dissolve into one warm being, they held each other tightly on the doorstep in the rain. The hall light fell in leaded patterns through the coloured glass of the front door. There was a noise inside, they fell back breathing heavily as a shadow moved in the hall.

'She knows we're here, she'll be out in a minute.'

'Love you.'

'Love you.'

'I'll think about you all the time.'

'It'll be wonderful. I want to know all about it when you get back.'

'I'll write you a poem.'

The shadow started to grow large in the hall.

She clasped him suddenly, her mouth slid over his, their tongues flowing together in affirmation of their love and then drew away. Her white hand turned the brass knob on the door just as her mother reached it.

'Love you.' she mouthed, her lips beautiful with kissing. The yellow gold light flooded over her as the door opened and she was gone.

Then, at sixteen and in love, he had arrived and felt he stepped on holy ground. Venice appeared before him at sixteen and instantly embodied the world of his imagination. Then, there was no nostalgia for lost opportunities, nor the attempted healing of a broken psyche. It was new and yet there was a familiarity as if the traceries of his emotions, thoughts and visions were here externalised. It was as if the intangible depth of all the music he had heard, the luxurious images of poetry he had read and all his own thoughts and feelings, dreams and ideas, inspired by them, had been sprayed into the air from a baroque fountain and formed, as they fell, the image of his inner being.

When, as a child, his mother read him fairy tales and stories of imagined worlds, he had strained to see within what was now visible. When he moved into his teens he read Keats, Byron, Tennyson and they created just such a world of decaying opulence, of carving and mosaic, of half hidden mystery where fact and reality had been left behind for an ever shifting haze of rich colour and a sensation of perfect beauty ever present, held within and beneath the surface. Porphyro half fainting with desire for Madeline, the high, carved casements, the moon and roses, amethyst and silver and the sensuality of the banquet, in the Eve of St Agnes; the ever dissolving darkness of flower and incense and longing for death of the Nightingale; the silver fire of steel, the heavy depth of cloth and pale perfection of female beauty in Tennyson's Arthurian romances; the Oriental domes, arches and latticework of Byron's world of heroes: all were here.

Schoenberg's Pierrot yearning in the moonlight, terrified

by black butterflies; Vivaldi's cascading strings and dripping pizzicato; Gilda sliding, still alive, from Rigoletto's hands into the dark water wrapped in a shroud of sacking; the unbearable aching, unfulfilled longing of Tristan and the heavy sexual riches of the Venusberg: all were expressed in the intricate, intense dreamworld of Venice.

Then his own response to these things was instinctive, he had read no criticism, nor commentary but allowed his imagination to ride these works through the adolescent blur of all-pervading love and the new world of experience it brought. After he had read Dante he dreamt over and over again of Jane as Beatrice, dressed in white descending in a pale rose halo, surrounded by candlelight, reaching out to touch his moist cheek with her gentle hand and guide him out of Purgatory into Paradise.

He emerged from the deep gully and faced the steep white curve of a small bridge. Two gondolas were trying to pass in opposite directions. There was a great deal of shouting though it was hard to tell if there was actually anger in it. The silver toothed heads tossed on their long necks like dragon chargers at the joust, the gondoliers clutching their lance-like oars. Suddenly one broke free and slid into centre stream. David stood leaning on the parapet of the bridge and watched the gondolier make two strong twisting strokes with the oar and then stand as the poised boat slid forward through the water with no further effort. He stooped and lifted the oar from the water as another small bridge approached and this time travelled smoothly under it vanishing from view.

The bridge the gondolier had negotiated with so little effort emerged from tall dark walls with crumbling plaster white and elegant, its high oriental curve creating a definite pause and space before leading into yet more high walls on the other side. A short white moment of light between two worlds of darkness suspended over the dark green depth of slowly flowing water.

He stood and allowed his mind to rest on the image. The movement of light and water drew shimmering golden hexagons along the pillared wall at the canal's side. His mind took on a stillness. The depth of the abyss and the fragile bridge above it seemed to span the borders of his being, his consciousness a small speck of light at the centre.

Through the darkness, slowly, quietly, like a soft breeze moving gently over fallen rose petals he became aware of movement on the bridge and the sound of laughter like silver bells. The darkness stirred and he found himself in a rose garden where the sound of a fountain playing drew him in. He floated past the geometrical patterns of a maze and into the centre. There the water of the fountain sprang like light from a lotus flower at the top and fell over scallop shaped dishes into two deep heavy bowls of green bronze. He looked down into the water of the green bowls and saw the moon rise through the darkness; in the distance across the field was a thatched cottage with its windows softly glowing. It was the one Jane and he said they would live in. She stood next to him her arm round his waist. There was a slight chill in the air and through her blouse he felt the warmth of her breast pressing on his ribs as she held him tightly.

'Let's go down to the little bridge and make a wish.'

She held his hand and led him down in the darkness to the small wooden bridge over the river. It was scarcely more than a stream, but it ran quickly over the pebbles and sounded bigger in the dark. They looked out over the rickety hand rail, poised suspended in the night above the running water with the moon just casting the faintest of long shadows and wished into the deep mystery of the eternity around them. Then she turned and put her head on his chest, and he folded her in his arms.

'I don't know how to say it.'

'Just three little words.'

'I love you.'

The surface of the water stirred in the darkness of the green bronze bowl as if a wind had breathed across it, the moon and the cottage and Jane faded and he saw a white bridge rippling gently; on the bridge was the girl in the creamy-white dress, the Renaissance girl from the ferry. The sun shone on her gold-blonde hair and pale skin and as she leaned on the white bridge the sound of her laughter brought David finally back to waking consciousness.

David watched as the girl and her friends laughed and played on the bridge. She posed for a photograph, leaning back on the bridge parapet tipping her chin and showing her profile to the camera in an exaggerated way as if for a magazine picture.

What painting was it she reminded him of? A painting he felt he had seen, Botticelli perhaps, he was not sure. The painting would not come to mind, or even the painter, it was just a sensation of an image, a feeling that beneath the surface waiting to be recalled was a picture rich in associations, sensual, emotional and in a way not readily explicable spiritual.

As his mind sank through images in deeper and older regions of memory seeking associations, he remembered creeping from the bed at his Grandparent's house and, in the semi-darkness, removing dust edged books from the shelves carrying them back and reading by torch light under the tight blankets. They were huge heavy books, darkly bound with faded gilt letters on the spines. They were full of coloured plates first seen hazily through a veil of protective tissue paper which peeled gently back to reveal the depth and richness of their colours. They were scenes from myths and legends; each picture a glimpse into a story that lived and eternally recurred within the books, a moment frozen by his eyes. He thought of the books as windows onto the worlds within them: Jason and the fiery bulls; Hylas and the Nymphs; Orpheus and the Sirens in their contest of song; Medea and the Brazen Giant and Theseus in the Labyrinth saved from dying with the Minotaur by the love of Ariadne.

Why was it that she had seemed so mysteriously joined with his journey of rediscovery when he had noticed her, so particularly, on the ferry. She was attractive, even beautiful but here there were so many attractive and beautiful women why was it she seemed to have some special significance? He could only think that it was an association from the past, a stirring of a deeply hidden memory formed early when impressions all seemed to fall into a dark clear pool and spread their essence throughout his being. At what stage the dark clarity of the water became muddied he was not sure. He felt the immanent presence of his childhood, invisible but making itself known in an almost unbearable sensation of energy filling his body as if in preparation for something that at present lay trembling, hidden beneath the rippled reflecting surface of consciousness.

The slight breeze along the canal rustled her dress and she held her pose until the dark-haired boy said something that made her laugh again and she rushed at him and went to hit him. She then turned, walked back to the parapet and standing on the bottom row of stone leant over, looking down into the water. The other boy joined her and said something, she looked quickly at him and then looked straight in David's direction.

Whether or not she was looking at David he could not tell but it took him by surprise and left him no time to look away. It was a strange sensation not knowing whether they were looking at each other or not. As his eyes started to lose their focus, he felt a gently pulsating energy go out across the divide. His breathing fell into the rhythm of the waves; he breathed in her gaze and exhaled his to her. He felt deep within him a sensation long forgotten, a hidden power filling his being, a force like first love. As the sensation grew, the bridge over the canal and the wishing bridge over the pebble rattling stream by moonlight, Jane's image and the girl in the Botticelli dress merged as one.

How was it he had not seen the similarity before? He was overcome by a conviction that Jane had returned to save him from the monsters of the labyrinth, to lead him up from the circles of his own private inferno through the trials of purgatory. He saw again the vision of Jane in white, haloed in a rose-pink light, leading him forward by the golden flame of a candle. He felt himself pulled forward and the stone of the bridge parapet dug hard into his ribs. The pain made him look away and when he looked back the girl too had turned to speak to her friend. She was looking at a book, a guide book David decided, as the two girls studied the page and then gestured to the boys to follow.

David suddenly confronted the possibility, even probability that he would never again see this girl who had been sent to save him. He felt panic and quickly reached into his bag to find his map. As he did so he began walking and started to work out how he could follow them. He tried to block out from himself what he was doing. It was a compulsion, something driving him when he knew it was foolish. A chance likeness between an old girlfriend and a sixteen-year-old tourist had created an obsession that interfered with his contemplation of Venice and yet he could not let go. Against his will and with an irrational excitement he turned through the narrow gap between the buildings, heading in the direction they had gone, in an attempt to make their paths coincide.

When he came to the calle that led to the bridge on which they had been standing there was no sign of them. There were fewer tourists here and he dashed forward looking to right and left. He thought he saw the girl's boyfriend and breathlessly sprinted into a turning that took him to a desolate and deserted corte. There was nobody. She had gone, back to the darkness of his mind. He leant on the stone well-head with its dry earth and drier plants to think and regain his breath.

He was making a considerable fool of himself; he was well aware of that. If he was concerned that his and the girl's fates were destined to coincide then he should have more faith in serendipity and if they were not then there was no excuse for such behaviour, rushing around for a glimpse of a girl he did not know. This perhaps was the pathetic madness of middle-aged desperation, even worse than the madness of old men who had simply ceased to see any convincing reason for sanity. The desperation, he had to admit, of Gustave von Aschenbach. The similarities were too close for comfort. He had read Death in Venice several times over the years and had always taken a rather superior view of Aschenbach's plight, his being cut off from the essential forces of the gods by his rigid attention to detail, the triumph of form over inspiration. And yet was this not the very situation in which he found himself? Not, it was true, from a conscious control and squeezing out of the life-force but from its progressive elimination nevertheless. The burial of Dionysus under barge loads of

Coca Cola, Seven Up and mounds of targets and sales figures.

Sitting on the stone steps beneath the well-head David felt the darkness of swirling water rising ever closer to his consciousness. He feared that it would bring with it more of the forgotten images that could drive him into such obsessional madness as led to his pursuit of the Renaissance girl. He looked around for the way out of the Corte and saw that it was through a low, narrow sottoportico.

3

THE FIRST DAY - PART THREE

Emerging from its cool, damp-plaster darkness he looked up and found himself in a deep gorge, the many-storied walls towering above him divided by a thin ribbon of blue. At the base of the dark walls, a gilt frieze of fashion windows, statues of glass frozen into long legged cranes and kissing couples. It was broken in places by the glittering, boiled-sweet colours of souvenir glass, lacking the supple liquidity of the large pieces in the fashion shops. There were windows of pizza, dark red with black olives on golden dough, and more Cola and Seven Up in over-bright red, white and green. There were dark caverns for drinking coffee, fronted by displays of ice-cream in plastic trays with dark haired Venetian girls in striped aprons shouting in their clipped and strident Italian, hands moving fast to scoop the ice-cream and take the money before leaning forward to hear over the clamour,

'Prego!'

'One strawberry one vanilla, one pistachio please,'

The scoop slid expertly round the ice-cream, landing it

in succession on the cones, each one placed in a wire holder like a flower arranger on top of the counter.

'Drei thousand...three thousand lire... grazie'

And leaning forward again the insistent 'Prego!' fired into the waiting press of hot and thirsty bodies with hands outstretched, their bare arms and legs patched with sunburn. Languages mixed and mingled into a single meaningless cacophony. The processions, with cameras and bags chafing, maps refusing to fold, pushed their way urgently through the narrow alleys. He felt cold, sweat chilled his forehead, he was dizzy, the roaring was getting louder, he had to put his head between his knees, that was what he had always had to do. He tried to make his way to the side.

Beneath London bridge, the Thames flowed swiftly; the tide drew it surging around the pillars. He was amongst the flowing crowd of the dead; he felt the bodies bumping and pushing, he was sinking, the gorge deepening and a flood rising over him the babbling voices turning into an overwhelming rush of dark water.

He was pushed to the side as he slowed to a stop. The bodies slid past him riding on the tide. Black barges moved in convoys past the Tower, and traitor's gate, through the deserted docks and past the walls of windowed flats in styles from Surrey's new estates, perched incongruous on the derelict banks, and by the great deserted heaps of rusting debris piled above shiny rat-grey slopes of stinking mud. They were plague barges, barges of dead, drifting unaccompanied out to the wide ocean.

The rushing water pounded at his head and, in the pulsating white noise of the water, hidden beyond its all-pervading flow, within the great organ chord always changing and yet remaining always the same like the ripple of golden light beneath the water, he could hear the sound of female voices, part of the chord but tracing their own path, recognisable as a threefold melody.

Other voices began to reach his ears. The rise and fall and rush of speaking voices, Venetian. He could not pick out the words. He became aware of a softness and warmth supporting him and the faint mingled scents of perfume, sweat and garlic. Warm scents, comforting. The rim of a glass pushed between his lips and touched his teeth. Cold water trickled into his mouth. The pillows were soft, the room floated, 'Thank you Mummy,' and his head nestled into his mother's arm the touch of her hand soothing away the burning in his forehead.

'Can you walk?'

'Come, you can sit in there.'

'It is very hot. Are you feeling better now?'

'Do you want a doctor?'

The voices, the street, Venice, the café, tumbled through the half-conscious blur. He was sitting on the stone ground, one of the ice-cream girls supporting him and holding a glass to his lips her breath warm against his face as she spoke.

'I'm all right,' he said trying to stand. 'It's nothing serious.' The ice-cream girl held his arm as he got unsteadily to his feet.

'Come. It is cool inside.' and she led him into the dark coffee cavern where giant fans turned slowly on the ceiling.

As he sat on the wood and wickerwork chair the darkness lightened. His ice-cream girl in her striped apron shouted and waved to a barman and, with a smile, returned to distributing gelati to the tired and thirsty crowd. The barman came over and David ordered an iced coffee. He checked for his wallet and camera and relaxed when he found them safe. The sweet strong coffee made him feel better. He had barely eaten since the day before. He'd not been taking his anti-depressants. Then there was the sudden removal from the safety of his routine in London and the accompanying emotional turmoil. What with that and the heat and the crowds a dizzy spell was hardly surprising. The cold clamminess of his forehead had warmed and dispersed. He started to feel in control again and sat back to watch the girls working at the bar and the ice-cream counter. They were warm and physical, their dark, earthy presence anchoring his mind firmly in his body.

His eyes kept returning to his ice-cream girl. It was difficult to say whether she was more attractive than the others, but their brief moment of intimacy seemed to have created a link, a bond. His head had rested between her arm and her breast, she had cared for him when he was helpless, holding him like a mother. Something seemed to be stirring beneath the surface of his mind, a recollection, a sensation that he had thought that before, but it remained a vague feeling and he could make no sense of it. He tried to remember when he had last been cared for by a woman and could not. Thelma believed that sympathy for the sick only encouraged malingering. His wife had never, so far as he could remember, held him like that and yet here was a complete stranger who had done so quite naturally and without any self-consciousness.

He began to feel more relaxed, less held in, as if life were starting to flow from the centre again rather than being fixed in a mould, dried and set. Suddenly the blood, the energy, the life that had escaped and flowed out to his skin retreated, disappeared in an instant and his head felt gripped by an iron band. His ice-cream girl had finished her stint at the counter and was walking towards him. This was ridiculous. All the new life, the flowing natural life had drained away, evaporated like a volatile spirit in the sun. She was an ordinary girl, earthy and physical, remember? Natural and uninhibited. He felt as inhibited as if he were wearing a strait jacket.

She moved closer, he was trapped; it wasn't even possible to run for the door as she was coming from that direction and the tables were full, with very little space between them. He swallowed. His head felt as though it had been pumped up like a balloon.

'May I join you please?'

She had her hand on the back of the chair opposite him and was already sliding round to sit down on it by the time he was saying,

'Please do.'

The brief pause helped him get his wits together and he half stood as he spoke.

'I'm very grateful for your helping me just now,' he said separating the words and emphasising them for clarity.

'Would you like some more coffee? On the house.'

'Yes, thank you very much.'

'Giovanni, due cafe Pronto.'

Giovanni waved his hand at her in a somewhat impatient way but brought the coffee. As he left, he muttered something to her. It was too fast and too quiet for David to follow.

'How are you feeling now?'

David realised that her English was good and that he did not need to continue to stress his words.

'Much better, I feel very awkward about it though. It was a stupid thing to happen.'

She turned to take the coffee from Giovanni. Her hands were delicate with sensitive fingers and long varnished nails;

'ordinary' and 'earthy' no longer seemed quite the right description.

'It is very hot and the crowds they are dreadful at this time.' Suddenly she smiled and her dark eyes narrowed at the corners. 'At first I thought you had been drinking.'

David smiled too. The terror that he had felt when she had first approached was gone, replaced by fascination and curiosity.

'You speak very good English, where did you learn?'

'In Bournemouth.' She laughed as David's face registered his surprise, 'I was an Art student in Milano until last summer. I used to go to Bournemouth in vacations to improve my English, when I wasn't working here.' She paused. 'This place belongs to my Uncle.'

This at least explained her cavalier attitude towards Giovanni and his muttered words to her.

He felt that he should say something about himself, but he always found this awkward. People were summed up by the job they did and yet it conveyed all the things that he felt least identity with in his life. He could say he was a writer but that was hardly true; writers were, after all, supposed to write.

'David, David Green, I'm a computer sales director,' he paused, 'as a day job.' Her attentive listening made him bolder, 'I used to write, I'm trying to again, begin to write again that is.'

He felt himself stumbling and stuttering and was angry with the fact that he had to try to cross this bridge. A bridge between the person who occupied his daily life and the person he felt himself to be, the person he was trying to recover.

'And I'm Francesca. I do this as a day job while I'm trying to paint. I've tried painting pictures of Venice for the tourists but it's worse than selling ice-cream. At least selling ice-cream doesn't mess up your painting.'

He had not needed to feel so defensive, she understood, and he was grateful.

'And do you paint better now you're selling ice-cream?'

'When I paint, I paint better but it's all in my spare time and I never seem to have enough of that.'

David smiled and found her eyes smiling warmly back. 'I know what you mean. I've neglected writing for too long.'

'So, have you followed all the other writers here? You are following many famous people who have come here to write.'

His glimpse of the Renaissance girl on the ferry and the wild and irrational pursuit of her as an embodiment of an image deep in his mind, a goddess of his mythology, surfaced. The plague ran in his mind and he felt a renewed sense of panic, a sense of déjà-vu, but what was it that he was seeing again? He felt images of blackness, plague and death rising within him but where had he seen them before? He smelt disinfectant and looked to see if a waiter was wiping the tables. The act of looking round helped him pull himself together. With an effort of will he obliterated the images.

'In a way I suppose I have. I find writing harder than I used to, I seem to have lost inspiration, but I thought Venice might be able to work its magic.'

'As long as you don't succumb to the plague.'

David felt a dreadful whiteness spread through his skin, beads of perspiration seeped onto his forehead and a chill struck through his body. He felt a tingling over his face and in his fingers. He gripped the table to avoid either passing out or being sick. He heard Francesca saying,

'Are you all right, I was joking, Aschenbach, Tod im Venedig, Death in Venice, you know?'

The implication of what she was saying, and the unconscious accuracy of her perception settled slowly on him. His grip relaxed and the panic passed. He shivered and felt drops of perspiration run down his ribs from his armpits.

'Sorry, I'm obviously still not quite recovered. Like him in more ways than one. I hadn't really thought about it. I'm OK now, sorry.' He sipped the dark, rich coffee. 'Where were we?'

'Venice working its magic. Are you sure you're OK?'

'Yes, fine.'

Again, her warmth and concern struck him; it was a feeling he had forgotten. It generated a new warmth in him which, as his eyes paused on hers, he felt flow between them. In the same moment her eyes had rested on his and he was sure she too recognised this undefined empathy. The moment passed.

'Is this your first visit?'

'I came here thirty years ago, it's a very special place for me, it represents so many things. Maybe you don't feel the same, living here.'

'Oh yes, it's special all right. I've never really lived here. I grew up in Treviso. I used to come and stay here during school vacations. Now I'm staying with my Uncle. It was a magical place then and it hasn't changed. That's what the tourist paintings miss. They just show the outside.'

'Yes! It's not so easy in words though. They have a habit of either being too mundane or too obscure.'

'Perhaps you should paint instead; or write music.'

'Perhaps, maybe once I might have.'

As he spoke, he saw Jane accompanied by her friend Emma at the music room piano, playing a violin sonata he had written. He had been annoyed that too much of it was derivative. The girls had apologised for their playing, but he was cross with himself not them. At least he had written it though, completed it, done something.

'Why once?'

'Why indeed. I'm afraid a lot of things have been left undone since I last came to Venice.'

Her face showed that she felt he was being deliberately obscure, so he added: 'Too much time spent earning money and neglecting the important things.'

'That is a shame. You must use such a talent; it is not our choice.'

Her own earnestness suddenly seemed to embarrass her, and she broke suddenly into a smile. 'At least that is what I was told when I stopped painting for only a few months.'

Their conversation flowed on through painting, writing and music and the elusive quality that set Venice apart. It seemed that they were old friends, or at least student acquaintances. Eventually the conversation paused. David did not want it to end.

'Can I get you another coffee?'

'I'm afraid I must get back to work, even the boss's relations can't take too many liberties.'

'I've enjoyed talking to you.' And then quickly before he could lose his nerve, 'Perhaps we could continue another time.'

'Are you are trying to pick me up now?'

'I don't think there's a right answer to that.'

She laughed, 'Probably not, though if you were Italian you would have thought of one.' There was a brief pause whilst she looked away. As she turned back, hesitantly he thought, their eyes met again, and this seemed to reassure her. 'Well we could meet later if you like, when I've finished. We can talk then.'

'I should like that very much. What time do you finish?'

'Oh, about five, come at five that will be OK. Now I really must go. See you later. Ciao.'

'Ciao.'

David stood up too, watched her thread her way through the crowded tables and then lift the bar flap, turning and slipping behind the bar with a single, graceful and rather theatrical movement. He felt as if he had somehow been caught up in a whirlwind, everything had been moving so fast and he seemed to have had very little influence over what was happening. He picked up the bag with his camera in and with a wave to Francesca made his way out.

Once outside, the blinding brightness of the sun, even in the crowded calle, mesmerised him. As his eyes adjusted, it seemed impossible to imagine that he had practically passed out here only an hour ago. There was none of the feeling of foreboding and doom that had hung round him earlier. Now he felt confident, alive and ready to enjoy the walk.

He started to walk, and the extraordinary nature of the events began to impress itself upon him. What had happened? What strange new turning had been taken within the labyrinth of memory and imagination, dragging in a mass of new and uncontrolled emotions, draining energy through its course and leaving a physically healthy body on the ground? Alternatively, what had allowed the energy to return so convincingly now? Was it all part of the same thing, events, images, feelings all swirled round on the tide or the wind, playing out their own story, or were these things isolated events, merely individual reactions to the heat or a meal?

And then of course there was Francesca. She was attractive, intelligent and with the most beautiful deep, dark, eyes. Certainly not the ice cream girl any longer. Where had she gone? Just a phantom of the imagination but what about the new Francesca, who was she? Was she a product of the imagination too? At least they were to meet again, and he would have another chance to find out.

He felt a sudden rush of excitement and apprehension hit his stomach. Excitement, well that was easy to explain but apprehension, why apprehension? A limiting, a closing in of the possibilities and perhaps most of all a dependence on another person outside memory and his personal experience of Venice. Someone new, what would she do to the inner world of memory and mythology and what effect would she have on this encounter with the past in the present? But then, if he gave way, avoided inviting another person in to his quest what new experience might be missed? There were after all another two hours to renew that inner, personal acquaintance with the stones and spaces, earth and water of Venice.

With a new vitality he pushed forward, the narrow passage, a cleft along the bottom of a gorge, now seeming the mysterious path to new experience not the threatening descent into darkness and despair. It had become the secret way of promise in books from his childhood that led to walled gardens or to Badger's tunnelled house beneath the snow of the wild wood; the green door into the hill; Aladdin's cave and the underground river leading through marvellous caverns to a domed jewel encrusted hall of all he could desire. The same tingling thrill ran through his body as it had when his mother read those stories to him and he felt himself carried into the creation of his own imagination, turning inside out and entering a world within himself.

Here he found it hard to know whether he was inside a world of his imagination or the world of his imagination was in him. The two ran together, the projection of his inner world, given images to build on when he was sixteen, and the outer world that had provided the images. They joined on a flow of light that made him seem curiously transparent, an intermediary who was no longer needed. He struggled to remind himself that Venice, important even primary though she was, was but one of the maps of myth and image within him and that whilst the force of the inner and outer patterns conjoining now reduced him to invisibility it had only eclipsed the rest of his psyche not replaced or destroyed it. He had to decide whether here, for a while, he should let it surge forward unrestrained and worry later about perspective or whether he should try to retain even now some sense of detachment.

He walked on at a more reasonable pace until, via an unplanned and circuitous route he emerged into a wide, open square the Campo Sant'Angelo. In spite of himself, he cast his eyes around the periphery in case he should catch sight of a creamy-white Renaissance dress disappearing into the darkness but there was nothing. Above the roofs on the far side, the perilously leaning campanile of Santo Stefano seemed to be mocking him, throwing doubt on his senses and making a drunken joke of his confusion.

He decided it was time to reflect and sat down at a table outside a small bistro. He ordered a beer. The bistro could not have been more different from Florian's or even Francesca's; it was cheap, friendly and relaxed with a few ageing white tables showing signs of rust. There were a couple of local workmen inside but no-one else sitting outside. His beer arrived. He tried it. It was very cold, and the outside of the heavy glass tankard had misted over. The afternoon was hot, the sun a brilliant pale molten gold blurring at its edges into the fierce blue of the sky. It made his shirt hot to the touch and sank through his flesh, at once revitalising and soporific. He felt the heat inside him suffusing even his bones. He drank the icy beer and all sense of urgency slipped slowly away. It no longer mattered who he met or who he knew or what he did or where he went. Not only his body but his emotions and his mind filled with the sun. It possessed him and dissolved his feelings and his thoughts. The sun gave life, the sun was life, there was nothing further to do.

Eventually he became aware of a slight cooling and looking up saw a small tuft of cloud had drifted in front of the sun. He looked at his watch: four o'clock. He was meeting Francesca at five and the Wagners at eight. He had forgotten the Wagners when he agreed to meet Francesca.

It didn't really matter, maybe she had only intended a chat over a glass of wine between finishing work and the evening. Alternatively, she could meet the Wagners, they were expecting his wife so some explanation would be required but at least the numbers would be right. There was an unreality in Venice, a sense of being cut off in time and place, drifting somewhere in another possibility, that made such things far less of a problem than they would normally seem. His clothes might be more difficult, he was dressed for wandering round Venice not for the Bauer Grunwald. His own things were back at his hotel room a ferry ride away. He was not even sure how he was going to get back that night or where he would stay if he did not. Would he need a tie? Perhaps George Wagner would lend him one. Judging by his previous performance he'd probably send someone out to buy one. Then again, they might not stay at the hotel for the evening anyway, they might go out to a bar somewhere.

With these things turning over in his mind he got up and, still filled with the sun's sense of lazy contentment, made his way towards the Grand Canal.

He came out onto the Ramo della Teatro at the quay Sant'Angelo. From the hot deserted silence of the square he was confronted with the sudden rush and bustle of water buses, vaporetti, the small fast motoscafi, and of course the nodding gondolas perched high on the water and riding the wakes of the insolent motor boats. There were tourists queuing and quarrelling as they waited at the metal shelter for the vaporetto. There were children crying and complaining and a sense of frenzied activity that came as a surprise and a shock after the stillness and space of Campo Sant'Angelo and his immersion in the steady heat of the sun.

He leant against a rail around the landing stage. In the distance was his first view of the Rialto bridge. Like the view of San Marco, it was a view so frequently seen in photographs and paintings that his own recollections were confused with them to such an extent that it was difficult to be sure which was which. He was feeling tired as well. Not so much physically since the sun had relaxed and refreshed his body but his ability to respond freshly to the experience of Venice was suffering from a surfeit of stimulation. His senses felt glazed over and his mind and emotions full up.

Much after all had happened since embarking on the ferry that morning. There was the tense anticipation and the experience of landing, the walk through the columns and on to the Piazza. There were the Wagners, the extraordinary vision of the girl on the bridge and the crazy dash to follow her. The embarrassing collapse outside the café, the beer in the sun and the meeting with Francesca. And now, what was happening now?

As he rehearsed the events of the day, he became aware that each was acquiring its own flavour, an emotional depth. Was he still missing what was happening to him, even here? Was his feeling of being mentally and emotionally full up just a sign that beneath the surface the missed reality of the experience was already spreading through his memory, ready to persuade him that the past is always more significant than the present? Perhaps it was just one of the cruel realities of life that we are never conscious of the total experience at the time and only in recollection can we make conscious its emotional depth. This was, he thought, both good and bad. Good because it meant that the idea that things were always better in the past and always getting worse in the present was just an illusion and bad because it meant that no golden past existed to hold the promise a golden future. But here was the paradox: the only past he could know was the past now in his memory, as sorted and interpreted by his mind. But what grip did that hold over the possibilities of the present? How free was the dreaming, image making mind that worked on without his knowledge, intervention or permission, ruling his experience and his recollection without any possibility of his control? He could not tell but perhaps here if anywhere, where the land and the water, the dream and the event, flow ceaselessly into each other he stood some chance of understanding whatever it was possible to understand.

He shifted his position on the rail but allowed the thoughts to continue. What should he do? In the past was his adolescent visit to Venice, consolidated, and made one with the deeper world that accompanied it; a visit made at a time when all things were imbued with an immediacy and significance even as he experienced them, a time perhaps when the divide between the two worlds was thin, and given greater significance still in memory. Now he could try to rediscover and relive that past, tap into the reserve of archetypal force filled then, when his senses and his mind were clearer, or he could begin a new phase of experience which may or may not draw from the mythology of the old one. He had a feeling that by saying yes to the Wagners and arranging to meet Francesca he had already committed himself to the latter. In fact, already new experience was bound up with the old, new images had quietly settled into the existing ones forming new patterns. He was only dimly aware of their nature, and not at all of how they fitted in, but the columns, his collapse, and the bridge were all accompanied by their own special aura as if during each he had had a dream and nearly woken in the middle of it.

Either way, whatever path he took now, he had to face the fact that his life could never again be the same. By coming here, he had chosen to tear up that phase of his life and begin rewriting. He felt a chill shiver run through him as the implications of what he was doing began to make themselves conscious. Before leaving for Venice he went into the office for a day to meet up with his old colleagues again and reassure himself that things could continue in the same way after the holiday should he wish them to. The familiarity of the concrete and glass, the air-conditioned tower block, struggled with an unwelcome sense that he was already a stranger there, distant from the people he had worked so closely with, shut out from their concerns, a visitor in his own past. When he said goodbye to Thelma as he left for Dover, he had thought that it would be only a week before the routine of that relationship continued.

Now he was on a dangerous path. Before even landing in Venice he realised that his sanity was in grave danger as he attempted to rebuild his mind, risking exposing it to the eruption of sub-conscious forces loosed as they encountered their images in the physical world; repressed fears and desires breaking free in the chaotic ferment like the demons from Pandora's box. But there was more. It was clear now that the sources of his material comfort were threatened too. His job at which he so often hurled abuse, seemed almost desirable now that he saw it was unlikely to survive what-ever transformation he would undergo. His marriage, whose emptiness he blamed more than anything for his failure, seemed to grow into a rock of stability, a foundation from which it was possible to make this journey of discovery. Yet, there seemed even less likelihood that it could survive even past the end of the week. What he was about to do would remove every source of support and replace it with what? The ultimate terror, the unknown. Words came to him rhythmically, words he had written many years ago. They were written about the hanged man of the Tarot, hung by the foot rather than the neck, with coins spilling from his pockets:

> *'Blindly step, the hand is gone,*
> *Only memory drives me on*
> *Beyond the measured, weighed, the known,*
> *Above the waters hung alone;*
> *Free from all that binds or ties,*
> *Only thus is man made wise.'*

He was interrupted in his thoughts by a sudden rush of activity. A vaporetto had pulled alongside the quay. The families of tourists gathered and collected belongings and children with much panic and noise and went cautiously aboard the boat that was rising and falling as its own wake arrived slapping and splashing against the side. No-one got off. As the vaporetto wallowed and turned he was left alone again. He wanted now to move on to the next stage, he felt ready for something new. He felt that the wall between himself and experience was already less dry, fixed and impenetrable than when he had arrived. It was still there but despite the long years of separation from himself, wandering in a wilderness, there was still the possibility of life. He paused in his thought. Now it was time, time to move on. He checked his watch. If he walked slowly it would not be much before five when he arrived at Francesca's.

4

THE FIRST DAY - PART FOUR

As he turned down towards the trattoria his heart thumped hard under his ribs and adrenaline poured through his stomach; the sensations of youth revisiting his habit hardened shell. There had been tense moments when he realised that he had not made a note of where the trattoria was and had resorted to retracing his steps. He had made one or two mistakes and gone the wrong way as, on the outward journey, he had not followed a logical route but had just been wandering. At last he thought he recognised the sun-blind but was still unsure until he saw the shop on the other side, against which he had sunk down before finally sliding onto the stone slabs.

Arriving outside the café again, at the spot where he had collapsed brought strange sensations of floating and foreboding that he could not explain; sensations reminiscent of his alarm when Francesca had mentioned the plague. Different girls were serving the ice-cream now and there was no sign of Francesca. Putting the floating feeling down to adrenaline and an association of the place with passing out, he walked into the soft darkness inside. It was not so busy now though most of the tables still had people sitting at them. He went to the bar and saw the waiter who had served them earlier.

'Is Francesca here?' he asked, suddenly feeling that she was not, that she had left and forgotten all about meeting him.

'I will see for you, wait here.' said Giovanni and passing an order on to one of the other waiters disappeared through into the back.

David waited awkwardly. He hovered between the tables and the bar trying not to look as if he were waiting to be served and yet to appear as if he had a purpose in being there. He looked around at the customers, couples, pairs of women with new clothes in designer carrier bags, businessmen in for a late afternoon coffee, all caught up in their own lives, following their own stream of consciousness oblivious to all the others.

He must have been staring too intently as he felt the people at the tables were starting to notice him. He looked away and began reading the labels on the bottles behind the bar. Just when it seemed he had been forgotten and would have to leave quietly, Giovanni returned.

'She will be here soon, please come in.'

Giovanni raised the bar flap and David went through. He followed the waiter up a steep, narrow flight of stairs and into a small sitting room. It had large mirrors and dark red heavily upholstered furniture. There was a heavy, ornate, wooden cabinet in an alcove on the left with glass and porcelain ornaments on it. Above it was an oil painting that he took to be Francesca's.

'Sit down please, she said she will not be long.'

Giovanni went back to work and David waited. He stood for a while looking at the painting. It was an evening scene of the grand canal in which the buildings and their reflections merged until it was not clear which was which. The gondolas were painted as black insects travelling through this half-lit gloom of illusion: not a comfortable painting for a sitting room. Certainly not the sort of thing that would appeal to the average tourist. He sat in one of the deep armchairs. The adrenaline was beginning to wear off and, as it did so, he felt alone and stranded, stretched thin and uncomfortable. His shirt was too tight, the bag he carried with his camera and notebook was a nuisance. He felt cold and sweaty. This was ridiculous, what was he doing here? Could he not leave quickly saying it was all a mistake and go back to his solitary musing on the warm comfortable past. An old wall clock with a carved, dark wood case ticked slowly and steadily with a resonant almost musical sound.

Suddenly the rattle of a door knob broke in on the clock's hypnotic sound and, in the gilt framed mirror, he saw the door open. He stood and felt himself draw an involuntary breath as he saw her. She was smaller than he had remembered her. She was wearing a plain white dress and a gold necklace that showed off her dark hair and eyes. When she had sat down at the table with him earlier, he had thought that she was attractive but now she had acquired an additional aura of beauty beyond that which he originally perceived.

'Hello, I'm very sorry I've been so long. I finished late. It was busy and some of the girls are so slow. Are you feeling better now? You still look tired; would you like a drink here before we go? I thought we'd go somewhere else; I see enough of this place during the day.'

She spoke quickly and with a light energy that made him feel instantly at ease, all the discomfort and self-consciousness slipped away. She looked at him when she spoke and smiled. He felt instantly warm and happy and grateful but was also vaguely aware of feeling alarm that his emotions were so totally at the mercy of things outside his control.

'Yes please. I mean, I'm much better but I certainly wouldn't mind sitting down for a while with a drink.'

'What would you like, we have just about everything.' She gave a quick smile as she opened the doors of the cabinet and laughed, 'It would be a surprise if we hadn't wouldn't it. We have beer and wine in the fridge.'

She turned and took a bottle of Campari from the cabinet, poured some into a glass and filled it with soda. She spoke as she prepared her drink. '

'I have to go to the kitchen for ice. Would you like something from the fridge?

'A beer please'

'OK, I'll be right back.'

The energy level in the room instantly collapsed as she left. At least, David thought, there would be unlikely to be any awkward silences. It was almost intimidating though to think that this was what she was like after a day working in the rush and heat of the café.

Francesca returned with the drinks and handed David his.

'Salute!'

She raised her glass and then sat down on the settee slipping off her shoes and putting her feet up in one continuous movement.

'Salute!'

David sat down in the armchair. He felt tired and he wished he had been able to change. He should have bought a shirt and tie when he remembered about the hotel but at that stage it had not seemed urgent.

'So, where have you been today?'

It was a simple and obvious question but not one that was easy for David to answer as he had not been anywhere in particular.

'I've just been wandering,' he said, 'following my nose, just soaking up the feel of the place again.' He felt that Francesca was looking slightly harder at him. 'Just looking at the bridges over the small canals, that sort of thing. I got as far as the Campo Sant'Angelo.'

Bridges over small canals. He tried to hide the picture that formed in his imagination: the white bridge illuminating the shadows, Jane's phantom projected onto an unknown girl and the wild dash that ended in a dried-up Corte with a disused well.

'That is the right thing to do. The tourist sights are too crowded, and you don't feel Venice there. You can't feel anything there, they come here, and we cannot do without them but there are too many.' She realised she was raising her voice and broke off suddenly and looked worried. ' Sorry, I didn't mean to be rude, but I have seen it at other times. In the summer, there are so many they are burying the thing they come to see. Then it is just a ...., just a Disneyland. But you did the right thing, there are places where you can find Venice even in the summer.' When she looked worried, she had seemed momentarily vulnerable but now she smiled again and said, 'And do you think it has brought you any nearer to writing again?'

It was David's turn to feel vulnerable as he always did on the subject of writing; it had certainly brought him nearer to one writer.

'Maybe, at least some sign that the imagination is still there. I'm afraid I didn't take my notebook out though. I don't know, I think I need to concentrate on just absorbing it at this stage. Perhaps later on, when I've begun to assimilate it, I shall get some ideas to work on.'

'You make it sound very cold, intellectual. I would think you would want to record the experience when it is strong, you know, most alive so you can use it later.'

'Perhaps you're right but I've always had to go sideways at it. If I go out thinking I'm going to write things down everything disappears. It's like turning a light on when a film's showing. I have to write later when I reflect on what's happened. It often seems more vivid then.'

At this Francesca laughed and said, 'Well, I'm glad you haven't got your notebook out now. I expect your way is best.'

David smiled and laughed too, 'It doesn't work very well I'm afraid but it's the only way I can do it at all.'

A more intense expression came over Francesca's face. 'I'm used to painting, it's different. I sit out and paint and combine what I see outside with what I see inside.'

He must have looked at the painting on the wall at that point because she looked at him and then at the painting.

'Yes, that's mine, sometimes what I see inside is worrying but there it is. If you start censoring, it's no good. If that's the way I see it then that's how I paint it. I need to be there to make it work. Often, I finish it later but if I do it all at home it gets stale, I just reuse the same ideas.'

'Oh, reusing ideas is a problem with writing too, you begin to caricature yourself and eventually you have nothing to write.'

'And then you have the writer's block, is that right?'

'Yes, I'm afraid that is right. And then, when all else fails you have to come to Venice. I suppose it's a bit like Lourdes really except that instead of being the last hope of failing bodies it's the last hope of failing writers.'

He said this with a wry smile and Francesca laughed but said:

'You run yourself down too much. You must believe in yourself. What sort of thing do you write?'

David began to feel that it was only a matter of time before this whole business of being a writer was exposed. He had omitted to mention that it was twenty years since he had published a slim volume of poetry and that he'd published little since. He had only written in rare surges of energy and then only two or three poems at a time. There was a novel half finished, accompanied by a pile of notes, a play that had been performed by amateurs but not made it any further and he'd had some stories appear in magazines but nothing of any substance. Nothing really since he had been married to Thelma. Francesca was intelligent and perceptive as well as beautiful and she would realise he was a fraud. He had not of course said he was a writer, only that he wrote in his spare time but, somehow, he felt that would not help.

'Poetry mainly, short stories, a play.'

'You must let me see some of your writing, the poetry in particular.' she said finishing her drink and jumping to her feet. 'Come on we're going out. Oh!' Her face suddenly took on that same worried look he had seen earlier. ' How inconsiderate of me, do you want to wash or anything first?'

David almost turned down the offer as just a gesture of politeness but decided he really would feel better if he did.

'Well yes, thank you.'

'Right, it's through here.' she said moving to the door and then, pausing, looked at him. 'You can borrow one of my uncle's shirts too if you like.' She said this slightly tentatively as if not wanting to offend him.

'Well if you're sure that would be all right.'

The caution in her voice disappeared instantly. 'Yes, of course, he's got hundreds. Come on, I'll show you the bathroom and you can pick a shirt from his wardrobe. He's away anyway.' She added this last comment with the same quick, dazzling smile she had thrown at him when she opened the drinks cabinet. 'He's with my mother and cousin at their house in the mountains. He will be back for the weekend when we get even more day trippers on top of the tourists.' She grimaced at the thought and then showed him through to the bathroom and opened the door of her uncle's bedroom opposite, indicating the wardrobe. 'Just come back to the sitting room when you're ready.'

He shut the bathroom door behind him. This was, he decided, taking on a life of its own. He had done little himself to make it happen and here he was being treated practically like one of the family, or at least an old friend, by a very attractive and intelligent Italian girl whom he had met barely five hours before. He looked in the mirror and assessed what he saw. At least he didn't look as bad as he felt inside. He still looked younger than his forty six years. His eyes looked tired but lately he'd been grateful to mirrors and shop windows for showing him he wasn't the shrivelled up old man he felt himself to be. He took his shirt off. His body was still all right from the outside, what was wrong was the mind that was driving it and the emotional turmoil that held it back. If he could sort that out maybe things could be good again.

He splashed cold water over himself and felt better. He needed a shave really, but it would do. He slipped his own shirt back on before crossing the hallway to go into her uncle's bedroom. He felt rather self-conscious about this but there was no doubt the offer was genuine. As he opened the wardrobe there was a faint smell of cologne. He chose from among the very impressive range of fashionable shirts one that he thought he would feel comfortable in and would also make him feel good. It was a dark blue with a pattern woven into the silk. He put it on tentatively. It should, he reasoned, make him feel more at one with Venice but as he felt the unfamiliar material next to his skin he wondered about its owner. What sort of man was it whose silk skin he was putting on? He checked in the wardrobe mirror and decided that whatever irrational misgivings he may have, he felt better, more positive, more in control. He rolled his own shirt up and put it in his bag. He then made his way back to the sitting room.

Francesca was reading a magazine when he got back. She looked up.

'Better?'

'Much. I really appreciate the shirt. I hope your uncle won't mind.'

She waved this away as something that was already agreed and picked up her bag.

'Right, let's go.'

David had hoped they would not have to go out through the café. For reasons he could not easily explain he felt awkward going out past her uncle's staff, but he was out of luck. Francesca led the way down the stairs and turned straight out through the bar. She waved and called 'arrivederci' to Giovanni and a couple of customers on the bar stools as they went, and David tried hard to look relaxed. The calle outside acquired yet another aspect now, it felt and looked different yet again in her company. Now he felt part of Venice, not a tourist any more though he wished he had asked to leave his bag behind. Just being with her made it more like going to a wine bar in Soho, or Covent Garden, where he felt at home. Would this detract from it or add a new dimension? Francesca walked quickly despite the uneven stones that looked as though they could easily snag a heel.

He was so caught up in the experience of being with her that he took no notice of where they were going. It took him by surprise when they finally turned down a narrow side turning. Here there was a bar with a green awning dipping low over the outside tables which were surrounded by ornamental wrought iron. There were archways in the white-washed wall that led through to the bar inside. The wall lights cast a pale golden glow over the white walls. It was still only half-past six but no direct sun reached this far so it seemed much later. Francesca went over to the bar and spoke quickly with one of the barmen who looked at David. Then, turning back, she touched his arm lightly and said,

'A friend of my cousin. Come on we'll sit over on the far side by the wall.'

As she touched him, her fingers made the hairs rise on his arm as if an electric charge travelled through them. Was this imagination, his own nerves or a flow of energy from her fingertips? When he was a student, he would have said a flow of life-force. Recently, until arriving in Venice, he would have said imagination or his own nerves. What he was aware of, as these thoughts travelled quickly through his mind, was his own reaction. He felt a tension, a resistance, a gathering together of his own body in defence. This was the last response that he wanted to give but he could not help himself and he felt her hand move away, subconsciously registering his own wall of separation. He could not tell if she was aware of what had happened.

They went over to the table and sat down. Again, routine came to David's rescue and he asked,

'What would you like to drink?'

'Wine I think, yes, red wine, vorrei un vino rosso della casa.'

He felt she had put in the Italian as either a reminder or a lesson. 'I'm afraid I don't speak much Italian.' but he added 'I can manage to ask for the wine though.'

'I wondered whether you could, but you didn't react when I spoke to Giovanni so I thought you probably didn't. I wasn't surprised, you English expect us to learn your language and, of course, we do.'

'Well I have tried but it's very difficult in England. You never meet anyone to practise on.' As he spoke, he gestured to one of the waiters. 'Una caraffa di vino rosso per favore.' The waiter looked at Francesca and said something to her that he could not understand. He then turned to David and said,

'Certainly sir.' and disappeared in the direction of the bar.

'You see what I mean, it's the same even in Venice.'

'Would you like us to have our conversation in Italian?'

'I don't think we'd be able to talk about anything very interesting if we did; I start to fade out after I've asked for wine, coffee and ice-cream.' Francesca grimaced,

'I think that would be too much like being at work, perhaps we'll stick to English for now.'

The wine arrived. They talked about the difficulty of translating poetry and Francesca's course at Milan. It was mainly art history, but she had made every opportunity she could for painting and had sold several of her pictures. David thought she was curiously and unusually evasive when he asked who had bought them. She changed the subject quickly to Dante and how she could not imagine how he could survive translation. David admitted that he could not know but that the sonnets of the Vita Nuova in

Rossetti's translation were among his favourite poems. He thought, but did not add, that the mid-life descent of Dante through darkened woods into the circles of the Inferno was too close to his own experience for comfort in any translation.

David looked at his watch and realised that he would soon have to broach the subject of the Wagners though he could, of course, just forget them. He was sure George Wagner would not be at a loose end for long, but he still felt guilty at the thought of not turning up. He also felt that he would like to show he was not entirely dependent on Francesca for ideas of where to go. Finally, there was a pause in the conversation, and he said:

'I met some Americans this morning. They invited me for drinks later on this evening. I left it open, but we could go if you'd like to.' He waited for a reaction and when it did not come, he added, 'You never know, they might be interested in buying some of your paintings.'

'Let's decide later. We came out to talk. I don't know whether I would find your Americans interesting.'

He had clearly not handled this well. He was not sure quite what he had said that had made a barrier come down over Francesca's eyes but he had no intention of letting the Wagners ruin his evening with her. Guilt and good manners had their limits.

'I don't know whether I would either,' he said rather defensively. 'I just thought I'd mention the possibility.' She did not react, and he added, 'George Wagner was interested in Byron.'

'Mad, bad and dangerous to know. I'm not sure whether that is a recommendation or not.' She had started to fidget with the cutlery on the table and did not meet his eyes. 'And why do you think he might be interested in my paintings?'

'He collects books, early editions. I just thought he might, you know, he might be interested in paintings as well.'

Francesca's energy and enthusiasm had suddenly dipped, or at least become shut in. She seemed both worried and exasperated with herself. Suddenly she stood up and reached for her handbag.

'I shall not be long. I had a phone call earlier, that's all, an old friend. It's nothing.'

David watched her walk quickly and purposefully through one of the archways dividing the tables and disappear from his sight. He felt an awful blankness fall over him. How many films and television plays had he seen where this happened, and the man sat waiting for the girl who never returned. She had left him, and he felt it was his fault, though he could not work out what it was he had done.

He sat and stared into his wine and the reflections on the surface. He watched the candle flame in the red glass of the lamp and settled into a flat, emotionless, unthinking state. A pool of glistening wax breached the wall around the top of the candle and poured, water clear, down the side, creating patterns at the base as it cooled; patterns like limestone cave formations, curtains of glistening rose-tinted rock, hardened, set and buried beneath the ground, the heat gone, leaving the cold remains. Caverns dripping coldly, piling rock on rock until it was lost; the cold emptiness of a wind-swept cemetery, raindrops dripping on petals until the mud covered them and they were gone. She had left him, and he felt it was his fault, though he could not work out what it was he had done.

A shadow fell over his table. David became aware of someone standing by it. He looked up fearfully and saw the barman that Francesca had spoken to when they arrived.

'Francesca sends her apologies and says please wait.'

'Oh, yes, thank you, I will.'

David stumbled over his words. He had been so sure that she had gone, and his mind had become so numb that he could not adapt. He had been away somewhere and was not sure what had happened, he knew it was significant but could not tell why. He felt as if he had slept but he knew he had not. Something waited for him beneath his thoughts, but he did not know what it was. He was still not convinced she would be back just because of a message.

'Is there anything I can get you?'

'No, no thank you, nothing.'

The barman returned to his work.

He thought back to what could have caused Francesca to break down so unpredictably. A phone call she said, probably nothing to do with him at all. He stared again at the candle and felt himself drawn in to its light again and through to the caverns beneath. It was just such blank, empty moments when his conscious mind seemed to switch off, that had enabled him to write, moments when he felt a dark quietude. Holding the focus of his mind on it, he had peered down into the depths to find that which was lurking beneath. And, as he began to write, the words had come in rhythm, like shadows from a cave. After that they needed working, revising, hammering into shape but without that first flow he was helpless. Did this mean that along with the instability, the panic and the anxious loss of control some part of his soul was flowing back to be reactivated again? How could he help it? How could he use it? He tried to remember what he had found in the cave, but it had gone; his mind was looking outwards again, and he could no longer see within. It was part of the problem that he found it so difficult now to see into himself, his eyes looked into darkness, his mind seemed to have a wall across it. He had lost his inward vision, become blind to himself and he did not know what he had done.

In the corner of the university grounds, on the grass mound that served as an amphitheatre, he had emerged as Oedipus, eyes closed, face running with stage blood and cried:

> *'O dark intolerable inescapable night that has no day.'*

and felt himself falling through space, resonating a hidden sound within, not acting any longer but standing in darkness over the Theban plain.

> *'Torture in the flesh and in the soul's dark memory.'*

He was locked into a recurring story on the rhythm of the words; he was no longer acting. He had put out his eyes on his mother's golden brooch pins before beginning his pilgrimage through the desert. Now his mother had gone, there was no-one to guide him and care for him as he tried to expiate his guilt. She had left him and it was his fault though he did not know what he had done. As Oedipus he had the tender hand of his daughter-sister Antigone to hold but now, for him, there was no-one.

'David.'

The sound of her voice travelled across the haze of his thought.

'David.'

He became aware of her voice but felt loath to leave the image of the desert, the hot clear air, the masks of fixed forms and archetypes, where there was no water to cause confusion. Then he felt her hand touch his arm. It was comforting now, and he did not pull back. He would have to answer soon, or she would speak again and perhaps be cross with him like his mother when it was time for school. He tried to speak but only turned to face her and as he did so her eyes melted through the hot, dry space and he saw that the lashes were damp and the lids slightly swollen.

'Francesca?'

'It's my turn to apologise I'm afraid. I'm very sorry about that but I couldn't help it. I'll explain another time.'

He stood and went to help her to her chair, but she shook her head and looked down.

'At least finish your wine.'

She looked up and gave the slightest hint of a smile. 'No, please walk me back. I want to go.'

They walked back in silence through the growing darkness: deeper in the valley of shadows between the high walls. David felt a tension in the silence that prevented him from speaking or asking about the phone call. She had said emphatically that she would explain another time. When they turned the corner, without looking towards him, she slipped her arm through his. He felt a warmth towards her spread outwards through his body but still the tension told him not to speak. He was concerned as to what secret pain had caused this previously energetic, lively, laughing, beautiful girl to suddenly collapse in upon herself. His concern sent the warmth of sympathy out around her like a mantle and he felt joined with her in a way that previously he had not. He could smell the faint fragrance of her hair as it moved softly to the rhythm of their walking and gently tightened his arm on hers. As they came near to the café, she led him to the side and, stopping, turned towards him.

'I want to be on my own now. I really am very sorry about this.'

She lifted her left hand and rested it lightly on his chest. She looked up and gave a weak smile, her eyes still tired with the hurt that had overcome her. 'Ring me tomorrow.'

He felt himself drawn by the sorrow in her eyes and bent forward to kiss her but the hand on his chest resisted.

' No, but please do ring tomorrow, about mid-day. I mean it, here......' She looked in her handbag and pulled out a card. 'Sometimes I do commissions, so I had these done. The Venice number is this one. Now I must go.' She turned quickly and walked away. David watched as she turned to enter the café.

5

THE FIRST DAY - PART FIVE

A few moments elapsed before he collected his thoughts. What was it that suddenly welled up inside Francesca? Was it connected with the black insect-like gondolas in her painting? What else was it she saw in her paintings that worried her? Who was it who had phoned her and what had they said? He tried to remember what he had said just before she became agitated and upset but could only remember that he had been talking about the Wagners. It was only about eight hours since he had first seen her, but he felt that he had been drawn inextricably into her drama as she into his. What that drama was and how it would play itself out he had no idea, but he felt that it would happen, that indeed it had already started.

He looked at his watch. It was nearly a quarter to eight and he could not stand where he was all evening. In his bag he had a timetable for the ferry. As he went to look inside for it, he realised his rolled-up shirt was stuffed into it and he was still wearing the borrowed one. It now felt more alien and awkward than ever. He would return it tomorrow. At least it could act as a sort of insurance that he would see her again. The timetable told him that the last ferry was at eleven o' clock so, if he wanted to, he had plenty of time for a drink with the Wagners. Alternatively, he could go back to his hotel room and try to write up some notes in his diary, he certainly had plenty to write. He decided to do both and use the ferry back as a reason to get away. The Wagners' card from the hotel said it was in the Campo San Moise. It would only take him ten minutes to get there and half an hour at most to get back for the ferry.

David approached the Campo San Moise via the bridge and paused on it to look along the Rio del Barcaroll. The gondolas each had a light hanging on its prow and this was obviously a popular place for tourists from the hotels to start a romantic evening ride around the dark canals. At night more than ever they held the mystery of the unknown. There was clearly something very basic and common to people, even those who had little interest in the imagination or travel into other dimensions of the mind, in the idea of floating into the centre of a fairy-tale maze at night. It was surely more than just another Disney ride. A common experience perhaps in dreams which now held an unexplained excitement as the dream became real. Whatever it was, it was something that people, who neither reflected nor thought about it, naturally sought without knowing why.

The hotel was large, luxurious and centrally placed but it was not an attractive building; impressive and modern certainly but with very little, if any, character. He went in and up to the reception desk where he asked for George Wagner. Sure enough, a flicker of recognition went across the receptionist's face when he said the name, showing that he was not just someone on the guest list. She rang his room and allowed the phone to ring for some time. As David waited, he realised that the possibility that George Wagner had forgotten all about his casual invitation had not occurred to him.

'I'm sorry sir, Mr. Wagner is not in his room.'

'Would you try the bar?'

'Certainly sir.'

There was a wait while she spoke to the barman and he tried to locate him.

'I'm sorry, sir, Mr. Wagner does not appear to be in the bar either. Would you like to leave a message?'

'Perhaps you could just tell him that David Green called.'

She gave him a message pad to write on and he tried to make it clear that he had not been put out at all and that it was no problem. Then, after thanking the receptionist, whom he noticed spoke English with an American accent, he turned to go. He was not entirely disappointed that they were not there, but he thought with some bitterness that had he not mentioned the Wagners to Francesca he might at this moment have been having an interesting and enjoyable evening with her. He went towards the front doors where the commissionaire stood. Even in the new fashionable shirt he felt underdressed. Then he heard a loud and unmistakable voice.

'David, David! I was just going to leave a message to say where we'd gone. Good to see you.'

He shook David's hand. 'Where's the wife?'

David had not really worked out what to say to this inevitable question. He had thought that he would be arriving with Francesca or possibly not at all. He had to say something that would leave him as many options as possible later in the week, and yet not cause problems should they meet after Thelma actually did arrive. He decided on the truth as being the only choice that would not lead to impossible complications later.

'I didn't really get round to explaining earlier but she's not arriving until the end of the week so I'm on my own at the moment.'

'No problem, Hilda is talking to some friends we've met from Chicago and she's likely to be bored stiff if we get onto Byron. I'll go tell her we're going for a drink. I'll get that edition of the poems I mentioned; I think that'll interest you. You just wait here, and I won't be a minute.'

The world according to George Wagner was straight forward and positive. You made things happen, there were no problems only opportunities. Whilst for David the whole ethos and attitude of his job involved his playing a role, putting on a new work persona utterly unlike himself, George was one of those people who thought and behaved like that naturally. Here was certainly a man who would be able to sell. The thought of his work shifted David into a different and alien frame of mind. From a world where flesh seemed fluid and existence relative, where dreams and images turned and transmuted beneath the surface giving an inner mythology to experience, it took him away into an outer, matter of fact world where such things seemed fanciful and irrelevant, the substance of illusion and possibly madness. The escape now from these preoccupations began to be almost welcome as a relief from the intensity of the last few hours but over a long period of time it was just an avoidance of the problem, an avoidance that had led to his seemingly endless years in the desert.

'O.K. No problems there. Let's go. Have you got any suggestions?'

David frantically racked his brain to see if he could remember passing a promising looking bar. His one concern was that it should not be the one he went to with Francesca.

He obviously paused too long because George Wagner broke in without waiting for him.

'There's a place just round the corner. I was talking to the barman earlier, he's a regular guy. Why don't we go there?'

David decided 'round the corner' sounded safe and agreed.

As they walked, he had an uncomfortable sense of being a little boy tagging along behind his father. He found himself falling back on his position as a sales manager to tell himself how unreasonable and unjustified it was. It was ironic that he should depend on this despised role as evidence of maturity.

When they reached the bar, which was indeed just round the corner, George hailed the barman like a long lost friend.

'Two beers Tony, make them good and cold.'

There seemed to be a considerable degree of long-suffering patience in the barman's attitude, but George appeared oblivious to it.

'We took in the Doges' Palace and the Rialto today. What about that Casanova getting out of those dungeons? He was some guy eh? I read where he once took up with a girl in a convent so a Cardinal could watch them. The Cardinal's mistress fixed it all up and she was a nun. They really knew how to live in those days eh?'

George clearly had a fascination with the exploits of the romantic adventurers of Venice. David forced himself out of his introspection and, trying to catch up with the conversation, said hurriedly,

'There's certainly enough material for several novels in his life.'

Tony put the beers on the counter and George paid him, pushing one of the glasses across to David.

'You a writer are you? It certainly would, a movie too.'

David observed his own, unexpected, reaction with interest and surprise. It was very different from his feelings when telling Francesca what he did. With George he felt instinctively reluctant to say he was a writer.

'I'm a computer sales manager, I do write a bit though, in my spare time.'

He was leaning on something he professed to despise and disliked himself intensely for it. Why was he so keen to establish his credentials as a man of business and play down the writing when he was with George and yet had felt compelled to do exactly the opposite with Francesca?

'Really? I'm in insurance. Loved it when I was selling. There's nothing like it. The freedom, the achievement; you make a big sale and you feel like a king, write your own pay cheque too. I push too much paper around now, but I still like to get as close to the sales team as I can. You the same?'

David felt the role of sales manager flooding through into his identity and taking him over.

'Yes, I know what you mean. I used to like being out on the road meeting new people. It's all bogged down with bureaucracy and accountants now.'

George nodded sympathetically,

'I just go in and kick ass, tell 'em it's the salesmen who pay their wages that soon shuts 'em up.'

'Absolutely, and yet to listen to the accountants you'd think the sales team were nothing but an expensive liability. They don't realise how vulnerable you can feel out there, how a few perks and pats on the back can boost sales.'

'What's the computer market like in England?'

Again, George was setting the agenda. David began to

question whether he really hated it, this world of computers and sales. Surely the enthusiasm and the flood of ideas that had rushed in disproved it. He was a man of the world, a successful businessman; someone to be envied. The glass tower block was a launch pad for him to conquer the world.

'It's tough in the defence sector at the moment. Politics on top of all the usual challenges.'

They discussed his latest project, without being specific he explained, because of security implications. David outlined the situation feeling strong and safe in this familiar role with its separate language in its separate part of his mind. George made some constructive suggestions and some that underestimated the amount of red tape involved. He talked about the way the internet and e-commerce had revolutionised his business and David found himself questioning George for new ideas and possibilities.

They were on their third drink when David felt the enthusiasm retreating and the words become vacant shells, speech become a reflex action. He felt his body drain of energy and the emptiness of depression take over. His mind reaffirmed his contempt for what he did, and he despised himself for falling into this false state of enthusiasm for something that was merely familiar. Certainly, there was a kick in getting a good sale, but it had gone in a few hours and meant nothing by the next day; all you could do was get another one and what was the point of that? Next to George he felt fraudulent, an outsider acting a part. He admired George's go-getting energy, it made him feel that perhaps there was a simpler way to success and fulfilment and yet he knew he could never do it.

'I tell you if I didn't enjoy it, I'd give it up tomorrow. You only live once.'

David found himself looking hard at George. Why had

he said that? Was there something in his face that gave away his thoughts? He hunted for a reply and found himself using one of those little clichéd bits of bar-room philosophy that somehow stuck with him.

'Life isn't a dress rehearsal.'

'Exactly.'

It was an image that had worried him when he first heard it and frequently since. It was just too apt.

'It's not always that easy to just give something up though, is it?'

'It's as easy or as difficult as you make it. Why, you had enough? If you've had enough, you'll be no good anyway so you might as well get out.'

This was said in an entirely matter of fact way with no sort of judgement behind it. It was impossible to take it the wrong way, but it was not a comfortable topic of conversation. Byron would be altogether more congenial.

'You said you'd got a book I'd be interested in.'

'Yes, here.'

George unwrapped the book from the carrier bag protecting it. It was handsomely bound in maroon leather with gold lettering on the spine.

'I picked it up last week in Charing Cross Road, London.'

'It's a beautiful edition.' David looked through it quickly. It had engraved plates and was in excellent condition. George had placed a bookmark in Childe Harold's Pilgrimage and David turned to the page he had marked, 'I stood in Venice on the Bridge of Sighs'. He read on through Byron's description of Venice crumbling yet retaining its beauty, of how he loved her from boyhood when she:

> *'Was as a fairy city of the heart,*
> *Rising like water-columns from the sea.'*

and of the spell her spirits cast over him later.

George looked over his shoulder and took back the book. He began to read, his deep American voice bringing out and savouring the rich vowel music of the lines:

> *'The beings of the mind are not of clay;*
> *Essentially immortal, they create*
> *And multiply in us a brighter ray*
> *And more beloved existence: that which Fate*
> *Prohibits to dull life, in this our state*
> *Of mortal bondage, by these spirits supplied,*
> *First exiles, then replaces what we hate;*
> *Watering the heart whose early flowers have*
> > *died,*
> *And with a fresher growth replenishing the void.'*

Replenishing the void. Byron too had come to this point in Venice; the point where his childhood and adolescent vision had faded and found solace in the world of imagination fired by her power of enchantment and, perhaps, a way to something more.

George stopped, drank from his beer and paused, still looking at the book. When the lingering resonance of the words had stilled into silence, David said, 'You read that well.' and then, anxious that he should not sound patronising, added, 'Like Byron I loved her too from boyhood, or not long afterwards. Now I'm revisiting, as he did.' He felt himself stumbling to a halt.

'I wish I had. Still I'm here now, that's what matters.'

David thought about Casanova's attraction for George and asked,

'Have you read Don Juan? It's got a strong line in satire as well as romance. It's a good story too.'

George looked upwards at the ceiling and said, 'Ah yes:

'And then he thought of Donna Julia's eyes.'

What a woman eh?'
David reached out to the book and said, 'May I?'
He intended to find Don Juan and read aloud from it but as he turned the pages he noticed, tucked away on a single page, 'Francesca of Rimini, translated from the Inferno of Dante'. The lines at the top of the second column caught his attention and without thinking began to read them instead. When he reached:

> *'And then I turn'd unto their side my eyes,*
> *And said, 'Francesca, thy sad destinies*
> *Have made me sorrow till the tears arise.'*

He faltered and saw Francesca's face and eyes and wondered what sad destinies of hers had caused the sudden sorrow that had overtaken her. A strange set of circumstances had led to him sitting there reading these words with a large extrovert American insurance salesman and yet it lent it a sense of inevitability as if the events were in some way connected like the threads of a plot in a play. Coincidence certainly did not seem an adequate explanation.

They talked on for a while about Europe and about Byron before David looked at his watch and said that he would have to catch the ferry back. The meeting had been altogether richer than he had expected. They walked back to the hotel together and parted with an open invitation for David to ring.

It was a short walk to the back of the great heavy stones that told him he had reached the way through to the Piazza.

He felt a reluctance to find the Sotto San Geminian and the way out; a reluctance to leave the inside of a warm and intricate maze of red walls, white bridges and dark green canals; a maze where now lights moved and flickered making its insubstantial nature even closer to a dream. It was a world of old stories and emotions that had grown familiar, a world like the inside of a theatre on a cold rain swept night in London. It seemed friendly and welcoming compared to the forbidding grandeur of the stones in front of him. And yet, as he came to the archway through which he had travelled earlier, he remembered his impression of it as the entrance to a tomb, leading away from the bright square teeming with people, its distance from the Basilica San Marco with its gold mosaic gleaming in the sun and the feeling of dark uncertainty that he had as he left it for the darkness within. Now from the other side he felt equally reluctant to go back as if he were leaving the womb for the outside world.

He stepped slowly into the archway and felt a darkness behind him. He moved quickly forward and out onto the wide-open space of the square. The sun and the press of tourists had left it. He breathed deeply, taking in its expanse and walked on, briskly now, aware that he was tired and wanted to get back. He checked his watch again; he would catch the quarter past ten ferry.

The ferry was waiting, and the queue of passengers had gone aboard. He sat on the lower deck this time wanting to feel enclosed and contained. The lights and shadows of Venice rippled over the dark water and, as they moved away from the quay out into the lagoon, her low line of palaces and spires was barely discernible between the darkness of the sky and water, vanishing into the star studded night like the castles of the Arabian Nights. They called at the Lido and when they pulled away again, leaving that too behind, there were few passengers left and the grumbling and groaning of the slow heavy craft was magnified in the space between decks.

The crossing in the morning, the thoughts and ideas, memories and reflections, Francesca, the Wagners and the Renaissance girl all slid quietly into the past. The darkness fell across them blurring their images. They would re-emerge. They would grow and mingle with the deeper past. Would they help to make him feel one again or would they just form further fragments scattering his soul across a wider desert? Like Augustine, 'To Carthage I came, where there sang all around me in my ears a cauldron of unholy loves.' But he was adding to them in order to find salvation not repenting. How could you tell, how could you set out intentionally to reconstruct a damaged soul? He felt he was letting experience touch him more deeply, opening his imagination and his past to its influence in a way he had not known for many years but what was coming in? Was it healing just to find a more open flowing contact with both present and past or did it depend on what it was that flowed in? He could not tell but it was that which he longed for, an unblocking of the arteries of the soul so that all his past and present was in harmony with itself.

He and the other remaining passengers formed a straggling line as they disembarked at Punta Sabbioni, all tired and some irritable. All had the lack of direction and purpose that comes at the end of a long and eventful day when the only thing left is to sleep. In the now nearly deserted car park, he walked over to the big B.M.W., comforting in its familiarity despite its links with work. David settled into the reassuring leather seat and relaxed. It was a secure haven after the day's experiences where every corner and thought had brought a new unaccustomed challenge. He started the engine, moved off quietly through the car park and then enjoyed the effortless ease with which it surged forward along the Via Fausta

Back at the hotel, he went to the reception desk to get his key. There was a message from Thelma. The message was timed 21.00 and said simply, 'Please ring when you get back. Thelma.' He looked at his watch and saw that it was just past midnight, rather late to phone or was that just an excuse. A conversation with her would sit oddly with today's experiences but he would have to face it. Either he rang her tonight at home or tomorrow in the office, whichever he did it was an intrusion of the life he was trying to avoid and a reminder of the temporary nature of this new one.

He climbed the stairs rather than take the lift. The big key fob rattled loudly as he let himself into his room, exaggerating its emptiness. He put his bag on the bed and looked around. He took a beer from the mini-bar and rang down for some sandwiches. He looked again at the message and pressed the familiar pattern of numbers, but the answering machine replied. Her recorded voice at the other end was worse. The familiar voice struck through him.

'David and Thelma are unable to take your call at the moment. Please leave your name, phone number and any message that you have, after the tone.'

An empty sound turning from reel to reel on command, an event waiting to happen again and again at the appropriate stimulus, a nightmare of recurrence like the life he was trying to escape. After the tone he left a message.

'Hello, it's David here. I got back late. I've had a good day. I went to Venice. I'll ring you tomorrow evening. Hope everything's OK. Bye.

He would not have said much more if she had answered, it would just have taken longer.

The sandwiches arrived and David got into bed. There was no chance now to write, he was too tired, but he got his notebook and pen out and put them on the side-table. He picked up the history of Venice he had brought with him and, as he ate the sandwiches, read about the barbarian invasions. He remembered Francesca's expression as she talked about the tourists. As he reached Paoluccio Anafesto the first Doge, apparently invented by John the Deacon, the book slipped from his fingers and fell heavily onto the floor. He leaned and switched out the light.

As he slept, dreams rose and fell through his mind, climbing into half consciousness when they coincided with his stirring. Water flowed dark, shaking with reflected colours, spears of light fell into the depths. He found himself suspended over the water. He travelled forward, sinking towards the water and passed through it. There was no water, the reflections existed only in darkness, images thrown against the void:

Darkness

There was a wood, he floated over wild flowers. He had wings but he couldn't move them, he couldn't move at all. There appeared before him a picture of an angel in a field that he'd had by his bed as a child. It said, 'All things bright and beautiful.' The angel had taken his place and he fell down through the blackness until movement ceased:

Darkness

Deep rumbling, thunder and through the sewer pipe poured a great tidal wave of water and excrement, he tried to hold onto the sides but he was swept away and on and on in the flow. The thunder grew until it filled the darkness and the foulness filled all space. There was no pipe and no flow just everlasting night:

Darkness

He lay across her lap with his arms around her neck, her hair flowing over his hands. Her arm supported him. She was all white and gold and through her dark hair flared the sun. They sat together on a shining golden throne that floated through the night. On his cheek was the warmth of her smooth breast. He sucked at the nipple and warm milk flowed through him. The warmth took away his pain:

Darkness

On a windy road at night a young girl beckoned in the distance. She had hair whose waves were dressed with rays of sunlight and a robe the colour of the sea. He floated over the road skimming its surface and the young girl went ahead. Stars formed around her and the walls of the buildings fell away. She sped on, until she became a star and leaving a silver trail fell into a great sea beyond space. He tried to follow but he could no longer move, he was fixed in a vast emptiness and she had gone:

Darkness

A blood red rose lit from within hung in the darkness. He flew to it like a bee seeking pollen. Inside, lit by the golden glow of candles, was a dark cavern. The scent of the rose encircled the candlelight and beyond that was the infinite space of night. A choir sang and the distant night sky folded its darkness into a black rose that constantly rolled in on itself, drawing the blood rose, the light and the cavern and himself towards it until they were all gathered into the dark:

Darkness

6

THE SECOND DAY - PART ONE

The square of the window glowed through the curtains. David turned over and reached out to look at the travelling alarm clock. It was quarter past six. He was warm and comfortable and went to settle back to sleep again when he saw the History of Venice on the floor. Vaguely he remembered the thud of it hitting the floor as he fell asleep. The sight of the book brought back a shadowy awareness of the events of the previous day. He leaned down to pick it up and his mind started working through what had happened and what he had to do. He was to ring Francesca at mid-day, he had to ring Thelma that evening. The image of the beautiful, young girl on the bridge came back to him. Who was she and would he ever see her again? He threw the thin duvet to one side and sat on the edge of the bed.

The hotel had little character and had not even the Bauer Grunwald's luxury to compensate; the rooms were uniform though they had everything that was necessary. Its great virtue, however, and he had chosen it for this reason, was that it had its own beach. David got up and stood naked by the window peering through the curtains. His room had a balcony and looked out over the sea. The beach was deserted except for a tractor, towing a rake, driving up and down cleaning and preparing it for the day. He decided to go and walk along it while it was quiet. He turned to look for shorts and a tee-shirt and noticed the blue silk shirt now lying on the floor where it too had slipped off the bed. He would get that cleaned and return it when he saw her next. He dressed quickly and took the lift down.

He came out of the hotel and made his way across the white paved sunbathing area onto the soft raked sand. He walked through the deep furrows left by the rake, sinking in until he felt the cold sand brushing his ankles. Beyond this, where the sea had washed and levelled it, the tractor had left the beach untouched and it was firm and smooth. Here his feet left slight, watery indentations that lasted just a few seconds before they filled again. Only the worm casts succeeded in remaining on its surface. He walked to one of the rocky promontories, built as breakwaters, and looked along the water's edge. The low, early morning sun sent a long gleaming ribbon of white fire along the still shining surface where the water had receded. Gentle, shallow layers of water slid over the smooth skin of the sand. Mooring poles stood in the water, like sparse trees, their spiral twists lost against the wash of light. He climbed onto the top of the breakwater and looked along the next stretch of beach. A gull flew steadily over the water, scanning the shallows for tiny fish. Still further along, towards the next line of rocks a solitary girl walked away. Her blonde hair glowed in the sunrise and spread over a white shirt; her legs were pale gold in the early light. She bent at every other step looking at shells, walking on sand like dark marble in the shallows. She might have been the girl from the bridge but was too far away for him to tell.

The shallow lapping water, the girl and the dark sand stirred in his mind images of last summer in Wales. Looking out through the windows of the boathouse at Laugharne, across the curving bay. he watched the sliding and slapping, licking and sucking of the soft waves over the smoothly rounded forms of the shining mud banks. A tape played. Dylan Thomas intoned the Ballad of the Long-legged Bait and the view of the bay rang with the notes of his voice. He watched and saw the fisherman cast a girl alive with hooks through her lips. The long-legged beautiful bait, thrown to the flood and drawn through the sea of loves and fishes on the end of a golden thread that rang from his reel.

Out across the bay, into the hazy distance he had felt himself drawn to follow that bait, slipping and bucking through the dark, turning, fish-filled sea. They would slide through the live, wild, sea whatever dreams and illusions dragged him into death; they would go wherever the gold gut took them, just so long as they stayed far from land and its still, fixed, stultifying silence.

Beyond the boathouse window the seabirds pecked purposefully along the shore. The taped voice added the priestly forms of herons nodding dark psalms to the congregation of gulls. Above the mud and the sea wall, away over the scrub green grass of St John's high hill a hawk burned sun-bright in the dusk. As the sonorous incantation ended and the conjured shapes dissolved into air, David was left suffused with a warm, spreading, sensual peace.

That afternoon in the sun, the desire for water to flow through the crusted dryness of his soul began to obsess him and terrify him. He was terrified of bodily death, and death in life; he wanted to live and yet feared that the life he longed for was only a terrible temptation that led to destruction. For months afterwards the turmoil of water haunted his imagination and his dreams. He knew that without water he was crumbling into dust.

He allowed his gaze to turn and follow the black breakwaters, magician's fingers pointing away from the sun's fire on the sand and out to sea. At sixteen he had stayed at a campsite a little way along the same length of beach. Then, in the clear water, he swam with the shoals of small fish, looking up to the sparkling golden dance of the sun on the surface above him, swimming, and seeing a tanned shoulder lifting above the blue-green of the sea, breathing in rhythm, he was at one with the water and the air. Swimming, breathing, rising and falling with the undulating waves, turning smoothly to slide beneath the surface, rising again, mouth taking in the air without any tension or struggle, a unity formed from the counterpoint of rhythms.

He would swim again and find out whether here the sea would have him back, whether the power of association would awaken some of this former union with the elements of water and air; help his mind float free again on the life sustaining seas within.

He watched the girl climb cautiously, barefoot over the rocks of the far breakwater and out of his sight. Now he was alone on the beach. The girl and the tractor had gone, and he was ready to return to the hotel for a shower and a shave before breakfast.

Over the coffee and rolls he looked through a selection of the brochures from the foyer: the opera in Verona, windsurfing, an arts festival in Jesolo and the market in

Cavallino. He had to ring Francesca at mid-day. He had wondered whether by this morning he would have decided against going through with it but now he felt a nervousness and excitement like stage-fright at the thought and knew he had no choice. Until then, the market at Cavallino would be a good way of occupying himself.

By the time he left the hotel, the sun had risen high enough to make its heat felt and the sky was already acquiring that brilliant luminous blue that gives it a tangible depth. It was not worth taking the car as there was nowhere to park and, as the bus went by a circuitous route, he decided to walk. Along the road were sun bleached houses with green, shady, well-watered gardens and dogs barking at the high wrought iron gates. On the other side, between the road and the endless fields of maize, were fruit and vegetable stalls piled high with home grown peaches, melons, grapes and plum shaped tomatoes. There were shops hung with beach umbrellas, inflatable crocodiles and sun beds. The traffic, from large Mercedes cars with double axle caravans to old women in black on bicycles had an air of purpose; everything around him exuded openness and plenty. As he walked, he felt good, positive; he would make things happen, he would make them work.

The market was already packed with people when he arrived. In his new positive frame of mind, he found the crush and noise invigorating. The tubular frames of the stalls bent and swayed under the weight of the tracksuits, leather jackets and hand-bags swinging from their roofs. There were stalls selling shoes and belts, records and jewellery, jeans and denim jackets; there were cuddly toys and life size ceramic dogs, from Great Danes and Mastiffs to Spaniels. There were cheeses and cold meats, hamburgers and hot dogs and, of course, stalls stacked so high with fruit it was hard to see the people behind them. The press of bodies between the stalls made the air heavy with sun-oil and leather, perfume and hot dogs, sweat and peaches. It was only possible to make slow, shuffling progress. German, American and English voices mingled with those of the Italian stall holders who called, cajoled and joked like any market traders but the sound of the language itself gave them their own strong, open, musical and dramatic quality. David looked at the contents of the stalls and bought a shirt. Then, conscious of the irony, he bought a can of Coca Cola and a polystyrene tray of chips and sat at a rickety wooden table by the stall to watch, smell and listen to the people and absorb the atmosphere.

He had nearly finished his chips and was looking idly past a stall selling decorated mirrors when he caught a brief glimpse, behind a large man and the hanging leather jackets, of the back of the head of a girl with flowing golden hair. It was only a glimpse, but he felt a sudden rush of irrational excitement flow through him. He stood to see if he could get a clear enough view to tell whether or not it was the girl from yesterday but now there was no sign of her. He sat down irritated. He was irritated that she had gone but most of all at his reaction. He did not know her; he had not spoken to her and he certainly did not want to repeat his performance of yesterday, yet his nerves and emotions would not let him ignore her. She had been a reflection of the image of Jane, projected by the secret mirror of hidden memory. Surely that was explanation enough. He forced himself to finish his chips and his drink slowly and calmly, he would not try to find her.

When he had finished, he stood, put the can and polystyrene tray on an overflowing bin and wandered over to the stall with the leather jackets. In spite of himself he looked through to where he thought he had seen a glimpse of her. She was there, just a little further along with her friends. She was definitely the girl from yesterday and he was almost sure that she was the girl on the beach that morning. She was young, only sixteen or seventeen. She had an energy that emanated around her, triggering emotional memories dormant since his teenage years.

She was the same age as Jane: her cheekbones, the spreading golden hair, her slim figure and something about the aura of energy joined them. He saw again the moment when their two images merged on the bridge and felt a shiver of power flow through him. As he watched their merged images on the bridge, he was aware of other strange, half dreamed forms welling up, crossing the void. In the darkness her head turned, her face became visible, the skin a radiant translucent white, eyes cast down shielded by the lids; behind her a fountain and a garden, a scent of roses. Flooding through the veins and nerves, in the body's memory, the stress and tension of adolescent love for Jane returned. The face in the garden dissolved entirely into hers. His consciousness reflected on the image and the image weakened. It was similar to the experience of not remembering a dream from the previous night until, halfway through the day, it emerged unbidden only to fade from sight as it was noticed. If only it were possible now to experience something for the first time, unburdened by memories and associations from the past.

It was easy to watch her without being noticed in this crowd and he tried to disassociate her image from Jane's, to break its power. Then, to his surprise the four of them, walked up to two older couples and began talking to them in such a way that he could only think they were their parents. From the way they acted he realised that his

Renaissance girl and the fair-haired boy were not girl and boyfriend but brother and sister and so too were the other pair. They were on holiday together as two families and had gone into Venice yesterday without their parents.

Suddenly she turned, on her own and walked in his direction. As she drew nearer, she looked in his direction and her lipstick, bow-shaped, blood-red, brought back the image of the long-legged bait that swam through his mind early, while he walked on the sun-streaming sand. He shivered and felt himself hooked and pulled by the singing golden gut, through the bucking, blood rayed sea. He hurriedly tore his eyes away, suppressing the pictures that roared in his mind. Was it really a good idea for someone with thoughts like these to go in search of the unrestricted fire and passion of Dionysus? He was a god after all who had driven the wild women of the hills, the Maenads, to homicidal frenzy; he had driven a mother to tear apart her own son. With a shiver he registered the significance of the myth. The son was killed for resisting Dionysus not for following him. He too had to follow Dionysus, awake again that elemental force, or be torn apart and scattered on the dry earth.

He raised his eyes again. She was next to him, stretching up to take down one of the suede, fringed, waistcoats hanging above them. She could not quite reach. The stall holder was walking towards them. He broke through his barrier of inhibition and, catching the man's eye to reassure him he was not about to steal it, reached up.

'Can I help?'

She was so close he could smell her skin and, as the darkness of memory released her, he could feel Jane close to him. He could feel the Dionysian fire burning for release. As he handed her the waistcoat, he felt beads of sweat appear on his forehead. It was, as the myth said, resistance to Dionysus that dismembered and destroyed.

She looked over the waistcoat and then back at him.

'Thank you very much.'

She spoke with a German accent. The links, the images and associations he had thrown over her were sent into confusion. The person he had created from her image was English. It had not occurred to him that she might not be. And yet, it should not have been surprising. There were relatively few English here and, really, it would have been more remarkable if she had been. It was just an idea he had got in his head to start with and had never questioned.

She tried on the waistcoat, looked at it carefully and then put it back on the hanger. She seemed uncertain as to whether to hand it to the stall holder or hang it up again; then, turning and lifting the garment towards the rail above the stall, looked at David with a smile of mock helplessness.

'Will you help me again, please?'

He felt his voice catching in his throat but smiled back and said,

'Of course.'

As he did so, he tried to think up something more to say but before he had got past his initial and totally useless ideas she was turning to go. He had to say something.

'Are you staying at the Serenissima?'

'Yes, with my parents, since Saturday. Thank you. Tschüs.'

And with a slight wave of her hand she walked away, back to her parents and friends.

After saying something to her parents, she and the rest of her group walked towards the gap in the metal fence that served as an exit and entrance for the market. David watched them, determined to resist the temptation to follow.

When they had gone from sight, he wandered on around the market for a short while but had lost interest. He felt relieved that the tension which had filled him had dissipated now that he had identified its source, but disappointed that with it had gone the excitement. He felt deflated and restless. It had just gone eleven o'clock and if he made his way slowly back to the hotel it would be time to ring Francesca.

As he walked, he thought back over what had happened. Did everything from now on have to be in some way nostalgia? When had he first begun to live through nostalgia? When was the earliest experience he could recall that relied for its energy on recollection? Perhaps when he was twenty-six, just before he was married: he felt a similar irrational fascination with a girl of eighteen or nineteen. She was dark haired with deep blue eyes and at drama college. He was living in two rooms of a large house at the time and had joined the family who owned it on a day out. Belinda was the daughter of friends of theirs. They went to an open-air production of The Tempest and the weather had threatened to live up to the play's title. The family atmosphere of the day out had already stirred something within him; it was a long time since he had experienced that. He knew that she reminded him of Miranda, the new love who had replaced Jane when he went to university. It was made all the more poignant because they were watching The Tempest. Even then he was recycling his past. The production was poor, and, during the interval, he had found himself alone with Belinda looking out over the wind and rain swept countryside. There was something about her that had called to a sense of innocent hope within him, innocent in a very basic and natural Blakeian sense. He had started talking about the play, but she talked about the rain on the trees and the clouds being blown through the sky. She quoted Shelley's Ode to the West Wind:

> *'Angels of rain and lightning: there are spread*
> *On the blue surface of thine aëry surge,*
> *Like the bright hair uplifted from the head*
> *Of some fierce Maenad,........'*

and he had replied:

> *'Make me thy lyre even as the forest is:*
> *What if my leaves are falling like its own!'*

She had laughed and said he wasn't that old. He felt it though.

Energy, innocence and imagination; even twenty years ago he had regarded these as things of the golden past. At what age does new experience stop and recycling begin? How long had the Maenads been chasing him and what was it he had done to those avenging daughters of darkness? As he had walked out to the market that morning, he had felt that he would make things happen. Again, he had been swept along by circumstances, stood paralysed when he might have acted. Why was he held like this, bound and helpless, fated to have his liver eaten by the dark scavengers of wasted life?

When he got back to the hotel it was still early. He collected his key, checked for messages and went straight to his room. By the time he had unpacked the new shirt he decided it was near enough to mid-day to phone.

He found the card. Adrenaline made his head pound again. It was crazy that all the most important actions and events take place with reason and senses distorted by adrenaline. He checked the Venice number and dialled out. The tones were unfamiliar, bleeping instead of a comfortable purr.

'Pronto.'

It was a man's voice.

'Pronto, vorrei parlare a Francesca, per favore.'

'Si, si, un momento!'

In the background he could hear the sounds of the bar. He had no idea what to expect, the abrupt end to their evening and the mystery surrounding its cause had undermined any faith he had in predicting events. She may not want to speak to him, she might look on yesterday as just a mistake, easily rectified by not seeing him again. She had been quite clear that he should ring though, it was practically the last thing she had said.

The earpiece clattered, a breath, then:

'Pronto. Qui parla Francesca.'

The voice was unmistakable. The pounding in his head accelerated. He steadied his voice.

'Hello, it's David.'

'Hello, I'm glad you rang, I didn't know whether you would.'

The pounding slowed.

'I wasn't sure you would want me to. How are you?'

'Fine, it is very noisy in here; I am at the bar.'

'Are you working all day today?'

'No, I will be finishing soon. Where are you?'

'At the hotel, in Cavallino, I could be there by two.'

He had not thought of going to Venice and phoning from there, obvious really.

'No, listen, has your hotel got a good beach? I should quite like to get away from here for the afternoon.'

'Yes, it's the best thing about it, that would be fine. Get

the ferry to Punta Sabbioni, I'll meet you there. It's a blue BMW.'

'Punta Sabbioni at about two then, ciao.'

'Ciao'

So, there was no problem. That was good. The beach, the sea, the sun should stop either of them from retreating into the infernal regions that had brought them down yesterday. It would be a day for hedonism rather than spiritual enlightenment, action rather than introspection. The blazing clarity of the Italian beach would contrast well with the dark maze of image and dream, reflection and illusion in Venice.

At this distance Venice seemed to be acquiring a malign and threatening character alien to any previous vision he had of her. A place to become lost amongst bridges and images, to travel within the imagination but to lose all reference to the outside world, a place where, without a thread to follow there was no way of finding a path back from the labyrinth where shape-changing monsters lurked. Where had the malign character come from? What was this he was perceiving in that most beautiful of cities? A terror before eternity? The awakening of a beast within himself? Or was it just the mind's resistance to change, creating phantom guardians at every stage of his attempt to journey back to the elusive idea he had of his former self. He would renew the search later but today, he decided, he would burn in the most sensual way he could.

He had two hours until Francesca arrived. He rang room service for a pot of coffee: he would give them the shirt to be cleaned. Feeling under the bed, he picked up his notebook to put down some impressions of the previous day. Gradually, he became immersed in the writing and the knock on the door jarred him back into the hotel world. His coffee arrived and he handed over the shirt.

Reading through what he had written in his journal, he searched for a pattern in the response to his return to Venice.

'It's the place you were aware of all the time but couldn't find, the place where all the experiences you thought were in your head turn out to have been real all along; a looking-glass world, another dimension. Monsters may be more frightening than Tweedle Dum and I think the board is circular. At least there's no way of telling which way you're going, maybe it's a sphere. Spherical chess, yes that's it. You become a king in the middle but how do you know where you are in a sphere?

And what of Francesca, is she destined to lead me to the centre? Perhaps, but there's no knowing. She may be a crone in disguise and blast me into hell. I can at least try to find out.

It's going to be difficult to force myself back into Venice, like making yourself walk with an injury: you know it's going to hurt but the exercise will make it better. It wasn't like this when I was sixteen but then the bubbles in the earth were full of angels, not witches. Angels aren't quite right somehow but at least beneficent spirits.

I find that the furies are after me. What have I done? Have I upset their daughters - possible - or am I just paranoid? Have I failed to pour the necessary libations? I still feel a close affinity with Oedipus, but I don't see what I can do about it - come to think of it neither did he. No doubt dramatic irony is great fun from where the gods sit but down here it's a bit of a sod.

Did everything go wrong when my mother died, I can't work out the connections or the implications but there it is.

I'm not even sure that things were right before that, maybe it's a matter of degree. It was certainly a watershed of some sort, alienation, freezing of emotions, safe-door slammed on the imagination: that kind of thing.

Everything and everyone here, appears to relate to something in the past. Is that how it works? Regression. I suppose that way you could even experience the past properly for the first time. Recurrence but with expanding consciousness each time round; sculling round the mind in a gondola.'

The only danger with too much analysis was that conscious thought could result in being shut out from further inner experience. The writing sounded posed, artificial, written for an audience, edited by the watchdog. A poem, one he had written not long after her death, a poem about the ultimate watchdog, the triple headed Cerberus. He opened the old manila-bound folder and sought through the poems. It was strange encountering it again:

'Night of the sun, far black through the earth,
Long beyond the staring eye,
Breath of darkness, far from birth,
Grim shroud of the forfeit sky.

I am the jaws of life;
You shall not pass.
I am the jaws of death;
The gate is sealed.
I am the jaws of God;
His Will be done.

Deep in the caverns, falling from flesh,
The trial of jaws possessed by Death

That black with nightshade semen wait
Three in one they guard the gate.'

Was this the door he had to open? Perhaps there were different guardians at different stages. Little ones like conscious thought: big ones like this. What guardian did he have to pass to reach his own soul?

7

THE SECOND DAY - PART TWO

David stood at the edge of the sea wall watching the black speck of the ferry grow against the dazzling background of undifferentiated sea and sky. Punta Sabbioni, at the end of the long low peninsula - so low that it scarcely interrupts the lagoon and the Adriatic, felt like the last outpost, the place where the known world ends, a suspended point from which one departs into watery space. Huge whitened mooring posts, cracked by age and salt water, jutted into the sky. Green shallows, full of tiny fish and pungent dark weed, rippled up to the wall. No cars went beyond so there were large areas of shaded parking. From here you could take only what you could carry with you; no worldly baggage could encumber you. Around the pier heads, from which the ferries departed, were frontier shops and cafés, welcome in this last place as an oasis before the desert. As well as souvenirs to act as charms, they sold ice-cream, cold drinks, coffee, pizza and advertised Menu Turistico. These were the things to see you into the other world.

But today David was not leaving to cross this blinding

abyss. The edge of the sea wall was as far as he was going before welcoming a being from beyond the divide, a creature of the shadows, a nymph from the dark pools of imagination. As the tall cumbersome ferry achieved its full size and began its wallowing turn in towards the pier, he scanned the rails of the decks for a first sight of Francesca. The boat was not crowded, as it would have been first thing in the morning or in the early evening, but there was no sign of her. It docked and was tied up, a sparse line of people trailed up the boarded way to the exit from the pier. She was not there.

Whilst he had grown used to the cruel vagaries of fate such frustration of his expectations at every turn still caused extreme swings in his mood. It really was too bad; anticipation of the future destroyed the present and invariably, it seemed, proved false. Always he was looking for something which would lift him from his present state and transform his life at a stroke; always whenever such a possibility emerged, he was roused to a quite unreasonable state of excitement only to be let down again into an equally unreasonable depression.

He wandered across to the timetables to see when the next boat was to arrive. She could, after all, have been late finishing or just have taken longer to get ready than she anticipated; the depression could be as ill-founded as the extreme excitement. He had forty-five minutes to wait until the next ferry, he would go and sit in the car. He began to walk along the sea wall, back towards the car-park. As he walked along the wall, he watched the weed floating, a little beneath the surface: dark, moving, magnified mats of leathery brown and green following the indolent, movement of the water. Against the quiet, irregular sound of this movement, as each undulation was brought to a halt by the wall, he became aware that the harsh drone of a speedboat had suddenly cut out and changed to a low steady throb. Instinctively he turned and saw a long, powerful white boat with its arched deck and sloping stern moving gently in alongside the steps on the opposite side of the pier from where the ferries berth. A young man with dark hair and a suntan who was driving the boat held it against the step. A girl wearing denim shorts and a T-shirt stood up and turned to face him, she waved. It was Francesca.

He waved back. Of course, ferries were for tourists. If you lived in Venice, you had a boat just as you would have a car anywhere else; she must have considered it so obvious that it was unnecessary to tell him. She had stepped out of the boat and started up the steps. The boat moved away with barely a sound until it was clear of the pier. Then the note of the engine rose, the bows lifted, and the boat traced a wide graceful arc of white on the still, blue surface. Francesca turned and waved to the young man who lifted one hand in acknowledgement. Now David thought he recognised him as the cousin she introduced him to yesterday. Not for the first time he felt old and puzzled as well as grateful that she should show an interest in him.

He walked back to meet her as she emerged from the covered section of the pier. She carried a beach bag and had her hair tied back with her sun-glasses tilted above her forehead. She was smiling and relaxed showing no sign of the stress of the previous night and was, of course, entirely unaware of David's emotional turmoil of the previous twenty minutes. That had been entirely in his head, causeless, self-generated and totally without any foundation in reality, violent emotion caused solely by illusion. And he remembered the panic that overtook him the first time he had been aware of her approach towards him, when he sat at the table in the café; that too had been groundless, created from a shadow cast by his own mind and relayed to his body. His body could not tell the difference, it was only a slave and churned out the same hormones for an insubstantial image, a painting of his fear, as for a physical threat.

'Ciao, David. How are you? I hope you are recovered. I'm pleased to see you again.' As she spoke, she walked straight up to him and put her arm through his, turning him and walking on without pausing. 'That was Carlo, you remember from the bar. He will always go anywhere in that boat. He is very proud of it.'

Everything, David told himself, was all right. There was nothing to worry about, nothing to be fearful of; it was all as it seemed to be, straight forward, simple and good.

'It's a very impressive boat. I'm glad to see you too. I must admit,' and here he paused, hesitant about what to admit, 'that I didn't know whether you had missed the ferry or had thought better of coming.' He was not sure whether her arm had tightened momentarily on his. He decided to change the subject away from his irrational fears. 'It's not far, it's in the next car park.'

Francesca's eyes narrowed and she lowered her sunglasses to shade them.

'It's very bright. You are lucky, last week we had storms and the week before, it was so hot and humid you could hardly move.'

David turned and smiled, he felt the smile come up from deep inside, a real smile escaping through the wall round his feelings, but she was looking across the lagoon and not at him. His lips held their shape, but the smile vanished. They walked in silence.

Something else from the past, meditation and hidden forces, someone else, a calm voice saying: 'What is a smile?

A contraction of the muscles of the face. No! Where does it come from, where does it go, can you use it up; when a smile appears on a crowd is it one or many? At-one, truth, Atma. The society he had once belonged to and believed in, the parallels he drew with Yeats, the long hours he had spent reading and mastering their spiritual exercises had all disappeared and become apparently irrelevant as if they had never happened.

He had dismissed long ago such ideas as muddle, super-stition, a net to catch cranks and charlatans but where had the smile gone and why? Suddenly he became irritated at this intrusion from the past, why should it come here both-ering him now? And he felt himself deliberately seal the breach in the wall that he had come here to destroy: what perversity was this? He was here for that very purpose, to revive the inner life of the past; he would get nowhere if he rejected those things which he did not like or against which he felt a sense of irritation; they were likely to be the strongest indications that he was approaching a warmer trail.

Careful to keep the irritation from his voice he said,

'It's not far now, down this one.'

They turned into the green shade of the aspens that protected the car park from the fierce sun. Francesca released his arm and raised her glasses again. Suddenly she stopped and said,

'Listen!'

He turned and saw her looking up at the trees. They whispered even in the stillness of this bright day, their silver backed leaves stirring to an unfelt breeze. He looked up, the sky dazzled him, and the whisper grew stronger. She spoke again, half to herself.

'When I was little, we used to listen to the leaves until we heard silver bells and fairy voices.'

He listened until words formed in their sound:

'The wind bloweth where it listeth.'

He listened, searching skywards towards the sibilant voice of the leaves. Where had the words come from and where did they go? He breathed the air softened and scented by the trees, slowly and deeply. How did the text continue? He could only remember that it was something about being born of the Spirit. A warmth spread out through his body like warm water rippling through his veins and along his nerves. He ceased to be aware of the ground beneath him as the brilliant light, the water and the whispering breath held him. He became aware of Francesca speaking again.

'My Grandmother used to say it was the angels. And who knows?' She smiled a warm smile, 'Perhaps she was right.'

The closeness of their thoughts and the experience left David only capable of muttering,

'Perhaps.'

It was an instant, immeasurable and unmeasurable; the intersection of time with eternity. Timeless, but it brought with it an extraordinary sense of peace, a spreading of his soul like the still waters of the lagoon on a perfect day. His consciousness, loathe to impose again the limitation of separation, hovered before landing, and then, softly as a circle of butterflies in a summer garden, fluttered and settled to define again the limits of his world.

Francesca, the car park, his own body: they were still there. The sense of peace still flowed through him in waves and it seemed that Francesca too had a new look of calm about her. She turned away from the brilliant fragmented light of the sun through the leaves and said,

'She saw one once, coming down out of the sky, all white and gold with wings. She seemed so sure it was impossible not to believe her.'

He felt the waves of peace envelop them both, flowing unhindered between them. How could he feel so close to someone he knew so slightly, closer than he had felt to anyone for such a stretch of arid years?

They reached the car. As he opened the door for her and walked around to the driver's side, he was aware that slowly but inevitably the moment was slipping away. He got in and the pungent smell of the hot leather seats, the feel of the steering wheel and the familiar actions of putting the key in the ignition, starting the engine and checking the mirrors were all pulling him back into normality, into separate existence. But, he vowed, he would hang on to that experience, he would try to recall it when he doubted his mission, it would be a fixed point against which he could measure the ever-changing flow of images. It was a reassurance that there was still a possibility of winning and no-one could take that away from him. He moved the car quietly out onto the long straight road to Cavallino.

The car was part of the world he had brought from home, its dark leather seats and the understated quality of its German interior belonged to his business life. The empty bracket that usually held his phone stared at him from the dashboard seeming to reproach him for not having made a call to a customer, or the office, for so long. The car itself seemed out of place, it should have been taking him to a meeting or a conference, assisting him in the organisation and exercise of power. It also carried a mental image of

Thelma and he had to glance repeatedly at the passenger seat to remind himself that it was Francesca sitting there. Not that Thelma often travelled in his car but nevertheless she was part of the same world.

Remembering Thelma, he thought about the phone call he had to make, he must not forget; about seven would be best when she got in from work. He felt a little cold as he remembered not only the phone call but the fact that at the end of the week she would be here. And what would happen then? Would he have begun to rebuild only to see the beginnings of a new structure flattened and the old put firmly back in its place? What was a week against the rest of his life? How could he possibly survive her arrival with any progress intact? He would wall himself in again and that would be that.

Again, he let his eyes be drawn left. Francesca seemed too fragile, too stylish, too energetic and alive for the weighty Northern strength of this car; her pale T-shirt, bleached denim shorts and lightly bronzed legs rested against the heavy blue-black hide, as oddly out of place as they would have been in the boardroom. Her fingers with their long delicate nails alighted on the leather. The image of the circle of butterflies returned to him: yes, she was like a butterfly lost in search of blossom and landed here in this alien place.

A bus slowed in front catching his attention and interrupting his flow of thought. He pulled out and overtook. He was doing it again, imposing the images of his own mind on her and trying to make them part of her; tie them to her and then possess them. Butterfly? Nonsense, she might not fit into this mobile office of his, but she would, he thought, be perfectly at home in a Ferrari and that was hardly a car for butterflies.

He slowed and turned into the hotel car park. As the car moved quietly, almost stealthily across towards an empty space he felt its presence surround him, a dark weighty cage of worldly wealth and success that had grown until it ensnared him, rendered him powerless to break its bounds, redefined him until he hardly recognised himself; a success that provided him with physical comforts which only made him a coward. It came to a halt and he switched off the engine. As it fell silent, his eyes rested on the magnolia bushes that fringed the car park. Without the air-conditioning, the dark blue exterior drew the sun to it and the temperature inside rose quickly. He could feel sweat starting to form on his forehead. He pictured them leaving this heat to walk through the cool darkness of the hotel and then out to the unlimited horizon of the water's edge where even he could be free.

'What are you thinking?'

Francesca's voice broke through the procession of images passing across David's mind. What was he thinking? What could he say?

'Just wondering whether this is real or a trick of the famous Venetian chiaroscuro.'

'And how will we tell?' Francesca's eyes narrowed and laughed at the same time in an unmistakably mocking look and David realised how far his fantasy of her had moved from the person with whom he had discussed painting and writing yesterday. He smiled rather self- consciously back at her.

'Silly of me.'

'There is no difference, it's all ..... ' and a shadow passed across her face bringing back the vulnerable look that he had seen yesterday, 'Oh I don't know.'

The look of agitation that had brought their evening to

so abrupt an end the day before made David apprehensive but, as his curiosity got the better of him, he asked,

'What were you going to say?'

'I was just going to say that it's all the same, all a trick of the light.'

'What stopped you?'

'It sounded pretentious. And if you believe it then there is nothing, well nothing to hang on to.' There was a pause as she stared through the windscreen. David could see things going seriously wrong unless he took some kind of decisive action.

' Come on we're supposed to be enjoying ourselves on the beach, not tying ourselves up in knots in here.' As he said it the image of being tied up in knots with Francesca flashed across his mind. He turned to make a joke of it but her face told him to keep quiet. He got out of the car. As Francesca stood up on the other side, she stretched upwards to the dancing brilliance of the hot sky above and as she relaxed the shadow lifted from her. She spoke half laughing,

'Don't worry about me. I get these crazy moods. Come on.'

David left Francesca in the foyer while he went to his room to collect the beach things and change into his trunks. He pulled on a pair of shorts over his trunks and left on the short-sleeved shirt. As he turned to leave the room, he caught sight of himself in the mirror. Who was it he saw there? He had dressed unconsciously; the person he was trying to leave behind taking over these automatic, mundane, tasks asserting by stealth, the power of habit. He removed the shirt. But what should he wear? He did not want to drag the person he had finished with into his relationship with Francesca. Increasingly, he felt she represented his new life, the Vita Nuova. Perhaps the shirt he bought in the market would be better but how could he tell? The last time he had felt so insecure about clothes was when he was an adolescent and then at least there was fashion to fall back on. It was the unfamiliarity of the situation that made the decision difficult. At home and at work he knew what was expected, the image he was trying to project, but that was part of what he wanted to leave behind. He did not want Francesca to identify him with the person he was trying to get rid of but who was it he wanted to be? He did not know enough about this new person yet and he had to hurry so he followed Francesca's example and put on a T-shirt. Glancing round the room, he took a pair of trousers off the bed and hung them in the wardrobe just in case she should come back later.

The beach was utterly transformed from the empty, shining sand, sliding under quiet lapping water along which he had walked that morning. Now it was a mass of sound and colour; a confusion of German, Italian and English voices whispering, arguing and calling to each other; children shouting from further down, near the water; cries of 'cocco bello, bello, bello!' from a beach vendor walking steadily across the sand, occasionally bending to sell slivers of coconut dipped in a bucket of iced water; sun shades sprouting like picture book toadstools, blue, white and orange, leaning at precarious angles above striped sun beds. They moved over the burning sand, between the near naked bodies, shining and scented with oil, that lay reading or sat perched on elbows to look out to sea. They threaded their way past children digging and crying between the beds, past the beach bags, plastic bottles, schnorkels, buckets of sand and sea water, and manoeuvred to avoid inflatable boats, balls, alligators and dolphins.

The tide was going out so there were a few spaces where

the water had been. They put up the sun shade, unfolded the sun beds that David had collected from his room and spread out the towels. It was odd doing these familiar things with Francesca who was so new, exciting and unfamiliar. It was disturbing, deeply so. She was moving everything along far faster than he could manage to assimilate the new experiences or their implications. When they put up the sun shade their hands touched and again a tingle of energy shivered through him. He found himself irrationally preoccupied with the thought of what she would wear to sunbathe. The majority on the beach were topless, even those who by aesthetic standards should not have been. It seemed perfectly normal, natural much more sensible than the frantic efforts of some to keep two square inches of bikini over their nipples and yet he did not want her to be topless. With strangers it made no difference, but Francesca was neither a stranger nor a lover. He remembered a thought he had when he arrived in Venice only yesterday - too sudden an intrusion would prevent the heart of her flowing inner being from unfolding - well, he felt that for them to be virtually naked together so soon, particularly in circumstances so devoid of intimacy as a crowded beach, would rob them of a stage in the unfolding of their relationship. He smiled ironically to himself as he remembered his vow to make it a day of unbridled hedonism. Francesca looked at him and smiled questioningly back. This was something he could not say. He wiped the sand off his hands and used his foot to give the sun shade one more push.

'Well, that's done; and we didn't quarrel once.' He had spoken without thinking and realised, immediately he had said it, what the response would be.

'What do you mean?'

' Oh, just that......' David had not mentioned Thelma and

did not see how he could explain what he meant without doing so.

'You mean you would have quarrelled with your wife?'

He had still not got used to how perceptive and open she was. There was clearly no escape, so David hesitantly agreed,

'Yes, I suppose I do.'

'Everybody does.' Francesca turned and sat down on one of the sun beds, 'But you didn't say you were married.' There was no accusation in her voice, but he still felt uncomfortable. He sat down on the other bed.

'No, it never seemed the right time.'

Francesca shaded her eyes with her hand and looked at him. Then she lowered her sunglasses over her eyes and reached in her bag. She took out a book. She found her place and then looked at him again, lifting her sunglasses briefly while she spoke.

'It doesn't matter.' And she leaned back against the raised end of the sun bed and began to read.

David watched her briefly, a little puzzled at her sudden disregard for his presence and yet feeling that in a way this disregard in itself signalled a kind of acceptance. He looked out to sea. The waves were small but large enough to break into curling white crests as they climbed over the sliding, backward flow of each former wave and spread across the wet sand, turning at the edge, as if not sure which way to go.

This was something that connected him to every stage of his past. He watched the sea on holidays with Thelma, often going alone in the early morning or late evening to let the regular beat of the waves flow like a mantra through the tension and circling thoughts in his mind. He had taken day trips or weekends by the sea in the period between university and getting married: Brighton, the Isle of Wight and his old stamping ground, Hayling Island; reflecting alone, hearing the ghost voices of his past even then. There were the visits to Weymouth when he and Peter had sat on Portland Bill and contemplated the emptiness before them as the best analogy with the infinite sea of space and time, minds that embraced the universe, consciousness reaching to the edge of the stars, later dissolved in cider.

Further back still, there were the teenage beach parties and long hot afternoons when the waves confirmed the insistent, forward rolling force of new emotion surging through him, emotion which first rushed to fulfilment with Jane. The inexpressible sensation the first time her breasts touched his naked chest; the first dissolving of their bodies into one while the surf hissed and rolled, roaring beyond the dunes, its sound and unfathomable depth joining with their boundless joy, joy everlasting in eternity though brief in time. Once and once only, nevermore could there be such a baptism of fire and water, such a reaching out and a breaking through the hard carapace of ego; the hard carapace that had exacted such retribution and left him alone like a crab scuttling across the bottom of a silent, empty ocean. But retribution for what, for breaking through, for moving on, or for drawing back in fear?

And through childhood with his mother, family visits to the sea, sandwiches packed in grease proof paper in tins with hinged lids, thermos flasks, sand castles with moats made like Portchester castle. The sea rushed through bringing down the drawbridge, cold, wet and gritty; leathery seaweed clinging round his ankles; the salt-green smell; seaweed and dead crabs as presents for his mother; the warmth of her body when the sea had chilled him and the happiness of unconditional love. The sea beat on, regular but always changing, always different, always the same. So many more coves, beaches, cliffs and rocky head-lands where he had watched her disappearing behind the curve of the world, the great blue all enveloping womb of life.

He became aware of the light touch of a hand on his bare arm.

'David.'

He turned, his senses struggling to register the present against the all-powerful, all-enveloping drama of the past, driving out the images, its glare submerging them.

Francesca was speaking quietly. 'I'm not being rude; I just didn't know quite how to react or even how I wanted to react. Silly really, it's not as if I was surprised.'

David tried to pull himself back to the situation and take in what she was saying.

'It's OK, it's all right, don't worry about it.' He paused to allow his thoughts to settle. ' Do you fancy a swim? It'll cheer us both up.'

'In a minute, I should like to sunbathe a little first.'

And as she spoke, she took off her T-shirt, easing it gently over her hair. She was wearing a one-piece navy costume, laced at the sides. Was he disappointed now, or relieved? She undid the denim shorts and slid them over her legs; her legs were smooth, shaped not skinny. Why was it that he felt himself trying not to react, trying not to be aroused? The lacing on the sides was very sexy, more so than a bikini; the cords against her skin, the hint that it could be undone. He was holding himself back, was this the threat, the real cause of his self-imprisonment? In his teens he would have let the blood flow, the images and emotions free to course through him, they brought the poetry and the will to power, the love and the freedom, the force of the green fuse. Blake knew: '*The cistern contains: the fountain overflows.'* Now the exuberance was contained, and the desire bred pestilence.

His head pounded, his muscles rigid with restraint. His emotions seethed in the milk that should have fed them. Soon it would be over, and life would go away. If this was the clue, the answer, and he had turned the whole force of creation against himself it was no wonder he needed anti-depressants.

Francesca took a bottle of oil from her bag, poured a little onto her hand and began smoothing it over her shoulder and down her arm. As she became more self-absorbed David allowed himself to watch, half sideways so that he could flick his eyes away if she looked up, still a coward. She cupped more oil in her hand and flattened the palm on her chest. Small scented rivulets ran from her fingers across the skin to the top of her breasts. She spread the oil gently over them and under the top of her swimsuit following the neckline to the straps over her shoulders. Her already lightly tanned skin became shiny under the oil, the smooth curves warming it and breathing out its scent to his nostrils. He turned his eyes away quickly as she lifted her head and shook her dark hair back but she took no notice of him and remained absorbed, running long rivers of bronze oil out along her legs and allowing it to spread and run down them before she smoothed it in around her thighs and along the cool underside of her calves.

As she reached her ankles, she clasped them lightly with both hands and rested her chin on her knees allowing her hair to fall forward. Her breasts pressed against her thighs. She paused as if soaking up the oil and the sun, breathing in the energy in its rays taking on a stillness that transferred even to David's turbulent emotions. He felt his breathing slow to the same rhythm as hers. The cadence of breath joined them for a time he could not count. A moment when the stillness became complete, and then she released the pose, sat upright and tipped her face towards the sky as if in acknowledgement of the sun. She allowed her hands to move back behind her and rested on them, straightening the knee nearest him for balance. Then, having made this intense communion with the sun she leant back along the bed, closed her eyes and gave herself up completely to Phoebus-Apollo and the fire of his rays.

Voices floated on the air, young voices laughing, building from the barely audible until they filled David's consciousness. Jane lay laughing and breathing heavily with her wet hair trailed across his thigh. Droplets of water ran from the ends, tickling down the sensitive skin on the inside. Her teeth were chattering slightly as she spoke,

'That was cold!' and she wriggled in closer to him, lifting her face so her chin rested on the front of his trunks. She slid her arms low round his waist. He was still trying to catch his breath after the run up the beach. The sun began to break through the chill film of water on his skin. As the effects of the cold wore off, he tried to see past her hair, uncertain that the waistband of the trunks would contain him. Again, she pushed closer and turned her head so that her warm breath brushed his navel. Her hair was wet and cold on his stomach and chest, but the heat of the sun now began to make his shoulders, legs and face glow.

Peter was chasing Lynne towards them; Lynne screamed as Peter lunged to bring her down, she dodged but fell anyway; Peter fell beside her onto the sand. Cold sea-water sprayed over Jane making her jump.

'Uugh! I was just starting to warm up.'

Peter reached into the bag, pulled out a towel and threw it to her.

'Here you are.'

Jane turned so that she sat between David's legs with her back to him and then held out the towel. David leant forward and draped the towel over her shoulders, rubbing gently on its rough surface to warm and dry her. She tipped her head back and he kissed her forehead. His hands moved under the towel and he held her to him. It was a new life, like being born again and experiencing everything for the first time. The sea stretched out in front of them, past the hazy shape of the Isle of Wight to the right: on, out and for ever. They too would last for ever with the sea. This was the fulfilment of life and he would never let it end. He brought his lips close to her ear,

'Love you.'

'Love you too.'

Peter tapped a Gauloise from its paper packet and put it to his lips. He held the packet out.

'Want a ciggy?'

The rich warm smell of the toasted tobacco reached his nose. It was a pleasant smell.

'No thanks.'

Peter flicked his lighter and the oily smell of lighter fluid joined the tobacco. It sparked but wouldn't light. He cupped his hands closely round it and Lynne put hers round too. It lit and the tiny puff of blue smoke rose and disappeared instantly in the sun. The sharp smell of the cigarette too was friendly, familiar, not the same as his grandfather's but close enough.

Peter spoke as he exhaled the smoke,

'Aahh! No more exams for two years. Well not real ones anyway. No need to feel guilty about not revising.'

Lynne looked at him with mockingly wide eyes,

'I hadn't noticed these attacks of guilt.'

'That, my little flower, is because you were too busy swotting. See what's on the radio, there's a good girl.'

Lynne poked her tongue out at him but rolled over and took the transistor radio from the bag. She turned the dial, to the accompaniment of hissing and shrieking, past unwanted stations. Guitar chords.

'Yeah! yeah! yeah! yeah!'

New love was vibrating through everything; it was all new: songs, clothes, not just them but everyone, everywhere, everything was new.

Jane turned to him,

'You'd better write.'

'I will, I will.' and he bent forward until his back stretched and began to hurt. They kissed, long and deeply until there was nothing but their lips and tongues and the warmth of their breath and a red haze as if they were in a new womb, this time together.

Eventually they drew apart, kissing lightly as they did so. Jane looked across at the others, but Peter was lying flat on his back on the sand, his cigarette finished. Lynne's head was on his chest. Jane turned back to David,

'Promise you'll always be there.'

'I promise.'

When the sun had cooled, they pulled on jumpers and walked up the beach to their bikes. The evening light gave a rose tint to Jane's blonde hair and pale skin. The pebbles at the top of the beach slid noisily as they staggered and tried to keep their balance, Jane's arm round his waist and her head pushing into his chest. The air perfumed with sea, dune grass, the distant smell of fish and chips and the warmth of Jane's body filled his nose and lungs until he seemed to float with joy. He rested his cheek on the top of her head, breathing in the scent of her hair, until walking became impossible. They stopped and kissed again until Peter, sounding irritated, shouted at them to hurry up. As they drew apart, Jane whispered,

'Everything's just so good. Can we make it last?'

'Why should it change? It'll always be us.'

When he went to university it survived a term until he began work on a play and he met Miranda. It was the first fall, the first loss of innocence, when he left Jane, but the real destruction occurred when he tore apart that relationship as well. He had destroyed it when his mother died, tried to destroy everything and had succeeded, created a desert from a rich and living garden. He had turned Eden into an arid wilderness of dry bones. He had fled away, away from her, away from himself, away from that vital oneness of thought feeling and physical sensation that he had known from childhood until that moment. Was that what had happened or was this just a mythology built for himself from edited highlights: not the rose of perfection but the rosy glow of illusion?

He looked across to Francesca. Even she seemed old, or at least worldly compared with that paradise of youth. He looked around, the sounds and colours unnaturally bright after his immersion in the past. To the left, further down the beach in the shallow water he was surprised to see the German girl who had reminded him of Jane. She and the dark-haired boy were hitting a small, rubber ball backwards and forwards with what looked like table tennis bats. She was beautiful, there was no doubt about that, but why had he behaved in such a ludicrous fashion yesterday: what was the matter with him? It was as if his body had been caught up in a dream, dream-walking perhaps, and pulled along the dark paths in search of the buried secret that he sought. Was it Jane he was chasing or was it his memory of himself?

Whichever it was, as he had come to rest at the covered well-head, he had abandoned the search yet again.

She laughed as she missed the ball and ran through white foam that edged the low rippling waves. If he let his eyes drift slightly out of focus it could be her, an image acting on a memory hidden deep beneath the rubble of his life, and the dark-haired boy, that could be him. They played with the same quality of innocence. Had they left a boyfriend and girlfriend at home? Did they too feel the whole world to be new as he had or was the world a darker place for everyone now?

'Do you know her?' Francesca's voice made him jump and look round guiltily. 'She is very attractive I think.'

There was no point in denying it. He could take her into his secret but then she could only ever be a confidant, a mother, not the one to make his shattered psyche whole again. She would be forever outside, looking in. He wanted her to be there, when he had passed through the trials of the labyrinth, waiting for him. He barely knew her and yet she had entered his mythology and acquired alarming importance.

He smiled rather awkwardly.

'She reminds me of someone I used to know a long time ago.'

'Oh, yes?'

'I saw her yesterday on the ferry and again at the market this morning. I didn't realise I was watching her.'

'Then perhaps you should go and speak to her.'

David's stomach felt as if it had suddenly been filled with iced water. Surely, he had not messed things up already. Francesca removed her sunglasses and he saw that her eyes were laughing. Instinctively he picked up a towel and threw it at her. As it left his hand, he felt a moment of fear as he realised that the act was spontaneous. As it landed, there was the briefest pause before, to his relief, she laughed. He laughed too, as the tension broke, and as they laughed their eyes met. The laughter subsided and their eyes stayed fixed, each on the other's. Laughter and something deeper flowed between them: empathy, understanding, a recognition, and a realisation that this was someone they could trust. A moment of quiet, and then David stood.

'Come on, let's go swimming.'

David paused after they had swum out beyond the rocky moles that acted as breakwaters and separated the small bays. The water changed here. It felt firmer, heavier somehow. It was deep and a darker blue, the surface moved in a smooth undulating movement that only accelerated and began to break when it got nearer to the shore. It was clearer too without the fine haze of sand stirred up in the shallows. They trod water. The water was warm around them but an occasional current of cold ran past. As a larger undulation passed them David felt himself drawn towards her by the water. The water joined them, filled the space between them in a way that air did not. Their movements sent out eddying ripples that met and swirled each circling around the other. Below the surface Francesca's leg brushed his and the water again caused them to draw closer. She put out one hand seemingly to stop them from getting still closer and colliding. Between breaths over the water she said,

'Thank you. '

'What for?' he gasped as a wave rose past his mouth.

'Being understanding.'

'That's all right.' he said unclear as to exactly what she meant.

'No, really. Let's go back.'

'Race you.'

'OK.'

David tipped sideways and took a breath as his feet rose and he lifted his left arm over aiming his fingers at the water in front of him. He moved through the water with the confidence of a strong swimmer, enjoying the blinding flash of light every time he tipped his head to breath and the cool darkness as he turned beneath the water again. Eventually the water changed, became warmer and cloudy, choppy and thin; colours and outlines of people registered in the brightness. He slowed and the tips of his fingers touched sand; he stopped, and his feet sank to the bottom. He stood thinking that Francesca would still be catching up and was surprised to see her stand only momentarily after him. They had separated as they swam, and they walked towards each other. David called first.

'You're a good swimmer.'

'So are you.'

David kept walking towards her and she towards him. The effort of swimming, the heat from the sun, the water dragging and swirling around his legs as he walked all combined to distract his body so that, as they drew close, he felt no panic or immediate tension to hold him back. As she smiled at him, he put his arm around her waist. Her hand alighted gently on his shoulder but this time, instead of moving him away, slid down his back and around him.

They walked through the shallows up towards the beach. So many sensations, emotions and thoughts clamoured in on him vying for his attention that they remained trapped beneath the surface of his consciousness. He was aware of not letting them through lest he should be overwhelmed and yet concerned that he should be blocking out the full awareness of the moment. There was the relaxation of a tension that had been there so long he had

ceased to recognise it; there was an opening out to everything around him such that the colours and sounds were
heightened. He felt he had arrived in the present with a
force that made time suddenly slow. He felt her body
against him, and a deep sense of warmth spread through
him. Elation spread with the warmth and bore him
upward beyond the mundane world. They rose from the
sea, transformed into two beings from the ocean depths,
children of Poseidon, alien to the shore they had left,
walking in a god-like world separate from, and infinitely
superior to, that of the other beings who crawled on the
sand.

As this intoxication of his mind subsided, he began to
think again. Was it just acceptance by someone of whom he
had felt so much in awe for her youth, beauty and freedom?
If so, he had surely been imprisoned in an appalling darkness cut off from so basic a need as simple acceptance. She
had held him like his mother when he collapsed and now,
again she was bringing him out of darkness. How she came
to possess the magic thread to lead him from the dreadful
labyrinth he did not know, it was beyond reason and for the
moment he would just accept. Her hand moved to the small
of his back and he released her as she moved away so that
only her finger tips touched him. She looked down and his
eyes followed, watching their feet moving with a different
cadence but covering the wet sand at the same speed.

'I said I would explain what happened yesterday. I will,
but I don't want to spoil today. Thinking too much about it is
bad.'

David let his arm drop and took her hand, giving it a
squeeze.

'Whenever you like.'

'You're a very kind person. When I said thank you just

now, I meant for not being too, how can I say it, pushing? Is that right?'

'Yes, I should think so, maybe pushy.'

Her English was usually so good that he was surprised at her hesitation but put it down to embarrassment.

They reached the sun beds. Francesca sat down. The sun had moved, and David adjusted the parasol before joining her.

As he sat down Francesca turned and looked over her shoulder, up the beach and then back at him.

'You may buy me an ice-cream if you wish.'

He looked round to see where she had been looking and saw an ungainly ice-cream wagon on fat tyres being half driven, half pushed along the soft sand at the top of the beach.

'You do eat it then?'

'Oh, yes,' she laughed, 'I love it. It is part of all the good things, childhood, family, having fun, the summer. You are not too sensible for ice-cream I hope.'

He smiled back at her.

'Of course not, but I thought perhaps selling it ....'

'I would not want to see it on my afternoon off. No, I should like melone e cocco per favore.'

'Si, signora,' he paused, ' bella signora.'

It was easier to say in a language he hardly knew. Francesca tipped her head to one side and struck a naive and innocent pose.

'Grazie singore.'

David wished he could speak to her in Italian, freeing himself from his inhibitions by taking on another voice but he could not and would have to manage. He found some money in the pocket of his shorts, put on his sandals as protection against the burning sand and went to get the ice-creams. She was right, ice-cream showed the good side of the present, good times ahead and a link with good times past.

Even in the short distance back it had begun melting. As he found the narrow, tortuous way along the thin strip of unoccupied sand, the ice-cream melting onto the cone made him think of a book he had as a child in which a family went to the seaside. The picture showed them standing with the daughter at the front, ice-cream melting down the cone and down her hands and wrists. He had often secretly tried to let his ice-cream do the same, but he was always told to eat it up before it melted.

As he got back to Francesca, she held out her hand and he passed her the melon and coconut ice-cream.

'What have you got?'

'Lemon and vanilla.'

'The coconut is beautiful, here try it.'

She held the ice-cream and he leant over to lick it. As he did so he touched her hand lightly with his to steady it. She did not move back and as his tongue followed the groove left by hers a strand of her hair brushed his face. He looked up and her eyes rested steadily on his. As he drew away from the ice-cream, he knew he could kiss her; he wanted to, and he knew that she did too. The thought took him a moment too long, he paused waiting for the barrier against spontaneous action to drop and then it was too late. She laughed, dabbed him on the nose with some ice-cream and smiled at him but, he felt a shadow flicker across her face.

'Thank you for the ice-cream.'

Then she leaned back on the sun bed and, looked out to the sea.

David watched a group of children with an inflatable tropical island. As they climbed onto it and then pushed each other off into the sea, the fat, air-filled palm tree nodded and rocked. He watched until Francesca sat up and David thought she was about to say something but there was another pause before she turned to him.

'I was going to explain. Something bad happened while I was at university. My Uncle is very good letting me stay in Venice and work, but he is still family and that is difficult.' She looked down and brushed sand from her foot. 'He's my father's cousin really and he and my mother may be getting married. My father died last year. It's very difficult.'

David thought that she suddenly looked very sad indeed. He did not want the happiness of the day to drain away like this and he wanted to comfort her. He felt more self-conscious now, though, about leaning and putting an arm around her. He placed his hand on hers instead.

'You don't have to talk about it if you don't want too, honestly you don't.'

She looked up, squinting a little in the sun in spite of the sun shade and gave a smile, a warm, gentle, intimate smile.

'I know I don't, but I wanted to; I will tell you the rest another time.'

He felt a warmth go out towards her, a concern and an empathy with the desperate misery buried within her, locked in by terror and hopelessness. It seemed hardly possible that she should harbour the same dark emptiness that he had been faced with at a similar age. Had there been some recognition of their shared but hidden torment, unspoken and divided by so many years? But she had hinted at something else as well. What more could there be, weighing down from within a girl of such warmth and natural vivacity?

She picked up her book again.

'You don't mind if I read some more?

'No, of course not. What are you reading?

'Umberto Eco, Il nome della rosa, The Name of the Rose.'

He had asked in a casual way, not wanting to allow silence to fall, and wanting to change the mood that had fallen with her revelation. He had not expected to know the book. It was one that had made a deep and disturbing impression on him when he read it. The dark air of menace, the secret hidden somewhere in the arcane mysteries held within the hand-lettered and illuminated books of the labyrinthine library, a secret that promised escape from furtive sex and sudden death in the mediæval Italian monastery and yet, seemed at the same time to be respon- sible for them, held a fascination for David, obsessed and excited him, hinting at something which could unlock a secret within him too.

'It's good, a good book, maybe rather sinister for the beach. I read it in English I'm afraid.'

At this last Francesca's mocking look returned and he felt it worth a little embarrassment just to cheer her up.

'Really?' she said, and added, 'Perhaps I am a sinister person.' She drew her knees up towards her and hugged her shins. She rested the side of her head on her knees and looked at him carefully before saying,

'When I was reading last night, before I went to sleep, the monastery library with its circular paths and mirrors that make you see things that are not there, its shadows and its old dark, hidden mysteries reminded me of Venice.' She paused and smiled. 'It made me have bad dreams: so now, I read it in the sun where there are no demons.'

'What did you dream about?'

'No, more.' She leant back against the raised end of the sun bed. 'Maybe later but now I am going to read.'

David searched in the bag for his notebook and pen. He lay back and stared at the white paper. The sun glared on it and he reached for his sun glasses. He wrote:

> *'Dark the water's voice that hides beneath*
> *Its mirrored surface images of lives*
> *Potential, incipient, alternatives we hide*
> *Or never take, the seeds that do not germinate*
> *But lie, lost among the tares.'*

> *'And in the flowing void their voices sound*
> *Forever cast into the vine's consuming fire;*
> *Cold flames leaping, lighting their watered shells,*
> *Taking life wherever they can catch a tired*
> *Or unsuspecting mind to give them form.'*

> *'Under the water's illusion shadowed face,*
> *Turning unseen*
> *Hidden from Creation's other light*
> *They wait, coiled in each others'............'*

Damn! The flow had gone. It was always the same. Quickly through the start, work at the middle and fail at the end. It seemed to be more than just a failure of imagination; more a buried pattern waiting to impose itself on everything he tried to do. He looked across at Francesca, she was engrossed in her book. He looked along the beach and saw that the German girl had gone. Then he lay back, closed his eyes and listened to the water.

8

THE SECOND DAY - PART THREE

The sun was still bright but without its earlier burning heat; its light turning to a rich gold. The beach was no longer crowded. Higher up, on the deep dry sand, small groups, now in T-shirts were playing boules and badminton. People were stirring, folding sun beds, deflating toys and airbeds, shaking sand from mats and towels. There was a sense of movement, and of getting ready for the evening. David looked at his watch: nearly six o' clock. He would phone Thelma later. The sun had stopped the churning of his mind and filled him with a deep animal contentment. The phone call wasn't important, it didn't matter, nothing mattered except being a good animal, here, in the present.

Francesca was standing at the edge of the water looking out to sea; the late afternoon light brought out the golden tan of her skin. There was a light dusting of sand sticking to the oil he had smoothed onto her legs after their second swim. She was familiar now; the strange tense fantasies, that had raced in his mind before, had evaporated. She was beautiful, mysterious, exciting, but a person he could relate to without a fog of tension and inhibition obscuring the space between them. They had swum again, put oil on each other's backs, laughed and talked, lying on their fronts, close together, watching each other's mouths as they spoke.

She turned, walked back to him and knelt on the sun bed.

'Carlo is coming to pick me up at seven. I have to work this evening.'

David held out his hand to her and said, 'It's been a good afternoon, the best I can remember for a long time.'

Her fingertips touched his as she answered,

'Yes,'

She spoke quietly and, he thought, almost absent-mindedly. There was a pause and David felt she was looking through him. Then she pulled gently at his hand and said,

'Come on, we'd better start packing up.'

As they cleared and packed David thought about her reply. He did not know what he had expected but he had hoped for a warmer response. Was he building another, deeper, cell for himself when he began to see her as the key to escape from his present prison, the key to unlock his soul's lost power? The fact that she was relaxed and happy did not necessarily mean anything. She was young, things did not have to have meaning. She had her own problems without being responsible for his salvation. It was undeniable though, that as they lay there, he had felt the knots and tensions of his soul as well as his body, begin to loosen and unravel. He felt on track, doing what he had come for, following his fate.

As they began to walk up the beach David looked back at where they had been lying. The small temporary island on which they had formed their relationship had gone, vanished leaving just a few indentations in the sand waiting for the tide to wash over them.

'Would you like a shower or anything before you go?'

'No, I don't have time but thank you for the offer. And David,' she looked ahead and hesitated as if not sure of what she was going to say, 'I have enjoyed it too, it was good to get away, thank you.'

David wanted to put his hand out to her, to hold her or touch her, but she seemed closed in, shut off and he, thinking better of it, said instead,

'We'll go straight round to the car. We can put the things in the boot.'

They walked up the long beach through the soft sand. He remembered again that he had still to phone Thelma. What would he say to her? He had four days left to reconstruct his life. Could it be done and if it involved Francesca what would happen when Thelma arrived? If he was not so intent on making things better, on rediscovering himself and coming to terms with himself there would be no problem. If he accepted his not uncomfortable life and forgot his adolescent aspirations, he could simply enjoy himself and Thelma would arrive at the end of the week without detracting from it. His stomach knotted. Somewhere within he knew that this was not a real choice, however much his mind liked to play with its comfortable possibility. In the place where deeper knowledge lay, he knew he could not now change course.

Even on the ferry as he had approached Venice yesterday, even before Francesca, he felt an inner conviction that his fate was sealed. He knew then that he would never be the same and that he would either have begun a slow journey of recovery or else be destroyed. It was Venice not Francesca that was forcing him into himself, uncovering and unravelling layers of image and myth that absorbed into themselves the substance of his life. But, without Francesca he would still have been wandering around in circles examining the problem, finding new aspects of the problem, being drawn further and further into the morass of his own existence. It was Francesca who offered him the chance to ascend above the infernal spiral paths, to move away from the dark shifting maze to an enlightenment beyond. It was she who would determine whether Venice would cause the forces of creation to once again flow forward, uncovering his true self, or to turn and destroy him, devouring their own children.

They arrived at the car and he lifted the sun beds, sun shade and the beach bags into the car boot and closed the lid. Francesca walked away a little and stood with her back to him, looking out into the distance. He watched her and felt a warm longing rise through him and go out to her. Could his sanity depend on a girl he had known for little more than a day? He was uncovering layer upon layer of fantasy and could no longer rely on his own mind or senses. Could a fantasy be used to find the way to truth: could a mask lead to the face within?

The car was like an oven inside, the dark upholstery blisteringly hot. They sat with the doors open to let it cool, Francesca with her back to him, her legs outside the car. She removed the band that held her hair back and shook it loose, running her fingers through it as she did so. A small shower of sand fell onto the leather.

'God, I feel a mess.'

He reached out with one hand and drew her hair back behind her ear.

'You look beautiful.'

She leaned backwards and rested her head on his shoulder.

'Thank you. I really have enjoyed today.'

'When can we meet again?'

'Ring me in the morning, about nine, I will know if I have to work by then. If I don't, we can spend the day together. Perhaps I can show you parts of Venice you have not found yet.'

'That sounds good. I shall pray that Giovanni has plenty of other staff.'

She turned, smiled, drew her legs into the car and, without hesitating or signalling her intent, gave him the lightest of kisses on the cheek. It was over before he could react.

'And now we must go, or Carlo will be waiting and I shall be late for work tonight.'

As they drove back along the straight road to Punta Sabbioni, he recalled the earlier journey: Francesca was no longer the butterfly in the boardroom, no longer seemed particularly out of place. Her presence now was warm and real, relaxed and without the barrier that had allowed his earlier fantasies to flourish. Even Thelma's phantom no longer intruded. He started to imagine Francesca accompanying him to company social events, showing her his favourite places in London and on the Sussex and Hampshire coast. Restaurants, pubs, theatres. She was only twenty years younger, plenty of men had wives twenty years younger.

Negotiating the pedestrians and traffic lights of the small village of Ca' Savio broke his chain of thought and made him suddenly aware that he had only changed one set of fantasies for another more extreme than the former. He laughed inwardly but a smile must have shown on his lips as well because Francesca turned to him and smiled too. She would, he thought, have smiled more and either laughed or left him for a madman if she had realised what had prompted the smile.

He did not pull into the car park this time and drove to the end where the coaches and buses turn. Carlo was already waiting by the pier. David pulled over and stopped.

'I'll get your things out of the boot.'

Carlo opened the passenger door and let Francesca out. He acknowledged David with a wave.

'Hello! You have had a good time yes?'

Francesca answered him in Italian before David could speak. Carlo looked at David, the look lasted rather longer than was comfortable.

'She is a wonderful girl our Francesca. I see you again I think,' and Carlo grabbed and shook David's hand. ' Arrivederci, we must go.'

David handed Francesca her bag.

'I'll ring tomorrow, early. Ciao.'

David watched them walk down the pier together to where the speed-boat was moored. Once, without turning, Francesca raised a hand and waved. He was very, very lucky; inexplicably so. She could have been with someone like Carlo but she had chosen to be with him. No more fantasies, no worrying about the future, just enjoy it:

> '*He who binds to himself a joy*
> *Doth the wingéd life destroy;*
> *But he who kisses the joy as it flies*
> *Lives in eternity's sunrise.*'

He had so often tried to take to heart Blake's lines and

always failed in the attempt. Now, if ever, with so short a time available to them he must try to accept a passing joy.

By the time David had cleaned the sand off the things in the car, showered and changed it was eight o'clock and he could no longer find any reason to postpone the phone call. He sat on the bed. It was quiet and he felt alone, irritated at having to make the call but unable to let it go.

He called the switchboard and gave the girl the number. He still did not know what he was going to say. After a pause, broken only by the occasional click and bleep, the phone rang at the other end, the familiar burrrr, burrrr of an English phone. It seemed to ring for a long time. His hand grew sweaty on the receiver. Then,

'Hello, Thelma Green speaking.'

The familiar sound, tone, timbre of the voice sank through him. A voice of such homely familiarity that he warmed instantly, a voice of familiar nuance and depth; a voice he knew so well he could make no connection between it and the person he had feared and been so reluctant to ring.

'Hello Thelma, it's me.'

'Hi, I got your message. How is it?'

His mind seized for what seemed to be minutes before his voice responded.

'The hotel's a bit basic but Venice is just as good as I remembered it.

'How's the beach?'

Nothing he could say would relate to reality; it was all just words.

'Fine, a bit crowded. I had a swim this afternoon.'

Pictures of himself and Francesca emerging from the water rose before him.

'Good, don't forget you're supposed to be relaxing. Not too much sight seeing, I know what you're like.'

There was a pause and he used the opportunity to change the subject.

'Is there any post?'

'Nothing exciting. You don't know where the bit for the end of the hose is do you? I can't find it.

'Have you looked in the shed behind the barbecue, or in that box in the garage?

Already domestic trivia were taking over. She was talking and he wasn't listening. He looked at his watch: they had been talking about nothing for fifteen minutes, it was some sort of substitute for communication. He must try to bring the whole sorry business to an end.

'Are you going to have everything organised in time for the conference.'

'I think so. I'll have to, I'm not missing the plane.'

'OK. Ring me later in the week and we'll sort out where I'll meet you.'

As soon as he had said it, he realised he should have said he would ring her but it was too late now; he would have to live with it, knowing the phone could go at any time. Well it could have anyway.

'OK, look after yourself and take it easy. See you.'

'Bye.'

'Bye.'

Click, burrrrrrrrr.

That was it. The end. Empty. Post-phone-call depression. There was a fullness in her voice, a sound that carried the vibrations of so many years. Could he live without her, throw so much of his life away? Was he doing the right thing in driving it to an inevitable end or should he accept what he had and make the best of it? Again, he knew it was an empty question and that the dice, the cards, the flight of birds, or the fall of their entrails, whatever messengers of fate he consulted would all tell the same story. He had come to Venice and now he was caught in the gods' infernal machine and could only submit to their will.

After dinner he went to the bar. It looked out over the beach to the sea. He had put his notebook in his pocket intending to sit near the windows and try to finish the poem. He ordered a beer. While he was waiting, a man he thought he recognised came over and stood by him at the bar.

'Grüss Gott.'

'Grüss Gott.'

'Herr Brandes.' He held out his hand and David shook it.

'David Green.'

Herr Brandes turned away, looked towards the windows and then back to David.

'The bar is empty tonight nicht war?'

There was a pause, the barman was returning with David's beer. He felt he had to say something.

'Can I get you a drink?'

'Ja, danke. Thank you. A beer please.'

He was around the same age as David, maybe just a little older. He appeared to be on his own. David paid for the beers and the German raised his glass.

'Pröst.'

'Pröst'

'You are staying here long?'

'A couple of weeks, two weeks.' David leant on the bar. Herr Brandes had probably come for a quiet drink away from the family but wanted someone to talk to. He was fairly tall, well built, with a pleasant relaxed manner and a soft deep voice.

'You have had a long drive.'

Yes, but I stayed overnight near Stuttgart. I prefer it to flying, you see more.' This David realised was an inane comment but, in the circumstances, it would have to do.

'That is right. I have come only from München. You have a good car ja? I too have ein bay em vay.'

There was a pause and they both drank. Conversation was going to be basic and although the German was pleasant enough David had writing to do.

' Herr Green. Do you know Surrey? I am often there on business..... but then I fly.' Here the German laughed.

'Yes, I know Surrey. Where do you visit?

'Camberley. We have bought an electronics company.'

David's sales instincts rose in spite of himself.

'Really, I'm in computer equipment, communications. We do a lot of business in the Camberley area.'

'Then perhaps we will do some business too.' He reached into his pocket and brought out a card. 'When you get home, ring me up. Maybe I will see you in Surrey, ja?'

David reached into his pocket for a card and then realised he had intentionally left everything to do with work at home.

'I don't have one, I'm afraid.'

'No problem. Another beer?'

David accepted and while they were waiting for the barman to arrive with the bottles tried to remember where he had seen Herr Brandes before.

Herr Brandes spoke again.

'Tomorrow we will go by boat around the three islands. The glass works, the lace and the church on the oldest island. Do you know them?'

It was a trip he had done with his parents. It was one he remembered with remarkable clarity. He had bought a glass cat for Jane. When he had visited her after she was married, she still had it. It was displayed in a cabinet along with a lot of other ornaments, the emotions locked up in it for good.

'It is a very interesting trip. The boat itself is enjoyable and the glass museums are good.'

'My daughter. She is very interested in history. She says she will be a teacher but, we will see.' He drained his glass. 'And now I must go or I think I will be in the dog's house eh? You are on your own ja. No problems.'

When Herr Brandes mentioned his daughter David suddenly realised where he had seen him before. It was at the market. He was the father of the German girl, the Renaissance girl; the girl he had made such a fool of himself over by chasing her through Venice. He felt embarrassed, particularly in view of the similarity of their ages.

'Yes, I am on my own here.'

David had nearly said that his wife would be joining him but suddenly wondered if he had been seen with Francesca or might be later. He decided to say nothing.

'Then I will see you again perhaps. Wiedersehen.'

'Wiedersehen.'

David thought about ordering another beer and going to sit by the window but decided to walk. Walking often helped the words and he had a poem to finish. It would be good to do the three islands trip again, perhaps another day, maybe with Francesca.

It was getting dark and along the path at the top of the beach there were seats set into the tall dune grass and dry hedge. Couples kissed, young couples, fulfilling every teenager's fantasy of the perfect holiday. They could be any nationality, German, Italian, English, Dutch, French. He thought about Francesca. Was he fulfilling an adolescent fantasy or worse, trying to revisit an old one?

He came to a slatted seat with a light by it. It was deserted. Good for writing but nothing else. He and Jane used to go at night to the benches by the cricket pitch on Purbrook heath. The wooden slats, the metal arms didn't matter. Sometimes it was so cold that their breath steamed but even that didn't matter. She warmed her hands inside his shirt, and they laughed at the shock. You grew out of that sort of thing, but you never stopped wanting it.

He took out his notebook and turned to the poem. Then he looked out to sea. There was a breeze now and the lines on the flag pole clinked and rattled like the rigging of the sailing boats moored in Portchester creek. The sea was breaking in the darkness, pools of dark ink fringed with phosphorescent white. The steady muted roar and hiss of the water filled his senses. He was in a different place, a place where the darkness of the water roared on to where it was absorbed in the darkness of the sky and beyond to the eternal roaring of infinite space. He was alone with the universe:

'Dark the water's voice that hides beneath
Its mirrored surface images of lives
Potential, incipient, alternatives we hide
Or never take, the seeds that do not germinate
But lie, lost among the tares.'

'And in the flowing void their voices sound
Forever cast into the vine's consuming fire;
Cold flames leaping, lighting their watered shells,
Taking life wherever they can catch a tired
Or unsuspecting mind to give them form.'

'Light moves on the face of the shadowed waters,
In the deep the failing, shattered fragments cry;
No sound can save their lives' relentless fall
But, shifting with borrowed light they glow
Raised briefly by the harrowing of a falling soul.'

It was finished. The sound and the darkness receded until he sat again, uncomfortably, on the slatted seat.

He got up, pushed the notebook into his pocket and walked back towards the hotel. As he got nearer, light began to spill out through the bushes and onto the path. The thumping beat of dance music reached him from one of the bars. Inside, flashing, coloured lights swept across the space, silhouetted dancers moved in dark rhythmic waves. Only by the windows were they identifiable as individuals. He stood watching, outside, an observer looking in.

A group of dark shapes broke off from the central moving sea and moved towards the table by the window. As they reached the table, talking animatedly, arms around each other he recognised them as the German girl, her brother and friends. How strange, he thought, that she no longer seemed to be the Renaissance girl, nothing was different, just his illusion had changed. Her appearance had not changed. She was laughing, drinking, dancing; taking part. He felt left out, jealous of their immersion in life. He had been at the centre once, when he was their age. Imperceptibly he had lost touch, been edged to the side, become a stranger looking in.

He stood until he began to feel self-conscious. He shook himself away from the images in the window; surrounded himself again in the cool fragrant, night air and felt alone but self-contained, apart but self-sufficient. As he walked, he reflected that it was hard to know if this was a sign of maturity, of adulthood or simply a way of coping with being left outside. He felt himself to be walking alone down a windy street, empty, emotionless, a ghost town of facades; he had been to such a place and had been led from it by Jane or the German girl or someone he had not yet met who was both of them and neither. Déjà vu, imagination, a dream revisited? He felt an irrational sense of excitement and anticipation but for what he could not tell.

It was late and he was tired. In his room he read through the poem again. He could never tell this soon after writing whether it was any good but at least it was written and charted just a small fragment of his mind beneath the surface.

The sheets were cool as he got into bed. He closed his eyes, but his mind threw up pictures of the beach and the sound of the waves. Francesca, her hair, her mouth, eyes and long smooth legs; the sand, its grains enlarged; the sounds, water and voices and the white swirling patterns at the edge of the waves turned repeatedly through his mind. He opened his eyes and they stopped but started again as soon as he closed them. When he was eight or nine, he had spent hours combing a pebble beach for fossils and at night the stones and their sounds had appeared magnified and amplified as though they had taken over and possessed his mind. Now they too joined the sensations of the day streaming between him and his consciousness. How could he claim to own his mind, or his consciousness when so little a thing as a day at the beach could take it from him?

He gave up the struggle and sat trying to read. His eyes worked their way along the words; he turned the pages, but he took nothing in. At last he felt his head plunge forward looked again at the page and again felt the sudden fall of his head. Putting down the book he slid into bed and with the cool pillow against his cheek fell asleep:

Darkness

Looking through the brambles he saw a large dark house. The guards would arrive at any minute. There were walls and he couldn't get away. His mother and Jane were in the house, but he couldn't get in. There was a secret and when you knew it you could catch the train. He tried the window and the glass was broken. It was dark and dusty inside. A rat ran across the floor. There was a piece of paper with some writing, Hebrew or Sanskrit, not clear. It was part of the plan, part of the way to reach them and part of the way to escape. The guards mustn't know, the guards would use it against them. There were more pieces of paper and when you had them all you knew the secret. They could all go together then:

Darkness

Steep hill, rolling chalk. In a dip between two mounds there was a building. Cars were parked. The building gave out a trembling energy. He paid to go in. Walking in the queue he came to an inner door. The waves of energy grew stronger. He went through. On a high pedestal, surrounded by a brass railed fence, was an animal. It was like a tiger but the size of a horse; the skin was like a carcass in a butcher's, parchment taut, striped but without fur. It was alive but held motionless, catatonic, radiating waves of energy but unable to move. The hills grew dark, the building faded, the tiger-horse glowed, stars shot through the sky. He was lost, looking on, the gulf too great to cross:

Darkness

Deep beneath the castle keep, heavy walls climbed upwards. Great oak beams straddled the space above the entrances to grey stone tunnels. Flights of stairs crossed from the tunnels' mouths. He stumbled slowly down a grey tunnel to a cell with a curved ceiling far into the earth. A single lamp lit the cell. Suddenly a flame flared in the darkness. Above the flame was an iron horseshoe. The metal glowed first red, then white, then gold. In the horns of the gold hovered an egg, bright in the fire. The egg was a stone and on it burned letters of fire. They were the secret, the key. The flame died and the egg and the horseshoe cooled leaving first an image of light and then darkness. The letters were lost:

Darkness

He emerged from a small tunnel into the great cave, cathedral high. Curtains of stalactites ranged across the walls like organ pipes. The rock glistened rose pink, shining with water. Rays of coloured light appeared; the far wall turned to falls of water. On a lotus throne sat a child laughing. The laughing grew until the walls faded and the stars shone, and the laughing reached out through the whole of the darkness of space. The lotus throne and the child travelled high into the distance until they became a golden speck among the stars.

As he watched he became aware that he too was sitting on a throne and behind him was a woman whose dark hair flowed over and around him. His head leaned back between her breasts. The throne floated slowly forward like a boat in the night sky. He could not see her; he knew her but did not know who she was:

Darkness

9

THE THIRD DAY - PART ONE

A long continuous sound like a muffled roar, not quite a monotone, a complex sound, richer than white noise but nevertheless seeming to contain all other sounds reached David's ears. It grew in his mind, his consciousness gradually stirring and expanding to apprehend it. He tried to analyse it, to hear it as chords, or dissonance, the pitchless reverberating hiss of a cymbal, deep rumbling timpani beneath. He heard long flowing phrases of strings, the stress moving almost imperceptibly as the bow changed direction. And yet all these sounds missed something, gave only a parody of the original. There must be notes in a sound which gave the impression of pitch and yet, as he listened, he could not find them.

His consciousness at last began to rise above the surface of the sound and he opened his eyes. What was it that he had been listening to? The curtains seemed less bright than they had yesterday. He looked at the clock; it was seven, they should be brighter if anything. The sound could only be the sea, and yet he had not been aware of it the day before.

He went to the window and looked between the

curtains. The sky was grey, and the wind blew a thin layer of sand along the top of the beach. The wet sand did not shine as it had yesterday but looked dull like mud. The sea rose into white curling breakers, crashing into great fans of spray on the rocky moles. It was the continuous thunder of waves, each wave always moving forward driving on over the sliding remains of the former that produced the complex, near musical sound that had made its presence felt in David's mind as he was waking.

From his window he could see that it had not rained on the hotel patio and so far as David was aware there had been no thunder. The storm must have been out at sea whipping up its surface until the waves reached the shore far from its centre. He turned away from the window, the change in the weather turned his feeling of excitement and anticipation into one of fear and uncertainty. Again, he was aware of his extreme vulnerability to external circumstances, as much an instrument of fate and circumstance as the sea was of the storm.

There were three more days to go after this one. He had still only begun to scratch his nails on the dry wall. He seemed to have made so little progress and yet compared with two days at home the events had been momentous. He had to search for a pattern, develop it, whether it was rational or organic.

He reached for his journal on the bedside cabinet. On his first day he had re-discovered Venice, joining the images of its mythology in his memory with those formed in the present by this new encounter with the same stones and water. The amalgam of the two formed his present, and now past, experience. He drew two circles, outer events and memory. At their intersection the conscious present. He placed the outer stone and water Venice and inner mythological Venice in their respective circles. He was pleased with the overlap representing the joined experience but concerned as to how to show the present instantly becoming the past and flowing back to change the new present via memory. He tried, unsuccessfully to match the flow with double headed arrows.

He had met Francesca in circumstances hardly propitious. They had met again, and it had ended badly; this time the cause was some dark shadow cast from Francesca's past. Was another person's past an outer event or some other category yet unshown? The shadow could even be indicative of a further past belonging to the initiator of the mysterious and unsettling phone call received by Francesca.

On the second day the Renaissance girl had become the German girl and he had spent the afternoon with Francesca on the beach, where the sea slid, merging imperceptibly into the sand beneath the burning heat of the sun and where their relationship had grown closer. He needed a three-dimensional diagram where the circles could become spirals growing and returning. He tried to draw them: conical towers meeting, rising and falling, strung on lightning flashes; spiral staircases, winding snakes conducting the force. Pencil lines proliferated until the whole became a grey and fogged confusion. It reminded him of the diagrams in Yeats' book, 'A Vision'.

On the third day? What would happen today, at the end of which he would be half way through his week? Which of the events and memories, images and reflections would pass each other on the spiral stairs that pulsed and vibrated with the force that flowed between these rich polarities? And what conscious present would he recognise as their amalgam? He paused to watch this moving, coloured model pulsing in his mind against a dark infinity, the fiery towers translucent with the flow of forms condensed from images, distilled from life.

As he watched, the force of returning outer consciousness became imminent, the images began to fade under its glare. He looked down at the page of his notebook. It bore little resemblance to the vibrancy of the creation in the world he had left. It was just a shifting indefinite mass, the grey ashes of his vision. He tore out the disappointing page and dropped it in the bin.

At eight o' clock he sat with coffee and rolls looking out through the windows of the dining room at the sea. He did not feel like going out onto the beach this morning. The roughness of the sea attracted him, but the bleak hostility of the weather deterred him more. Today the life guards would hoist the red flag and shout or blow whistles at anyone who went into the water. It was rough, but on a Cornish, Welsh or Scottish beach it would have been a normal sea with children desperately trying to stay on surf boards, swimming hard against the waves, and coming out covered with bright red blotches from the waves' battering.

The wild force and primitive power of the sea had always held a deep elemental fascination for him. Once, in March, he and Miranda drove in his van to meet Geoff at university in Lampeter. They bought wine from the off-licence and stayed in for the evening talking with Mike, a friend of Geoff's at university. By eleven, the nature of existence and the significance of the evidence of the senses were becoming blurred. Miranda lay on the bed with a book having declared the discussion pointless in its arid intellectualism. The verdict was that all possible solutions were somewhere between self-evident and irrelevant. Neither the good Bishop Berkeley nor the bad Marquis de Sade could provide the answer though there was a general preference for de Sade.

As the discussion reached this unsatisfactory deadlock, Miranda put down the book and announced that she wanted to do something radically different and considerably more exciting. They all agreed. Walking was considered but rejected as both too energetic and insufficiently exciting; flight was ambitiously suggested but the bounds of probability had not been pushed back far enough to make this a serious consideration; finally, swimming was proposed, elaborated on and accepted. Mike enquired as to whether the University might contain one or two girls of a sufficiently adventurous nature to accompany them. Geoff was pessimistic but thought that Vicki and Karen might possibly be prevailed upon, particularly if Miranda would help persuade them. Mike, who liked but feared Miranda, was concerned that she might frighten them off, but she soothed him with reassurances that she would be meek as any lamb. She then made him very nervous by whispering in his ear. They collected together Geoff's guitar and as much wine as they could and made their way up to Karen's room. Miranda and Geoff went in and with unrevealed subtle blandishments persuaded them to come and bring much needed towels.

Drinking and driving was not something that anyone took too much notice of in those days, particularly at midnight on back roads in Wales and, singing to Geoff's guitar, they drove out to a deserted rocky cove. David remembered them taking special note of a life-belt hung on a sign saying that swimming was forbidden because of dangerous currents and hazardous rocks. They backed the van to the edge of the shingle where it became the bathing machine. Miranda by this time, much to the disapproval of the other girls, had drunk most of a bottle of wine. She suddenly knelt up, her long luxuriant hair looking particularly wild, and announced that it was time to commune with the deep. Mike opened the rear door of the van a few inches and an icy blast of air blew into the comfortable warmth of the van. He closed it quickly declaring that, whatever Berkeley said, the evidence of the senses was in this case likely to prove reliable using the well-known 'more wrinkles than inches' test.

'Well,' declared Miranda, rejecting such exclusively male evidence, 'I am going swimming.'

The other girls protested, and David, Geoff and Mike had not put the case for swimming particularly vigorously, feeling that there were worse things than being in a warm van with three girls, several more bottles of wine, a guitar and the sound of the sea firmly outside. But Miranda was adamant.

'I am not coming all this way and drinking all this wine just to sit in the Stygian depths of a van. Excuse me while I undress.'

And undress she did, except for an Indian cotton shirt sewn with tiny flashing mirrors. She then flung open the back doors of the van, screamed loudly as she leaped out into the spray chilled wind, and then weaved and swayed into the black, crashing, freezing cold sea. David, Geoff and Mike saw this as both a challenge and a potential crisis where assistance might be needed. They stripped quickly down to their T-shirts, or in Mike's case vest, and made for the water.

By now the madness of the occasion had taken hold and they shouted, laughed and then began a full-throated rendering of 'For those in peril on the sea'. The water was deep, rough, stony underfoot and icy cold. Diving and swimming just a few strokes took away all breath and energy. Miranda was waist high in the water between waves but staggered and was almost submerged each time the darkness of a new wave broke and burst over her. She was holding her hands above her and shouting something that seemed to be an incantation to the moon. Her long dark hair straggled wildly over the thin soaking cotton that clung to her body moulding itself around her breasts. In the wild water, against the background of the black rocky cliffs she shouted against the sound of the sea and the wind as the clouds blew fast across the full moon; she had all the appearance of a crazed Celtic priestess. David felt himself possessed by an uncontrollable surge of passionate devotion that her displays of pagan madness always invoked and he stood possessed by the simultaneous force of the sea and Miranda.

Through his trance and the crashing and howling of sea and wind he became aware of Geoff shouting that it was time to go back to the wine. As he returned to normal consciousness he could only agree. All three of them shouted and waved wildly at Miranda to come back but she seemed not to hear them.

Finally, David turned and made his way out to her, barely able to keep his footing. As he drew close, a particularly thunderous wave broke over them and lifted them both, flinging them forward and then dragging them as if bound together in a vicious undertow. Somehow, against the rattling, tearing force of pebbles he managed to stagger upright and drag her with him. She clung tightly with her arms but limply with her body and seemed still transported into some other dimension. They reached the shallower foam but still she took no notice of his voice. She would not stand so, now the water no longer took her weight, he lifted her forcibly and carried her. She clung on to him and, as the bitterly cold wind cut into his wave-numbed, pebble beaten, skin, he felt warm droplets touching his neck. She was crying. Mike and Geoff helped them into the van, but she would not let go nor make any attempt to dress so they put the rest of the towels over her, started the engine and put the van's heater on full. Geoff picked up his guitar and played again. Soon Miranda's sobbing stopped. She looked up from David's arms and in a quiet voice said,

'Wine, give me more wine.'

And so they did.

Mike drove and by the time they got back both Miranda and David were dressed. She still seemed elsewhere: possessed. They climbed the stairs and along the corridor to the room of a friend of Geoff's who was away for the weekend. In the borrowed bed she still clung to him in her sleep.

At breakfast the next morning she seemed to be virtually unaware of what had happened. She and David were both bruised and cut, and she listened to his explanation without any recollection of what had happened after leaving the van. That, in a way, made it even more compelling as it seemed to suggest that the whole episode had occurred at a deeper level than mere rational, analytical consciousness. It could also have implied that she was too drunk to remember but mere alcohol did not seem an adequate explanation for her previous night's intoxication. The experience of such elemental power, and irrational emotion and behaviour, impressed itself forcibly on David. He could not put it out of his mind for months which became some of the most ardent and intimate of their relationship.

Geoff said, years later, when David and he were reminiscing about what had happened and the effect that this episode had exercised over him: 'Miranda was a great girl, we were all sorry when it broke up but she was completely round the bend you know. In fact, all the women you go for are totally bonkers.'

And he was right. Women with a certain kind of unpredictable, irrational and frenetic energy had always appealed to him. Even when he knew he was asking for trouble he found their attraction impossible to resist.

Perhaps he had married Thelma because she was sane and did not have this violent and exciting madness. Perhaps he had hoped that such a relationship would be more stable because of its lack of volcanic emotion and also provide a way of avoiding the turmoil it created in him. It had lasted, but was that why the relationship stirred no inspiration to poetry and why he resented it so much? Did he need the furies to tear at his soul, allowing the creative chaos to spin new patterns of words charged with magic and emotion? Miranda was an extreme and special example and the instinctive witchcraft she performed that night compared, in its total surrender to instinct, with the raving, murderous chase of the Bacchae as they tore apart their victim. In a lesser way though, was that not what he sought in women, liberation from his own rational consciousness, liberation from convention and the freeing of the god within. And was it not the absence of this over so many years that had caused his soul to wither and shrivel until its dryness left only a thinking, reasoning shell? It seemed that his instinct might have been right after all in identifying Francesca as a cure for the sickness of his soul however irrational such a cure may seem.

As David's mind returned to Francesca, he looked at his watch: twenty minutes to go. He ordered another pot of coffee and looked out at the crashing waves.

He forced himself to wait the full twenty minutes and

then went up to his room to phone. Today there was little of the tension that had characterised yesterday's call, just a sense of anticipation. He felt certain she would have found a way to avoid working and be able to see him. He felt even more certain that his relationship with her was central to his purpose for the week.

The phone rang and was answered. He gave his name and asked for Francesca. There was a pause while the man at the other end went to fetch her. It was a long time before she came to the phone.

'Hello, David.'

There was a flatness in her voice that troubled him.

'Hello, Francesca. Are you still O.K. for today.' He held his breath, less confident now.

'I tried, David, but we are very busy at this time of year. We do not have enough help. Maria is not well, she is pregnant, and they really can't manage without me. You will enjoy yourself anyway.'

David felt everything crumbling before him; his plans, his newly discovered path to salvation in ruins. He tried to gain control of his breath and his voice before speaking.

'That's a shame, I was looking forward to it.' He felt the tension rising and his breath catch as he asked, 'When can we meet again?'

'I think it will be all right tomorrow, at least in the afternoon. Ring in the morning about this time again.'

At least she had not tried to stop the whole thing, there was still a possibility, but he had to lose a whole precious day.

'I'll ring and I hope you can make it. I want to take you up on your promise to show me Venice and to talk about things, everything.'

He did not want to push too hard, but he wanted her to know that it mattered.

'What will you do today?'

Francesca spoke in a cheery, matter of fact way that increased the distance between them still further.

'Oh, I don't know, the weather's changed so the beach is no good. I might try to write a little and then go into Jesolo.'

He had made no alternative plans and at this moment could think of nothing worth doing.

'The weather will be better later. The storm was far away. When the tide turns the clouds will go and the sun will come out again. I must go now, enjoy yourself and ring tomorrow. Ciao.'

'Take care, I'll ring. Ciao.'

He did not want to let her go but could think of nothing further to say and the phone went dead. She had hung up; their conversation was finished so why should she not?

The things in his room mocked him with their uncaring, superior passivity. They had not been changed by the phone call; nothing mattered to them. He picked up a pair of trousers, screwed them into a ball and threw them hard across the room. The revenge over these inanimate objects made him feel, if not better, then at least more resigned to his fate for the day.

He thought of going into Venice anyway but felt that he would be constantly drawn and distracted by the presence of Francesca's trattoria. He decided to have a lazy day, go into Cavallino, maybe Jesolo, write a bit, read, that sort of thing. He would even buy an English paper and see what was going on in the world beyond this retreat of dreams and illusion, therapy and insanity. He would even see how the stock market was doing.

He went down to reception to ask for The Times and

said good morning to Herr Brandes who was collecting his edition of Die Frankfurter Allgemeine Zeitung.

'The weather is not so good eh? Perhaps we will not go to the islands.'

David remembered Francesca's local advice on the subject.

'It will clear later, when the tide turns the sun will come out.'

'Ah, maybe. We will ask the receptionist.'

The receptionist said the same as Francesca and Herr Brandes said, in that case he would persuade the family to go on the trip. He could not, he said, bear to sit around all day.

David took his paper upstairs and read it with growing irritation and lack of interest. Too much had happened, too many things circled in his body and his mind; like Herr Brandes, he was not going to be able to sit around. Eventually he rang reception and asked the times of the trips to the three islands.

'You can take the vaporetti or join an excursion with guide from Punta Sabbioni. We have timetables for the vaporetti and the excursion leaves at eleven. If you don't want to take your car, Mr Green, you can catch the bus outside the hotel. Have a nice day.'

Well that was simple. He could do either and it would be far better than hanging around the hotel. If he took a vaporetto, he could go at his own pace, but he felt he would like to be looked after today, told what to do, fed on the standard information for tourists. He would join an organised excursion and even catch the bus to Punta Sabbioni.

10

THE THIRD DAY - PART TWO

They sat deep in the varnished wood interior of the small boat. The bows rose too high for anything but sky to be seen through the forward windows but through the side windows he watched the thick white foam stream and spread behind them. He was anxious, unsettled and felt as if he should be elsewhere dealing with the cause of his anxiety. The boat took him away from any possibility of contact with Francesca, the low growling power of the engines thrusting it into the blue sky ahead. He felt cut off, artificially removed from his new world of feeling and imagination and perhaps even frightened that those recent experiences, that had created their own emotional map within him, would fade and become unimportant, robbing him of his new-found sense of purpose.

Opposite David sat Herr Brandes with his wife who was blonde, tanned and long legged. Her face was lined, particularly at the corners of the eyes, from repeated tanning. He found her attractive though it was difficult to define why; was it perhaps the signs of experience, the Weltschmertz mapped out on her face? Her eyes reminded him of his mother's eyes, partly remembered and partly recollected with the help of photographs from his childhood. Warm caring eyes. On Herr Brandes' other side sat his daughter, once the Renaissance girl, whom David now found was called Eva; she was engrossed in a guidebook and took little notice of the boat. Her brother sat next to their mother and stared out of the window. She had addressed him as Boris when they first boarded the boat. David recalled that when he had first seen him, he had impressed him as an athletic, clean cut youth but now he seemed remarkable mainly for the bright penetrating blue of his eyes. Herr Brandes and David had exchanged formal greetings when they met at Punta Sabbioni, but since then the family had spoken only to each other and then only rarely.

David tried to look through the window and at the same time study Eva from the corner of his eye. This was the girl after whom he had dashed through the streets so foolishly, the girl who initiated his vision of the fountain and Jane as he contemplated the bridge, the long legged bait drawn through the sea to the sonorous tones of Dylan Thomas and whose close proximity had so confused and threatened to overcome him in the market place. She was the shadow he had seen dancing and laughing the night before in the sensual crowded heat of the disco. Now, he told himself, he was sitting calmly opposite her unaffected. He noted dispassionately that she seemed younger now, sitting reading, just a school girl with her parents.

How was it possible, he thought, to create any kind of order or sense from his life when his perception and experience proved so utterly false, a pattern of constantly shifting illusions and shadows; shapes and impressions without form or substance; a sea of reflected images stirring his being into waves of emotion, rising or fading with no more cause than the random play of light through the water.

The lagoon had widened; the lively female guide, who seemed genuinely fluent in at least four languages rather than only familiar with set scripts, had just finished describing the history of the Arsenale and, having pointed out the Cimitero San Michelle, was now talking to a pretty, fair haired five year old about her dress: in what language David could not quite hear. The water had changed colour, it was greyer and evidently shallow except for channels marked by bricole, the ubiquitous clumps of heavy wood, whitened, cracking and banded with metal. All the captain had to do was keep within the markers and all would be well.

All would be well: just follow the markers, keep to the well-used established deep water between the dangerous shoals, and then he could not go wrong. They would lead him safely through the tempestuous seas; he did not need to find his own way. All would be well, and yet why could he not really and honestly believe it, why did he feel that this was at best just an avoidance of life. He was not convinced that he could be led safely by the hand according to the regulations, the rules and a creed such as that held by the religion in which he had grown up.

He felt more like the Ancient Mariner adrift in a boat that mysteriously took off, of its own volition, on courses out of his control; one day ice-bergs and a strong wind and the next becalmed amongst slimy things on a still sea with the sun drying out every cell of his body.

And what of the ghost ship that came between him and the sun, its rigging the dungeon bars? Death and the golden haired, red lipped temptress Life in Death dicing for his soul. She was the long-legged bait with whom, impaled crimson lipped, he slid through the teeming life of the sea, bound to her body, dying in life and living in death. He wanted to escape but with every movement he was tied more tightly and dragged more deeply down into Davy Jones' coffin-cupboard under the sea where they all went into the dark.

It returned, the fear in bed under the sheets as a child when he contemplated his own death; the certain knowledge that he would cease to exist, that whichever way he turned, whatever he did, he could not avoid it; how he, everything he knew, thought, remembered, experienced, even the sensation of his own body would cease to exist. He felt again the blind panic, the gripping dread that had wrung his body until it ran with rivers of terror. He shivered uncontrollably. Three whistles, she had won, he was to spend his life, that brief window of light, revisiting the past, torn by a compulsion to relive it, seeking release. Francesca, George Wagner, Herr Brandes: he had held them all with his skinny hand and fixed them with his glittering eye drawing them into his ring of recurrence.

The water, the boat, took on a new significance; he wanted to get off, not play this game any longer; he was diving deeper and deeper into the circles of hell; he would follow the channel, sell computer solutions, be faithful to his wife. He looked round wildly, breathing hard, cold sweat reappearing on his forehead and saw the people. Who were they, their eyes upon him?

The guide looked at him, clearly believing he was suffering from sea-sickness,

'We will be landing on Murano in a few minutes.'

He mumbled back that he was fine but cursed to himself as he realised that this lapse had been noted by the Brandes family. It was the same thing again, the same as the day of the presentation in Birmingham; that which was inside his head taking over from what was outside so that he lived and acted in a world projected by his own mind. Perhaps he was schizophrenic, seriously mad not just under stress, perhaps this whole world problem that he had set himself to solve was not a problem for the world at all but just a malfunction of his own psyche. How could he know? How could anyone know? He could only believe his own experience even if it was the experience of madness; without that belief the whole substance of his mind would be reduced to nothing and with it would disappear anything he could meaning-fully call himself. Somehow, he had to keep separate the two worlds, liberate the inner world whilst maintaining order in the outer. But would it work? If he kept this rigid control over his mind it was surely unlikely that he would liberate anything. And again, what was this liberation? Was it in fact the freeing of the demons of madness, the Pandora's box of the world's evils wilfully freed to destroy the tender remains of his mind?

'On your right you see the glass factories of Murano famous since the thirteenth century as the centre of Venice's glass making industry.'

She had reached the English version of her commentary.

'Glass making was transferred to the island at that time, officially because of fire hazards but the real reason was probably to safeguard the immensely valuable secrets of their method of glass making, famous all over Europe. The glass makers were well paid and enjoyed many privileges but never allowed to leave the lagoon. It was rumoured that when on rare occasions one did leave, they would be followed by the Doge's secret police and killed with a glass dagger, the handle of which could be snapped off thus leaving no trace of the cause of death. Happily, it is now possible for you all to watch the glass makers in action without any such fear. When we land, we will go straight to one of the oldest workshops. Thank you.'

Order in the outer world, the mind's secret police at work: those who let the secrets pass will be killed with a dagger of invisible glass. Order the mind like the Venetian state, all lapses reported through the lion's mouth. Only then can the canals, the dreams, the visions run freely without danger to the Emperor. He shivered as he remembered Yeats' Emperor of Byzantium, the Emperor of the Tarot cards. Yeats would have understood. He knew there were other coexistent worlds with their own order. At least, if he was mad, he was not alone. Dante took Virgil through the dark wood into hell; he could, perhaps, take Yeats as his secret guide. And now forward, if not to the goldsmiths of Byzantium then to the glass blowers of Venice.

The boat's engines faded to a quiet chugging, the bows came down and, carried mainly by its own momentum, it moved, quietly bobbing on the small ripples, around into the narrow Rio del Vetrai.

'We will now go straight to the workshops for a demonstration of the traditional method of glass-blowing still practised in Murano and then you will have free time to spend in the show rooms.'

David did not get up immediately but allowed time for his mind to recover from its harrowing journey and for the first eager members of their party to climb the short companion ladder and disembark. When he stood, he found himself waiting behind the Brandes family. He felt a little kinder towards himself as he looked again at Eva; she was, despite being so young, very beautiful and exuded around her an aura of magnetic attraction that was impossible to ignore. As she climbed the ladder in front of him, the sun lighting golden rays in her hair as it had in Jane's, he felt the sensations of the chase through Venice returning, the chase through the labyrinth of memory and dreams. He made a new, strong and determined effort to destroy them. He would not be tossed uncontrollably on this sea of emotion and memory; he would take control; he would, and here, almost before the thought had formed, he realised the irony and the futility of his determination, be Emperor of his soul.

Wrong, wrong, wrong: but what did he have to do? It did not work to be a helpless victim of his thoughts and emotions, nor to be a tyrant over them but there seemed no middle way that was anything other than compromise and that surely was against everything he had believed and stood for at sixteen when he believed he possessed the secret. It was against Blake, Lawrence, Nietzsche, Byron, Yeats, everyone he respected and looked to for inspiration.

They entered the glass factory and ascended the stairs. At sixteen he had climbed these same steps, at Eva's age, and rather than grow in wisdom he had simply lost his way. He wondered what she was thinking and what was happening beneath her conscious thought that might be recalled when she was forty. Would she look back to this as a time of power and integration in her soul before it was drained and dispersed, or would she somehow find the secret of retaining her true centre and identity regardless of what she went through?

As he watched her, he longed to share her strength and certainty. Could he connect, tap into that power that he failed to locate within himself. He watched her fair hair falling over the pale skin of her neck and shoulders. Alarmingly, he saw a cloak of darkness fall around her and a shape move in closely to her neck, to draw her blood, draw out the red knowledge of eternity. He saw himself bereft of life force doomed to draw it out from others, from her. He had lost the source within himself and he could only wander, searching for those who still retained the secret of that magic spring. Two small roses of blood appeared on her neck, fountains of life. He drank with the thirst of one who had crossed a desert.

He stood still, the knowledge of what had arisen in his mind spreading into his consciousness and felt horror and repugnance at the desperation within himself. This was not the way. This was not the way at all and yet on reflection was it not a perfect image for the way in which he sought to slake his thirst for lost life. The image could not hurt. Rather than reject it, should he not welcome it as a parable of the sickness of his soul, a story that could lead him into truth. He recalled his experience and his fear on the boat; the image could not hurt so long as he could keep the two worlds separate, so long as the image did not, as the others had, become so strong that it took over and became the outside world in which he acted. Even Dionysus no longer seemed an adequate expression of what he was releasing. Who could tell what distortion and perversion of that force could have occurred within such a long period of imprisonment? He climbed on, up the narrow stair.

In the workshop, fresh from the furnace, the molten glass glowed on the end of the craftsmen's pipes with an intensity that baffled the eyes. They twirled and pulled at the incandescent bulbs, drawing out a handle here or a spout there, the ancient craft reduced to simple jugs, ornamental snails and butterflies. The skill and dexterity were impressive, but it was a tourist show empty of art; the Doge would not have killed for this. The centuries had emptied it, modern life had trivialised it, it was just as clever, but it had lost its soul. David reached into his bag for his notebook; he felt the vampire tower over him and possess him again, drawing the warm blood of youth into his withered veins. Like Dracula he too roamed, haunted, across the centuries feeding on the blood of the living. He sought for words to encapsulate the images, to pin them into patterns that would recreate themselves in other people's minds. Something grasped and clawed within him forcing him to make only cryptic mnemonics on the paper, not write the words. Something seemed to dwell within him gripping his hand but he would, he told himself, remember what had happened, he would beat it yet.

The group was moving on, through into an impressive room hung with glass chandeliers like frozen cascades; heavy wooden furniture and a grand piano were ornamented with large glass sharks, dolphins, coloured birds on glass trees and embracing couples. In such profusion and in the carefully placed lighting they looked magically attractive. It was hard to tell whether they would retain their attraction on their own in another, perhaps less congenial, setting or whether they would be like sparkling coloured pebbles collected from the water's edge that turn dull and lifeless when taken dry from their bag at home.

David found himself by the piano with Herr Brandes whose family were inspecting the large and expensive pieces in this first display room.

'It is impressive, yes?'

'Uh, yes, very impressive.' David spoke without conviction, partly because Herr Brandes had taken him by surprise by speaking and partly because he was genuinely not sure.

'The selling I mean,' said Herr Brandes clearly amused

at David's awkwardness. 'It is very clever, the demonstration, this room and then we will see the cheaper ones. First, they make you believe you want something, then show you the ones that are too expensive and then show you the ones you can afford. It is very clever and all without saying a word.'

David found it difficult to make the transition to thinking in terms of selling but he agreed and found himself released from the weight that was dragging him down from within. If only he could live on the surface, then there would be no problems to solve. But he had tried that and, not only had it not lasted, it induced a deep sense of self-betrayal.

At that moment he noticed that Eva was coming back to speak to her father.

'Papa, kommst du hier. Wir haben die schönste kleine glas vögeln gefinden.'

'Ja, ja, ich komme.' Herr Brandes looked round resignedly at David and then back at Eva. 'Eva, this is Herr Green. He is staying at the Serenissima. Herr Green, my daughter Eva.'

She held out her hand and David registered their eyes meeting briefly as they touched fingers in a ritual remnant of a handshake. He fought back images of blood and stolen life that accompanied the chilly handshake from beneath a cloak of night.

'Hello, I think perhaps we have met.' Her eyes had already left his. 'Papa, komme, schnell!' And she took her father firmly by the hand to lead him to the glass tree full of small coloured birds.

The child-like outburst redrew her image in his mind. She was a schoolgirl, enthusiastic and naive; beautiful, probably intelligent but still a child. If there was a sixteen year old female from whom he could draw life she was a spirit within his own psyche, a goddess to be invoked within, not another person, not Eva. Eva mirrored that internal force, but she was not it.

Relieved at this internal reassurance of release from the threat of future obsession and danger of potentially violent behaviour, he wandered around the glassware. There was no-one he could buy glass for, no-one to take Jane's place. He paused looking at the kaleidoscope of glittering light above him. A small chandelier might fit the living room at home. He would mention it to Thelma, and they could visit again if she were interested.

As soon as he had had this thought, he realised how far his mental world had drifted since his phone call that morning. He had been right to think that the boat was taking him away from his new matrix of thought and feeling involving Francesca and in which the final eclipse of his marriage seemed inevitable. He had been right to think it, but was he right to fear it? Even now, was it really too late to consign the emotional chaos of the last two days to the vast store of past experience and simply carry on being a sales manager with a tolerable marriage and a pleasant house and lifestyle? Why destroy it all, why turn it all upside down because of insubstantial feelings of discontent within? No damage was done, he had had some pleasant and disturbing experiences that could be of use in his writing, he had completed a poem, and now he could return to his comfortable former existence. Venice was only a city, Francesca only a woman and Eva only a girl. Thelma knew none of it. Nothing had changed.

The inner sense of depression and betrayal that went through him after these heretical thoughts had passed through his mind dragged him into a state of dark melancholy. His energy was drained, his sense of even the possibility of emotion left him and his head felt as if it were stuffed with cotton wool soaked in treacle leaving thought impossible. He moved to the window and leant on the ledge looking out at nothing in particular.

Slowly he became aware that the room had emptied, he had no idea how much time had passed. The depression and melancholy had subsided leaving a flatness, a state in which nothing much mattered; he was here in the room, breathing, existing, that was all that registered on his consciousness. Practicalities began to make their presence felt: was the boat still there, if so where was everyone and how long had he got left on Murano? He went downstairs to the rooms filled with cabinets of progressively cheaper glassware. There were cats with lean hooping backs similar to the one he had bought Jane. He wondered if it still stood in the china cabinet in her room and what thoughts came to her when she went to dust the contents of the cabinet and picked up the cat, her hands still touching the same glass that he had put into them when they were both sixteen.

He walked on and then paused by some vases. He ran his eye across the shelves and then quickly returned his gaze to the shelf directly in front of him. There at eye level in the centre was a vase identical to the one his mother had bought when he stood with her by these same cabinets thirty years ago. It had been placed on the mantelpiece when they returned and had remained there, usually with a drawing pin, a paper clip and an elastic band in it; the design would not allow flowers to stand properly.

They had laughed a lot together, especially in places like this, and in museums and art galleries; he could remember what about. How was it that mere things, places, even a shop were more durable than a living human being, made in the image of God. Why was it she had to go, leaving him to wander in this empty wilderness chasing one mirage after another? Where was she now? And in the emptiness, he said a quiet blessing, a prayer that, if the laws of the universe allowed her to be anywhere, she would be peaceful and happy wherever she was. Then looking furtively around he crossed himself as a sign of the religion that had once joined them. His eyes watered at the corners as the sadness rose to the surface and feeling started to seep back into his being. He dried the tears from his eyes with a tissue intended for cleaning the lens of his camera and then turned and walked with steady conscious steps towards the doors.

He was totally unprepared for the brilliance of the light on his eyes made sensitive by tears and his mind dark with introspection. He felt himself to be temporarily blinded by its whiteness. He was in a cocoon like state floating in a temporary stillness, the light took away the stone under his feet and the need to move in any direction. He was here, now; the present poured through him with such force that past and future ceased to exist. A still consciousness, without the syntax of thought, sensed him to be at the centre of the light, a centre which expanded infinitely and yet never moved.

Gradually the light filtered back down through his consciousness until he became aware of it as sunlight and of himself as standing on the side of the Rio del Vetrai. In front of him the water fragmented the light into golden hexagons on the walls of the canal and behind him the cases of glass scattered into an infinite variety of tiny rays the light that fell through its shapes, colours and forms. Glass, the perfect symbol of Venice, earth ground and melted by fire until it turned to fixed water, water that could be turned by breath into art that reflected and refracted the sun. A perfect unity of elements and spirit.

Still he felt no need nor desire for movement or action. He was filled with a warm comfortable stillness from which he was in no hurry to emerge. The sense of light and oneness had faded in its immediacy but left its influence to suffuse his body and mind. There was no hurry because there was no compulsion, no pressure on him to be anywhere or other than he was now, here and in the present. It was not the only time he had had such a sensation, they happened frequently when he was an adolescent and then became rarer and rarer. The last time must have been at least ten years ago. This was, however, unusually intense and he knew that the after-effects could continue to affect him for several days. Perhaps this was a turning point, a point from which he could see more clearly, a reference point from which to measure his actions.

He looked along the canal and identified the boat on which they had arrived. The captain was still on board. David asked him how long remained before they were due to leave for Burano and was surprised to be told that they had half an hour.

Still feeling detached from his surroundings and with an unfocused but heightened consciousness of all around him he walked along the side of the canal. The sun seared the air with a dry furnace heat. The small shops along the canal were closed with sun bleached cards in the windows showing that, in contrast to Venice, they would not be open again until after the summer. The owners had clearly fled the heat. The heat created a stillness in the air that discouraged any motion and with only a short time left, not long enough to visit the museum, David sat down in a locked doorway feeling rather like a Mexican at siesta but without the hat for shade.

Nothing mattered in this heat and stillness, none of

them mattered, women, work, writing; all seemed far away, farther than the glittering sky. Perhaps he could go south from here, pick olives or grapes, have enough to eat and drink and sit in the sun. There was too much doing, all that activity was confusing, stopped you from being aware you were alive, came between you and yourself. Was that why the Ancient Greeks understood things so well: they just sat in the sun and contemplated life. It was an attractive thought and for the moment it would do. In its stillness, his body felt full, calm and alive in the way of an animal in the sun. Even his hands felt more conscious in a warm, relaxed way. Any movement would have his full attention, like the Buddhist monks whose meditation was just to walk with their whole consciousness focused on every step. He closed his eyes and fell into a slow rhythmic breathing, the air flowing past his nostrils charged with the sun's life.

'Herr Green, Herr Green, the boat is leaving. We are waiting for you.'

David struggled to take in what was happening. The voice, the brilliant light, the very hard ground. As he looked up and around, he realised that it was quite straight forward; he had fallen asleep in the sun. He tried to get to his feet, stiff with sleeping in such an awkward position. His mouth felt dreadful, as if the blood had been squeezed from his tongue and replaced with dry rags.

'Sorry, sorry, I'm coming.'

Herr Brandes helped him to his feet.

'No problem, we saw you from the boat. I said I would get you.'

David was standing now and moving stiffly and awkwardly along the canal.

'Thank you, thank you very much. I must have just fallen asleep, missed the museum too.'

Again, this week, he had been helped to his feet and rescued by a stranger though at least this time it was something that could have happened to anyone. As he walked, he became aware that he was desperate for a drink but could not possibly hold the boat up any longer.

He climbed aboard the boat apologising to everyone in as many languages as he could manage. The captain did not seem particularly bothered about his late arrival and the courier asked him if he was feeling better after his spell ashore, still clearly convinced that the flat waters of the lagoon were too much for him.

Seated again in the wooden interior of the boat he felt awkward and glanced several times at Eva hoping to renew contact and somehow re-establish himself as something other than a rather foolish figure who appeared seasick on totally calm water and held up the boat by falling asleep in doorways. He thought at one point that he caught her eye and he smiled at her, but she did not respond. He concluded that she must be looking past him, through the glass of the window to the water. He turned on the hard, wooden seat and looked through it himself. In the distance an airliner was landing at the Marco Polo airport. That was where she would arrive. This separation, detachment, new life with its new sense of perspective was as fragile as that. There was no escape in this new world of communication, a world that, ironically, he was helping to create. You might want to just sit in the sun, but someone could always fly in, land like a mosquito and your isolation was gone. Back flowed all the unwanted contents of the old life; no need to look back, these days it came to get you.

They were approaching Burano. He remembered it as a good island, colourful and cared for. The guide announced that the people of Burano took great pride in the painting of their houses. Many people lived there, fishing and making world famous lace by a method unknown elsewhere. They should visit the Scuola dei Merletti and watch it being made.

As they walked in from the small quay to the Piazza Baldassare Galuppi his memory was confirmed. It was a comfortable island, like Venice on a lower scale and without the peeling and flaking walls. There seemed more working inhabitants too, not just tourists and people to sell them things. He had thought idly of going south, well this was a foretaste, a painted southern fishing island, small but with a feeling of spaciousness, nevertheless:

> *'O for a beaker full of the warm South,*
> *Full of the true, the blushful Hippocrene.'*

There he could sit and write beneath the vines and the olives, the sun soaking away the pain. There Hippocrene, the spring of the muses, would feed him as it had fed all those others who had fled to Italy. Why not? It was hardly an impossible dream.

He paused where the canal turned abruptly right under the Japanese bridge and between the wide Fondamenti and low, two and three storied houses painted in green, red and pink. Small boats lined both sides. The rest of the party were walking on to the Scuola to see the lace being made. He pictured old women in black sitting round, the threads from their bobbins weaving spider patterns of lace, spinning the threads, like the Norns, the fates, the witches of the blasted heath. The weird sisters spinning their influence out across time and space to ensnare him, to trick him, to bring him down. Were they at the dark heart of his soul, spinning his destruction? Irrational though it was he did not want to go in to where the old women, pleasant and friendly as they almost certainly were, sat round their sociable task. The image was stronger than the reality and he had no wish to feed it.

He looked towards the Scuola and felt it as a centre of sinister power, an invisible web of force spreading from its innocuous walls that held all the appearance of a convent. Weird sisters, Eumenides, Furies, Bacchae, Maenads: what troops of fateful women were these that harried and controlled him and why should he feel their presence? What was it that beat beneath the surface of his brain; what avenging frenzy sought to invade and destroy him and what was it he had done to invite their attentions? He moved his gaze away and let the brilliant sun flood through the darkness within. The main street was wide, open and friendly, the sense of menace was, he told himself, entirely a projection from his own soul.

He walked round to the wide street off the piazza. A poster announced a concert of Galuppi's compatriots whose fame had survived the centuries more successfully than his own: Gabrielli and Vivaldi. It seemed strange to find a concert out here in the lagoon. Who would come and what would draw them? A singing violin with organ continuo played distantly in his head, a slow movement from a Vivaldi concerto but he was not sure which. Vivaldi came from so long ago, his early teens when he had first made music his own rather than something borrowed from another generation. The violin sang of peace and contentment, not the pure clear notes of spiritual peace, but the secular peace of beauty and love. It vibrated with the emotional, sensual ease he sought in his vision of the warm south; and yet beneath it, constantly, were the chords of the organ, God's instrument, underpinning, giving stability, referencing the free roaming notes of the melody to its tonal centre. There was more here, more for him in those brief and isolated bars but, as he turned his attention to it, it faded and would not return. A barrier fell between him and the faded sound so that he could not recall it and without the music the thoughts crumbled, their meaning left them. He was left with a sense that something important had nearly happened but with no way of discerning what it was.

He looked back across the piazza to the souvenir shop. From the sun-blind in front of the shop hung white dresses frothing with lace like sea foam and beneath them, like decorated reels of cotton, were round tables draped with ornate lace cloths in white and pink. The party from the boat had returned from the Scuola and was just entering under the green shade of the blind. Towards the rear of the party were the Brandes family. Eva was not with them. Puzzled he looked back to the Scuola in time to see her coming out through the arched doorway.

He felt himself call to her, she was late, and the boat would go; his mother was already aboard.

'Jane! We're over here, come on; it's leaving.'

The time-worlds co-existed, concentric spheres; the two that had been selected as his past and present and the others, the possibilities that he had not experienced. At sixteen he had wanted Jane to be there so passionately, to share what he saw, that he had seen her phantom with him as he walked. Suddenly that phantom had returned, she was here again not aged like him but unchanged sending him plummeting back through the years. Another cycle of what might have been, caught in the ring of recurrence. Nothing was lost, nothing forgotten, the emotions rose freely from beneath the weight of time and lived as if the years had not existed. Deep, overpowering, adolescent love brought from the depths by an illusion, a fantasy tricked by the golden hair of a girl who had not been born at the time. An image of a girl raising an image of love. Yeats' images, the dolphins rise, the dogs of Aphrodite; the gong sounds, and the soul responds with unwanted emotions and a phantom from the past. All these things were held, undimmed, in the minutest of detail, complete with the least tangible and subtlest layers of feeling just waiting for some chance icon to release them. Nothing was lost from life, but every detail stayed, held in its entirety within his mind, creating the present from the action of its unfathomable depths on a thin film of sensual experience. He was held powerless, impotent to recreate himself, by every second of his past.

The present, the thin film, reasserted itself. Eva had not gone on towards the souvenir shop but instead had turned and was walking towards the main street where he stood. She must have noticed his stare as, before he had a chance to turn back to Gabrielli and Vivaldi, she turned her head and looked straight at him. She was too far away for him to have seen her eyes, even had she not been wearing sun glasses, but he was sure it was not a coincidence. A moment later his suspicion was confirmed when she acknowledged him with a small casual wave of her left hand. He responded, automatically, and the contact even at this distance, and however brief, reasserted Eva over Jane and the inner turbulent and troubled depths sank from his sight.

Before he had even finished his wave of reply, Eva had looked away and turned up towards the shaded tables of a pizzeria. He watched her walk, her legs, her slim waist and her long hair, loose except for a hair band. He focused on the experience of the moment; he told himself emphatically that he was watching Eva not Jane. Jane was a forty-six year old woman whom he did not know. She was out there somewhere but the passage of so great a stretch of time would have changed her beyond all recognition. She might even be dead. All worlds that involved the girl he knew were now only possibilities and choices not taken. The girl who still held a part of him in thrall was now only a phantom and the emotions that the phantom evoked were the reflex twitchings of a corpse. He must gain momentum and go forward if he were not to be sucked down into the darkness of the past. He must enjoy the sensual experience of the present.

Eva re-emerged from the pizzeria carrying ice-creams in cones. David caught sight of her from the corner of his eye. As she walked, he shifted around from the concert poster to one for an exhibition of paintings by Salvador Dali.

Dali looked down triumphantly from a mock throne through absurdly long mustachios mocking him for timidity and conformism, for failing to realise his desires, for not living his life, goading him to act. If Dali could do anything, however outrageous, live out fantasies of the most bizarre and wild kind then why could he, David, not dare to put into practice his more modest and simple ambitions.

Eva paused and turned her head to lick the trickling streams of melting cream from the backs of her hands, flicking her hair away to one side as she did so. The emotions of the day before returned and David felt a warm energy flowing through him. He recalled the ice-cream he had shared on the beach with Francesca. They had been so close, her eyes had been soft and open to him, he had nearly kissed her, he had nearly done so much that would have changed his life but in the end, it had stayed in his imagination.

Eva had rejoined her family outside the souvenir shop and was laughing as she handed them the ices. The memory of Francesca made David feel irritated with himself for expending so much time, emotion and imaginative effort on Eva. He must act, he must change his life and Francesca was offering him an opportunity to begin.

The contrast between Burano and Torcello was made all the greater by the short distance they had to travel. It seemed that they had barely settled into the boat and felt the bows rise before the engines slowed again. Burano was all sun, bright colours, the south; but now David looked out across a grey-green expanse reminiscent more of the salt marshes, mud flats and islands tufted with coarse grass along the Sussex shore line.

The boat rocked and bobbed against the small wooden landing stage and the captain stood helping each passenger off. David noticed him say something to Eva and laugh as he held her hand. She too laughed as she jumped clear. The voice reached him but not the words. Her laugh floated to him but her reply to the captain was lost. He could not tell from the snatches of sound what language they had used. He felt himself again to be an outsider, a watcher while others related naturally and easily to each other. It had not always been so.

The green of the grass, the short vines and the small fields like allotments seemed far removed from the other islands and from Venice itself. It felt odd to be walking on grass along the side of a green watered canal and yet to still be on a Venetian island. Rising above this flat green deserted island with its air of neglect was the heavy and secretive shape of the cathedral, with its high unwindowed brick walls and heavy red Mediterranean roof tiles. It was as if he had arrived at some hidden verdant centre; an island within islands and at its hub the church of Santa Maria Assunta.

Ahead of David, at the door under the portico, an old

woman dressed in black was taking the entrance money. She stopped Eva by gesticulating at a notice on the wall and then at Eva's legs. Frau Brandes took out a large silk scarf from her bag and Eva arranged it as a makeshift skirt which seemed to satisfy the doorkeeper. David thought it a bizarre, irrational requirement; from whom, after all, was she covering her legs? And yet this largely symbolic act of modesty seemed charged with significance. He tried to focus on it, to interpret the meaning of Eva and by association in the depths of his memory Jane, veiling themselves from his sight. He could find nothing but the implied innocence of their youth and of the unquestioning faith he had in his first love both lost, both returning into the unknowable eternity from which they had come.

The woman in black exacted no penance from David to make him fit to enter though he was sure he needed one more than Eva did. He felt that he too needed to make some ritual gesture to mark his passing through the blind heavy walls into the other world within. He paid and looked about him. He was relieved when he noticed the stone stoop of water in the doorway and as he entered, he dipped the tips of his fingers into its clear still surface and crossed himself.

Sunlight streamed down in slanting rays from the small clerestory windows and landed at the feet of the columns supporting the great height of the blank wall opposite. A power radiated in the place despite its unused and deserted air. He felt himself to be in a sunken temple, the rays of the sun descending through water. To the left, covering the entire west wall, was a rich Byzantine mosaic of the Last Judgement. Waves of grey-green marble floated the fate of man from crucifixion, through judgement to damnation or reward. Between the simplicity of the crucifixion high under the rafters and the imageless sea beneath, hung the story of the soul, his soul, played out against a cloth of gold. There was no appeal against the judgement of the figure of Christ in his royal blue robe, no escape from the mighty archangels in pale blue and gold, towering above the waking mortals. He had no doubt as to his fate after years torn between heretical beliefs and atheism, and now he was sealing it with a lustful dash for comfort in Francesca's arms.

Above the doorway, dark winged figures confronted the angels and sealed the fate of the damned as they entered into everlasting darkness. Thundering chords, echoing the chant of the Dies Irae, reverberated in his head. The angels protected the blessed and kept them apart. The beating wings and claws of his breakdown returned, he had seen the distant emissaries of damnation and had been powerless against them. The voices that had forced themselves into his head, driving out reason, driving out his very sense of identity gave merely a foretaste of his ultimate destiny. He knew himself to be destined for the darkness where the naked and wretched souls lost all individuality and were lost.

Long ago he had contemplated this living wall with his mother. They had marvelled at the way in which it brought to life and reality concepts impossible to imagine, a demonstration to all, not merely the illiterate, of the principalities and powers and the fate of those who strayed. Then he had marvelled and felt his imagination stirred but now he grew cold with terror at the sight of the hopeless figures, fading into the deepest black, the coffin-cupboard that buried even the soul. The waves beneath were the timeless sea of eternity in which he knew now he would have no part.

Cold and sweating he turned to the east. Dark oak transoms spanned the nave. The cathedral was a secret sunken temple but also a ship, an ark, and the ark was a refuge from the flood, the wrath of God. David walked a few steps up the centre aisle and, feeling the marble and mosaic of the floor move beneath him, held the side of one of the simple wooden pews. He slid along its seat and without thinking found himself kneeling.

Now the sensation of being within a ship grew. The tortured and crucified God hung above a transom before him. Beyond, at the east end, past the candled catafalque of an altar, the high domed apse formed the bows. There, light dazzled through a window in the centre of a mosaic frieze of the apostles. The brightness of the light made it blur and float and standing above it, her feet supported by light, was the Virgin Mary arching over the golden field of the sky. In her arms she held the child risen above the dying man and from her eye fell tears. The images constructed their own patterns in his mind and told their own story irrespective of creed or dogma. They fell deep into his consciousness so that the golden bowl of the universe stretched within him and Mary looked down on him, her gaze healing his tortured mind; the Lady of Sorrows wept, and her tears washed out the dust of death from his body. The Queen of Heaven gathered him to her and cradled him in her arms. Beneath, far below in the darkness he saw his own tired and beaten body, worn out with separation from her love. His mind became an endless space of blue and gold and he was taken up into the space.

Form once again began to impose itself on his consciousness, his mind began to reflect on the form before it. The ark settled on dry land. He felt warm; peace beyond comprehension flowed where the turbulent emotions of terror had been. The feelings and sensations descended into his body and he shifted on the wooden seat. The craftsmen of Byzantium had built their icons well.

He sat, held simply by a reluctance to disturb the stillness. Everything around him seemed clear and strong, presenting itself with a sharper, stronger impression of reality. It was as though a veil that usually blurred and obscured things had been lifted. Whilst he stayed still, the clarity remained. Gradually, thoughts began to rise and move in his mind, his eyes moved to scan the church, his breathing broke its harmony with the breath around him and, as these assertions of individuality took over, the veil fell back into place. There was still a peace and clarity but now he was separate from it, his body felt recharged with energy and strength, but he had broken away from its source. It was inevitable, in life there was no other choice.

It was, he reflected, like the consciousness of childhood; time was slower, all things imbued with meaning and significance, perceptions brighter, clearer:

> 'Heaven lies about us in our infancy!
> Shades of the prison-house begin to close
> Upon the growing boy,
> But he beholds the light, and whence it flows,
> He sees it in his joy.'

Outside, along the covered ambulatory, a large iron gate rising nearly to the top of the arch arrested David's progress. Through the gate, rough, uncared for, grass was visible, broken in places by large stones and the remains of broken pillars. Beyond was the small domed church of Santa Fosca. He had half thought of visiting it but having arrived at this dead end found the motivation for the visit ebbing away. As he contemplated the overgrown grass and scattered lumps of white stone he shivered, and his thoughts turned back to the mosaic and the terrifying justice it portrayed. He imagined the fear and torment hidden beneath the placid sight of gravestones. Who could tell which mound, peaceful in a green churchyard, hid a world of everlasting torment?

The warm sun and the sight of the rounded church helped to keep away the fear and he brought to mind again the image of Mary floating on golden light. He pictured her form again before him, reaching out, offering mercy, offering warmth and love but this time there was a difference about her. Her eyes were warm and dark like his mother's, like the picture his Grandmother had of her at eighteen. His Grandmother had set up a shrine in the corner of her sitting room after his mother's death and the picture was at the centre. He had often sat and stared at it until it seemed to come to life. Now, once again, a picture had brought her image back. Although this time he had intentionally created the image, still it had begun to live, to change. Her eyes were warm and dark like his mother's but as he watched he realised that they were Francesca's eyes as well. As the warmth and comfort flowed from them, he felt an overwhelming desire to go to her; he felt that it was she who held the key to healing the pain of the malevolent chaos within him.

The boat, the lagoon, Eva all seemed irrelevant; it was Francesca he had to see. Venice seemed to have become irrevocably linked to Francesca. Her eyes were the eyes of the golden mosaics, her dark hair and golden jewellery were the shadows and splendour of Venice, the balance and proportion of her figure were the harmony of the stones, her mocking sense of humour and its flashes of dark irony and mystery were the costumes and masks of the carnival, her voice, soft and sensual but also bright and laughing, teasing and enticing but with a deep secret understanding, was the music that breathed through the very soul of Venice. He saw her as she was on the night they went for the drink at

Carlo's bar, her white dress against the darkness of the Calle, the lights of the windows glinting on her necklace and earrings and, later, the unspeakable sadness in her eyes. Even her sadness seemed to be a part of Venice.

There was no decision to make, he knew he must leave the tour and take the next scheduled boat to Venice, he knew they must be together.

11

THE THIRD DAY - PART THREE

As he stepped onto the white paving slabs leading to the first bridge on the Riva degli Schiavoni, David paused and allowed the dark centred archways and the soft glow of white marble to beat into his consciousness. He tried to recall the moment, only minutes away, when he had stepped off the boat, an action that two days before had been one of intense meaning and significance. He could not. It had been only an effort of will and an inner prompting from some unknown source that had allowed him, even now, to open himself to the influence of Venice and the contrasting patterns of the Doges' Palace. How far he would otherwise have walked in darkness he could not tell, the curtain of his preoccupation with meeting Francesca again shut out all else.

He walked, out into the Piazzetta. Street vendors at handcarts selling corn for the pigeons, a photographer with a hooded camera and the milling diversity of tourists struggled in his mind against images of Francesca, half formed conversations and nervous anticipation.

He found himself looking around, half expecting to see the Wagners descending again on a table outside Florian's. This return was a strange and unexpectedly complex experience. Two days ago, he had been stepping back across thirty years and every image had burnt itself into his mind seeking out its counterpart buried beneath strata of debris, inseparable from the emotional fire and trauma of his adolescence. Now, compelling though the arcades and vast space of the Piazza San Marco were, the effect was less overpowering. He paused, a hint of fear passed through him, a fear that he might lose Venice as a symbol and a land of his personal mythology. As he stood, however, allowing her to speak to him, he sensed that whilst she was less overpowering, she was at the same time more pervasive; less a torrent breaking through the darkness of rocky clefts and more a spreading flood filling him with her presence.

Reassured, he retraced his steps, past the Bacino Orseolo with its waiting gondoliers, and into the deep gullies between the high walls. He breathed deeply and the damp, cool, powdery smell of the walls sank into his lungs and ran through his blood; evocative as perfume, or incense.

It was quieter and darker than it had been when he had walked this way before. Many of the day trippers had left and the air felt still, settling gently between the buildings, warm but no longer with the oven-like heat that had overcome him and filled his mind with images of a private hell. He felt tense but invigorated, convinced that at last, he was in tune with his destiny and following the way marked out for him. Several times in his search for the trattoria he faltered, unsure of the turning he had taken but each time, when he let his instinct take him, he found himself still on the right path.

At last he saw an awning above the ice-cream counter that told him he had arrived. It seemed smaller and somehow less significant than he remembered it, though whether this was because of the change in the light or because its significance had caused his memory to magnify it, he could not say. Now the calm induced by the afternoon gave way to anxiety and an urge to walk past and not precipitate the great and irreversible change that he felt was bound to follow if he went in.

He tried to recreate Francesca's image in his mind but only managed brief flashes, impressions of her eyes, her hair, the white dress and gold necklace; nothing definite, not an image that he could hold and see. Without the image, he began to tell himself that perhaps she was not so significant after all; without an image his emotions did not turn spontaneously in his stomach but had to be sought and encouraged; surely, he had experienced enough of forced feelings.

From the shop window ledge opposite the cafe he looked cautiously and apprehensively into the semi-darkness. It was nearly empty. He realised that he was standing on the spot where he had collapsed and that without Francesca, he was no further forward than he had been when the black river of hell overtook him, when his worst fears and the meaningless current of time overwhelmed him. As he felt the dark river flowing nearer and nearer to the surface of his consciousness he felt too, Francesca's arm and warm breast as his head had lain cradled against her. It was a deep warmth, a comfort that reached into his soul. He could not remember having felt like that since he was a child and his mother held him when he was ill. The memory of that warmth told him that she had come to return to him all he had lost, all that had left such a gaping emptiness across time. It seemed incredible that he could have doubted. She would not lead him into the whirlwinds of hell but guide him from purgatory as Beatrice had led Dante: she had come to return to him the life he had lost.

He went in, nervously looking to left and right, not knowing how he would respond if he saw her immediately, cleaning the tables or standing at the bar. There was no sign of her, however, despite the fact that she had said she would be working. He had been apprehensive about the effect of his unexpected appearance, but he had expected her to be there. He breathed deeply, pushing back the growing feeling that all was not right.

Giovanni stood with his back to the bar, drying glasses and, fighting back the growing tension, David went over to him.

'Scusate.'

Giovanni turned, the cloth in his hands continuing to dry a glass. David's sense of apprehension grew; his limited hold on Italian left him and he continued in English.

'Is Francesca here?'

Giovanni looked blankly for a moment.

'I'm David. I was here the other day.'

Recognition crossed Giovanni's face and the cloth stopped moving.

'Francesca is not working today, my friend. She went out early.'

David's stomach sank and his throat caught; the apprehension was justified; she had not been working at all, it had been an excuse, a way of avoiding him. One day on the beach and it was over. David steadied himself.

'Do you know where she has gone?'

'No, my friend, she does not tell me.' Giovanni began to

turn away and then, putting down the glass, added, 'Perhaps, you telephone, she is working tomorrow.'

This time he turned and picked up another glass and began drying it; David took it as a signal that he had nothing further to say. He tried to think of some way of reopening the conversation, but it was clearly finished; Giovanni either genuinely knew no more or was not prepared to tell him. There was no point in staying now, there was no point in waiting until Francesca returned. If she did not want to see him then that was that.

He moved to leave, saying 'Arrivederci' to Giovanni who acknowledged it with a slight wave of his glass cloth and a shrug before returning to work. It occurred to David that perhaps Francesca had been intending to work but at the last minute had changed her mind and left it all for Giovanni, hence his taciturn mood, but it made little difference really; either way she had decided to do something other than meet him.

Once outside, David began to feel the emptiness, the pointlessness, the lack of any way forward without her. He turned the corner and leant against the wall. The darkness rose and pushed through, flooding into his mind. Thoughts rode on the back of the darkness. Without Francesca his first three days had achieved nothing. The voice of the spirit in the aspen leaves; the breaking of his writers' block when he had, at last, written a poem; the whole experience of Torcello, were all inextricably linked to Francesca. Without her everything disintegrated and disappeared like a handful of dust in the wind. Dust blowing like petals from the wreaths, petals that went one by one until there was nothing and she was gone. The wet icy wind returned and clawed through his heart. Despair rose through him gripping his chest and closing around his throat. There was nothing left behind the mask of existence, but chill darkness and it was folly to think otherwise.

He looked down at the stone flags and as he rested his gaze on them, transferring his attention to the irregularities on their surface, he felt the pain spread through him, softening as it became more diffuse, easing, as if by filling his whole body it was diluted. The hard reality of stone brought him back to himself and he looked up. The shade of the calle went before him, a dark valley, the way forward through the pain lay within him. He told himself that he could not give up so easily, he must move forward and try to find again the new awakening that Francesca had stirred in him. He must discover what had happened.

Carlo was the only other possible contact he had with Francesca. If he was not to accept that everything was finished, then he could try Carlo's bar. There was something about the way Carlo had spoken to him at Punta Sabbioni that made him think Francesca had discussed their relationship. Carlo had spoken as if he knew there was more to it than just a day at the beach. The way he had said, 'I see you again, I think.' had subconsciously registered the fact at the time but so many sensations were vying for his attention that he had not really brought it into awareness. Perhaps Francesca would have confided in Carlo again; perhaps he would know where she was.

Although he was cheered a little by this possibility, and felt more positive because there was something he could do to find Francesca, he realised that when he had walked to Carlo's he had followed her and had not taken much notice of where he was going. It was also a grim kind of hope as when he found her, she would probably confirm to his face all his worst fears.

He set off, confident that he was at least starting in the

right direction. Francesca and he had set off briskly and walked for some way before having to turn. The shadows were climbing higher on the walls, the line of light drawn above him marked the surface of a shadowy river beneath it. He walked through the shadow and an involuntary fear rose like cold water through his stomach.

As a small child he had read an episode of a picture story in the children's corner of his father's copy of the Church Times. It was a dark shadowy valley and a winged monster with a lion's head descended and attacked the lonely man walking through it. The name of the monster, Apollyon had fixed itself instantly in his mind. He had thought at the time that the valley was the Valley of the Shadow of Death from a psalm they had learnt at school. He had dreamt about it for months and had not dared to look at the later episodes. In the dream he would find himself walking in a valley that kept getting darker, the black mountains rose higher around him, and he was alone on a stony path. Suddenly from high in the mountains a shadow crossed the deepening sky. Above him there was a great beating of wings; he was enveloped in darkness; the air became thick and suffocating with the smell of the monster and all he could see were claws and dark veined skin and rivulets of blood. Every time, he had awoken screaming and soaked in sweat, gasping for breath until his mother came and drew away the fear with her warmth. He knew now that the story was from Pilgrim's Progress and that it was the Valley of Humiliation, not Death, that Christian had walked through but still its early meaning lay buried within him and controlled his reflexes in a way that later learning could not.

He forced himself to go on and finally had to decide whether to turn right or left. He turned right and found himself on a small bridge looking down at the heavy green canal. The tops of the buildings were still lit by bright sun and their reflections were thrown into sharp contrast by the darkness around them. A short way along the canal was another bridge, white with dark railings rising from between the buildings. It was empty and its emptiness disorientated him, in his mind she was still there just as he and Jane were still standing on the wooden bridge looking at the stars. He tried to bring her back. Laughter floated from the bridge but now its silver bells mocked him; the Renaissance girl posed by the railings, then turned to meet his eyes and vanished, the laughter ringing behind her. This time he could not follow her. She had emerged from the ferment of his own mind, a mythical being summoned by Eva that had a life of her own.

She was like Eliot's hyacinth girl who came with arms full of the blue grape-flowered blooms, dripping with dew, hair wet and eyes sparkling with desire. A girl, or image of a girl, who filled the desolate and empty sea of time. He felt a rising, unendurable longing that vibrated into a sea of suspended dissonance that promised harmony but never found it, the Tristan chord. He heard a voice mounting over its desolation:

> 'Frisch weht der Wind
> Der Heimat zu
> Mein Irisch Kind,
> Wo weilest du?'

She was his Isolde, his Celtic priestess, she had healed him before and now he lay wounded, waiting. A glimpse of eternity through the sensual, then silence:

'Oed' und leer das Meer.'

Empty and desolate the sea of time that separated them, her healing presence lost. Long wailing notes struck through him, music slid, ever seeking, never finding rest. A voice alone, bleak and hopeless followed by the surging of ceaseless unresolved chords, notes that pass and lose the moment raging against hostile fate.

He was drained by the music that swelled within him; music that, like much else, he had shut in and forgotten. It might even have been near here that Wagner wrote those notes. Francesca was the returning healer for his soul, she must be and he would go to her.

He left the bridge, plunging again into the shadows and when he emerged it was to find himself confronted by the entrance to La Fenice. The reconstruction beginning its rise from the awful ashes of the fire. It was empty, silent, a shell of scaffolding and plastic; the worlds of light and colour and the intense complex patterns of emotion woven into music had gone and left, vanished into airy nothing. He had no memory of passing this with Francesca and it was not something that would have gone unnoticed. He walked beneath its high wall with windows staring into nothingness; a barrier built to contain a dream filled darkness inside; a skull wall to contain the imagination. Now the fire had blasted it to desolation; grey ashes of the living towers in his mind. Francesca was the one who would help him rebuild himself, his life. Again, he heard the tormented waves of Tristan and Isolde, swelling, seething, rising and pouring through his head and resonating through his stomach:

'Oed' und leer das Meer.'

He had to find her, he had to go on. Turning beneath the Sottoporteggio San Cristoforo, enclosed beneath the builders' wooden covering and by the still, paler water around La Fenice he felt safe but also entombed. At the end, in near darkness the St Cristopher shrine was untouched, undamaged. He felt that he could lie down here and 'cease upon the midnight with no pain'. He walked to the edge and leant against a pillar. New rails had been erected or he could have slipped, still and quiet, into the water. He was sure he had not walked here with Francesca; he would have remembered this; somewhere he had taken the wrong turning; he had lost the way and would never find her now.

He walked on until he found himself again in the Campo Sant'Angelo where on his first day he sat and drank in the midday sun, lazing in soporific, sensual, satisfaction after having met Francesca. Now as the shadows continued to deepen, the leaning campanile of Santo Stefano seemed more threatening than mocking, like a high-hatted witch peering down to find him out and spread darkness through his veins. He hurried on to escape her, seeking out the darkest calle and turning away from the light.

He was alone, it was deserted, and he turned into a calle so narrow he could touch both sides. The windows were sealed with rusted bars and the glass crusted over with dust. Here he was hidden. He slowed and felt the momentum that had driven him, drain away. He had no map; it was getting dark and he had no idea where he was. In the gloom he peered into a window without bars and there looking back at him were faces of the Commedia dell'Arte: long-beaked sinister masks of the plague doctors, wide dark-faced hooded masks, Pantalone and Arlecchino, dark leather faces of maroon and black, old men with long phallic noses;

masks that fixed the of follies humanity, the attempts to live, the treacherous guidance of desire. He saw in the dust rimmed window a graveyard of personae, of the characters created by people trying to live. They were his faces, all his faces and every one was empty, its strings tied around darkness.

Above him a piano began playing, restless driving quavers like running footsteps. It stopped and began again running on deeper and darker until the patterns of quavers disintegrated into circling broken chords hunting and turning until they rose in a spiral and finally came to rest in the centre.

He knew it, his father had played it but he could not place it. Then it lightened and the tripping subject of a fugue began, simply at first and then growing in complexity weaving the statements together into a perfect balanced pattern that life could never equal, a balanced pattern that lay as an ideal never to be reached. The most life could manage was an occasional rest at the centre as at the end of the prelude. He knew now what the piece was: one of the Bach '48 Preludes and Fugues' that he had heard his father teaching to music pupils from his very earliest childhood, dense patterns of black on the page that he turned into the clearest, the most lucid, music. Somehow his father had become obscured in the story David had created around himself, the story that he identified as his mythology but now, in this dark centre of empty masks, the chance playing of a piano by a stranger had brought him back, placing him at the centre too.

Where this fitted into his present attempt to rediscover his creativity he could not tell. When he was at college, the wife of a poet who taught there read tarot cards for him. She had said that he would not make sense of his life until he came to terms with his father, but he could not fit this into his concept of himself. His relationship with his mother had been so close and cut short so cruelly that he could not find room to explore what was only the voice of cards read by someone who knew nothing of his past. It had always stayed in his mind though, and he had returned to it many times but always left the idea as too difficult to cope with.

The narrow calle with the rusty barred and dust filled windows became oppressive rather than safe. The window with the masks grew into a dark emptiness, a glass that let him see through into himself; a darkness full of vague empty images hiding yet more emptiness. There was nothing there; nothing behind the flickering light of waking consciousness; the masks themselves floated, caught in the darkness, husks of ideas created to hide the dreadful truth.

The piano was playing the fugue again now and its ordered perfection cleared some of the emotional turmoil within him. His mind cleared a little and he decided that he should find his way back; there was no point in going on with his search; he would ring Francesca in the morning and face whatever she had to tell him. He looked about him wondering how best to return to St Mark's.

The far end of the calle appeared blocked by a wall of some ten feet high, a garden wall, though what kind of garden was found here in the heart of Venice he did not know. He walked to it and found that he could in fact turn either way. There was an iron barred gate in the wall but through it, in this light, all he could see was some tangled undergrowth and a vague image of a statuette. Beyond the undergrowth was darkness. He could not tell what, if anything, lay beyond it.

At school they had played a game they called 'psycho-analysis'. Imagine you are in a wood and there is a path running through it - describe it: that was your attitude to life. You find a cup: that was your attitude to love. You pass a waterfall: that showed your attitude to sex. You found a key: that gave your image of religion. Then you came to a wall with a door, you described the door and that told you how you felt about death. Finally, you went through the door and described what was on the other side and that revealed your view of the after-life. This wall was like that, it seemed to hint at something held beyond it, it was haunting and hypnotic, drawing him to it. He pressed his face to the gate until it hurt; he strained to see through the undergrowth and past the statuette, but it was dark and tangled and the iron bars were locked, firmly shut.

At last he fell back and looked each way along the wall. For no particular reason he went left and walked rapidly now that he had found a way out of the narrow calle. The walls of the buildings drew back, and he reached a canal. Here there were lights reflected in the water and gondolas with lanterns swinging unevenly. It was no longer deserted, and the activity of tourists gave him something more substantial to cling on to, something to take him away from the masks filled with darkness and the tangled but inaccessible garden. The canal was familiar and signs 'Per San Marco' began to appear on the walls. He focused on the rhythmic pace of his walk, fast and regular, independent and utterly within his control, taking him reliably to the Riva degli Schiavoni.

He found the ferry ticket in his bag and punched it in the machine that rang, announcing his departure. On the ferry, the comfortable throbbing of the engines filled the silence. He rested his mind on their drone and let it drive out thoughts, a mechanical mantra that allowed him escape, of a kind, from the incessant activity within him. He was tired, empty of the surging tides that had carried him through the day.

They stopped briefly at the Lido and then moved out into the darkness of wider waters. He shivered as a chill breeze blew across the boat, flapping the canvas awnings of the decks. The isolation and the emptiness, the lack of direction now Francesca no longer acted as a focus for his future, induced a momentary panic. He was lost on the dark water: all effort, all purpose, all meaning had abandoned him:

'Oed' und leer das Meer.'

The Tristan chords rose through him, distantly now as though his mind had lost the energy to bear them.

He shifted on the metal seat and listened first for the music and then, when it would not come, for the stilling sound of the mantra. He tried to let it take over again, but the moment had passed, and it was now just the sound of engines. He was impatient to be back in the hotel, to close the day and rest.

At Punta Sabbioni he cursed his decision to use the bus and leave the reassurance of his car behind. A row of darkened buses stood in the centre of the turning point of the road. Lights sprang on in one and its engine churned whined and coughed gutturally into life. He climbed aboard and rang his ticket in the punch again. The engine throbbed, waiting as he waited. Eliot again padding his footfalls in the mind, the taxi throbbing whilst Tiresias watched.

Back at the hotel and in his room, he sent for some sandwiches. He had not eaten since breakfast but worked his way mechanically through them without enthusiasm or enjoyment.

Later he stood for a long time looking out through the window at the darkness of the sea. Empty and desolate: the aching waves of Tristan once again flowed as an accompaniment to his thoughts. He had glimpsed something briefly but now with only endless darkness before him, life at home with Thelma began to seem warm and attractive; a safe world that was comfortable and predictable. The quarrelling, the tension, the shouting seemed trivial compared with this awful lonely emptiness in a limitless night. The lack of close shared romantic love or passion seemed only the loss of a luxury compared with this aching chasm that stretched into eternity.

There was a line of Beckett's that stuck in his mind permanently after reading it only once, a line that said we were born over an open grave and life was the flash of light as we fell. He had played Pozzo, blinded like Oedipus, and knew as soon as he had spoken it for the first time, that it was a terrible statement, one of appalling honesty, one that faced what he had never been able to bring himself to face even as a possibility. Now he had been forced to confront it and he felt he had to hang on to anything that could fan the flame of light, even for an instant. Perhaps he would phone Thelma in the morning.

In bed, tiredness would not bring sleep. He pulled the duvet down hard over his head but, when his eyes closed, the darkness rushed before him. Lights sped into its depth like the traces of fireworks against a November night, borrowed lights living only in the persistence of memory.

He turned and sat up quickly, staring into the room. Looking into the darkness he felt his own identity dissolving without light to feed it. His own persona was no more than the persistence of memory; he was no more than a trace of light, already dead but appearing to fade slowly through a trick of the mind. The mask was empty, the darkness had won.

He grabbed at the table lamp and forced the sliding switch across. The room glowed; the illusion of existence returned. He was the things he saw, nothing more: put out the light and then put out the light. He leaped from the bed and walked determinedly around the room asserting his existence through physical movement, through the feel of the carpet on his bare feet. He gripped the window sill, hard to make his hands hurt: I hurt, therefore I am.

Gradually the panic eased and slipped away. Either a brief glimpse of the illusory nature of reality left or the reality of his existence returned; either way, now the panic had gone, he felt more comfortable but not tired. He sat down in the chair with his notebook and allowed his mind to rest on the images that had coursed through his mind during the day. He tried to decipher the notes but could not. The images formed into new chains:

> *'Upon the stair she climbs and turns*
> *The winding corner, out of sight,*
> *White gossamer on stone.*
>
> *A shadow, curling harsh as smoke,*
> *A cloak and mask of darkness, falls,*
> *Aching, hungry and alone.*
>
> *The darkness draws her ivory down,*
> *Two roses bleed upon her neck,*
> *Two fountains feed the air.*

The billowing cloak is filled with blood
And rises on its borrowed life;
The mask is sated there.

The cloak and mask, then hung on thorns,
With blood in rivers feeds the ground;
A wasted thing in agony.

She turns; and tears like crystal form
And fall across the night as stars
From eyes that sound eternity.

They reach the tomb and, from the rock,
A mother's tears that wash out death
Stream down upon the reddened earth;
The waters of a second birth.

The act of writing left him drained of tension, as if a barbed chain of words had been there, enmeshed in his nerves, waiting to be untangled and drawn out. He could not tell so soon whether it was any good or not, that would take time. He felt tired again now and slid into bed. The duvet was cool and comforting around him. He turned out the lamp and drifted quietly into sleep:

Darkness

Beneath the bridge a river ran, teeming with fish writhing and swirling. Closer and the fish were human, faces drawn, agonised or empty with despair. The dark water flooded into their mouths. Ahead, in the shadows, round a corner, a figure disappeared. Held by the bridge, he tried to follow, the water swirled fiercely, and the laughing started. As he ran on the bridge he slipped and slid through the rails and into the mass of silver bodies, sinking in their struggle to stay afloat. He grabbed at an empty caricature of a girl as she slid past, but she disintegrated into fish scales and slime:

Darkness

He sat in the hold of a wooden ship. Casks rolled with the movement; rats scurried across the boards away from the swilling of green water. The ship wallowed and turned, heaved and rolled. He was being taken somewhere; it was important; he had to get there. He tried to reach the ladder to join them, but the water drove him back; it poured in from the hatches. He could not tell whether he would get there but he must, it was important:

Darkness

The sea was receding; he was left stranded on the grass. There were white stones and he had to leave them; he had to get into the building. There was no door or windows, he could only reach the bottom of the wall; he had to get in. There was a ditch by the wall, and he walked along it. At the end was an iron gate. It led under the building. The roof was low, there were old crumbling pillars, it was dark. He saw white stones and went to them. They were bones and skulls; they were heaped all around him. He tried to climb on them to reach a trap in the roof but kept sliding back. A voice called. He had forgotten that she was there too, she must be outside; he tried to go back to find her but wherever he turned was blocked by bones. She called again, faintly; she was leaving. He called but there was silence; she had gone. He was left with the bones and the skulls:

Darkness

He half awoke aware that something had gone, something important that he had to find but it blurred over, and he sank back again into darkness.

12

THE FOURTH DAY - PART ONE

Towards morning, light trickled into David's consciousness and then dimmed again leaving behind a vague feeling that he should be doing something significant, something that mattered. Light returned and with it an awareness that, above the layers of sleep induced calm, the surface of his life had been stirred into a turbulence whose broken reflections were waiting for him.

As he lay in bed, through semi-consciousness, he saw the tangled garden and the masks; he heard the mocking laughter on the empty bridge and beating wings over the Valley of Humiliation; he saw the tears of the Blessed Virgin running over the icon in Torcello and felt again the fear of the Last Judgement. Heat and confusion swirled around Eva and Jane and the shadow on the stairs swept past, chasing them through his mind into darkness.

He forced his eyes open to banish the procession of images and, as he did so, he remembered the chain of thoughts and feelings that sleep had broken. Francesca had seemed to offer him a new life but when he turned to find her she had gone. Everything had depended on her: she was the healing embodiment of Venice, the soul and centre of his search, and now she was gone.

His notebook lay on the small table by the bed, open at the poem written late after the darkness had tried to draw out and destroy him. He read it through.

It was a spare poem with exposed words, nowhere to hide: but was it any good? It was difficult now to imagine the poem not existing, he had uncovered it: but was it any good? He could not tell but he could not imagine it changed. It would do. The week had not been wasted even if it had not transformed his life. He had written and finished two poems in three days. He had not written at that speed for years. If Francesca was to be a momentary flicker of light in a life that would continue dull and pointless, then at least she had shown him that somewhere within there was still a living being.

The room was becoming claustrophobic and he felt a sudden need to escape beyond this circle of fate that was hemming him in. He went to the window and pulling the curtain a little to one side looked out. The sky was blue and bright though flecked with white clouds. A light wind blew the halyards of the small dinghies that had been pulled onto the sand. It flapped the hotel flag that showed it was safe to bathe. There were already people on the paved terrace unfolding sun beds and smoothing striped towels. He looked at his watch: nine o'clock, he had slept late.

The day having started without him, and Francesca having gone, he felt little sense of purpose or motivation. He did not feel particularly depressed, just stranded by point-lessness. Logically he was no worse off than before except for the loss of hope; the unspoken, even unthought hope that had lain beneath the surface of his life supporting him even in those moments when the desert seemed most arid.

He turned away from the sight of people staking out their section of beach and sat on the bed. He had tried to create a new life, moving into it and leaving the old behind. It had not worked. Now what was he to do? He could return to his old life. Perhaps when Thelma arrived, he would see that the marriage and his life were not as bad as they had seemed. Perhaps Thelma was right, and he simply had unrealistic expectations of life. There was no reason to believe that it was normal for the intensity of adolescence to continue through life, quite the reverse and why should he be any different? He had reached the beginning of middle-age and this feeling of disappointment at a lack of achievement was quite usual. He had at least acquired a comfortable cushion of relative prosperity to insulate himself from any real deprivation. He should be reasonably content even if he could not be happy.

He grimaced. Look at it a different way. It was a nice try but there was no possible chance of his believing these platitudes. It was all self-deception and unconvincing lies. He could pretend to himself, suspend disbelief, live as if he thought they were true, but if he had known otherwise before his return to Venice, how much sharper and clearer was it now? He could choose untruth; he could voluntarily blind himself so as to exist cocooned from the pain of reality, but he could never fool himself into forgetting he had betrayed himself. Too much had happened for that. He did not know any longer how to begin to create that new life but, if he was to follow this inner voice, he had no choice but to find out.

Here then were two views; two alternative ways of looking at his situation but which was the truth? What was truth? It was the first view that had the corroboration of a third party: Thelma looking with her cold objective eye. The second had no point of reference but an inner hunch, something with no reasonable claim at all to objectivity but at the same time something that could not be ignored. Certain things felt true, certain things felt false; the better something was, the more beautiful and profound it was, then the greater the urge to feel it true. Hardly a reliable test. There was no reason to believe that beauty and profundity were any more true than ugliness and superficiality, but to believe the opposite would be to cast darkness over his world in preference to light. It was illogical, but to him inescapable and not a comfortable conclusion. To believe that beauty is truth in middle age was a hard doctrine:

> *'Beauty is truth, truth beauty, — that is all*
> *Ye know on earth, and all ye need to know.'*

Keats conformed to Nietzsche's advice and died early before it became too hard. 'Many die too late and some die too early. Still the doctrine sounds strange: "Die at the right time".'

Agitated, David got up and went to the wardrobe. He pulled out the first pair of long trousers and shirt that came to hand. He dressed automatically and absent-mindedly. There must be another answer. He did not want to die, he wanted to find his way back to the centre, to the hidden stone, to the fountain, to his Beloved, to the Self, to all the other images and symbols held up over the centuries as a way of visualising the journey back to the start. And what was the connection between this and his conviction that Francesca had offered a way forward? He tried to recall some words of St John of the Cross that he had found scrawled almost illegibly in one of the notebooks discovered before he left:

> *'For love is like fire, which ever rises upward with the desire to be absorbed in the centre of its sphere.'*

But was this what he meant? Francesca could simply have been a snare, a distraction, a siren to draw him away from his journey to the real source and centre of his being where all was still as bright and fresh, as innocent in love, as it was when he began. He had remembered St Augustine as he returned from Venice on the first day: 'To Carthage I came' and did Francesca sing from the cauldron of unholy loves or was she the voice that led within? He thought she had descended like Beatrice to lead him from Purgatory into Paradise. It did not matter now; she was gone, and he had to try another way. He would try another way but how and what he did not know. There was little he had not tried at some time.

Over breakfast in the restaurant, rolls and coffee in a heavy silver pot, he looked out at the sea, and the growing number of people already in the sun. He thought again of phoning Thelma.

He could not begin again in Venice. Deep though it was in his consciousness and central as it was to his imagination, Venice had been temporarily overlain by Francesca and whilst it would surely survive in the longer term, even the thought of her now was dangerous to him. Venice would play a part again in the future, of that he had no doubt; but, for the next few days, he could not trust himself. He would pass the time here on the beach, spend a day in Verona and go to the opera, read, do some writing; he would leave Venice until Thelma arrived. With Thelma he would be just a tourist and that would help break the spell of the last few days.

It was after making this decision that David realised to what extent he had been driven against a timetable culminating in Thelma's arrival. Now he sat back facing the fact that this decision removed it, there was no rush, no pressure, nothing to achieve. The odyssey was over almost before it had begun: almost, because something had been achieved, the last three days had been lived at an intensity rare, if not unique, in the last twenty or so years. If it had not provided him with a new life, it had at least given him a store of emotions, ideas and experiences that he could draw on in the months ahead.

The two poems need not be all that came out of it. He had invested too much in Francesca for the original aim of the week to survive and now the current of excitement and tension, fear and exhilaration that had carried him along was a spent force. He would plan and prepare, for the longer term, a way that did not depend on chance or emotion; he would treat the remaking of himself as a project to be managed as he did sales and installation projects at work. He would create himself, be Emperor and gold smith; untouchable ruler of Byzantium. It was a project he had attempted before, whilst still a student.

Miranda lay on the grass bank in the college grounds. The buildings were half hidden by the thickly layered leaves of the sycamore and horse-chestnut trees. Her eyes, a deep blue, were overlain with the reflection from the green of the grass and leaves around them. Her white hand moved to a tall field buttercup at her side and she slid her finger and thumb along its stem. Her skin was always very white even in summer, a dramatic contrast to her dark hair. She turned her head and looked at him, narrowing her eyes a little against the patches of sunlight, and thinking before she spoke.

'It's so intellectual, it pretends to be about the soul, but it hasn't got one, it's all ideas without feelings.'

Her voice was warm and rich, deep but very feminine, a dark, clear, sensual sound that impressed everyone, male or female, who heard it.

'I still think you'd find it interesting. You like Yeats and he was a member. There's a meeting tomorrow you could come to.'

'I'll see but I'd much rather stay here with you, not go to a meeting full of old women smelling of moth balls.'

David laughed, leaned over and kissed her.

'They don't all smell of moth balls.'

'Just most of them.' Her eyes softened and she whispered, 'Come here.'

Her arms encircled him, and she pulled him down to into the comforting warmth of her body.

She kissed slowly and deeply, drawing him into the darkness of her heat. When he opened his eyes and looked up, the trees and the dazzling pools of blue sky showing through their leaves took him by surprise. Their lips parted and she smiled up at him.

'There, that's better than any old Theosophical Society.'

And he had to admit that it was.

There were many times when he loved her so deeply that it hurt, when her long dark hair, sea-deep eyes and rich voice sank into every corner of his mind and imagination;

when she was the woman who existed inside him and they were at one with each other. He knew that other people thought so too, and it was easy to see why. She lived in a world of poetry, music, dance and theatre so what could possibly be missing? She was intelligent as well as talented and creative so how could anything be wrong?

He tried to accept that she was rather possessive. Although both students in London she was at a different college and they were only really able to spend time together at weekends. He still wrote poetry for her, they had friends from both colleges and their passion had grown and deepened in over two years together. The nearest he could identify as a reason was that she had no time for the purely intellectual, everything had to be immersed in feeling, Mahler not Bach, but with so much to outweigh it why should that matter?

Now that his mother was in hospital for another operation, he knew that, emotionally, he depended on Miranda more and more. She visited with him and his mother was always happy to see her. It was a good relationship so why did he goad her with these things that he knew were meaningless to her and which pushed them apart? It seemed as if the closer they were the more he wanted to find something to separate them as though he were afraid of losing his identity entirely.

They went to the Theosophical Society and it smelled of sandalwood floor polish, not moth balls. He had been there on his own before and was fascinated by the systems of evolution and re-incarnation, the mysterious Sanskrit names and the promise that he could achieve enlightenment through his own efforts. They went into the lecture room and sat down. Miranda seemed tense and kept looking across to a picture of Madame Blavatsky.

'She has powerful eyes, even in a picture.' she whispered. 'I don't think she'd be very impressed with this lot though.'

David grinned and looked around. Why was it that organisations devoted to the highest ideals of truth and wisdom always attracted such an odd assortment of people?

The lecture was on Raja Yoga and given by a large lady who was adamant that the first steps were to give up drinking, smoking, eating meat and most especially the desires of the flesh. At this Miranda relaxed visibly and ran her fingers lightly along the inside of David's thigh. She was clearly confident that her knowledge of him was such that there was no chance of his reaching even this preliminary stage. He could only acknowledge that she was right and hope that the large lady's strictures on the dangers of travelling the path without sufficient purification were exaggerated. Now he was with Miranda, he too saw the eccentric and unbelievable side of it.

He felt very close to her as they walked, arms around each other, back to Marble Arch. The tube whirred and rattled through the darkness first underground and then from tunnel to tunnel with brief glimpses of stars and street lights in between. The train reached Putney bridge and they kissed until it had crossed the Thames. As they parted, she whispered in his ear, 'Against the bridal day, which is not long:' and he whispered back, 'Sweet Thames! run softly, till I end my song.' It was a ritual begun the first time she had visited him in London and then re-enacted every time they returned on the tube.

Back at his room, Miranda lit candles and sandalwood joss sticks. They rested their gaze in each other's eyes and the fragrance lifted them into a timeless space, a Tibetan temple, high and unassailable. She knelt on the bed naked under her green robe with gold braided cords and, holding it open for him, wrapped them both in its cool silk. She was at her most sensual and if there was anything in re-incarnation, he could only see her then as a Tantric priestess who knew how to make the erotic reach into the inner heart of their combined souls.

Later in the semi darkness they lay quietly, listening to the breath of the night air over the bamboo wind-chimes that hung in his window. The curtains were open, and they floated in a magic space under the stars.

Here was the transforming power that he sought, the sense of peace and oneness with everything; samâdhi without mantras, a yoga of their own not dependant on abstinence but on love, desire and fulfilment. But for it to work, he depended on Miranda: it was more than sex, it was a special kind of magic that they worked intuitively together. At the Theosophical Society he had sought a way that he could achieve it alone, intellectually by learning and work until his mind embraced the Universe as Madame Blavatsky had promised. Now he did not feel ready or inclined to recreate himself alone. He drew her warm body to him and held her tightly.

Before dawn, together in the narrow student bed, he felt her breath brush through the hairs of his chest and felt the rhythm of her slow heartbeat on his ribs. As light began, almost imperceptibly to enter the room he slid gently from her and went to the desk in the window. While the pigeons cooed on the roof, he wrote to the rhythm of her breath and her heart:

> 'A feathered moonlight skein of dancing,
> Night rocked and swayed in the water's swell,
> Air poised soft as the breath before dawn
> Singing in the sighing reeds.

Naked in the forest,
Sinew on softness,
Light in floating,
Heart beat soft as the breath on skin,
Soft as the breath before dawn.
Breath of life,
Life light as breath,
Before dawn
Is love.'

At university, he had not been ready. Since then he had worked to establish himself in the material world. Now was the ideal time to begin the inner journey. He had been brought to the start more than once before but always something had stopped him from getting further. Now he was not dependent on anyone and no-one was dependent on him. Thelma and he provided company and a home for each other without the emotional dependence and entanglement that a more satisfactory relationship would demand. He would phone her to check what flight she would be on. It was almost a relief not to be facing the destruction of his old life but rather its regeneration.

He finished the pot of coffee and left the dining room. As he passed the reception desk the girl behind it called out to him.

'Signor Green. Mr Green, there is a telephone message for you.'

It seemed one of those extraordinary coincidences; he was sure that it was from Thelma. It would not be the first time their thoughts had coincided over a phone call. She had said that she would phone him later in the week to tell him about the flight and now, just as he was about to phone her, she had left a message.

He felt a great sense of relief as if he had been on a particularly exciting and terrifying fairground ride and had at last stepped back onto firm ground. The ground still seemed to sway, as if his body had not yet accepted that the ride was over, but the danger, the churning in the stomach and blood rushing to the head had gone. Now, it seemed, he could look forward to nothing more alarming than hot-dogs and hoop-la.

He went over to the desk and the girl handed him the message. He noticed her long, curving, red-varnished finger nails on the paper, smiled at her as he took it and pushed it into his pocket. He was beginning to feel more active, more physical, more externalised, a separate entity in charge of himself. He would ring Thelma from his room rather than the desk.

Back in his room he sat down on the bed and lifted the phone. He started to dial and then stopped. He tucked the receiver between his jaw and his shoulder and took the message from his pocket to check whether Thelma had said he should ring her at home or the office. He looked at the paper and for a moment he did not take in what it said. Finally, he lowered the phone and sat staring at the words:

'Please ring before 12:00. Francesca.'

Everything that he had thought and everything he had repeated to himself since he arrived back at the hotel last night; his arguments in favour of continuing his life with Thelma and his acceptance that the quest was over were all based on the assumption that Francesca's disappearance was final. He had intentionally set out to destroy his original aim of moving irrevocably from an old to a new life; avoided bringing to mind anything about Francesca; firmly decided to avoid Venice as too dangerous with her power to awaken images and forces from the past; consciously determined to seal the cracks opening in the dry shell of his present and take a longer, slower less radical route to healing himself.

He had seen again the danger of pinning his hopes of renewal on a vulnerable relationship with a woman subject to all the unreliability of any relationship never mind this one, barely forty-eight hours old. Already she had walked out during a simple evening drinking in a cafe because of problems of her own; already she had pretended to be working in order to avoid seeing him. What possible justification could there be for him to trust anything of importance to him to anything so fragile? There was no reason why this message should change his resolve. She had let him down and had every right to do so but equally he had every reason to ignore the message and keep to his new plan. He would phone Thelma.

The travelling alarm clock by his bed said it was now nearly half past ten. In England it would be half past nine and Thelma would be in the office. He would ring her there. He lifted the receiver and for a moment could not recall the number. The phone seemed heavy and he had to consciously push himself forward to dial. He picked out the code for England and London and by then had remembered Thelma's number. He felt nervous and his hand was sweating slightly. He pressed the buttons deliberately. It was a direct line so she would answer. He had decided that this was the best way and there was no good reason now for him to change his mind.

The phone rang for a long time and he would normally have put it down and tried again but he was determined to get through. Finally, a voice answered.

'Thelma Green's phone'.

It was her secretary. The delay should have told him

Thelma was not at her desk, but he was convinced that she would answer.

'Hello Caroline, it's David here. Is Thelma there?'

He usually enjoyed chatting to Caroline on the phone but now he did not want anything to get in the way.

'She's in a meeting at the moment but I can give her a message. I suppose you're disgustingly brown by now.'

'Absolutely disgusting. Do you know when it'll finish?'

'Well, it's supposed to be over by half past eleven, but you know how it is.'

Despite the tension, David laughed and agreed, he knew how it was.

'Can you tell her I called, it's not urgent.'

'I can get her to ring if you like. Has she got the number?'

'Yes, it's in her diary.'

'Right, well, you'd better get back to your sun-bathing. I don't suppose you've got room for a little one.'

'I'll put out an extra towel.'

'I'll be there for lunch'

'Sea-food and chilled Soave.'

'I can taste it now.'

'Bye.'

'Bye.'

That was it, he had committed himself. There was certainly a feeling of anti-climax, of a mission aborted; but at the same time the tension, the anxiety and the sensation of an approaching thunderclap that would tear away everything he knew, had also gone. It left a worn, tired sensation in his body but also one of relief.

He was left with an hour before Thelma could ring and he could not sit there watching the phone until she did. He did not feel like going onto the beach and it was not worth going anywhere in the car. There was a small group of stalls and souvenir shops on the opposite side of the Via Fausta. He would explore them. It was something trivial and undemanding that would pass the time.

As he passed the reception desk on the way out, he noticed the girl with the long, painted, finger nails talking on the phone. Francesca's call returned into his mind. What was it she had wanted to say? Perhaps he should have phoned anyway, just out of politeness. No, it was too dangerous, better to leave it as it was and then, after twelve o'clock, she would be just a memory to be moulded and formed into part of the past along with all the others.

He walked briskly out of the hotel and, pausing to remember which way to look for traffic, crossed the road. The stalls were stacked high with boxes of peaches, plum tomatoes, pears and grapes. By the side of each was a mound of large dark green melons bigger than footballs. The stall holders were not actively selling, as they had been in Cavallino market; they just talked and pottered about, stacking and re-stacking the fruit. David wandered along the stall fronts and then looked into an apparently deserted, flat roofed building that declared 'Cambio/Wechseln/Change' on its sun-faded sign. He idly calculated the value of Italian lire and then Deutsch marks in pounds sterling.

As he moved to look away, he noticed a clock at the back of the office. Eleven o'clock: half an hour until he had to be back in the hotel ready to take the call that would settle him firmly back in the life he knew; the house in Wimbledon; shopping at Sainsbury's; Thelma; a pint at the One Tun and possibly, though only possibly, the office and selling computer systems. It was not an exciting prospect, but neither was it unknown, unpredictable, terrifying nor the product of a delayed adolescent fantasy.

The souvenir shop was built like a long, low, wooden

supermarket. It was surrounded by rail after rail of silk squares, casual shirts, shorts, jeans and beachwear. The inevitable, inflatable alligators, airbeds and tropical islands hung nodding above him. He riffled through the scarves until one caught his eye. He would get it for Thelma, a sort of arriving present and a gesture to himself that he was committed to forgetting the wild barely formed ideas that had been coursing through his mind since his arrival here. Sitting on sun drenched slopes under vines and olive trees was the stuff of travel brochures not real life. And as for Francesca, that had been the most absurd fantasy of all. He quickly closed his mind to consign her, and her phone call, to darkness.

He took the scarf that had caught his eye, from the rail and went into the shop. There was row after row of multi-coloured glass: gold-rimmed goblets, red-based bowls, sets of glasses with decanters, bowls of coloured glass fruit, dolphins, ballet dancers, Bambi deer, elephants, cats, sharks and snails. He worked his way along the rows to use up time, trying not to look at his watch, looking at prices, looking at things he could not imagine anyone wanting but that they bought anyway. Souvenirs, reminders, things used to mark out time, things done and acquired because they were there. He tried to ignore the parallel building up in his mind; a parallel with the life to which he was returning. Finally, he paid for the scarf and allowed himself to check the time. It had just gone twenty past eleven and he decided that he could allow himself to go back.

At reception he ordered some coffee and a copy of the Times, to be sent up, and then took the stairs rather than the lift to his room so as to use up a little more time before Thelma's call.

He sat at a small table away from the phone and tried to

read but all the books he had brought with him were about Venice. He opened a simple travel guide to plan the first day in Venice with Thelma, but it opened at a photograph of a beautiful Venetian girl who looked back at him with Francesca's eyes. The coffee and his newspaper arrived. He poured himself a cup from the heavy pot and tried to read the paper but everything in it: wars, murders, rapes and collapsing economies; all seemed trivial compared with the approaching phone call. He tried to do the crossword but could not keep his attention on the clues for long enough to solve even the most straight-forward of them.

Eventually he got up, went over to the bed and took the scarf from its bag. He held it up against the light and then sat on the bed to re-fold it on his lap. As he did so he looked at the phone and saw, tucked under one corner, the message from Francesca. The clock told him it was ten to twelve, and she had asked him to phone before twelve. Would she be feeling like he was, waiting for Thelma's call? Unlikely, but he did not know her side of the story and this was a bad way to end it, just letting it drift into the dark. If he rang, they could part amicably, perhaps even write; it could be useful, after all, to have a contact in Venice.

He put the silk scarf back in its bag and slipped it into the drawer in the cabinet by the bed. He lifted the phone and dialled Francesca's number. This time the phone was answered quickly.

'Pronto.'

He thought he recognised Giovanni's voice.

'Pronto. Qui parla David Green. Vorrei parlare a Francesca per favore.'

'Si, Si. Un attimo.'

What was he doing? It was against everything he had decided, against common sense and all reasonable caution and yet the energy returning to him, the sense of excitement made it difficult to keep down the feeling that this was not just a good-bye. That might be all Francesca was offering, a more orderly, polite, even friendly good-bye; but a feeling began to flow irrepressibly through him that he was moving back on course, coming to life again, foolish, even foolhardy though it might be.

'Hello, David?'

He knew now that if he had intended to have nothing more to do with Francesca he should never have phoned. Her voice cut deep tracks into him, it sounded right through him, it transformed everything.

'Francesca.'

'When it got so late, I thought you weren't going to phone.'

David thought he heard an undercurrent of anxiety in her voice.

'Sorry, I've only just got your message.'

The truth would have been too complicated to explain.

'Look, Giovanni told me you were in last night. I don't want to talk about it on the phone. Can you come over now? I have still got this afternoon off.'

He did not realise how much he had sealed up inside as self-protection. Now it all came flowing out through him, there was nothing he could do against such a flood. He could not reverse it; he had no choice but to accept. He steadied his voice.

'Of course I can. I'll just check the ferry times.'

The timetable was in his bag and he went quickly to the wardrobe to get it. He grabbed the bag and took it back to the phone.

'Hello, Francesca. I've got it here, hold on.'

He rummaged through the bag and pulled out the

timetable. — Cavallino to Venezia via Punta Sabbioni; the next boat left at one o' clock.

'I can be there at one forty. Where shall I meet you?'

'I'll be on the Riva della Schiavoni, where the ferry comes in.'

'I'll see you there.'

' See you soon. Ciao.'

'Ciao.'

He put the phone down and held his hand on the receiver for a moment. That was it, he had done it now. There was no going back. He didn't know what she was going to say but she would not make him go all that way just to say good-bye. What should he do about Thelma? He could phone her now on the off chance that the meeting was finished but if she had not phoned then the chances were that there was a good reason. If she rang while he was getting ready, he would just take the flight details, talk as usual, there was no great problem. If she did not, then there was nothing more he could do. He had to go. The call from Thelma was no longer the one single significant move to decide his future. It had become an inconvenience, a problem of his own creation; something he wished now he had not so hastily initiated.

He checked his watch. That morning he had dressed carelessly and not even shaved. There were fifteen minutes before he had to leave; long enough if he did not waste time. Which shirt? He had worn the new one already. The pale linen one would do, it would fit in most places they were likely to go, and the cream trousers. It was the best he could manage from a wardrobe intended for a solitary week wandering and writing.

He laid the clothes out on the bed, checked the clock, and then went to the bathroom for a shave and a shower.

Twenty minutes later he left the hotel. The mid-day heat engulfed him as he left the air-conditioned lobby of the hotel. He turned towards the car park but as he did so a bus swept around the curve of the hotel's drive. He did not want to be tied to what time he returned or, the involuntary thought flashed through his mind, which day. He would, once again, take the bus.

13

THE FOURTH DAY - PART TWO

D avid stood against the white painted rail, looking past a peeling life belt at the white foam topped waves pushing away from the ship. It was as if he had been returned to the start again, chosen the wrong thread, gone down a snake, taken the wrong path into the maze.

The waves moved backwards and away, always renewing themselves, never changing. When they had played themselves out, they merged back into the water with a swirl of bubbles and were indistinguishable from the rest, movement without change. Constant motion, travelling over the surface of the water but nothing moved because the waves were the same as the water beneath and returned to the water. In my end is my beginning. Try again, another one of the infinite possibilities that co-existed, each seeming to go somewhere whilst always remaining ready to merge back into choices not taken. And each possibility taken was enriched by the others, changed by the others as it rose to the surface. There was nothing to lose whichever choice he made, there were just different ways of seeing, different ways of refracting the same light.

The Renaissance girl no longer existed: he had chased a phantom through the calli and the phantom called and released images of past paths. An image of another Renaissance painting: the hunted unicorn. What painting was that? And another: the unicorn in the brake, symbol of the captive soul. Now, the unicorn was trapped again in the thorn bush, waiting to be free.

Miranda had worn the stag's horn ring he brought back from Scotland. They had joked about it but somehow it seemed right, better than a proper one. She talked to the unicorn in the field on the hill under a full moon while the snowflakes fell. The stars in the sky were the dome of a great cathedral and they were wrapped in a vortex of power, together, joined in the images of the gate of horn. It was real then, totally real. Only weeks later the force fell away from their eyes leaving a pony in a field and two people, separate, ready to go in different directions, walking across a dead land, devoid of dreams; a hard, cold, unyielding land, dry and dead as bones. Surely reality could not be just dry bones.

It was a time he remembered only as a blur, as a dream; the time around his mother's death. He felt that it was a deep underground lake of images and emotions; memories sealed in and out of reach. Occasionally something would surface, like the unicorn, but even then, it was stripped of its emotional power, its essential reality. After only a short while searching the inner darkness for the story of those months he would become exhausted and have to surface for light and air. Somewhere buried inside him was a part of his life he could not reach, a critical part to which he was denied access, a reality that could not be born.

His eyes looked distantly and bleakly across the lagoon:

'Oed' und leer das Meer.'

He looked out across the flat water and, as his thoughts spread out over its surface, thinner and thinner, until they disappeared into silence, he heard Francesca's voice.

'I'll be on the Riva della Schiavoni, where the ferry comes in.'

'I'll see you there.'

' See you soon. Ciao.'

'Ciao.'

Her voice was perfectly clear in his memory, like cool water running through his brain. He felt a smile begin to form deep in his stomach. It rose steadily through him, seeping out through his chest and into his arms; it rose through his neck and into his head; it spread out to fill his head and finally to register its presence on his face. He became aware that his lips were fixed in a broad smile. He was beginning again, sailing back; this time with a clear purpose in mind.

This time, as they pulled away from the green of Napoleon's gardens and the framework of metal by the gallery of contemporary art, he felt uncontrollable elation. Not the tension of anticipation and fear that he had experienced four days ago but pure, unmixed, elation. Water lapped around the green bronze-finned monster that lay by the wall. An ordinary piece of sculpture perhaps, but in its position in the water, covered and uncovered by the wash of the tide, it became extraordinary. David felt the water lapping around himself too; around him and through him, unblocking the hard clay in his veins, allowing the reawakening of the flowing, responsive, spontaneous life within. No doubt this was only a first layer, a clearing away of the most obvious and superficial blockages but it was a significant step forward and enough to convince him incontrovertibly that he was doing the right thing.

The ferry made a gentle arc before turning in towards the Molo and the Riva degli Schiavoni. The assortment of tourists who rushed to photograph their first glimpse of St Mark's seemed to be separated from him by an even greater gulf than before. This time his attention was all on Venice and Francesca; the ferry, the first sighting, the kaleidoscopic reappearance of images from the past were all things of a different cycle, another phase.

Four days ago, he had seen nothing but the Campanile, the columns on the Piazzetta and the Doges' palace as the ferry approached the quay. Now he strained to see amongst the crowds around the entrances to the piers. It could not go wrong this time. She had to be there. The momentum had built up and could not be thwarted now.

From the crowds by the piers he let his eyes spread their search along the covered tables where people sat drinking coffee or beer and then back along past the stalls of gondolier hats and coconut slices. Finally, they reached the steps of the Chiesa di Vivaldi, Santa Maria della Pietà. By the heavy black, studded doors, closed now against the sun and tourists, stood Francesca.

He fought against the hesitancy, the fear brought on by the knowledge that she was no longer only an image in his mind, an idea to be weighed against others, but a being made unpredictable by her own life. Within the image that he wrapped around her was another person. This time he would not let his cowardice hold him back, this time he would let the flow of life and energy that had returned to his veins, carry him forward on its tide.

The other passengers surged towards the steps down to the lower deck. They seemed unremarkable and undifferentiated compared with those of the first day. Then, he had noticed the girl with snake earrings, affluent Germans, quarrelling English and, of course, the Renaissance girl and her companions. This time they seemed no more individual than the crush on the London Underground in the mornings.

As he moved with them, he tried to glimpse the steps of the church, but they were obscured by the ugly metal and glass shelter that controlled and separated the passengers leaving the boat from those arriving. He felt a tautness and excitement, a confident anticipation that joined him unexpectedly to a sense of his own physical presence at sixteen. He felt the sixteen year old leaving the ferry and walking down the slope to the edge of Venice, felt the dark brown and blue patterned shirt he had worn then, felt his body young and, most of all, his spirit and imagination held poised on the jet of a fountain of energy. The air and the sun were suddenly clearer, he felt conscious of himself and the colours and sounds around him with a long-forgotten clarity and force.

He broke away from the crush by the souvenir stand. The gondolier hats, shining slivers of coconut and T-shirts printed with gondolas and views of St Mark's, shared in the immediacy of his state of consciousness and, as he turned to where he had seen Francesca from a distance, he felt himself lifted on a wave of adolescent energy. He felt it filling his muscles and releasing the knotted tension in them; he felt it as an invisible sea of light flooding him with its strength as he breathed it in.

Francesca still stood at the top of the steps. As he walked towards her, she waved but did not move. She was wearing a simple, terracotta, fitted dress and her gold necklace caught the sun as she waved. He felt that he had walked through into another world, a new life, a return of his early life, an alternative that he only had to choose.

As he reached Santa Maria della Pietà she descended the steps. She smiled and he struggled to emerge from the world inside himself and meet her as another person rather than a symbol in his personal mythology. She took off her sunglasses as she drew level with him, and their eyes met warmly and openly without barriers or confusion. He touched her arm lightly and kissed her on the cheek. Her skin was soft against his and he felt her respond, though her lips touched only the air. He had gone forward; he had not held back and everything was all right. He wanted to hold her in his arms, to hold her and to kiss her, but this, he knew, was not the moment so he tried to put as much as he could into his voice.

'It's good to see you again.'

'And you.' She looked briefly past him and then said, 'Let's find somewhere we can talk.'

Her fingers touched the bare skin of his arm in a movement that told him they were going to walk back towards St Mark's and then gave a momentary squeeze to his forearm. He took it to be a reassurance, a gesture of sympathy with what she guessed he had felt yesterday, a recognition of what had happened until they could talk.

There was a completeness about walking back over the bridges with Francesca. When he was sixteen, he had walked there with his mother and they had talked excitedly about the history and, most of all, about the paintings of Venice. He had walked there on his own at sixteen when he had been allowed to come and explore without his parents. Jane had not been with him, even though his first visit seemed so closely linked to their relationship. He had imagined her there, created her image beside him, but she had not been there. Francesca was there and within her was a deep knowledge and understanding of Venice. She would lead him further into Venice, both the outer Venice and the maze of images, shadows and reflections that made up the inner Venice - an inner Venice that she too must surely share within her own mythology.

The painting on her wall came into his mind: those sinister and insect-like gondolas were beings from her inner Venice; and he looked at her as she walked beside him wondering how much their mythology had in common and to what extent the gods and demons that inhabited it were different.

As he tried to see beyond her dark hair and into the world of her imagination, she felt his look and from behind her sunglasses he was sure her eyes met his. How could they penetrate this veil of darkness that separated one person from another? With speech? By intuition, whatever that meant? He wanted their inner worlds to meet and to flow into each other, forming one inner Venice as they walked through one outer Venice and shared it with their senses.

They had reached the bridge that looked towards the Bridge of Sighs and turned together to lean on the balustrade. They looked down between the palace and the prison and at the bridge between. The petalled eyes of the bridge stared back, petals over dark water. Francesca spoke first.

'When I was a little girl, I thought that dying was like crossing the Ponte dei Sospiri. A wonderful palace full of beautiful things gathered together over many years, then a narrow bridge with a last broken look at the world and then into a dark lonely prison with no windows and nothing beautiful.'

She paused and then turned to look at David, a smile lifting the darkness created by the image.

'I was supposed to believe it was the other way round of course: unless I didn't go to Mass.'

David smiled but the mixture of emotions churning inside him prevented him from speaking at first. She was too beautiful, sharing these things with her was too good, even the sadness of an image of death. He saw another image in the Bridge of Sighs; he saw this sharing of Venice and sharing of minds as the palace and the way back to his old life as the bridge into the dark, walled cells. It was too soon, he felt, to share this with her, but he wanted to, desperately.

'I feel I've been living in the prison and now I'm here to escape.'

As soon as he had said this David thought it was the wrong thing, too gloomy, too negative, not the image he wanted to project at all, but to his surprise Francesca gave a broad and slightly mocking smile.

'Then you must be like Casanova and take risks, live dangerously. It is too safe in prison.'

David felt both excited and alarmed by the perceptiveness of this response. How could she know this already? What had she read into the conversations they had on Monday and the next day on the beach? And when she said he should be like Casanova did she only mean he should be more adventurous in his life? Despite his new found energy and confidence he could not stop something in him from drawing back and he despised himself for it.

He managed to return her smile with one of self-mockery.

'You're right! Do you know Byron's Prisoner of Chillon?

He made friends with the mice and got so used to prison that he sighed when he left. Perhaps that's me, friends with the mice.'

To his surprise she seemed to take the remark seriously and looked distantly along the canal before saying,

'Yes, I know Byron.' She turned to look straight at him. 'Everyone makes a prison for themselves: not many people dare to escape.' Her eyes clouded and she looked away and then down at her hands. 'You're not the only one who finds it difficult. I didn't want to lie to you yesterday.'

Their arms touched as they leant on the bridge. As their skin touched, David felt his stomach contract and relax. If he had felt sixteen when he arrived today, he felt it even more so now. David slid his hand over hers and squeezed it. She tightened her hand too and then stood up and let go.

'Come on, let's go somewhere quieter to talk.'

'Yes, I don't know how many tourist photographs we've been in standing here.'

She grimaced, 'Hundreds I expect.'

They emerged into the Piazzetta by the handcarts selling corn. A small child of four or five suddenly ran into the mass of feeding pigeons stamped behind them and chased them round in circles. The birds all took off simultaneously and swooped low over David and Francesca, veering sharply over their heads with a beating and whirring of wings. Francesca ducked involuntarily and caught David's arm. She exclaimed something in Italian that he could not make out. She held his arm tightly while she said,

'I'll never get used to that; I think they are trying to attack me.'

The Valley of Humiliation came back to David, and the winged demons of his breakdown and he shivered.

'You did not like them either?' she asked.

'I've never minded pigeons but I'm off winged things coming at me at the moment.'

'I have never liked them. Keep walking. They are like the tourists; they stay in the Piazza and make a mess.'

The band had started playing outside Florian's and he suddenly thought it would be good to sit there with Francesca, the band would keep them from thinking too much about prisons and other depressing subjects.

'Would you like to be a tourist for a little while and have coffee here?'

To his surprise she almost shouted back at him.

'You must be mad, I would not pay those prices for coffee, especially when the band is playing.'

'It would be my treat.' She looked puzzled at this, so he re-phrased it. 'I would pay.'

'Don't waste your money, that is just for tourists and it is too crowded. We are going to talk, remember?'

He was puzzled as to why she was quite so aggressively against the idea, but he was not certainly not going to risk things breaking down at this stage. As they walked past, he said,

'Isn't it something you would ever do?' and then the tense look that re-appeared in her face and the sharp way she said, 'No.' made him regret he had said even that. He was sure there was more to it than just an aversion to tourists and spending money, but he determined to say no more on the subject, however innocent it seemed.

There was something in Francesca's silence that kept him silent too, that and the fear of saying something that would precipitate another cold or hostile response. They walked on and David, held within a tense shell of his own, could feel one around her too. As they neared the end of the Piazza, Francesca turned and brought him to a halt.

'If it is still O.K., I have changed my mind. It is not just the tourists, there is something else. I should like to go there now.'

David felt bemused but also a sense of excitement that he had moved nearer the secret that would unlock the complex tapestry of emotions that drove Francesca in these irrational moods. He had little else to go on. He agreed, smiled and they turned back to Florian's.

Nearer to the secret he might be, but still he had only a disordered assortment of facts that dared him to link them. There were the menacing gondolas, something that happened at university, her father's death and the mysterious phone call mentioned in Carlo's trattoria after he had spoken of the possibility that George Wagner might be interested in her paintings. She had been relaxed and apparently happy on the beach and then had made up the story about working so that she could avoid seeing him. Now there was this change of mind over Florian's. Maybe there was a sort of pattern in these things but there was far too much missed out for him to create any kind of picture from them.

As they walked back, she said, 'You must think I am crazy, instabile;' and then quietly, 'Maybe you are right.'

David thought of his own predicament before he left for Venice; he was in no position to pass judgement. He gave a short laugh,

'Don't forget, when you met me, I was so unstable I had fallen over.'

She hesitated and then, to his relief, she laughed too.

'And you were frightened of the plague. Perhaps we are both crazy.'

The memory returned, the smell of bleach on the cloth and the resonance back to 'Death in Venice'. He had not realised that his fear had shown so obviously. There was always the possibility that in his case he really was mad, the borders between external reality and his inner world seemed so thin. As he faced the possibility again, he said with emphasis,

'You could be right.'

Francesca looked at him briefly but with a questioning look that made him realise that he had replied with rather too much conviction. If it were true, he would rather keep it to himself for as long as he could.

They arrived back at Florian's where the band was temporarily reduced to a trio, consisting of piano, bass and drums. They were working through a medley of show tunes. Francesca walked determinedly to a table on the edge, slightly hidden from the main array of tables by the bandstand. She sat down and stared tensely at her hands on the table. David sat too, aware that a struggle, in which he was not involved, was going on within her. Finally, she looked up and faced him with what seemed a slightly forced smile.

'There, I have done it and it is all right. Now, we will have some coffee please.'

David had noticed before that her usually excellent English became strained when she was worried or tense. Whatever she had just overcome had clearly taken a considerable effort of will. He ordered the coffee and they sat and listened while the trio played through the selection of arrangements from musicals. They finished with 'Lullaby of Broadway' and then they too left the bandstand. The sounds of voices and pigeons returned, strangely enhanced by the space that was neither outside nor inside.

Francesca sipped at the coffee and then said,

'I'm sorry about yesterday. I wanted some time on my

own, that was all. I thought it would be easier if I just said I was working. '

'That's all right, it was just a shock the way I found out.'

'Why did you come?'

'I felt I had to.' He hesitated, wondering how far to go, 'I wanted to see you and I thought you'd have finished work by then.'

She took another sip of coffee and then turned to look at him. She paused, watching him for a few seconds before saying,

'I'm glad you phoned back. I feel I can talk to you. You were not part of it and that makes it easier.'

There was a warmth in her voice that reassured him, but he felt worried that if they entered too much into the world that troubled her, she would be overcome by emotion again as she had been in the trattoria.

'You don't have to tell me anything. We can just walk and see Venice, have something to eat; just enjoy it, like the beach.'

Her voice took on a harder edge. 'Is that what you want?'

What he wanted was a closeness, a sharing, an intimacy that set his stifled emotions free again; he wanted to enter into her world where his dried and encrusted soul could be dissolved in new life. As he tried to reach out and through the barrier between them, he felt a growing concern, an ever-strengthening desire to free Francesca from whatever it was that tormented her.

'I should like to share it with you properly. If whatever it is gets in the way, then I should like you to tell me.' He hesitated, 'And if you'd like to, if it would help.'

A look of decision and determination came over her face.

'We should stop talking round in circles. The reason I

didn't want to come to Florian's was that I came here last with my boyfriend from University.' Despite her obvious intention of saying it all in one go, she paused and looked down again. 'It was the last time we were in Venice. He was killed in a car accident. I have not been able to come here since, even in winter when it is quiet.'

David felt awkward and inadequate. Their relationship was not established enough for him to know how to react. He saw her hand resting on the table and remembered looking at the Bridge of Sighs. She had accepted the gesture there. He moved his hand and laid it over hers.

'I'm sorry. We could have gone somewhere else.'

'No, I wanted to come. It was time and I felt you would understand. I think you have felt sorrow yourself.'

Again, David was struck by how much she seemed to know about him; how much he had revealed about himself to her without saying anything. He recalled their conversation on the beach.

'Was that at the same time as your father?'

'No. A few months later. My father died suddenly from a heart attack. We were skiing, he felt ill, and then, that was all.'

She waved her hand in what seemed to David a helpless gesture that said she could not describe what followed. He felt the waves of sorrow rise in her and resonate through him. He put out his arm and she moved towards him. He held her and felt her head rest briefly on his shoulder and her breath against his neck. Then she rested her hand lightly on his chest to get her balance and sat up. A conciliatory smile passed fleetingly over her face. She finished her coffee and then said,

'Come on, let's walk. There is more but we will walk first.'

As they stood David put out his hand to her and as they moved, she did not let go.

They had been partly shaded where they were sitting. As they walked out into the clarity of the Piazza the brilliance of the sun and the blast of heat had a disorientating effect on David. The direct rays of the sun combined with the reflected light and radiated heat shimmering over the stone flags to blur his senses like an over-exposed film. Francesca led them directly across the middle of the square and he felt that they were floating over the stones in the middle of a sea of voices. The one clear sensation was that of Francesca's hand on his.

The Byzantine, gold encrusted arcades and lead topped domes of San Marco moved through his heat misted sight like the images of Xanadu floating midway on the waves. Again, the doubts flowed in. Was he building just a pleasure dome; a garden walled with towers that breathed with the fumes of incense and illusion? Or was he set to rise on the mighty fountain of the sacred river that cast the stones and rocks away before its regenerating force? At this moment he did not care, he would build a dome in air, a dome of sun, with glittering caves and driven wild by honey-dew would drink the milk of Paradise. Intoxication with Coleridge's vision ran through him. Music sounded behind the images. What he heard was not a girl playing a dulcimer but an orchestra, a rising tide of music surging and swelling until it burst through and filled his mind. He felt himself possessed by the uninhibited, whirling, ecstatic dance from Beethoven's Seventh: the apotheosis of the dance. Around him span a wheel tongued with fire. His mind shook with light and heat, there was nothing he could not or would not do to live this vision. This he felt was the true breaking of the dry wall.

Onto his vision fell a shadow. His skin cooled, his eyes darkened, the air in his nostrils lost its heat. They had walked into the shade of the clock tower. He turned his head to Francesca who was unaware of the cascade of sound and images showering through his mind. She too was held in thought but as they entered the Mercerie Dell'Orologia her hand loosened on his and she lifted it to remove her sun-glasses. Her eyes glanced sideways at the window of a shop selling beautifully crafted and expensive leather. As she put her sun-glasses into her own bag he noticed that it was of a similar quality, far above the normal purchasing power of an art student. He told himself that it must be a present from a relative; he knew nothing after all of her family except that her uncle ran a busy trattoria.

She seemed to notice him looking at the bag but was still preoccupied as they turned and walked past the mixture of boutiques, fashion houses and more shops selling hand-made shoes, handbags and other accessories. Francesca had taken control of their direction and, partly to break the silence between them, and partly to gain access to the thoughts that held her, he asked where they were going. She replied almost absent-mindedly, in a way which seemed to suggest that he would have to fit in with her arrangements,

'A friend of mine has an exhibition. I said I would drop in. I think it will interest you as well.'

She had pulled back from the intimacy of the shared moment at Florian's when she had revealed a part of her fear and had put her head on his shoulder. He felt that she was repossessing herself, taking back any dependence on him that the sharing of her pain might have created. He wanted to reassure her, to tell her that she could rely on him, to let her know that his vision of the future could help both of them to heal their wounds. He also knew that he could not. Fear that such a direct approach would tear apart the fragile threads that had begun to join them held him back. He felt he must wait for the moments when they could both spin further strands into the web, when they could share and grow closer by mutual assent as fate allowed.

14

THE FOURTH DAY - PART THREE

The gallery was in the corner of a small square. At first, he took it to be a small chapel but as they approached it, he saw that a board outside was advertising the exhibition. They had spoken little as they walked but David felt that Francesca had become more relaxed and that the emotional turmoil of Florian's and the tension immediately after had slipped away. It was evident, as he grew close to the gallery that it was indeed a converted chapel. As the white of its walls, made brilliant by the sun, gave way to darkness as they entered, David was temporarily blinded.

He waited near the entrance whilst Francesca went straight to the desk where a woman sat reading a magazine. So far as David could tell in the semi-darkness, she could be in her late thirties though she might have been much older. Her hair was almost black, and she had strongly moulded features emphasised by heavy make-up. When she saw Francesca, she stood up and they embraced and kissed each other in what David could only think of as an excessively theatrical manner. Despite the apparently artificial effusiveness of the greeting, when they spoke it struck him as being with a genuine warmth, though he could not understand enough to tell what they were saying.

David began to feel rather awkward and solitary. The sudden energy and enthusiasm that had filled Francesca made him feel correspondingly dejected. During the walk she had been gradually returning to normal, but he felt that in his company she had been upset and tense, whilst here she was suddenly transformed, and he wished he could have had this enlivening effect on her.

He had begun to think about looking at some of the pictures when Francesca turned and waved to him to join them.

'David, this is Cristina Matozza; it is her exhibition. We are old friends.'

He held out his hand feeling unwanted reserve in doing so.

'Ciao, Cristina.'

He did not want to reduce the warmth and spontaneity of the feelings that were flowing but did not know how else to react. He need not have worried. Their hands barely touched before Cristina reached under the counter and brought out a dog-eared and well used catalogue. She handed it to David and then waved towards the exhibition and said,

'Molto piacere. I hope you enjoy l'esposizione. Francesca, she is a good guide.'

She then turned to Francesca again and began saying something at great speed. Her voice was husky as if she were a heavy smoker and to David the words were barely distinguishable from each other. Close to, he could see that she was older than he had first thought but it was difficult to say how old. Francesca appeared at first to be resisting whatever it was that Cristina was suggesting but finally she seemed to agree and even became enthusiastic.

When Francesca turned away and back to David, she retained the energy of the conversation and put her arm through his as she walked towards the first picture. He was aware that she was taking control of the day but in Venice where she was at home and with people that she knew, he told himself it was only natural. All the same David was concerned that she should not see him just as someone to be led around but without breaking the natural flow and rhythm of events he could not see what he could do about it.

The pictures were large, many of them over six feet high, and a combination of painting and sculpture. They consisted of exquisitely painted pictures of a romantic idealised Venice surrounded and overlaid by plaster and stone crumbling around them. The decaying masonry formed spaces of varying shapes in which the pictures lived. Even the plaster was enhanced with colour, maroons, blues and gold, but beneath the colour it gave the impression that it was crumbling. The concept might have seemed pedantically obvious had it not been for the quality and ingenuity of its execution.

David paused in front of a picture whose heavy use of perspective behind the raised plaster drew him into its world in a particularly powerful way. He was aware of Francesca pausing too. The openings in the layers of plaster, and what appeared to be cut away tiles and brick, curved and revealed two lovers in a palace whose walls were painted in the styles of Titian and Tintoretto. They were embracing on a throne at the end of the room made distant by perspective. He wanted to say something to Francesca about it but everything he could think of seemed trite and trivial compared with what he was feeling. It was Francesca who broke the silence.

'I thought you would like them. This was a new idea for Cristina, her last exhibition was all sculpture.'

He felt he had to say something about the picture,

'They really distil the contrast between the romantic decay and the richness of the past, when it was a glorious imperial power.'

It was an obvious comment and Francesca did not react immediately. When she did, she spoke tentatively,

'They are more than that. I find it hard to say but they try to capture the metaphor that Venice provides for life. You must see into them. They are not about Venice, but they try to capture the meaning that Venice has had for so many people.'

He felt at that point an almost over-powering desire to say ' I love you.': to use it as a key to break through the division between them that forced them to utter struggling phrases to join their experience; to speak when there were no words that could adequately convey even the experience of looking at a picture together. Instead, he slid his arm around her waist and as he did so he felt her lean slightly towards him. He felt the warmth from her body through his shirt; he breathed the faint perfume of her hair and it permeated through him opening his veins and making his head swim. He rested his eyes on the lovers on the distant throne beyond decay and the crusting of experience. As he did so her head rested against his shoulder and she said quietly,

'It will never change for them; they will be happy always.'

He held her tighter and whispered,

'But they need us, or their happiness is wasted.'

She turned her face to him, the softness of her eyes in the shadow of the room met his and for a moment he was filled with sadness and joy, longing and contentment.

As the moment fulfilled its natural cadence, she shifted her weight and gently loosened his arm at her waist. She called to Cristina who had left the desk and was rearranging some heavy drapes around two dark carved wooden chairs that formed part of the display. Cristina called back, gesturing with her hand but without turning around. Francesca turned to David and explained,

'I said we would look after the desk for her while she has a cigarette.'

Cristina was already climbing the wooden stairs at the back of the gallery.

'If there is no-one here, she sometimes leaves it unattended; these pictures are very valuable, and anything could happen.'

Francesca sat on Cristina's chair and David sat on the desk. Again, there had been the pattern of growing close and then the break away, but this time far more gently and she had not cut herself off as she had before. In fact, she seemed very happy and relaxed. David watched her squaring up the catalogues and realised that small exhibitions like this were a normal part of her life in Venice.

'Have you ever held an exhibition here?'

She did not look up as she replied,

'Yes, I shared one with Cristina in the year before I went to University and again the following summer.'

'Nothing since then?'

'Not here. Earlier this year in Milano a friend organised a small one for me but not here.'

David thought he detected a note of tension returning to her voice.

'Were they a success?'

'Do you mean did I sell many pictures?'

'Partly, and what people said about them.'

She picked up a pile of catalogues that she had already tidied and tapped their edges on the desk to square them again. There was a pause while she held them upright on the desk and looked intently at them. Finally, she broke her stare and turned to David.

'I have told you a lot about me. You must talk about yourself more....., but I will tell you. My friend in Milano, Renato, he is about your age, perhaps a little older. He came to my first exhibition and bought three paintings. He has helped me ever since; he has introduced me to friends who have also bought paintings and some drawings, and he arranged an exhibition this year. He is a banker not an artist and has many rich friends who like to buy work of new artists.' She paused and then said, 'He has been a good friend too.'

She put down the catalogues that she had been holding throughout this speech. 'There, you will have to tell me more about yourself before I say any more.' She thought for a moment and then went on as if she had made a decision. 'When we arrived, Cristina was telling me that some of our friends, mainly artists, are getting together tonight for a party. She thinks it would be good for me to mix more. We could go if you would like to. I think it will be fun and there will be people of all ages.'

It seemed to David a skilful change of subject but one that he was happy to go along with.

'You mean old fogeys like me won't be out of place?'

'Fogeys? You will be with me, so you won't be out of place anyway. I just meant that it will be a good party and you'll enjoy it.'

The tension had suddenly disappeared again, and she was more relaxed than she had been since Tuesday on the beach. Whatever this party would be like, he would be with Francesca and that was what mattered now.

'I should love to come and I'm sure I shall enjoy it. I was just a bit worried I wouldn't fit in.'

'You mustn't worry. Enzo, he's a sculptor, he will be there, and he is more than sixty; he is still dancing when most of us are trying to sleep. Maybe it will be good for you as well - good for both of us.'

To David this picture of Enzo was not entirely reassuring but there was no doubt that if he was seeking spontaneity and the natural inspiration of youth, if he was serious in this quest to break through the accretions of dead matter that had collected around his soul, then a party could indeed be good for him. It could be particularly good in the company of Francesca and, to a lesser extent, the others who sounded as if they had found ways of escaping the malign influence of time and retained their youthful enthusiasm and creativity.

Footsteps on the stairs announced the return of Cristina. She called to Francesca, and David caught enough of what she said to work out that she was thanking her and asking about the party. Francesca's reply brought about a sudden switch, by Cristina, to English.

'So, I will see you at the party. Francesca says you are a writer, that is not so easy. If you are an artist or a musician the language makes no difference but,' and here she paused, ' my English is not so good. You have enjoyed the pictures, I think?'

'Very much, particularly this one.' He pointed out the work with the enthroned lovers.

'Ah yes, that is one I like too. If you like it, then I can arrange the transport to England.'

David was a little taken aback by this, though on reflection he realised he should not have been as that was how she made a living.

'I'll come and see it again. I'll think about it.'

'Do not think too long. Carpe diem David. When you like, you must take. You miss life if you think too long. I see you tonight and you can tell me.'

There was no doubt that this advice was relevant to his position with Francesca and to his problem with life in general, but it was not necessarily transferable to the purchase of the painting. Francesca had already hinted that the paintings were expensive, though he would not make a decision on whether to purchase this work of art that had unquestionable significance for him solely on the basis of cost. He had to consider where it would go if it were sent to England, whether by then he would have a home to go to, let alone one large enough to be host to a painting such as this. If he went to the party tonight with Francesca, and he had no intention of refusing, what implications would this have when Thelma arrived? He was more than half way through his week and possibilities were beginning to close in.

He felt Francesca pat him on the arm as she spoke.

'Come on, let's look round again. Don't mind Cristina, she has a warm heart, but she never misses an opportunity to sell.' As she moved David back towards the pictures, she called out to Cristina who laughed and went back to her place at the desk and the magazine.

They walked past the pictures and Francesca talked quietly about them, picking out some of the scenes Cristina had used and giving David the background to the originals.

As she talked, she gradually seemed to become preoccupied. Finally, they paused in front of a picture at the far end and she said very quietly:

'Perhaps you had better wait until you speak to your wife before you buy it.'

It was the first time there had been any mention or even hint of Thelma, or even of his having another life elsewhere, since he had admitted her existence after they put up the umbrella on the beach. His stomach felt as if it were descending rapidly after being punched; there was no question of his being able to answer straight away. His heart appeared to beat only once every five minutes, his breathing had all but stopped. He had been standing in silence for a time that he was sure should be measured in hours. It was like the time he span and crashed the car; he was in a different time world and did not know how to get back.

He had placed Thelma and Francesca in two separate parallel worlds; alternatives that could never meet; different ways in his life that could never be joined. Now he was faced with a direct challenge to talk about Thelma to Francesca, perhaps that had been what she was hinting at when she said he must tell her more about himself. He had been ready to discuss his situation, his wanderings in a sterile waste land or even his breakdown but had not prepared himself in any way for this.

'I don't really know what to say to that.'

'You have not said why she is not on holiday with you. Do you always go on holiday alone?'

There was no aggression or malice in her voice but why, he thought, had she decided to ask these things just as they seemed to be getting so much closer and they had an evening to look forward to? What answer did she want? Did she want to hear that he and Thelma had nothing in common anymore and were on the verge of splitting up: which would be an exaggeration. Or did she want to hear that he had just one week and at the end he would go back to his wife and she could go back to her life leaving just a few days-worth of memories: the classic holiday romance. On reflection the second seemed rather more likely.

He decided to stay as close to the truth as possible, the truth that was as far as he knew it but without adding any unnecessary detail.

'No, not usually, but this one was unplanned, and she had to work. She said she might come out later if she could.'

Francesca had been staring ahead at the painting and at this, to his surprise and immense relief, she turned and, giving a quick smile, said in a conspiratorial whisper,

'Not unannounced I hope.' She looked back at the picture. 'You look very nervous.'

'I never know quite what you're going to throw at me next.'

'Neither do I.'

How would she react, thought David, if he told her what had precipitated his holiday? It was true that she had revealed more to him than he had to her, but it would be a gamble. To reveal what could be interpreted as weakness could destroy such interest as she had in him but to move further into their intimate secrets could equally bring them closer.

In the centre of the small room there were bench seats and he moved towards one of them, indicating to Francesca that she should follow. It was opposite the painting of the lovers. He had to tell her. He watched as she sat down, her thin dress against the old brown leather of the seats, her smooth skin against its cracked and flaking surface.

'This wasn't exactly a planned holiday. Work and everything were getting me down; it's been building up for years. I was told to take a break. I felt that because Venice reached back into part of me that existed before things went wrong it would help, be a good place to reflect and sort myself out.'

He paused. Francesca had turned her eyes away and was looking at her hands. Her attention directed his own gaze onto them as well. He had noticed her hands when she first sat opposite him in the café; the delicate fingers with long nails as she took the coffee cup. It was her hands that caused his first image of her as a natural and earthy ice-cream girl, to dissolve. Her hands moved and parted; her eyes returned to his and smiled softly as she spoke,

'It's hard to live your own life, from the inside, and still be part of life outside. I had to leave university for a term because everything else was too difficult.'

Again, their experience joined them. He need not have been concerned; he should trust her more, live from the inside. That was exactly what he had done in the past and it was what had gradually slipped away. When there were moments of quiet, when he could return to himself, he found such a disjointed and fragmented story, broken by the long periods of neglect, that he could do no more than patch over a little of the damage. It would take a long time to do more than that; all he could hope for from a holiday would be a turning in the right direction.

He put his arm out and drew her to him. He turned to speak, and her eyes looked into his. He felt her breath against his face; he moved closer and allowed his lips to touch the soft warmth of hers. They moved under his and he felt her hand touch his waist. Knotted clumps of energy, broken and distorted, imprisoned around his body, came to life, flowing into the centre like water released by breaking dams. He shivered as it washed through him. Francesca moved and her forehead rested on his so that their lips parted. He breathed in the smell of her skin and felt it running and dispersing through him. He kissed her forehead. Her hand moved on his waist and she sat up. There was a softness in her smile and the dark centres of her eyes that made him want to blurt out an adolescent stream of pledges of undying love. Instead he ran his fingers through her hair and past her ear and said,

'I can't get used to how much you understand, how close we seem after so little time.'

She put a finger to his lips and whispered, 'Don't say too much.' and then, drawing away, let her fingers run along his arms until their hands met and said, 'I think we should go now.'

David stood, not letting go of her hand. The colours of the painting, the purple, maroon and gold, mirrored the sensual intensity of his feelings, a warm and decadent richness. As she got up, Francesca looked again at the painting and then gave him a push, 'Come on or Cristina will be sending it to England.'

Cristina was engrossed in a book when they reached the desk but after she and Francesca had spoken, she turned to David and said, 'I will see you this evening. It will be a good party; they are good people; you will have fun I think.'

'I think I shall. Ciao.'

As they left the cool darkness of the gallery, the warming brightness of the afternoon light and the still hot air washed over them like a bath of bright water. The shadows in the campo had moved and rose deeper into the far wall. An expectant calm hung in the waiting pool of air over the flagstones. They walked, not speaking until they had left the square and moved into the shadow of the callé that ran from the opposite side. It was narrow and moved them closer together. He glanced at her profile, quickly so as not to attract her attention. They had certainly found much in common: but the party, would it just serve to emphasise the difference in their ages and backgrounds or would it be an occasion for loss of emotional inhibition, for action without reservation, an opportunity to escape from the paralysing encrustation around his soul?

'Is the party because of anything special? Somebody's birthday perhaps?'

'Most of us make money during the summer but the others, they don't sell ice creams, they draw tourist portraits and the Doges' palace and gondolas in canals; they draw and paint them over and over again and eventually they need a party. That is all.'

He could understand that. The image of the sixty-year-old sculptor, mentioned earlier by Francesca, came into his mind.

'What about Enzo, does he make sculptures for tourists?'

Francesca turned, a smile breaking across her face until it turned into a laugh.

'I forgot I'd told you about Enzo. No, he doesn't do sculptures for tourists, at least not unless he wants to. He does what he likes but he always needs a party. You will like him; I will introduce you.

Originally mentioned by Francesca as a way of reassuring him that he was not too old for the party, Enzo was beginning to take on a life of mythical proportions in David's mind: an amalgam of Zorba the Greek and Picasso with maybe a hint of Hemingway; a big man who danced and drank and created his own world from the images inside him; a man who didn't need to compromise. He, David, had compromised, his father had compromised; both to survive so they thought, for material security, but they had lost themselves as a result. His father had become defeated and bitter whilst he had driven himself to a break-down with perhaps the defeatism and bitterness to come. What sort of security was that, what sort of survival? For what is a man profited, if he shall gain the whole world, and lose his own soul? And he had only gained a tiny corner of the world, he had not even sold his soul on a grand Faustian scale but merely won a small patch of Wimbledon.

The warmer light of the late afternoon fell on alternate walls of the narrow calle as they walked. Its soft comforting glow tempered the harsh anxiety engendered by this contemplation of his own destruction in both time and eter-nity. In darkness such a thought would lead to the sort of uncontrolled panic that he had experienced the night before: at mid-day the harshness of the light and heat would not let him hide. But now, by Francesca's side, in the light turning gold with evening, the fear melted away.

The tourists too had deserted the alleyways and squares leaving each well-head solitary at the centre. In channels of deep shade, under green awnings, tables with clean linen stood empty outside the trattoria and restaurants. Waiters stood leaning in doorways or making the last adjustments to the tables ready for the evening.

The fiery, frenetic energy of the day had passed leaving a vibrant calm: a sense of being supported by still warm light; a peace that soaked through David and eased away the tension and the fear, the panic and the insistent sense that he must act to save himself before it was too late. The images that had swirled dizzily through his mind and taken over his body since arriving in Venice slowed and dissolved leaving all around him etched out with an unfamiliar clarity. A veil seemed to have disappeared from between him and the buildings which now appeared as strangely bright as old oil paintings, newly cleaned.

He had time, all the time, to turn his eyes and allow them to rest on Francesca. She moved before his eyes, but he remained still. The walls, the paving stones moved past him and he was at the centre.

'We'll go back to the trattoria. I must shower and change.'

Francesca's voice moved across the clarity before him. It disturbed the stillness like a light breeze through leaves; like the breeze in the aspen trees at Punta Sabbioni. He did not want to break in on the calm, the stillness by talking; he did not want to leave this state that had visited itself upon him with no further cause apparent than the still light of the evening. He must have paused too long because she turned and said,

'Are you O.K.?'

Instead of answering he put his arm around her shoulders. A ripple blurred the reflection on his consciousness. It could only be a momentary state; action ruffled the surface like a wind on a still pool. He knew there were those who, through long years of study and practice, managed to move with a still consciousness but even they could only do so by absenting themselves from anything that could be called normal life.

They moved out onto a small bridge.

'I was just thinking what a mess I'd made of things when Venice and the evening took over. It's very peaceful now. A stillness when everything falls away and you can see again like a child.'

'Yes, I often come out at this time and find a quiet pool at the corner of a canal. Sometimes it will be so still that everything is reflected in it and I feel like God watching the world. Then eventually a boat comes and breaks the reflection. I have tried to paint the moment when it breaks but I have never managed to paint the breaking. It is always too soon or too late.

His arm slid to her waist and he drew her to him until it was difficult to walk. He stopped and she folded in towards him; her lips slightly parted at the centre, rose towards his. His head tilted and their lips met; her arms tightened around his waist and, for the first time, passion and desire, moved in their kiss. In the gallery the kiss had been one of warmth, understanding and affection, those things missing from his life for so long. But now she let her body relax in towards him in a way that was new.

What had brought about this change he could not say. In the short time since leaving the gallery he had been brought again to despair at the futility of his life and its lack of essential energy when compared to the image of Enzo; he had felt a beatific peace and oneness, a clearing away of the clouds that darken consciousness and now Francesca seemed to have made some sort of commitment to him, at least for the moment.

Francesca shifted her back against the parapet of the bridge and their lips parted. Her breath and the faint sweetness of her skin ran like a drug through his head. Their eyes met and each searched beyond the darkness of the other's pupils. Any remaining barrier now was buried deeper than they had so far reached.

15

THE FOURTH DAY - PART FOUR

Back in the apartment above the trattoria, and seated in one of the dark red, heavy chairs, the cold sweat of apprehension that had accompanied his first visit to Francesca's sitting room seemed incomprehensible now. Francesca was still changing and getting ready and he was again alone in the room. This time he was filled with a warm excitement, an anticipation encouraged by laughter and by their closeness as they walked back. The shutters that had periodically barred the flow of energy from Francesca had gone and with them the crippling inhibitions that David had felt were destroying everything good. Her warmth had melted the crust of wax that held back the red flowing energy from within. Sometimes her laugh seemed a little too long and then he felt the tension of sexual excitement behind it. As the need to prove himself receded so he found a true source of energy rising through him.

When they had entered the room, they kissed and it seemed that they would make love there and then but as desire engulfed him, Francesca moved her lips away and said they should get ready. This time there was no closing off of the energy, more a sense of heightening it, not allowing it to earth too soon but building it to an ever-higher level. The force ran through him at a pitch that shocked and renewed his body and revisited emotions on him at an intensity he could only associate with adolescence. In Francesca he had found the bridge across the abyss, the link with the life of his past.

It was not that he had never had an affair. There had been several brief relationships including one with Caroline, Thelma's secretary, but he had always felt them to be nothing more than a momentary glow in the terminally fading embers. They had elicited a poem or two and made his blood run faster than its usual Lethe-like pace but that was all.

This was different. Now everything, all the forces of existence seemed poised and focused on the moment, and the moment was focused on the point at which he and Francesca touched, a vortex that drew into itself body, emotions, mind and soul. The intricate maze of myth and poetry, music and art, philosophy and experience created in him by his past, conducted through its golden mesh a force that met its opposite polarity in her: both channels of force finding their completion within the windings of the transforming labyrinth of Venice.

He had showered and changed back into his own clothes, declining this time the offer of a shirt. He wanted to keep about him as much of himself as possible, he did not want anything to allow the leaking away of his new found power. She had suggested he find some music amongst the collection stacked in the corner and partly hidden by a substantial sideboard.

He walked over to the shelves and to the piles stacked on the floor. They were a strange assortment showing a taste, or tastes, that ranged through every style and period. There appeared to be several distinct collections but when he thought of the differences in his and Thelma's tastes this was perhaps not surprising in any family. At one end was a collection that could only have been built up by a knowledgeable and sophisticated enthusiast for serious music, or perhaps a professional musician. It was a collection that had clearly been gathered over many years as there were vinyl records with old and yellowing sleeves as well as a row of compact disks. David studied them with interest and admiration.

They were not stacked in a way that made browsing easy and he realised he should turn his attention to choosing some appropriate music that would set the right mood on Francesca's return. In his teens, when Jane and he had held each other closely on the settee in the new and unexplored world of love and sex, finding each sensation and emotion for the first time, he most frequently played Chopin nocturnes or waltzes. Now he found himself seeking them out again. He had seen a selection of Chopin that included some Nocturnes but as he eased it from the pile, a recording of Liszt's Années Pelerinage in Italy came out above it. He looked through the titles, Sposalizio, Il Penseroso, the three Petrarchan Sonnets and, perhaps most persuasive of all, the Dante sonata; this was the music that reached into the world he and Francesca inhabited now. He took the record from the pile, put it onto the turntable and settled back into the large armchair.

The plaintive, hesitant melody of Sposalizio emerged, unsteadily until flowing arpeggios supported it and it rose to a climax. The melody appeared again, simple and trusting, rising by modest steps, notes dancing and turning like a flight of small birds, strength in the supporting chords, affirmative, then peace and the rippling of downward flowing notes like trickling falls of clear water.

Il Penseroso began, a dark meditation. Through the darkness, chords struck with the firmness of a tolling bell, a death march. Against this, and through the darkness, came a subterranean longing, a hope and a solitary light at midnight that struggled to lift the falling semitones, a dying fall against which the will of the thinker could only produce a momentary rise into discord: thought alone insufficient to find harmony. The square, tripping melody of the Canzonetta del Salvator Rosa danced against infinite darkness, simple, almost trite; a trivial human attempt at happiness. Dancing and laughter in the face death:

> 'Hence vain deluding joys,
> The brood of folly without father bred,'

But how else can man strike against the darkness and survive?'

Another change as the Petrarchan sonnets began. A rush of chromatic harmony and rippling arpeggios surged forward; the melody faltered and turned over its surface like perfumed smoke. The warm, longing caused an ache within him and he let the notes absorb and control his spirit and desire: beauty rising, lost and longed for. Cascades of notes fell through him and, in the sensual fragrance of the music, so roundly sensual it seemed to take on form, he became aware of another fragrance, a warmth in the air behind him and turned to see Francesca standing rapt, like him in the tangible world created by the sounds around them. As he turned, she put her hand on his shoulder telling him to keep still. He covered it with his.

As the last of the sonnets closed in notes that fluttered

like the wings of angels she moved to sit on the arm of the chair, her arm around his neck. He turned and kissed her cheek as the opening tritones of the Dante Sonata raised above them the Infernal gate. The howling of demons and the damned whirled downward through the circles of hell until arrested by chorale-like chords and celestial bells; thematic transformations in which the celestial is contained in the infernal and the infernal in the celestial. Both inter- twined in the fall of Francesca da Rimini and Paulo; love burning in its descent and burning to ascend whirled will- less in the maelstrom of lovers; both intertwined in the ascent, led by Beatrice, into Heaven. As the final chords rose around them David felt drained and invigorated by the trial and overcoming; detached and disorientated he found it impossible to speak; anything he could say would be trite and facile when compared to the experience that had joined them.

After a long pause, Francesca was the first to move. She walked quietly to the record player, lifted the record from the turntable and slipped it back into its sleeve. She was still not dressed and wore a long, silk, brightly patterned dressing gown. When she turned, he saw that her eyes and lashes were moist. David moved to get up from the chair, but she gestured to him to stay where he was, pausing before gaining enough control of her voice to speak.

'It's all right, I have not heard that for a long time. Those records at the end there, they are,' she hesitated and took a deep breath, 'were, my father's.'

'I'm sorry.' he muttered and then aware of the inade- quacy of this response said, 'It's a fine collection. He was obviously a knowledgeable musician.'

David felt her eyes searching him and then seeming

reassured she sat in the other chair, drawing her knees up and curling sideways so that she still faced him.

'Even when I was very young, I used to sing, and he played the piano. They were our best times together. He worked for the bank and came home late, so I didn't see him much except at weekends.' She spoke softly, the side of her face resting on the high chair back. 'Music and skiing were the things he loved.'

There was an intimacy and love in her voice that made David's throat close and his eyes grow wet in the corners.

'My father was a musician too. He was an organist and a school teacher.' and then aware that he was moving the conversation away from her, asked, 'Do you still sing?'

'No, not really; the painting took over from that. Sometimes, when I went home in vacations I sang again, and he played. When I was little, I imagined I was a great singer and we were on the stage together but later I knew I wasn't very good and that he would always work in a bank even though he was good.'

'It still brought you together though.'

'Oh yes, and he used to add to the piano part to cover up the places I found difficult.' She paused, her eyes inward as her lips smiled, 'Your father, he taught music? He didn't have to work in a bank.'

'He taught music but not just to pupils who wanted to learn. It was in a school and many of them were only there because they had to be. He used to get very cross and upset. The orchestra and choir were good though and he had the church choir and organ. He gave recitals too.'

She looked at him again in the same questioning way she had earlier and then said, 'We do have quite a lot in common, don't we.'

David smiled and said,' We do, don't we.' not sure quite

what it was that troubled her, and the meaning behind her look. Perhaps she still felt worried or guilty about the boyfriend who was killed in the car accident.

There was a silence whilst Francesca turned and sat up in the chair, her knees still drawn up and her arms around her legs.

'Look at me! I'm still not dressed, and we should go soon.' She wiped her eyes with her dressing gown sleeve and smiled. 'At least I had not done my make-up. I will be quick now.' She uncurled herself from the chair and went towards the door before saying, 'Help yourself to a drink if you want one.'

David went to the drinks cabinet, poured himself a whisky and then found there was no water. He did not feel like playing more music and wandered to the book case. There were many large format art books. He selected one on Titian and sat sipping the neat whisky and flipping over the large colour reproductions.

Francesca was not long this time and returned in a thin cotton shirt and frayed denim shorts. It was a contrast to the more sophisticated side he had seen to her and, at first, he wondered whether she had dressed in this way in deference to him. When he thought, however, that she looked more like an artist, he realised that it was just a matter of dressing to fit in with the people she would be meeting. She looked good in anything. He stood, closing the book,

'You look,' he hesitated.

'Yes?'

'Beautiful,' He moved over to her and putting his hands around her waist said quietly in her ear, 'and very sexy.'

She laughed and put her bare arms around his neck. She lifted her lips and as they pressed on his, they opened.

Their tongues touched lightly and slowly before her lips closed again and moved to his ear, whispering,

'Just look sexy?'

Their eyes looked deep into each other's pupils as he said,

'No definitely not.'

And they kissed again.

At last they separated for long enough for Francesca to say,' Come on, or we'll never get there'

David waited again whilst she re-touched her make-up and then they set off for the Dorsoduro.

They emerged from the high walls and narrow calli into the Campo Sant 'Angelo where, on the first day, David sat suffused in sunlight, the golden heat running as a drug through his veins. Where, in contrast, only yesterday he had seen the leaning spire of Santo Stefano transformed from mocking to sinister and threatening when he thought that Francesca had rejected him. Now the soft light of late afternoon had turned to the pale, reflected, wash of early evening. There was no direct sunlight now between the high walls, but the low reddening sun glinted in places through the gaps.

At the end of the Campo Frances Morosin were flower sellers with stalls and Africans who sold handbags arrayed temporarily on the stone flags. A profusion of trees and green bushes climbed behind the iron railings enclosing a private garden. The lush green was surprising after the stone and plastered walls.

The wooden structure of the Accademia bridge looked oddly temporary and out of place. A utilitarian crossing, thrown hastily across the Grand Canal in contrast to the permanence and extravagance of the Rialto bridge whose basic function seemed almost incidental. It was odd that one of the most typical views of Venice, along the Grand Canal to the lagoon, past Santa Maria della Salute, should be from this incongruous vantage point.

Across the bridge, they turned in front of the Accademia. It was quiet with only the occasional bar and shop. They turned again and in a small square was a gallery and shop that seemed unlikely, through its position, to attract much trade. The beat of music from between the slats of shutters above the gallery announced that this was where the party was being held. David felt nervous, he enjoyed parties where he knew people but here all was unknown, the people, the language, the society that they came from, even what was expected of him. His nervousness must have shown because he felt Francesca squeeze his arm as she said, reassuringly,' Don't worry, you will like them, it will be O.K.'

Francesca pressed a named bell push and a voice came crackling and distorted through the narrow metal slats. The metallic voice was made even less distinct by the background beat behind it. Francesca gave her name and, laughing, added something else that David could not translate. The door buzzed and Francesca pushed it open. A heavy aroma of glue, linseed oil and turpentine, greeted them. It mingled with the mustiness of the walls as they climbed the steep dark staircase. The smells and the darkness increased David's sense of apprehension as did the pounding of the music.

The door opened and light flooded through onto the staircase. Standing in the doorway was a young man of Francesca's age. He had dark hair, a beard trimmed scarcely longer than stubble and wore jeans and a red T-Shirt. She called him Angelo and he put an arm round her and kissed her when she greeted him. David felt annoyance at the feelings of jealousy and ownership of Francesca that arose in him and vulnerable because he was an outsider. The feelings, he knew, were irrational and an obstacle to enjoying the evening with Francesca but his annoyance pushed him forward and instantly Francesca took his arm and introduced him. Angelo shook his hand and then flinging his own arms wide said, 'Come in, come in. I shut the door quickly or we have complaining, I think. I will show you to the drinks.'

The room was lit with spotlights. On the walls were several abstract paintings, unframed and apparently still attached to their stretchers. The floor was varnished wood and the furniture tubular, chrome plated steel. The rugs were worn and showed signs of paint splashes and white marks that looked like plaster of Paris. In the far corner was an upright piano, its dark varnished case sitting oddly with the rest of the room. The room was empty and as they passed through it David wondered if they were the first to arrive.

Angelo showed them into a dark hallway and, having left the source of the music behind, David could hear voices coming from another door that led off it. It was the kitchen and Angelo gestured to them to go in. It wasn't much different from parties at home, he thought, everyone clustered together around the wine bottles in the kitchen.

Cristina was not there but from Francesca's description he instantly recognised the tanned, white bearded Enzo. He was pouring wine and listening to a woman in a loose-fitting dress of cotton batik. She had blonde, rather wild hair and reminded him of the late sixties world of new age ideas. She was probably in her early thirties. When Enzo spoke, he put his arm around her shoulders and gave her the wine. He spoke seriously and quietly at first and then paused and added another comment in a louder voice, from which David deduced she was Elena, Angelo's partner. She smiled and Enzo threw his head back and laughed loudly.

David was aware that he had begun to build Enzo into a role model for uninhibited action, the man who was himself, who lived from the centre, who had achieved the object of his own present quest. As Enzo talked, he emanated a vitality that David found himself envying. It was a vitality that he had once identified in himself and here was another man, considerably older, who had found the secret of retaining it.

Suddenly Enzo spotted Francesca and surged across the room towards them. He greeted Francesca with an enthusiastic hug and kiss. She introduced David briefly, as though she had already spoken of him which unsettled him. Enzo, however, grasped his hand as she spoke, and shook it with a firm grip. The warmth of the grip and the radiating power of his eyes replaced the feeling of failure with reassurance and he felt himself buoyed up by the energy emanating from Enzo's personality.

'If you are friends to Francesca then that is good, you take care of her eh?'

As he said this he turned towards the door as more guests arrived. David registered the fact that everyone seemed very concerned that Francesca should be looked after.

He became aware of a glass of wine being pressed into his hand. As she gave it to him, Francesca kissed him on the cheek.

'Are you all right?'

'Yes, just a lot to adapt to, that's all. I see what you mean about Enzo.'

'He's special isn't he.'

Enzo turned back and gestured to Francesca. She smiled and said,

'I'll be with you in a minute,' and was immediately absorbed into this new group with Enzo again in charge.

David felt vulnerable in the face of her admiration of Enzo. Was she playing games with him, or maybe a joint game with Cristina, or an elaborate plot controlled by Enzo. Isolation, nervous insecurity, the sword of Thelma's arrival hanging over him: surely he was an easy target, especially when it involved the degree of emotional warmth and sexual power that flowed so naturally from Francesca. None of this made sense, he did not even believe it. It was a way of punishing himself, making himself hurt for being an object of his own contempt.

He sipped the wine. Enzo's laugh grew blurred at the edges. The expectant energy with which he arrived had ceased to turn outward and drained into his blood causing a dull frustration, an energy with no object, a restless discontent. He did not feel a part of the laughter and conversation. Francesca was absorbed in an earnest discussion that he could not begin to follow, and a creeping paralysis prevented him from initiating a conversation of his own. He was irritated with himself; he'd always said that only boring people got bored at parties; usually he enjoyed them and had contributed to some memorable ones. Here he was surrounded by conversation he could not understand; a flow of animated sound with individual phrases and words rising to the surface, the clarity of their individual meaning teasing him to guess at the context and create ever more fantastic stories for them; a world of chaos onto which he tried to impose meaning from the briefest clues.

The tension inside him was getting worse as he tried to resist the force pulling inward. He looked across at

Francesca in the hope of catching her eye, but she was looking away and he moved back to lean on the kitchen worktop. The music from the other room seemed vaguely familiar; probably an English pop song sung by an Italian group. He tried to remember what it was.

The door-bell rang again and David heard the sound of Angelo's voice without being able to discern the words. He heard another voice that seemed vaguely familiar and then the sound of the door shutting. As the voices neared, he recognised the second as Cristina's. He smiled inwardly to himself at the feeling that he was about to greet a long-lost friend on the basis of at least a dozen words of conversation.

Cristina entered, animatedly talking to Angelo in her deep and smoke roughened voice. She was wearing what David thought was a rather affectedly artistic black outfit: long, shiny and draped. It was certainly dramatic like something from a Greek tragedy, Medea perhaps. As Angelo poured her a drink, she appeared to greet at least six people simultaneously. When she turned to Francesca, she again threw her arms around her and they held each other before Cristina spoke. David could not help but wonder whether there was more to their relationship than was apparent. Francesca whispered something to her and, laughing, led her over to him.

With a rustle of shiny black material Cristina leaned and kissed him on the cheek.

'So, then. You come to the party. You are wanting the picture too, perhaps.'

David must have looked momentarily worried because she instantly laughed and patted him on the shoulder.

'You must not be always serious. Remember: no thinking, just live.'

Laughing, he said, 'I'm always nervous when someone is selling me something. I'm usually on the other side.'

He was aware of Francesca moving round beside him and putting her arm through his. Perhaps Cristina's diagnosis of his psychological problem, first given at the gallery, arose from something Francesca had said though it was equally likely that it just represented her own view of life that she recommended to everyone. Still holding onto him, Francesca reached across to a bottle of wine and poured him another glass. He bent his head and kissed her on the temple, feeling her eyelashes brush against his face as he did so. He took her arm and led her through into the other room.

The flat gradually filled and Angelo turned up the volume of the music. The pounding of its beat fragmented David's thoughts until they gave up the struggle. It was getting darker and the small spotlights broke the darkness into irregular shapes. The plain walls receded, and the physical space seemed bounded only by darkness, cut off, self-contained; they were moving, breathing and drinking within its circle of sensuality. It was hot. The scent of warm skin rose from bare arms, backs and legs. The Italian voices added another layer of music. Two girls began to dance, conscious of how well they moved, a theatrical performance. Couples began to join them.

Francesca had left to get more wine and had clearly been delayed in conversation. The two girls still controlled the centre of the floor, their performance becoming more extravagant, increasingly wild and more sexually provocative as other dancers appeared. As he watched, the darker of the two undid her hair and shook it loose so that it moved rhythmically over her face and shoulders.

As she did so, he saw Miranda. She had loved to dance

and the effect of her performances on male guests at parties had led to several difficult situations culminating eventually in an escape, with body guards, from a party near Hampstead Heath.

They had spent the day at the wilder end of the Heath filming an epic about Boadicea. A friend of hers from college, was trying to break into films and was going to send the result to Elstree. David had observed at the time that it was hardly a suitable choice for a low budget amateur movie but as Miranda was starring in it, she was very much in favour and told him to keep his opinions to himself. Part of her costume was a leather bikini in which she had to crawl along a cold rock-strewn stream at the bottom of the wood, trying to avoid being seen by Romans. He had laughed and said people paid a lot of money for films like that and she had said she would wear anything or nothing if a producer at Elstree were going to see it. Between shots she had cuddled up to him under a coarse travel blanket. As she wriggled against him for warmth, she nibbled his ear and whispered,

'I'm going to wear this to the party tonight.'

He laughed but when he picked her up that evening, he observed with a certain amount of relief that she was wearing her gypsy skirt and a black embroidered bolero top.

The party was a mixture of friends from college, the cast and others involved in the film and another mainly male group of rather hearty types from the rugby club. There was a shortage of girls and the hearties were drinking hard and watching those girls there were with increasingly blatant leers and louder and increasingly obscene comments. Miranda's dancing was well known and someone from college found some Spanish dances and put them on the record player. David wanted to leave but Miranda had finished off several vodkas by now and told him not to be boring. She started to dance, and the hearties began to gather, initially restricting their response to clapping and the occasional shout of: 'Get 'em off!'.

David, knowing there was nothing he could do, left for the kitchen and the wine. He grimaced as he noticed that it too was Spanish.

The kitchen floor was wet and sticky with beer and its inhabitants were reduced to misfits discussing stamp collections and those who needed the worktop for support and the sink for comfort. David contemplated gloomily the depressing end of an otherwise enjoyable day. Suddenly there was a roar of cheering and shouting from the other room. He rushed through and behind a wall of cheering men, in the middle of a rapidly shrinking space, was Miranda still dancing but now wearing only the leather bikini and a pair of high heeled dancing shoes. Her skirt and top lay crumpled on the floor. She seemed oblivious to the fact that this was not the good-natured appreciation that might have greeted such a dance had the party been exclusively friends but that things were becoming dangerous. He tried to push through to stop her but was pushed back against the wall by two of the hearties.

Quickly he went to find Chris, whose party it was. He was a useful friend in a situation like this as he was well over six feet tall and strongly built. He found Chris in a dark room with Angela, apologised for interrupting and told him what was happening. With two more friends, they managed a military style capture of Miranda from the dance floor and she and David got away in his van whilst the hearties' cars were blocked in by Chris's father's Range Rover. Dancing had largely countered the effects of the vodka on Miranda. There had been no time to pick up her clothes and, as they sped along the dark edge of the heath, she pulled the car rug around her, saying,

'What are we going to say if we get stopped?'

'Tell the truth?'

She giggled. 'I was doing a Spanish dance officer. It was very hot, and I just happened to be wearing my leather bikini.'

They laughed and she turned to him, sliding her hand inside his shirt,

'We don't have to go back yet, it's only one o' clock.'

He turned off the road and parked a discreet distance from several other cars whose windows were already steamed up. She pulled his shirt open and they kissed uncomfortably over the handbrake. The light from a passing car broke through the trees and reflected palely on Miranda's skin. Their lips parted and Miranda looked around.

'I think we've escaped.'

'And no police either.'

Then, as they both laughed, they climbed into the back and under the thick blanket.

David smiled at the thought, and how the party and the dancing girls had brought that distant memory to life again, still a part of him, still changing his life from within. He reflected on how different his life would have been if he had not destroyed that relationship. His life might have suffered from an excess of danger, emotional heat, and imagination but would that not have been better than the cold empty wasteland across which he had actually passed, the only warmth coming from memories such as these. It was a decision that he could not rationalise adequately, even in retrospect, and it had utterly changed everything.

He turned and saw Francesca moving towards him with

two full glasses. As she moved, she swayed in rhythm with the music and as she passed through a spotlight, he saw her breasts moving under the thin cotton of her shirt. When she reached him, he put his arms around her and kissed her, her bare arms close to his face as she held the drinks high to stop them spilling. Now he would give himself up to the opportunity of the moment. He would not make the same mistake again; the rest of his life could be better.

They drank and kissed again. As they kissed, she moved against him to the music; he moved with her and they danced. It was now too loud to talk. He put his lips to the smooth curve of her ear and said it was hot and then became aware of her fingers undoing the buttons of his shirt, her long fingernails brushing the skin of his chest. The overpowering force of his senses beating through his blood drove all thought, memory or reflection from him. The music slowed to a strong blues. His hands slid down the warm dampness of her shirt; he was aware of the urgent pressure inside his trousers as she pressed herself in closer to him. A contentment, a warmth flowed through him as all the anxiety of relating to another human being dissolved and their desire joined them.

As the music stopped, he put his arm tightly around the bare skin of her waist and whispered,

'Is there anywhere we can go?'

Her lips slid over his, bruising them slightly against his teeth. He breathed her breath and the scent of her lipstick joined with the scent of every passionate kiss from the past, bringing them to life and adding to the present.

She took his arm and, stopping briefly to speak to Angelo, they crossed the dance floor as if going to the kitchen. In the darkness of the doorway they kissed again and turned to go up a narrow flight of stairs and into a bedroom.

It was barely cooler than the dance floor as the night was hot with the heaviness of an approaching storm. By the small table lamp he could see that their clothes were patched dark with sweat and the ends of Francesca's hair stuck wetly to her neck. The music began again, the beat rose through the floor. He put his arms around her, and they swayed to the rhythm. His hands met the bare skin below her short shirt, and he moved them inside and onto the smooth skin of her back. She wore no bra and he let his thumbs move down her ribs touching the soft sides of her breasts. Her ribs moved sharply as she breathed in; her lips and teeth pressed hard on his neck. He felt her hands pull his shirt from his trousers and then push down past the waistband. He tried to speak, to say her name, to stay conscious that it was her, Francesca, and not let the years of automatic sex take over. She silenced him with a kiss and moved against him so that the softness of her breasts filled the palms of his hands, their hard nipples pressing at the centre.

The beat of the music and the haze of his blood wiped out all but the sensation of their bodies and the soft searching of their tongues in the hot wetness of their mouths. She pulled again at his shirt trapping his arms behind him and he fell back onto the bed. He pulled his arms free and lifted them to her as she knelt over him. He slid her shirt over her head and as she knelt there in the dim light, the perfection of her full, young breasts and slim waist threatened to overcome him and he repeated her name to himself like a mantra until he believed that it was her.

He reached out and undid the waist of her shorts and then, cupping her breasts in his hands moved them to his mouth letting his tongue circle and slide over and around the erect nipples. Her hair fell against his face and again it seemed more than he could bear. These were the breasts that had cradled him and this the woman who had unlocked the life within him. His trousers loosened at the waist as she undid them, and he felt the freedom as she released the heat of his erection from its containment. Her hands pressed down on his ribs as her lips and hair slid lightly over his stomach and the soft warmth of her mouth stroked gently over him, her hair cascading over his thighs.

As her lips returned to his, he slid her shorts down over her legs and she moved, twisting to kick them free. The sweet scent of her arousal reached his nostrils and he moved his hand over the silk smooth skin of her thighs and into the wet heat between them. She moaned and pressed down over his fingers moving against them until her head fell back and her breasts moved violently with the force of her breathing. Shaking, she grasped his wrists, her nails pushing on the veins and pushing them wide slid herself down over him. Together they moved and turned and fell, sliding in ecstasy. He was aware of nothing without her, they breathed together, their pulses beat together, their sweat ran together and a world of infinite beauty and limitless love grew as they moved and sank in the joined juices of their bodies. When he turned above her, kneeling up and looking down along her body there seemed no limit to perfection or to beauty or to the depth or breadth of their perfect world - beauty is truth, truth beauty, he could know no more. At last, her cheek childlike on his chest, her lips lightly against his skin, her arm across him and their minds washed clean by love, they glided as softly as a gondola into sleep:

Darkness

There were trees, tall straight trees. It was night and there was a full moon low on the horizon. Owls hooted. He walked alone carrying her body on his shoulder. He walked and could see the edge of the wood where the moonlight shone on the full ripe corn. He kept walking but got no nearer to the edge of the forest. He could not leave her, or he would be unable to walk; but whilst he walked with her on his shoulder, he could not leave the wood:

Darkness

Thunder crashed violently with searing white lightning. Black mounded rocks, curved, sprayed and beaten by towering dark waves. Terror in the darkness, no moon, air knife-sharp with salt fears. Foam, lightning-lit, fringed their peaks as the dark sea beat and drew at the rocks. Thunder cracked and the rocks split across. The sea surged in through the fissures, greedily pulling and breaking rocks into boulders, boulders into stones and stones into black sliding sand that it sucked into its depths:

Darkness

His eyes opened in the darkness, unseeing. He was soaked in sweat. Thunder again, this time a long angry rumble. A bright slatted square lit the wall. He was awake. A storm was circling. He got out of bed and went to the bathroom. Walking naked he cooled and dried. He went to the window and heard the wind rise. He opened the shutters and saw the trees in the little square moving wildly. He could hear the muffled roar of the distant sea. There was another rumble, darkly receding, and a flicker of blue-white light. No rain. He closed the shutters again but left the windows open. The storm had passed over. As he got back into bed Francesca turned and moaned gently. She clung to him, and he to her, as they drifted back into sleep. Once, moving between sleep and waking in the dark warmth like water, the soft curves of her body and the hardness of his, joined again in love: a waking dream in which their bodies shared:

Darkness

Floating on warm darkness, he was cradled by a stream in twilight; a stream emerging from a dark journey through undergrowth and black trunked trees sliding out into the open between reed lined banks. Around and beneath him were lily leaves and pale salmon cups of perfumed flowers lit by the sheen of the sky before morning. By his side she floated, trailing flowers from her hair, her dress flowing until its flow joined that of the water. She floated among the fallen petals not dead but sleeping. Sleeping in the quiet before dawn:

Darkness.

16

THE FIFTH DAY - PART ONE

S trange scents floated on the air as it moved softly in his nostrils; a deeper yet coarser touch of a different pillow pressed against his cheek. A glow, deep as a rose, filtered through his eyelids. He turned and felt warm skin, smooth against his leg.

His breathing deepened and the scents grew clearer, warm perfumed skin and wood polish scented with sandalwood. Sandalwood sank, turning its fumes in his mind, awakening images that free floated in his semi-consciousness: Miranda, joss sticks, smoke wreathing their bed, the secrets of tantra. A tingling of sensual energy ran through his skin, unlocked by the atavistic key of the warm richness on the air.

Rose turned to pale gold as his eyelids parted, slowly taking in the forms around him lit by the slatted glow passing through the shutters. Over the white of the pillow fell dark hair, spreading from Francesca's forehead, her face still with a childlike peace, like a warm image of the Madonna.

David moved his head against the bare skin of her

shoulder, his lips resting against the slow beat of the pulse in her neck; he put his arm across her and as he did so she stirred slightly, her hand moving to rest on his arm, holding it against her. The scent of her hair and skin replaced the sandalwood, driving out the ghosts and he sank back into sleep.

He was woken next by Francesca moving slowly from under his head and arm. Her lips melted their softness onto his forehead, and he opened his eyes to see her kneeling by him, naked, with her hair falling across her face as she looked down at him. He lifted his arms to draw her to him, but she smiled and turned to sit on the side of the bed.

'It is getting late; I have to work this morning. You can stay here; Angelo will not mind. I will be back at about one.'

David moved his hand and held her wrist.

'I've woken somewhere different, beautiful,' he paused, 'Paradiso.'

She turned her head and answered reticently, almost questioningly, 'It was good, very special, it is a big thing to sleep with someone.'

He ran his hand down her arm, she was holding back inside, and he wanted to dissolve their separation again, as they had last night.

'It's like feeling all the force of being in love at sixteen as well as being rescued from a purgatory of years.'

She held his hand still against her arm.

'It was very special, but don't try to make me say things, it shuts me up inside. We can just be ourselves, now; we don't have to make promises.'

He shifted his position, his head now on the pillow she had left. 'I'm sorry, I'm trying to grasp the butterfly again.'

'Don't apologise, but now, I think, you are being mysterious.'

'A little, a poem about not trying to keep beautiful things because you destroy them.'

'Maybe that is true.' She leaned closer to him, her elbows on the bed and her hands against the sides of his face. 'Does the poem say what you should do instead?'

He slid his hand beneath her hair, 'Kiss the joy as it flies.'

'Then,' she said with a slight mocking edge to her voice, 'that is good advice.' And her lips covered his, her breasts warm against his chest. His eyes closed and the kiss took away the confusion and tension of their words. At last she drew away and sat up again.

'And now, I must shower and go, or I will be late.'

He lay back again in a half sleep. It was interrupted when Francesca leant over him, dressed now and smelling of soap. Her wet hair dripped on his face and the pillow as they kissed. She left, and as he drifted again into sleep he remembered thinking of Jane on the beach, her wet hair across him and the surge of adolescent emotion burning through the chill English sea.

When he awoke again, the light through the shutters had acquired a hard edge and the gold had given way to white. Music floated up from one of the rooms below; not the hard pounding rock of the night before but the subtle, changing rhythms of a saxophone playing jazz. He got out of bed and walked to the window. Through the slats of the shutters he could make out the square below: the dry flaking pinks and dusty white of Venice; leaves and small branches on the flags showed evidence of the storm but there was no sign that it had rained.

Now Venice was outside whilst he had moved inside. He felt that he had passed through a gateway, had found the secret song that lulled the guardian even whilst he himself had slept. Always before he had been outside looking in, whether in on the Venice around him or in on the Venice within him, it made no difference. Now he had moved, the world was reversed, and he was looking out.

He picked his clothes up from the floor and dressed. His shirt smelt of Francesca's perfume. He breathed it in and thought of the night before. As he tried to recall it, his memory blurred over. There were physical sensations that came back to him and the sense that this was supported by layer upon layer of unconscious experience: emotional, mental and spiritual. The sense that being aware only in the present precluded all reflection or conscious memory; that the very power of the experience prevented him from having access to immediate knowledge of it. The watchdog had been asleep but now it was on guard again.

He pushed back the shutters and the room filled with light. A small hand basin with mirror became visible in the corner and he washed and tidied his hair. For the morning after a party and a night when he had had little sleep, he thought that he could have looked worse. He needed a shave, but the twenty-four hours of stubble added something to his feeling that he had broken free from a dungeon that had been holding him prisoner.

A rhythmically irregular and wandering melody on vibraphone greeted him as he descended the narrow wooden staircase. In the room which doubled as living room and gallery and where the dancing had taken place the night before, Enzo was clearing up. David looked around. It looked smaller this morning than it had seemed last night. A floorboard creaked and Enzo turned,

'Ah, David, Francesca said you are sleeping. You sleep well I think.'

It was not clear whether this was a statement or a question, but David decided to treat it as the latter. 'Yes, thank you.' And added rather obviously by way of conversation, 'You stayed too.'

Enzo chuckled deeply and said, 'I think so. But I cannot remember. I make a mess maybe, so I tidy now.'

He had a mellow purring voice, not stopped in the throat but thrown forward onto his teeth, an actor's voice.

Enzo went over to the hi-fi unit and turned the volume down to background level. He picked up a clutch of wine glasses from behind the speakers.

'You want some coffee?'

He did, large quantities of it; he had not got a hangover but was beginning to feel a little vague and shaky. Enzo went off towards the kitchen with the dirty glasses. David picked up some more glasses and a bottle, hidden between a chair and the wall, before following him.

The filter machine had been left on and the jug contained a dark and thickening sludge. Enzo removed it and put it straight under the tap. It hissed as he ran the water into it and David feared that the glass would crack. The new filter paper gleamed white and the grinder seemed unnaturally loud. The coffee filled his nose and mouth with its rich, pungency as Enzo tipped it from the grinder without measuring it.

'There, soon we will have coffee.' He pointed at the untidy mountain of glasses stained with dark rings like dried blood. 'Now we wash.'

He threw David a cloth and began washing and rinsing the glasses. Soon the derelict pile had been transformed into shining rows along the cupboards and the jug filled with fresh aromatic coffee. Enzo took down four cups and filled two with black coffee.

'You pour some coffee. I give these to Angelo and Elena. They will be in bed until late, I think.'

David poured himself some coffee and went through to the other room. The isolation and vulnerability he had felt the previous night had gone. Last night his uneasiness had been exacerbated by his general nervousness, his uncertainty over Francesca and lack of anything, even a language, that he could use for security. He was surprised that Enzo appeared to be alone but glad that it would give him a chance to talk. Despite having initially been intimidated by Francesca's description of him, and by the force of his first impressions, David felt a warmth and approachability in Enzo that led him to think that this artist who lived successfully and forcefully from within might be someone who could help him in his quest.

The vibraphone had struck up with a new urgency against a repeated syncopated beat from the piano and string bass. It was familiar, itself a source of security. He turned up the volume a little and looked at the CD case. It was the M.J.Q., a transfer of a 1960 live recording. No wonder it was familiar; it had been after midnight music, talking over cups of powdered instant coffee with Peter, Mike and Geoff. Jazz was a music he could share at college parties late, after the pop music had died down. Coleman Hawkins, Charlie Parker linked by the art students with the smell of linseed oil and turpentine as home-made psychedelic oil slides bulged and broke their shapes, coloured amoeba turning and swimming over the walls and ceiling. There was the enigmatic music of Thelonius Monk played by the piano trio at the Mermaid and the raw excitement of trad. at the Dolphin. Then there were the quick 'jam' sessions played on the school piano until a lookout called to say a teacher was coming. Another buried world of energy and experience parcelled away and acting from within.

He wandered over to the dark upright piano and lifted

the lid. He let the fingers of his right hand find the key of the music and fill in the melody with riffs that flowed from the past without plan or thought. Hidden patterns waiting to emerge, fragments loose in his mind looking for a chance to slot into a jigsaw of sound. His mind a jumble of unfinished, unresolved pieces of an unseen and, as yet unknown form, hunted like the jazz riffs for a melody to join. Somewhere he had read that Freud, (or was it Jung?), had said that neurosis derived from a break in the story of a person's psyche; if that was right then the kaleidoscope of unconnected images, torn and incomplete jottings of experience randomly buried in his mind could only have resulted in disaster.

He stopped the CD and sat at the piano. Without the rhythm section he had to begin again, letting the chords mount up into sequences and the melody follow. The structures, the patterns began to flow, his mind and emotions held poised over the notes absorbed in the present. Sometimes his fingers fell from the shapes that formed in his mind, but he did not pause, his mind flowed on and his fingers found their place again. Finally, he began to emerge from the music and the chords separated; his mind looked for a close and his fingers supplied it, ending on a seventh in a safe cliché.

He heard a coffee cup being put down on a table.

'Francesca said that you write but not, I think, that you are musician.'

The words pleased him, but he felt an instant need to deny them. He turned on the stool.

'I play a bit but I'm hardly a musician.'

Enzo sat down on the armchair, leaned forward and picked up his coffee. He stirred the coffee once and took a sip. At last he spoke.

'Why are you saying that? It is good to be a musician.'

David was thrown by this; it was not what he meant at all.

'It is very good, but I'm not good enough.' He added, 'My father was a musician, a good one.'

Enzo sat back, balanced his coffee on the arm of the chair, tapped a cigarette from a soft packet and lit it. He did not smoke casually but drew in carefully on the cigarette and focused his attention on the returning smoke. At first David thought the sudden introversion out of character but, as a successful sculptor, it was hardly surprising that there was more to him than just the late-night dynamo at parties. Tim Whiteman, the poet and lecturer at college had smoked in the same way. He watched the smoke rising as though from a thurible, following it into hidden regions where inspiration lay, beyond the world where the mind was enslaved by solid objects and into the insubstantial where Yeats and Blake found images for poetry.

The ash had reached a point where it was ready to fall, and Enzo's hand moved out and over the table. The movement caused it to drop just before the ash tray. The need to brush it from the table and into the ash tray broke his concentration and the out-flowing energy returned. He waved his hands outward, one holding the ashtray and the other the cigarette.

'My father made wine. You should make wine he said. But I make sculptures. Maybe I should make wine but then I have to be good like him. So, I make good sculptures and he made good wine, no problem. You, and Francesca, you like to come to my studio tomorrow? We can drink, talk. You see my work; you will be interested I think.'

The point of what Enzo was saying was not clear; did he mean that you should not do what your father did or that he regretted that he had to find a way of not competing? Perhaps he was being intentionally mysterious.

'I'd like that very much. We're meeting later; I'll ask her.'

There was a fleeting pause whilst Enzo's eyes fixed on David.

'You come anyway. You have a problem I think; maybe Enzo can help.'

A little of David's apprehension returned. He found himself resisting the very offer that he had earlier hoped for; feeling that allowing someone else in to help would weaken him. He had hardly been a great success without help, perhaps he should start to accept it.

'Yes, if Francesca can't come, I'm sure she'll tell me how to get there.'

Enzo felt in his pocket and withdrew a business card; it had a wine stain on it which Enzo vainly rubbed against his trouser leg before handing it over.

'On the back there is a map, there.'

David turned it over and looked at the diagrammatic sketch map. It was surprisingly clear.

'Now.' said Enzo rising, 'I go and get bread and the news-paper for Angelo. Then I go and work, I think. You come tomorrow and we will talk some more.'

After Enzo had left, David went back to the piano and played for a short while, but it was repetitive empty stuff. He was going through the motions; the former feeling of music flowing through him had gone. The creative centre had gone and all that was left was the crumbling and decaying shell: clouds without water, trees without fruit, wandering stars condemned into everlasting dark. He recalled the painting in the gallery, the decaying frame and the ever-lasting lovers on the throne within, the generating and

enlivening force sustaining the rest. Words began to form
from beyond the darkness.

> *'Beyond a crumbled frame of clay and broken*
> > *stone*
> *Within still lies the image we would have*
> *The ordered room rich cased in ageing/mellow*
> > *oils/painted thought*
> *And at the centre an icon of the soul's harmony in*
> > *love.'*

He looked around for a pen or pencil. There was nothing. Repeating the words to himself he went hurriedly to the
kitchen and found a message pad. He returned and sat in
the armchair caught now in words, shut off from everything
except the focus of the point where the words could be
teased out of night. This fervent love, this gesture against
decay, the light in the forces of duality; the attempt to breed
flowers in a desert:

> *'Image looks on image, desiring each new*
> *Creation of the anguished mind*
> *To set itself against the smell/rot of death*
> *To bring the form of love to life.'*

The light and creation only possible in duality seeking
immortality in unity, in the sweat that seeps from skin
through skin:

> *'As if the sweat could breach the walls of flesh*
> *We try to break the bounds that separate*
> *To merge the phantom in the soul*
> *And make a copy of the secret there.'*

And when they fail, the clouds without water and trees with withering fruit, wandering stars condemned to darkness, broken images:

> 'Fallen images fade against the night
> Broken in their coupling desiring/ against/de-
>   feated in love
> To match the copy of their mind's creator
> Consumed in darkness and in fire.'

How to leave the images, to find the eternal light, to move from two to one without invoking death; to peer into the centre of light, the silence:

> 'Seeking blindly in the darkness of our unseen
>   hearts
> And bless for
> Trust/We sink and leave the images
>   touching/behind
> On the throne/bed within the room beyond decay
> Touching the lineaments of their unchanging love
> And make our longing one with them.'

> 'Now in the room's dark centre, built
> Upon their pattern, in the heart we live
> One rose, one world of satisfied desire
> Until the spinning images return and hide our
>   sight/knowledge
> Behind the patterned light of their mask/disguise.'

Attention had held through the draft. He tore the rough sheets from the pad and took them up the narrow stairs. The shutter darkened room with slatted shafts of light helped as he crossed out and selected. Finally, he found on the dressing table a writing pad of larger paper; he wanted to be able to give this to Francesca, properly written, when she returned.

He finished copying it out and propped the sheets against the mirror looking as he did so at his reflection. He had lain on the bed as a teenager writing poems to give to Jane, and to others who, for a moment, possessed the power to unlock his imagination. The individual was not discernible from the poems when he looked back but always the motivation had been to give them to the girl who had provided the light on the words' path. Now, in the mirror, the face that looked back was no longer the same. It was one that had looked on and seen how the trick worked, glimpsed past the scenery into the wings. Tiresias, the old man who had known and suffered all; not the wounded hero Oedipus whose ignorance of self had caused the plague. But, if the blind prophet whispered now these intimations of light and darkness, how could he use them? Where was the possibility of growth, of recovery, of progress? How could he make this corpse begin to sprout? He lay back on the bed and watched a ray of light from the shutters shine on a handful of dust.

When he woke, it had passed one o' clock and he could hear the murmur of voices downstairs. He could pretend to be asleep until Francesca came and kissed him awake as his mother had or he could act with new resolution, new freedom. But he was not yet ready. He tried to move, to force himself to do the rational thing but an ever-increasing force pulled at him and bound him to the comforting fantasy, the reassurance of the past. It was as if a huge magnetic force acted on his emotions and his body's responses.

Roughly, he raised himself from the bed. The force held

him from the door, and he went instead to the window; he dragged back the shutters. The white-hot sun, like glass iridescent with heat, blinded him and blurred the outlines of the buildings. His eyes adjusted, the crumbling pale rose of the walls mingled with the green and red of window boxes and the greys and creams of unpainted stone. He could not see a canal; he could not see water. Turning to the basin in the dark coolness of the room he ran the tap. The pure glistening flow spiralled and splashed, both clear and shining, spreading and seeking over his hands before disappearing into the darkness. He shook them and wiped them once on the towel.

Steps sounded on the wooden stairs: a woman. When he was ill as a child, he had heard the door go and tried to guess from the turn of the knob whether it was his mother or his father. Was it Francesca? Too late to go down but he could meet her at the door. He passed the dressing table mirror with the poem propped against it and saw his reflection: the outer self that showed no sign of the changes within. He reached the door as the steps slowed, he breathed deeply and turned the handle.

The darkness of the landing confused him at first, hid her face. Then he saw that it was not Francesca but Elena; it was her flat after all, hers and Angelo's.

'Buon giorno - you have slept well I think?'

She was a little taller than Francesca, her face suggested experience and the world, an open acceptance of things. Her golden blonde hair was tied back rather than wild as it had been when he had watched her last night with Enzo.

'Yes, thank you, I went down earlier though. Enzo made coffee. It was a good party.'

She smiled the appreciation of a hostess and then said,

'Francesca rang. She will be a little late. She said you are not to worry. She will come.'

He thought he detected an amused smile behind the words; she had obviously worked out that there was reason for Francesca's reassurance.

'Please come down and have some more coffee, if you like.'

A phone call the day before yesterday and he believed Francesca had deserted him. He had decided never to see her again. Another phone call had changed it. He had resolved to go back to Thelma; when she arrived, there would have been no problem, just an exchange of pleasantries and a resumption of routine. Now? Armed with a poem on one hand and on the other an awareness that he had no strategy for dealing with what seemed like an approaching wall of stone, he did not know. Confusion and apprehension returned. Had Thelma rung the hotel when her meeting had finished? He should find out.

'Yes please, I should like more coffee and may I use your phone,' he paused to think of a reason, 'to see if there are any messages at the hotel.'

He was not sure whether she had smiled, or how much she knew.

'Of course. I will show you.'

She was a relaxing person to be with. Attractive but not with the overwhelming sexual force of Francesca. Good vibes, sixties again: he could imagine her at Glastonbury.

At the bottom of the stairs she looked into the living room. Angelo was reading a paper. Elena spoke to him, but David was only able to pick out isolated words, including 'telefono'. Angelo lowered his paper.

'Buon giorno David. There is coffee here when you are finished.'

Elena showed him the phone, which was by the kitchen door, and left him.

He paused for a moment unsure of the number but, as he thought briefly that he would be unable to call, the number came back to him. He dialled and imagined the girl with long red fingernails.

'Pronto.' It was her voice.

'This is David Green, room 305. I've had to stay to do some business in Venice. Are there any messages for me?

'Ah, si. Room 305; from Mrs Green. She will arrive at Marco Polo airport tomorrow, Saturday. You will please meet her at 11.40. If you have problems, you will call her at work this morning. The number is here if you require it.'

He thanked her and assured her that he knew the number. The message had been given very efficiently; there was no room for doubt. He saw the scarlet of her nails on the white paper of the message and then around the receiver as it was replaced. They slashed across his mind and the blood ran.

It was inevitable, there was no surprise and yet all the time it had seemed to be a different parallel world that might sail past, not touching, if only he did not think about it. They had touched briefly at Cristina's exhibition when Francesca spoke through the divide, but only briefly. Now it seemed there was no escape, no place to crouch down unseen. He had to go to the airport and bring her back into his life, or rather bring her for the first time into his new life. He shivered at the impossibility of coping with what seemed inevitable. This was not he thought ruefully, an ideal way of diverting a breakdown.

Elena called from the living room.

'The coffee is in here.'

There was still a gap. His new life, the coffee, Angelo,

Elena, Francesca, Enzo, Venice, were here and now, real. Thelma was a second-hand message on a hotel phone, no more real than the memories he had been trying to discern in the turgid and unpredictable waters of his mind. She could be turned, organised, manipulated like them: until that is, she appeared at the airport tomorrow.

He sat with Angelo and Elena, and talked of Venice and London, of galleries and art, David tentatively, aware that he was at best an informed amateur when it came to the visual arts. Angelo left to see someone about a sale and Elena went down to the combined shop, gallery and workshop below. As she left, the pervasive smell of spirit gum invaded the room. A smell for him associated with theatre and false beards but here with masks: the smell of disguise and new faces and personas in either case. How easily welcome, a friend, a part of the family he was in his persona as an appendage of Francesca. In any other guise he was an outsider, a tourist. He could not back out of the relationship and still keep anything he had experienced or achieved. And Francesca: what was she expecting? This was her life he had come into and she would see him as someone who had joined it temporarily, a tourist in her life as well as in Venice, before returning home; or to be more precise, before home arrived in Venice.

Francesca and he could agree that was how it would be, voluntarily split their paths again with Thelma none the wiser. They could, but then what would he have gained from all this struggle and unearthing of the soft, vulnerable layers within and reawakening the charged images of the past. What was there to gain? He was attempting the improbable task of healing himself, repairing a fractured soul by means of an extra-marital affair - not after all usually considered a healing salve for anxiety and paranoia.

It did not conform to the recommendations of Freud never mind the Church though, superficially, it was easy enough to explain. He was desperate for affection, for warmth, for acceptance by a woman but now the last state was worse than the first. He had given the child the childish things that it wanted and left the man to recover and attempt to put together the pieces.

He was alone. It was tempting, very tempting to just get up quietly and leave. He could put the poem in an envelope and leave a brief message. If Francesca rang the hotel at all, she would be discrete, he was sure of that. He could harden his heart, make himself cold, shut off the emotions, bury them inside with her image. He could bury them from sight until the winter rain had washed away the flowers, the petals like dead butterflies drowned in mud.

His throat closed and his eyes stung. The images traumatically seared into his memory. They were what controlled him from within, mocking thought, reason and free will. He could hide them, hide from them but there was no escape; they would pursue him and overcome him rending him apart as a sacrifice to their power. He had seen them at Cavallino market but now they were nearer, so much nearer they were almost upon him. All he could do now, to hide from their blood reddened nails, to put off the inevitable was to get up and leave. That way he would gain a little life, or life of a sort; he would slide slowly to destruction rather than be overcome in an instant by a leap of frenzied power from the avenging images.

The door to the gallery below banged. Female voices rose up the stairs, laughter. A clatter of heels on the lower wooden stairs and then more voices, more laughter. Elena and, unmistakably Francesca. Voices again and then the heels resumed their ascent.

He was ready to finish the whole business. The phone call from Thelma brought home to him what a total destruction of everything that he considered normal life would be brought about if he maintained this new, and almost certainly temporary, relationship and confronted her with it.

He would be calm, quiet, explain the phone call and tell her that it was better if they ended it now.

The door opened and Francesca entered; or rather a flood of energy, of sunlight, of sea, of water that shone like Murano glass filled the room with Francesca at its centre. She brought with her the whole panoply of Venice and surged through his dark decisions, convictions, and gloomy nihilism like a new tide removing old castles of sand, shining sunlight on the water's edge washing with light the dark sand beneath. Thelma too in her absence faded before Francesca's real and substantial presence.

He stood and her body folded onto his, her arms were around him and his hands rested on her waist, the slight dampness of the cotton dress moulding it to her skin. The warmth and smell of her body climbed on the air through his nostrils and suffused his brain with fumes as drowsy as those of Keats' poppies. What were his vague and unreal thoughts and fears when compared to the reality, the force of this.

They drew apart and, clearly a frequent visitor, she threw her bag into the armchair and offered him more coffee. She called from the kitchen asking what he had been doing. He thought back to before the phone call.

'I'll show you, wait a moment.'

He climbed the dark, narrow wooden stairs with their faint odour of sandalwood polish and pushed open the bedroom door. Last night they had entered wet with sweat and inflamed by dancing. Now he saw himself and

Francesca on the bed embracing in the transforming fire of love. Around them formed a window, a frame of his dry and crumbling past. The past he had, a few minutes before, been vowing to preserve by destroying the life within. What stupidity, what life denying cowardice!

He turned to take up the poem from the dressing table. From the mirror, Tiresias, all knowing, stared back and shook his head, 'This too is an illusion, this too is another set of images to control you. You cannot be free and slave to emotions, to thoughts, to desires.'

David paused and said, 'I can if I choose to be their slave.'

But Tiresias shook his head again in pity at such enfeebled thinking.

'You're a miserable old sod,' replied David but shivered and, less sure than he had been when he arrived, grasped the poem tightly, a charm against blind prophets.

'I'm in here', she called as he paused at the bottom of the stairs and looked into the sitting room. Her voice came from the kitchen. The smell of coffee no longer held the rich attractive warmth that it had earlier, and he was beginning to feel the effects of the seemingly non- stop intake of caffeine. How was he going to give her the poem? He would have to wait for the right moment: she would ask him again what he had been doing.

He stood in the kitchen doorway and watched her as she took cups from the cupboard. The simplest of domestic actions and yet it elicited a wave of emotion that flooded through him daring him to imagine that this was permanent, that this was their kitchen and that Francesca, who exerted over him the power of a goddess, was his wife. For this, was it not worth hazarding all?

As she turned from the cups to the refrigerator, she

noticed him watching her; she smiled and flicked her hair from her face as she leant to open it.

'Have you eaten yet? I had something while I was working.'

David's stomach was responding to his strong and mixed emotions, but food seemed the best possibility for countering the effects of the coffee and perhaps calming his feelings as well. He slid the poem into his pocket to wait for the right time.

'I had a roll for breakfast with Angelo and Elena but if you're sure it's all right I could do with a snack.'

She found some cold meats, long Italian tomatoes and rolls, poured the coffee and they went into the sitting room.

David sat and Francesca went over to the hi-fi. She opened the tray of the CD player.

'Modern Jazz Quartet; Enzo?'

'Yes, we listened to it early this morning. We talked. I like him.'

She slid back the CD in its tray and pressed 'play'.

'He's been a good friend to me. More like an uncle - one I could talk to without worrying he would be, I don't know the right word.'

'Disapproving?'

'Yes, but more, he would not say it was right or wrong, or good or bad. He would listen until the pieces start to fit together.' She paused. 'He has been a help in many things.'

David laughed a little self-consciously, recalling that Enzo had appeared to already know about him last night, and yet he had the feeling that the pause was not initiated by anything to do with him. Her eyes flicked up quickly at his laugh and he felt the need to divert her from any questions that might be forming in her mind, questions that might require commitment of some sort from him to give an answer.

'He said we should visit his studio. He said he was worried about my problem.'

To his relief, she too laughed.

'Was he? No, we should go. There is a good feeling there. He is sometimes too much the guru, yes? But he does understand much.'

There was a pause as he ate. Francesca sipped her coffee, watching her hands as she did so. Her English too was beginning to show the signs of anxiety. Music covered over the gap, its relaxed swing out of step with the increasing tension. Francesca looked up from her hands and said, with artificial brightness,

'You know he plays the saxophone.'

David felt his breathing relax in response to this simple and undemanding statement.

'No, we talked about music a bit. I played the piano when he was making coffee. I'm surprised he didn't say.'

'Perhaps he was going to surprise you with it when we went there. You can never tell what he's planning. For someone who is so, what is it, outward, he is full of secrets.'

He fingered the poem in his pocket, he had to make a time. He had also to tell her about tomorrow. What was he going to say? What did he want to say? - I love you, live with me, marry me, you have transformed my life and the world - how could he possibly, it sounded like the gushings of an adolescent and he had no idea of what she was thinking or feeling, of what caused her sudden mood swings. She knew roughly how long they had left and yet she had not mentioned anything; she had said little and certainly not committed herself to feelings of any sort. And then there was the cynical face of Tiresias in the mirror - the spoiler of life or the voice of truth?

Francesca raised her coffee cup and paused, 'We can't go tomorrow. My uncle is coming back for the weekend, I need to be at the trattoria tomorrow. Maybe on Sunday I can get away for the evening.'

Sunday. Sunday was after Thelma, across the abyss, the unknown. By Sunday his fate would be decided. He must tell her. If they were to be together for the rest of the day then he must tell her now.

'I rang the hotel after you phoned.' As he spoke, he watched Francesca's face closely for any clue as to what was going on in her mind; he observed a tightening in the corners of her eyes. He needed clues to help him, he needed to know how she felt. 'Thelma had left a message.' Had he told Francesca her name? 'That's my wife. She's arriving tomorrow at mid-day and wants me to collect her from the airport.'

There, that was it, or at least the first stage. He watched her nervously, as nervous of the questions she might ask him and his lack of any answers as of any final dismissive statement she might make.

She stood up and, without putting down her coffee cup, turned away to the window. He had only her back to tell him her thoughts, her reaction. He did not even know what he wanted her reaction to be. She put the coffee cup down on a small table by the window and then rested her hands on the sill, looking down at her fingers. She spoke quietly, tentatively. 'We have not been very honest with each other I think.'

David began to mumble a protest, but she continued,

'We pretend that there is only us, that because we are on an island, in Venezia, nothing else exists. I am sorry.'

David's stomach tightened sickeningly around the food he had just eaten. She clearly believed that whatever it was she had not been honest about was as significant as Thelma's arrival. Indeed, she was apologising to him. Her eyes moved from her hands onto his face. He searched their depth and darkness in vain as she went on,

'There was not much time. I think we both wanted an escape from our problems, not to talk about them.'

The xylophone started up at an energetic pace and Francesca moved quickly to stop the CD. Silence, ominous, threatening, took its place.

She sat down in the chair opposite, her hands held together, and her eyes fixed on them.

'What will you do now? Go back to the hotel?'

There, that was it, the straight, basic honest question that he had been dreading and that he had somehow to answer. There were only two answers, stay or go, any hesitation or prevarication was the same as go. Stay seemed to be more in the realm of fantasy but could he be the one to destroy it? He had come here looking for a new life, a vita nuova, he should be prepared to make himself appear foolish, to dare humiliation for even the slightest of chances that Francesca might be the means to that new life.

' I came here with a whole set of problems that I have only hinted at. I came here looking for a solution, for a way to begin again a life with meaning and purpose, a life lived from the centre.' His mouth was dry, his throat closing, his voice had difficulty emerging, he must go on. 'I met you. I feel as if I have begun a new life. You've always stopped me saying anything before but now you must let me. I love you and I want to stay.'

There was a long space before he managed to breath in again. He had committed himself. Not perhaps in the words of a poet, not much of a script, but it could have been worse, a lot worse. He felt relief, terror also but mainly relief.

Francesca's hands tightened on each other, the small slim knuckles whitening, her stare fixed. When she spoke, it was in little more than a whisper.

'I have told you some things about myself, more perhaps than you, but there is more that now you should know. When I..., when my... Oh. !'

And she strangled a muffled expletive, her face in her hands. He could not see her eyes, but droplets fell onto her fingers and ran along them onto the backs of her hands. She stood, looking quickly away and walked to a box of tissues in the far corner of the room. He wanted to go to her and comfort her but did not want her to feel he was pushing himself onto her. She wiped her eyes and turned to him, her voice breaking,

'I'm sorry, I really am sorry.'

The helplessness in her voice was too much for him and he got up and went to her. He took her in his arms. Her head went down onto his chest, her hands grasped his shirt and her back shook with tears. He let her cry. Eventually her breathing returned to a regular rhythm and the shaking stopped. He smoothed her hair with his hand, and she looked up. She sniffed hard and, peering through rainswept eyes, said with a half smile,

' Do I look awful enough to put you off now?'

He felt his throat tighten and eyes sting at the words but smiled and said,

'Nowhere near, you look unbelievably beautiful.'

'My God! you really must mean it, in this state!'

And he held her tightly again until she pushed him, gently, away.

'Come on, I'll do something with my face and then we'll go out.'

She squeezed his wrists, kissed the backs of his hands and picking up her bag, left the room.

Alone, he walked over to the window. It was like waiting in the wings before a first entrance: the fear, the tingling of the nerves, the constriction of the chest; stomach descending fast. These were the same but on stage all was order, pre-ordained, the same new thing every night. This was different. He could not remember when he had last put himself into such a precarious position for such high emotional stakes; surely not since he was a teenager when life was constantly played for all or nothing. He could not sit down or stand still. He paced, listening hard for Francesca's approach.

When she returned, she had re-done her make-up. Her eyes were still shiny. He remembered the trattoria on their first night out, its sudden and unexpected ending. The falling wax of the candle into underground caverns, rose-tinted rock; dripping until all was lost. Words echoed in his mind, 'She had left him, and he felt it was his fault though he did not know what he had done'. She had left petals to lose their beauty in the wet and windswept mud.

'David?' She put her arm through his. 'Come on, you look as if you have seen a ghost.'

They went in single file down the narrow stairs and Francesca looked into the shop to call to Elena. Her voice sounded artificially bright to David's over-sensitised ear; his head seemed to amplify and reverberate the sound like the inside of a cave. As they left the darkness of the stairs and went out onto the campo, a flash of brilliant white burst through him and he floated, motionless. The black cat, Jane, the glass vase, his mother's laughter, Miranda: all were present. She held his arm;, they were together; he turned, and her dark hair and brown eyes met her image. He could not speak but held her tightly and she soothed him as she always had speaking quietly.

The blinding light slowly gave way to brilliant sun and his mother's voice transmuted imperceptibly into Francesca's. He put his arm around her shoulders, and she put hers around his waist.

She walked purposefully, leading him, until they came out onto the Zattere. Even in the searing heat of the early afternoon a breeze blew across the wide open water of the Giudecca canal. Waves slapped and sprayed against the wooden platforms with sheltered tables. A barge, rusty and workmanlike was pulled alongside. The width of the water made it seem almost higher than the land. Francesca walked away from him to the edge, her thin dress rippling in the light breeze. She pushed her hands up under her hair and shook it as if to free it in the wind. David too breathed deeply and the stretch of clear water and fresh salt air dissolved, for the moment, the walls that hemmed him in. She half turned and held her arm out to him. He went to her and she put her arm through his but stayed staring out at the water.

'I told you about my boyfriend, the car crash. That was not all. This is very difficult, but it is right that I tell you. I told you about Renato who helped me with the exhibition in Milano. He is your age and married. He bought paintings from me and introduced me to his rich friends. They like to buy paintings also. The exhibition was a success and he is easy to be with. We went to restaurants, opera, things I couldn't do with Marcello, my boyfriend at university. Students are too poor for that sort of thing. I felt guilty but I pushed it away; if the present is good, it is not difficult to forget other things.'

David allowed an emphatic 'Yes!' to interrupt her. She squeezed his arm and flashed a half smile at him.

'There was nothing to feel too guilty about but when my father died that changed. I was always crying for no reason and flying into tempers. Marcello tried but he did not know what to do. Renato was very good; he knew how to make me feel better and what to do when I was bad. We became closer and then we started to make love. He would book a hotel for the weekend in the mountains or we would go to the lakes. It was so easy, and I couldn't do without him even if I had wanted to.'

Her grip tightened on David's arm and she looked away down the canal to the deep-water port.

'We were in a hotel near Lugano when Marcello was killed. I didn't know. I was laughing and eating by the lake and in bed with Renato while he was dying in hospital. I went back but I had to leave university for a term. I was in hospital for a while - with nuns.' She gave a small shiver, 'Hospital for the mad people.'

He laughed quietly, ironically: 'I was also in a hospital for the mad people, though not for long. They thought I should come here to get better.'

She turned back and looked at him again. The fresh air had dried her eyes, despite the strain of telling her story. 'I forgot. You told me at Cristina's. Maybe this is the place for mad people. No inconvenient reality.'

'You might be right.' How could he ask the question? He wanted to care for her, to help her; he didn't want to seem selfish, but he needed to know.

'Do you still see Renato?'

'I didn't see him for a while. I stayed here with my uncle.

Then when I went back to university, we started to see each other again. It was no good, the guilt got in the way. He said there was plenty of time and we saw each other for meals and opera as it was in the beginning, platonic.' Her voice cracked. 'Like father and daughter.' She paused until she was calm again. 'It lasted for a while but this February he came to Venice for Carnival. He said he could not carry on with it as a platonic relationship, that he wanted it to be as it had been. I couldn't, I said I needed longer but he said he couldn't bear it any longer. He would still help to sell my pictures, but we would not meet any more. There would never have been any question of him leaving his wife. I must seem awful, with no morals, a whore. It didn't feel like that.'

'I'm hardly in a position to judge anyone am I?'

She looked away, across the water.

'That first night, when I was so upset at Carlo's. The phone call, it was from Renato. It was about a picture but always, in his voice, there is a kind of, what can I say, hope.'

He could see now why she had been so tense and reticent at times; the unpredictable rushes of apparently irrational emotion now made sense. Sympathy, empathy had flowed out to her whilst she told her story and the difficulty was that now he loved her more rather than less.

17

———

THE FIFTH DAY - PART TWO

The steps of Santa Maria della Salute spread, curved and white as scallop shells, the ridges stained with sea. Spiral shells rode like chariot wheels above the entrance and high on the dome, looking out over the lagoon and the Adriatic: Maria Capitana del Mar.

They had walked in silence around the Punta della Dogana, exposed, adrift on the wide water. They walked a path in the sea, seemingly unsupported, precarious as though the water might swallow them at any moment. As they rounded the point, the white domes of the church rose above the sea like dolphins to balance the golden lions and brass horses of San Marco; twin rulers of water and stone.

Francesca held his arm tightly. He moved to the steps and she followed, still holding him as he sat down. He raised his arm and put it round her shoulders. They clung together as if on a rock that the tide would soon engulf.

David had no idea how much time had passed when Francesca released her hold on his arm and stood up. It seemed short but the pain in his legs and inertia in the joints suggested otherwise. Turbulent emotion had temporarily played itself out and he felt a blank emptiness inside. Francesca reached her hand down towards his and he held it, cold and fragile, for balance as he stood. She looked, with similar emptiness, into his eyes and then away up to the doors of the church. The outer doors had opened marking the end of siesta. She turned back to him and said,

'Come on, let's go in.'

The flamboyant external decoration like bubbling sea foam and shells, peopled with statues, was left behind at the entrance as though they had dived beneath a breaking sea and found a deep green calm. They entered a domed under-water cavern, circular, more temple than church, like the Roman Pantheon. Light spilled through arched windows above the six dark chapels arranged equally around the circle. Across the intricate mosaic of the floor, a vast unfolding lotus floating at the foot of the eight pillars, glowed a spot of golden light in the entrance to another cavern. As David's eyes adjusted, he could see that it held the chancel and the high altar.

Francesca went to the stoop of holy water and crossed herself. David went to do likewise but felt suddenly self-conscious in her presence and stopped. Francesca looked questioningly at him; he had made it more obvious than he thought. His body tensed and grew warm with embarrass-ment – ridiculous; on his own he would have simply crossed himself but with her he felt an impostor.

'This church was built when Mary drove away the plague from Venice.'

At the mention of plague, the warmth of embarrassment turned to a shiver of fear: his collapse outside the bistro, dark water and black shapes floated in front of his eyes. Chanting reverberated in his head; a rushing filled his ears.

He was floating, swaying with the water. He felt again the supporting arm and cushioning breast; the faint memory of garlic and sweat merged with the spicy sweetness of incense.

'Over here, sit down here, on the steps.'

He lurched towards the cluster of burning tapers by the side chapel and she held him tightly against her, steadying him. The warmth from her body ran back through his emotions calming, secure. In the darkness of his mind he could smell wool and faintly scented soap, feel the rough softness of a cardigan against his face. The dust of an armchair by the fire.

'Put your head between your knees.'

The rushing slowed. He felt his forehead, cold and moist like a fish or a corpse from the water. He became aware that he was gripping Francesca's hand. He released his hold and looked up. Her hand was white where the pressure had driven out the blood.

'Sorry.'

'What for?'

'About your hand I mean.'

She smiled faintly and reached out, putting one hand on the back of his neck and the other on his forehead. He felt the tension draining away between her hands; he did not want her to take them away, ever. It was Francesca who could save him from the plague, and he whispered,

'For me you are Francesca della salute.'

She dropped her head as though concentrating or perhaps praying but did not move her hands or speak. He wondered whether she had heard.

At last she lifted the palms of her hands, leaving her fingertips only touching his forehead and neck and then moved those away too. He could still feel them even after they were gone. He felt almost weightless as though he were floating above the lotus floor. She spoke quietly.

'Maybe this is our last day. We should not waste it. Come you must look at something.'

She stood and held her hand out. He straightened his legs and felt himself float upwards. His hand moved out towards hers, apparently of its own volition and she led him across the lotus towards the golden spot of light above the high altar. The light became an icon and the icon a Byzantine representation of the Virgin. The darkness above the altar cleared to show figures in dark marble.

'There.' Francesca pointed at the figure of a beautiful young girl pleading with the Virgin to drive away an old crone. 'That is Venice praying to the Virgin to get rid of the plague.'

David let his gaze rest on the figures. As he looked, the figure of Venice became unmistakably Francesca. On Torcello too, Venice and Francesca had become one, again under the influence of a golden, Byzantine Virgin. In the gold mosaics and the icon, he saw her eyes; in the darkness and the light her moods, in the shadows of her hair, in her voice and in the sensual perfection of her figure she was one with the mystery and harmony, brilliance and hidden soul of Venice. Now she had driven away the black hag that tormented his mind, the plague that ran on rats' feet and burst its pus-filled boils into the depths of his soul. Tears formed in his eyes, blurring his vision and he reached his arm out to encircle her shoulders. She turned and whispered, her warm breath against his ear,

'Now you must light a candle.'

He did so, lighting it from another. Francesca lit one too. One light on many candles.

They sat and watched the candles burning and flickering in the semi-darkness. Wax ran down, as it had down the candle in the bistro when Francesca had rushed away with tears in her eyes. He had thought then of the crematorium, its desolation as the petals were torn from the flowers by the wind and how the rain drove them into the mud. Now he prayed fervently for the warmth and safe-keeping of her soul. For once she seemed less far away.

'What is it you haven't told me?'

How could he begin to say? How much did he know himself and how could he even begin to communicate the parts he did know? He had to try.

'It's vague, difficult to explain, I'm trying to find out. I hoped that Venice would help.'

'And has it?'

'It is doing something but whether 'help' is the word I'm not sure.' He paused but she looked at him and said nothing. He struggled to go on.

'There are some things that I'm sure are important but why and what they have done I don't know.'

Still she said nothing.

'I was very close to my mother. When I was twenty-one, she had cancer. I don't think I could take it in. Everything about that time seems vague, unreal. It's as if I dreamt it. There were rituals I had to go through to make her better. There was the White Hart, it had no significance except as the name of a pub and a bus stop, but suddenly it was filled with symbolic power. The sign showed a white deer with a golden crown caught in a thorn bush; maybe that was it. I had to walk past it every night and then clockwise round the castle by the sea. Sometimes a deep voice spoke across the water, but afterwards I could never remember the words.

The night she died, my grandmother was there; she told me to speak to her even though she seemed unconscious. I couldn't find anything to say but thoughts of sea spray and tides seemed to flow between us, something to do with life running into eternity. At the crematorium, afterwards, the freezing rain blew, lashing the birch trees, but it smelt of salt. The flowers were beautiful, but the wind tore at their petals and the rain bore them down into the mud.'

Her hand closed over his, tightening, and he looked at her face. She stared into the distance above the altar. So much more recently she had lost her father, suddenly, expecting years ahead and then on holiday..... .

'I haven't talked like this to anyone since.'

She still did not look at him but said,

'I'm glad you can talk now. Perhaps that is what is needed, at least to start with, to help.' She still looked towards the icon on the altar. 'Perhaps she is helping now, you must pray to her, she will always listen.'

He felt towards his neck and ran his hand down his chest to the opening in his shirt. It was at home, in his desk drawer. She had helped him before.

'What is it?' Francesca's voice had a note of concern.

He was about to say lightly that he was not on the verge of a heart attack when he remembered her father and stopped himself

'No, no. I'm all right. It's just that, I had a pendent. A girl-friend gave it to me many years ago when I was a student. It was from a convent in France. Mary was on one side and the Sacred Heart on the other. It was just before my mother died.'

There was a moment's hesitation and then she said,

'Are you a Catholic?'

It was a straight forward question but one that made him uneasy and anxious, like the embarrassment he had felt when he went to cross himself when they entered the building. It went further than just an Anglo Saxon reticence about religion. Symbols, images, the common currency of religion, went deeper to where the trouble lay. His relationship with his mother, with both his parents, something about his relationship with himself caused him to be at once strongly pulled towards, and at the same time to resist, Catholicism.

'No, I'm not. I'm not really anything anymore.' Despite himself, he felt his hand pull away from hers and clasp his other one and his eyes turn to the floor.

'But you still feel something, I can tell. What happened?'

'I've tried to work it out. It's a mess. I left the choir and stopped going to church regularly when I was sixteen. I thought I had found God elsewhere. The usual stuff, in the countryside, the sea, on mountains. Wordsworthian Romantic stuff.' He could hear himself deprecating the experience that had once meant so much to him. He could feel Francesca listening and so continued. 'What really finished me with the Church of England in particular, I mean after that, was the funeral: my mother's that is.'

Francesca's hand moved and took his again but still she said nothing.

'It was a long service, with communion and everything, and yet not once in the whole time was Mary mentioned. It just seemed so incomplete. A mother's funeral and Mary was shut out. I thought: how could I belong to a church that was so one sided, and - ?' He searched for some way of conveying something so vague and yet important that he had never been able to explain it adequately to himself. 'So sterile, without warmth and understanding; dry stones without water.'

He felt the softness of her eyes turn onto him, a softness that emanated light. The image of the golden Madonna on

Torcello floated again before him, a tear on her cheek. Francesca spoke quietly.'

'So, you stayed with the countryside and the mountains?'

'To start with, but then even that began to fade. I studied Eastern ideas, yoga and meditation. Sometimes I went to a small Roman Catholic church for Mass. I could never make myself take the last step of talking to the priest though. I just came in quietly, didn't take communion and then went at the end. Something stopped me just as something pulled me towards it. My girlfriend at the time, the one who gave me the pendent, became a Catholic. We split up after my mother died. I seem to have just been in a desert ever since.

Francesca's eyes moved away, and he felt a darkness encircle him. They moved quickly around the church and settled again over the high altar.

'Here in Venice, in Italy, especially studying painting, the images grow to be part of you: Giovanni Battista in the wilderness, Moses striking the rock in the desert and water pouring out; the Virgin among the rocks. They are part of you as well, part of trying to find God. San Francesco, he too found God in the mountains and the countryside. You are lucky to have known that. Mostly we live in the wilderness, the desert. When someone dies who is close, then we see the desert more clearly and feel more alone. Even Venice begins to crawl with scorpions.'

He shivered. It was a powerful image and one that he felt he had experienced before. She looked back to him, this time her face had lost its radiance and become lost and vulnerable.

'Now you understand my painting. The one on the wall in the flat.'

And he realised where he had encountered the image.

That too had become a part of him. Gondolas as scorpions, stalking the crumbling city.

'San Francesco, he came to Venice. There is an island, San Francesco del Deserto - Saint Francis of the Desert. It is owned by Franciscani, they are the only ones who live there. It is very peaceful, beautiful with many birds singing. I should like to take you.' She hesitated, 'but if that is not possible then go anyway.'

It had returned, their hopeless situation. He still did not know what she felt. Whether she intended to return to Renato when the pain had eased or whether both he and Renato, were ways of coping with the loss of her father. He had committed himself at Angelo's; he was determined not to go back.

'I told you what I want. I love you. I want to go there with you.'

'You have a wife. I can't give you any commitment. I am with you now and I should love to show you the island, but you must not leave her thinking we will be together. Everything, it is too complicated already. In the future, sometime perhaps.' She stopped abruptly and looked suddenly down at her hands. 'And that is wrong too, I should not even say that. I don't know what will happen and.... '

She broke off, her earlier calm authority, the truth that had been speaking from within her, broken up and submerged under turbulent emotion. She shook her head in nervous anger and waved her hands helplessly as uncontrollable tears welled up again from within.

David cursed himself for feeling self-conscious and looked around to see if they were being watched. No one appeared to be taking any notice of them. As he turned back, his eyes were caught by the pyramid of candles and the two they had lighted in particular. The golden light, small spears of fire, casting out intermingling haloes against the darkness of the sanctuary. Light in darkness: he had to hang onto any speck of light he could find, and yet his light must not darken hers.

He turned to Francesca. She sat perfectly still, her head in her hands, a wall of separation around her. He did not disturb her but turned his eyes back into the candlelight. Candles around the crib at Christmas, a candle at baptism, candles on the altar, candles around the coffin, the paschal candle. Light in darkness, life in death, the candle was peculiarly appropriate: warm and intense and yet fragile and susceptible to the slightest draught. It was the same with the inner light, the guiding light, so easily obscured if not extinguished by the turbulence of life. What had happened to the fragile flickering that lay behind the brief story he had just told Francesca?

Sitting cross-legged on the wood-block floor at school, the smell of dust and sand in his nose, he looked into the rays of sun that poured through the large, metal framed windows. The piano played cradle-rocking chords:

> *'Jesus, good above all other,*
> *Gentle Child of gentle Mother,*
> *In a stable born our Brother,*
> *Give us grace to persevere.'*

They were comforting words - Gentle Child of gentle Mother - like being by the fire at home and listening to stories. Her cardigan was warm and rough on his face and smelt of soap. It was his song for her and while she looked out of the kitchen window and did the washing-up, he tried to see above the edge of the sink as she sang to him, that he was her only sunshine. He loved those words too, except the last line which made his stomach feel funny and then he held onto her sleeve.

One Sunday, when his father came home from church he said,

'Would you like to join the choir?'

The darkness in the church went out in all directions. It was cold. He tried to imagine being in the choir, holding the manila bound anthems sewn into their covers by his mother and lettered in special writing like very old books. It made him feel nervous and lonely.

'No. I don't think so.'

'Why not try it for a while?'

He felt nervous and lonely again.

'No. I don't want to.'

And his mother said,

'Perhaps when he's a little older. He is only seven.'

And because he had said he didn't want to join the choir he asked his father to play on the piano from the Little Organ Book. It was bound in dark green leather with gold lines and writing and was the biggest book he had ever seen. Everything about the organ had to be big and that must be why even this book was called little.

At Christmas he sat on the organ stool while his father played the voluntary. At the end, when his big hands pressed the thumb pistons under the keys and the stops shot out, it filled the whole church and made his chest vibrate:

> *'Omega and Alpha he!*
> *Let the organ thunder,*
> *While the choir with peals of glee*
> *Doth rend the air asu-under*
> *Doth rend the air asunder.'*

And so they did.

When they got home, he said,

'I think I'd like to join the choir now Dad.'

At his first Saturday morning choir practice he realised that it was nothing like he'd imagined it would be. He was able to go home and tell his mother he had enjoyed it.

In the beginning it was the music, choir practices, the other boys calling Dad, Mr Green. Unaccompanied motets at the Eucharist, anthems with the organ at evensong. At evensong they sang the Psalm, the Magnificat and the Nunc Dimittis. These were new words, special words. As well as the green Hymnal he had a brown Psalter and Chant Book. You had to learn what the pointing meant in the Psalter in order to sing the chants. You knelt down in the creed when you sang 'of the Virgin Mary' and the Magnificat was Mary's prayer:

'Gentle Child of gentle Mother.'

It was mysterious and important. It was about some-thing you couldn't understand. Only servers and priests were allowed in the Sanctuary because it was God's altar and He was there when the priest held up the wafer and the shining silver chalice. Not all the priests were the same. Father Stevens knelt down very low at the altar as if he had collapsed and then he kissed it. Some people in the congre-gation didn't think that was right. He was a kind man and very clever; he had been to Oxford University. If you loved God why shouldn't you kiss His altar?

He heard someone in the congregation say that Father Stevens was copying the Catholics. That didn't make sense because in the creed they sang, 'I believe one holy Catholic and Apostolic church.' His father said the Church of

England was Catholic and that they were called Anglo Catholics because they were English. When he walked to school with his mother, they walked past a church that said it was Catholic but that was Roman Catholic. He asked her what the difference was, and she said they sang in Latin. He had seen Latin on grave stones and memorials on church walls when they visited them on days out. Magnificat and Nunc Dimittis were Latin and so was Agnus Dei but Kyrie Eleison was Greek and that was even older. He played O Come All Ye Faithful from his book of piano pieces, but it was called Adeste Fidelis. That was Latin too. He thought it was good to have a special language for speaking to God.

Father Graham took his confirmation classes and he had to pray twice a day when he wound his watch up. He didn't think Father Graham believed him when he said he had done it every time, but he had. He already knew about the colours of the altar cloths and the vestments so that was easy too. The Trinity was difficult. God was Father, Son and Holy Ghost but they were all one. God's son was Jesus and Mary was His mother so Mary was God's mother as well. He liked that, it seemed right, but he couldn't understand it. It was right that you couldn't understand God.

He had to make confession before he was confirmed, and he had to write down all the things he had done wrong. He told them to Father Graham in the Lady Chapel where there was a light that never went out. It was difficult writing it down, but he liked Father Graham and there was a statue of Mary holding her hands out. He had to read Psalm 23 when he got home as a penance and then it would all be forgiven. Father Graham left to become a monk and people said it was a waste because he did such good work as a priest. They were wrong though because if you were a monk you could still do good work and you would get to know God better.

He was twelve then and soon afterwards the magic started to fade. The church changed too. Father Stevens left and they moved the altar. The new Vicar stood behind it facing you, so it wasn't so mysterious anymore. The statue of Mary disappeared from the Lady chapel and she wasn't mentioned again, except in the creed, and he thought extra hard about her then.

He still enjoyed the choir, but he only sometimes felt as if God was there in the way he had when he was younger. The feelings came back, or feelings like them, when he walked to the woods near Southwick in the afternoon and stood alone in the trees by the small river. He just waited and, particularly when the sun started to set, he felt that he had dissolved into everything else. It was the same when he sat alone by the sea and listened to the waves or sat on the Malvern hills and let the wind join him to the great spaces over the valleys and the warm rough-grassed mounds beneath him. This was the mighty rushing wind that brought the spirit of God; but was it the same God or a different one? Were there different gods or just different ways of knowing the same one? It wasn't until he read Wordsworth and Shelley that he realised other people had felt like that as well.

When he moved to London, that faded too. He still felt it a little from time to time. When the mist hung round the trees in the college grounds in the morning and he leant on the old bark of their trunks. He began to try to find ways of making it happen which was when he joined the Theosophical Society. They talked about the long years of meditation and yoga that could lead to Samadhi, oneness with all. He had been given it free, without effort and had not realised it.

Perhaps he had spent long years learning in previous lives but in that case why had it gone away again?

The candlelight flooded back, and he felt Francesca's hand grip his arm. He looked back at her. Empathy, sympathy, love without desire welled up in him and held him as it went out to her. She took several long breaths and her hand relaxed. She turned towards him and her other hand covered his. Between their eyes flowed a stream of sadness, longing and confusion. Her eyes filled his consciousness until they became his own staring back at him. Eventually she spoke, her eyes still on his.

'Thank you for not talking. I needed to be quiet just for a short while.

He turned his hand to hold hers. 'I did too.'

There was a silence as their eyes slowly parted. If this was their last day what should they do? If it was their last day what would become of what they had done? What of the bed enthroned in the centre of the crumbling stone and the search for salvation in a shared soul's image? If there had been progress was it not inextricably bound up with Francesca and if that were so, then would their tearing apart not plunge him further into darkness?

He became aware of his hand now in his pocket. There was a folded sheet of paper and he drew it out. He moved his other hand, releasing Francesca's, and opened the paper. It was the poem he had written that morning as the inspiration faded from his music and turned to words. The poem he had honed and beaten and finished in the room where they had made love and where the sun fell as he let the water fall over his hands and where the blind prophet looked back with disdain at the idea of running after truth in the form of a woman.

'What is that?'

Francesca looked past his arm at the paper, the words in shadow.

'A poem I wrote this morning, before you came back, before everything; well, before I told you about the phone call from Thelma and we had other things to think about.'

The phone call from Thelma. That was real. Tomorrow she would arrive and what would happen then? On Sunday he would know but until then the darkness was full of terrors.

She did not look up but kept her gaze on the paper. She reached out her hand to it.

'Can I see. I should like to read it.'

'Of course. I went upstairs to get it for you, but it never seemed the right moment after that.'

She held the paper so that the candlelight fell across the words:

For Francesca - A poem on the picture by Cristina
'Beyond a crumbled and decaying frame of
  broken stone,
An opening in the purple cloth that shrouds the
  past;
Within, the ordered room, rich cased in aged and
  mellow oils
That bring the balanced spirits near and draw
  their song.

'Upon each image looks another, desiring every
  new creation,
Breathing of the anguished mind, forms embodiment of fear;

Caught in terror on the rim of death above
    eternal darkness,
Desire cries out to find its pattern love and in it
    live.

'In the sweetness of our flesh, dissolving in sweat,
    we fall
Into the dark, soften the bounds that separate and
    merge
Each phantom in the other's soul and copy there
    the secret
Held beyond all vision, within creation's robe of
    light.

'Fallen images fade as burning stars against the
    night,
Broken in their coupling, defeated in their love;
Fragments that fail to match the copy of their
    creator
Consumed in night and everlasting fire.

Seeking blindly in the darkness for the unseen
    heart
We leave the fickle light of images behind and on
    the bed,
Within the room, beyond decay, we join that
    perfect love
Whose lineaments are set to never die.

Now, as the lovers at the centre of that inner
    room,
At peace, absorbed, entwined within the secret
    rose,

We are subsumed, transformed, transcending all
    desire:
Until the spray of lighted images returns and
    hides again
The heart within the patterned show of their
    disguise.'

As she read, her hand moved and held his. One in the eye, he thought, for Tieresias, and then he smiled: perhaps not in the eye, one somewhere anyway.

Francesca continued to stare at the paper for some time after David sensed she had stopped reading. At length she said,

'There is much that I don't understand but there is warmth and there is darkness. Love and death. It is like the painting. I shall read it again if I can keep it.

'Of course. It is for you. I'm afraid I don't think I can be much help in explaining anything.'

She began to fold the paper. 'No, you should not explain. There was something in the picture for you but not anything Cristina could have explained. Even some things, I think, that had not happened. Perhaps there are no choices and we worry over nothing.'

He felt his stomach suddenly tighten. What was it she was saying and how did it apply to the unknown pit before him? There was no point now in holding back.

'And in the future? Are there choices there?'

She smiled, 'Is it in the stars or do we make our own fate? You do not think I can answer that.'

'We seem to make our own fate but afterwards it looks as though we had no choice.'

'And what controls our choices? If we knew that, then we would not be in this mess, I think.'

His choices were controlled by a sea of hidden images that swirled and seethed in storms that came, wrought their havoc and then subsided as if they had never been. Storms of past emotion, the unreconciled forces of his life that lay in apparent calm until from nowhere a sudden squall whipped them into a frenzy that drove him before them. Against such forces as those, reason was an irrelevance, a maker of fragile and superficial order. Even if reason had been in control there was too much unknown, even what outcome he wanted to achieve. It was too vague, too emotional, too subjective. He wished to feel better, to be happy, to relieve the awful pressure in his head and the lethargy in his body. These were not aims that reason understood or could prescribe for.

Francesca turned and looked steadily at him.

'David, it might be better if we stopped now. I cannot make choices or decisions. You must see your wife before you decide anything and what you decide should not depend on me. I will stay here, and you leave, go back to your hotel and tomorrow you will meet your wife.'

Panic began to make its way through David's body. His thighs and hip joints felt as though they were dissolving into liquid that tingled and ran through his spine, poured icily into the clenched knot of his stomach and rose into his skull, numbing his brain with fear. She was taking the decision, taking the control away from him; he had made no use of it, so she was taking over. She would vanish, leaving behind a tangled mess of old emotions and nothing else. It was like a falling dream, falling helplessly in terror through dark space to an unknown and unseen fate. He tried to force his mind to imagine the future without her, without even the possibility of her being there. What would he feel facing joblessness, a breakdown on his medical records, a marriage without comfort, much less love. He would probably draw back from finishing the marriage just to keep something that was familiar, whether it was worth keeping or not, but Francesca had filled the void where meaning was supposed to be. All he could see as he tried to peer forward was an emptiness like a distant horizon over the sea.

'After all,' she continued, 'we have known each other less than a week.'

City of unreality, city of illusion shaking under the summer haze, a cauldron of unholy loves. Blind eyes looked back, pitying one who chased after phantoms in search of happiness. Sometimes the phantoms were in his head, sometimes they alighted on a body or place and possessed it, acquiring a semblance of reality. Embodied or not, all were vanity, there was nothing there, a shadow play, a ghost sonata. Whose ghost was she?

'We met here less than a week ago.' he agreed. 'But we have, we seem to have.....' It was clumsy, he struggled to bring himself to say it. 'We have known each other much longer.'

True until it had left his mouth, and then a tired cliché. It was true from the mythology woven together in his head but only there. It was the phantom he had known for much longer; it was only this week that it had entered and possessed her body driving out whatever reality was there, whatever other tangled mythology that was a stranger to his own. Who was he to throw ghosts about, much less chase them and insist their hosts co-operate.

She did not laugh or wave aside the tired phrase. 'I know.' she said. 'I was trying to make it easier.'

When she spoke to him, when her emotions stirred and care and sympathy welled through her words and actions, what phantom did she address? An image cast about him like a net; a character formed from her mind and memory for him to play. No love was possible except that for the mind's own reflection in a pool: the warmth of being loved was just a vain illusion. All men were islands in love with the productions of time; all knew those productions only within their own minds, there was nothing more. Love led only to the whirlwinds of Hell.

Despair wet his eyelashes and blurred the candle flames. One light with many flames. He could not reach it, could not know it; he was falling into darkness. He bowed his head, hiding his eyes and tears fell. He knelt still, his mind transfixed, his emotions paralysed until a kind of peace returned. He pressed his palms onto his eyes and wiped away the last stinging remains of drying moisture. He sat back on the seat and turned to her.

There was nothing. Pillars, space, muted light, the door to the sacristy with the sign that said it cost two thousand lire to pass. He looked round quickly, stood and cast his eyes around the great space of the nave. From one chapel to another, one dark painted scene to another but she was nowhere, gone, torn from his web of images. The broken membranes of his imagination contracted, shrivelled; unsupported images bled into the darkness and he fell back. The falling dream, the helpless terror he had imagined now was real. Words he had turned to in his teens came pacing back, stepping through his mind, imposing funereal order in the dark chaos:

> 'Dark night, vague shapes of trees, embalmed
>   darkness.
> To cease upon the midnight with no pain,'
> A dark cocoon held in night.'

In this darkness with the memories that had flooded here: in her presence perhaps this would indeed be the time to sink into the ultimate darkness and forget:

> 'No, no! go not to Lethe, neither twist
> Wolf's-bane, tight-rooted, for its poisonous wine;
> Nor suffer thy pale forehead to be kiss'd
> By nightshade, ruby grape of Proserpine.'

There was no comfort, only a recognition of shared anguish spelt in Keats' words calling on myths and symbols without which he could not even comprehend his own soul. Without illusion life was impossible, reality an unbearable darkness. Only images cast against the night could make it possible to go on.

Many candles and the one light shining in darkness; shadows flicker, and a tangle of dancing shadows was all that it was possible to know:

> 'Then glut thy sorrow on a morning rose,
> Or on the rainbow of the salt sand-wave
> Or on the wealth of globèd peonies;'

On the altar the golden icon of the black Madonna, Mater Dolorosa, Mother of Sorrows. Shadow of light in darkness:

> 'Hail Mary, Mother of God;
> Pray for us sinners
> Now and at the hour of our death.'

18

THE FIFTH DAY - PART THREE

From the darkness, through the heavy door, he emerged onto the white stone. He scanned the small clumps of people tufting the edges of the steps. He looked across to the bridge that left the wide white Fondementa della Salute and arched over the canal into the darkness of the narrow clay-red calle. She had gone, left as though she had not existed, no more substantial than the net of images he had thrown over her; it was his weakness, his imperfection, his indecision and she had gone.

He turned and looked out across the wide mouth of the Grand Canal. Light reflected brightly from the water and white stone but without its earlier penetrating glare. The colours were clear, without the false tint of sun-glasses and a cool breeze blew from the lagoon. On the other side of the water, the Molo and the great pillars at the entrance to the Piazzetta still swarmed with scarcely differentiated, ant-like, bodies. He felt disturbingly detached from his arrival and entry through the pillars that had been so momentous such a short time before. He felt detached too from Francesca's disappearance. A protective skin seemed to have re-formed over the raw and sensitive layers of his inner mind and memory.

Perhaps this was it; this was as far as he was going. Francesca had left him sightless in the desert; Eva was as much a shadow as Jane whose ghost had come to life through her. He had turned over layers of memory and submerged emotion, exposing them to light but was at a loss as to what to do with them. He had relied on Francesca to lead him to a new place of self-discovery, a new life where the old would become either insignificant or be reconciled and lose its restless power to drive him obsessively and irrationally to places he did not want to go. Now she had gone and in the morning Thelma would arrive bringing the anaesthesia of familiarity and meaningless activity. He would forget; layers would again pile up as sediment over the remains of the past, burying its forces, destructive and creative alike. In some ways it was a relief.

The thought that he could give up the uncomfortable and dangerous quest made him look round again, expectantly and fearfully; Francesca might be there just out of sight; he might not be free of the dangers or deprived of the possibilities that were focussed on her. Voluntary self-deception of heroic proportions had allowed him to entertain the belief that he could escape from his own past, and from himself, by escaping from the person who had promised to be the key to his self-discovery. It was a desperate attempt to rationalise the easy option. The layer of self-deception was so thin that he had to pretend not to be able to see through it. If only he could really believe in this comfortable illusion and not be aware that he had only to allow his mind to look sideways for a moment to see what a sham it was.

There were two inescapable facts that he had to find a

347

way of accepting: Francesca had gone, and Thelma was arriving. It was up to him to make what he could of this for now and for the future.

Thelma was arriving but he had not spoken to her. They had not made any arrangements for meeting other than the information that her plane arrived at 11.40. He looked at his watch; it was nearly five. It would be four at home, but she would have taken a half day and he could ring from the public phones near the Accademia. They would sort something out. He could drive around the lagoon and meet her with the car, or she could use the motoscafo direct to San Marco. She would not have much luggage as he had brought most of it in the car so that was probably the best solution.

Practical matters, solutions to day-to-day problems, these were the things to distract from too much reality, to distract from Francesca. He could go back and have a shower, change and, he ran his hand over the sharp, thickening stubble, shave. The thought brought with it an image of the bathroom at the hotel. Yesterday at midday he had shaved and showered there before leaving to meet Francesca. Before that he had tried to ring Thelma at the office. He remembered the scarf he had bought for her and tucked into the drawer and then Francesca's uncle's shirt. Where was it? He thought he had put it in to the hotel's cleaning service. If it caused a problem, if Thelma came across it, he could always say he had bought it: more dissembling.

Yesterday he had decided to forget Francesca and had rung Thelma. It was all decided; he would take the safe way. Then one phone call, Francesca's voice and he was on the ferry to see her. The same at the flat that morning, he was ready to end it, to hide from the avenging furies by returning to suburban life in Wimbledon safe in the knowledge that it would take time for them to find him there. Then one glimpse of the light that flooded the room with Francesca and all resolve was gone.

But how was he to know which was the right course, which was resolve and which cowardice? At one moment he thought he knew: he should be bold, should strike out, to hazard all he had. The next, he thought he should be rational, measure his life by reason and build his house carefully on good foundations. There was no way to know. If you thought about it for long enough everything became a meaningless blur, a fog in the head; peals of hollow laughter receded in the darkness beyond the fog, will o' the wisp spirits dancing through the marsh lights until you were lost and dizzy in a maze of dark mires sucking at your feet as you struggled to find a path without map or guide.

His hands went out, involuntarily, to steady himself, to find his balance on the dark perilous turf; the Grand Canal rushed back into his sight. He looked around to see if anyone had noticed what would have appeared a strange and irrational gesture. No-one. He was as alone here as in the darkness of the moor that sucked darkly at his feet.

He was without emotion, in a timeless transfixed state. He struggled to bring to the surface an image trying to make itself felt: thick cellophane, folded, wrapping something that may have been an egg - sugar flowers on chocolate, an Easter egg: flowers wrapped, sprayed out in cellophane, a face beneath the creased transparency, floating with flowers cast onto the water with dark weed a funeral veil beneath; white steps like a wedding cake through a film like rippled water - birth, death, a marriage all wrapped still in cellophane, held still, distant and preserved. Fear began to creep through the wrapping, eating the stillness, gaining speed dissolving and destroying until there was nothing but a small pile of white ash.

The coffin was open in the sitting room and he prayed: for what he did not know and to whom he was not sure. It was all that was left, the only channel for his whole emotional world to flow. Every thought and feeling for twenty-one years was related to her and all were unsupported now, one half of his being wrenched away. He could only pray that she was at peace now, the dreadful pain that tore apart her body had finally gone; pray also that released from her body that had held him so warmly, she was still there somewhere to know that peace. And as the praying came to an end the tears began uncontrollably again draining him until all that was left was empty and unable to feel anything.

The breeze across the canal dried the salt water on his eyes, made them cold and sore. He shivered in the sun. He became aware of the heavy thump of a door shutting behind him; he turned and heard the bolts shoot across. Santa Maria della Salute was closed.

He felt drained by the involuntary journey through yet more apparently unconnected images that supplied no answers. Tension and conflict were not resolved but had temporarily worn themselves out. He forced his mind to emerge from the image world. There were still practical problems to solve; he had still to find out how and where to meet Thelma.

He descended the steps to the small wooden bridge leading away from the wide, open water. From the open space of the Salute, the Grand Canal and the Zattere, the arched tunnel through into the interior of the Dorsoduro appeared closed, dark and claustrophobic like an entrance leading to a labyrinth of caves. He crossed the water and entered the cool shade.

Once inside, the darkness ceased to threaten; he felt welcomed, drawn in and held by the familiarity of its walls. Their shadow ruffled the unnatural quiet that had lain over his feelings since he had fallen away from the candlelight into darkness and looked up to find Francesca gone. He inhaled the smell of damp plaster tinged with garlic, it suffused his blood and rose again from where reason could not reach. He found himself back in the world where he had known her. All that had been searched for, and which had in part been found, bore down upon him. The thin defence, the attempted protective illusion, had been circumvented and an uncontrolled tangle of images was once again free to drive him where it wished. Without this illusion, the light that entered his eyes, the sounds and particularly the scents were those of his time with Francesca: a time which itself drew on the deep pool that reached back into his own past; confirmation that here was that for which he sought when he first decided to revisit Venice. True, he was aware that it frequently disappeared behind walls and into areas of impenetrable darkness, but he nevertheless felt a sense of continuity that had, for so many years, existed only as an item of faith and vague memory.

Briefly, along the Rio della Fornace, like a glimpse of sky from a deep cleft between caves, he saw the wide water of the Grand Canal on one side and the expanse of the Giudecca on the other: open water, open sky. Francesca had been his guide through the dark labyrinth, but he had voluntarily entered that tangled world of confusion which defeated thought and whirled emotion into an impenetrable fog. Now that she was gone and he had no guide, he could not stay. Thelma and his recent past before his breakdown were clear, straight forward and rational. It was a world where he did not need a guide so long as he looked firmly forward and outward. He struck out determinedly. He would ring Thelma and make all necessary arrangements. Now Francesca was gone, the real continuity lay in his marriage, his home, and possibly his job.

In the Campiello Barbaro an iron pump splashed continually into a drain below it. He held back whilst two women, Americans with rucksacks, filled plastic bottles. One, the fat one, marched purposefully away calling,

'Come on, it's this way.'

The other, curiously listless, whined back, 'Oh do we have to? We could sit here.' but as the fat one disappeared, and she followed anyway.

It was quiet again; he went to the pump and ran water over his wrists. He had run water over his hands at the flat after he had written the poem for Francesca and talked to Tiresias, a washing away of impurity of purpose and a preparation for the sacrifice but then he had looked back, pulled away, been unprepared to lose his life to gain it. He observed, with a certain amount of irritation, that this simple act of putting his hands under the pump had, through raising associations from his memory, acquired a wholly inappropriate level of significance: a masquerade of images parading as meaning, an emotional charge lent by memory giving them a false sense of importance.

In the dark window of the antique shop beyond the pump hung marionettes, Comedia del Arte figures, stereo-types whose predetermined actions and reactions were controlled by the pull of strings. He too was controlled by the pull of strings stronger than reason. Reason could not provide meaning and the forces that provided the appearance of meaning were irrational; he felt helpless as a puppet to decide or act on anything. Like the listless woman he too could see little reason to keep moving on but knew also that at any moment an irresistible force might suddenly emerge and command him to go its way. Will-power could pull the strings before they were pulled for him, but he did not know what to will. All things were the same; the dark confusion that hinted at salvation and the clear sky that seemed so arid.

He stood and looked at the marionettes and the cracked oil paintings, crucifixes, and statuettes, swords and medals with cases: symbols of battles of the spirit and the flesh that pulled the strings from a turbulent and confused world beneath consciousness. He turned away, back towards the constantly running stream from the pump head. The running water and the cool breath of the unaccustomed trees inclined him to clarity, provided enough of a distinction to allow him to continue in his decision to phone Thelma.

At the Guggenheim museum he looked into the small garden courtyard, through the wrought iron gates of thorns that held large glass fruit drops. The walls were heavy with creeper and a large well-head stood in the centre. Just the fact that it was an art gallery was enough to make him search the courtyard and the visible part of the office. He caught himself in the act and dragged his eyes away. He was trying to leave confusion behind, to focus outward and away from everything she stood for.

The sound of an American voice made him turn again and look to the far end where the steps were. Coming out of the glass doors and onto the steps were George Wagner with his wife and another couple, also American. He felt an instinctive need to turn away and try not to allow another intrusion into his thought processes, but George waved and called out,

'David! Hi! How's things?'

There was no way to avoid it now, so he walked towards them.

'OK, fine thanks.'

The American voice and the familiar and friendly forms of the Wagners brought back thoughts and feelings of the excited anticipation of his first day. George shook his hand and introduced the others, fellow guests at the hotel. David took part in the ritual greetings whilst trying to keep down the confusion of rising memories. George was talking again.

'We're going on to see the view from the end here, by the church. Ring the hotel, we'll have another drink, your wife too.'

He had forgotten that he had mentioned Thelma; this might now indeed be a possibility. Now Francesca was gone there was no reason why not.

'Yes, I'll do that. She's arriving tomorrow.'

'Good to see you. Look forward to another talk. We'd better be moving on. Take care now. We'll see you.'

With that they turned and walked off towards the small square with the running water, the marionettes and the flaking oils.

They had welcomed him to Venice and George had provided congenial company after Francesca had left him in hurried, and mysterious, circumstances. Now that she meant so much more to him, she had gone again, and George's fleeting appearance served only to highlight the significance of the short time in between. Memories only a few days old came stealing upward, threatening his precarious decision, urging him to find Francesca.

He watched them, detached himself from their

emotional power and saw them subside again. It was an act of will, but it seemed an empty achievement that left only reason remaining in its sterile mesh. Francesca filled him with life, energy, hope and a renewed sense of being but what it meant and what it was for was outside the scope of reason. It had vanished as quickly as it had come, like the fiery will o' the whisp dancing through his mind's night, the image he had seen on the steps of the Salute. To the rational mind it was an illusion, potentially a treacherous one, that flashed its light over the black mouth of the mire and would leave him trapped, sinking into oblivion as he listened to fading laughter after he had thrown all away.

In confusion, he left the Guggenheim and came out onto a quiet canal glowing in the low sun of late afternoon. There was a mysterious comfort in the last rays of the sun, a redder gold before the darkness, a dance in the fading light on Blake's Ecchoing Green, a dance of innocence leading to experience. Along the fondamenta were studios and galleries avoiding, in the main, the conventional pictures of Venice though still inspired by her. It was reassuring: a gesture against despair; the vision of artists coming out against the dying light. It was a metaphor of overcoming and carried with it an unverifiable sense of truth. This too may well be an illusion, but it was a comforter against the darkness, a good lie.

High walls with shutters clinging to them closed over him. Could he commit his will to a lie? If truth could not be discerned from illusion then surely one reality was as good as another: Thelma as Francesca, Wimbledon as an Italian vineyard, selling computers as being some kind of artist. Why should one lie be better than another?

In the open space of the Campo San Vio, by a newspaper stand with Il Gazzettino across its roof, stood a row of perspex topped public telephones. He had given himself until he reached the Accademia where he knew there was a line of phones at the end of the bridge. To be faced with the possibility of phoning Thelma now, just as he had reached a point when all things seemed equal and nothing was to be preferred was an instant challenge - why not here and now, why wait for the Accademia? The drone of the motoscaffi and the splash of bow waves from the Grand Canal blended with voices from the kiosk. He moved towards the telephones, fumbling in his pocket for a credit card. Now, close to the phone, the voices and the water paralysed his mind and the telephone stood issuing a challenge to interfere in the flow of things. Ridiculous, he told himself; all he intended to do was arrange how to meet Thelma; she was coming, that was decided, and he had to make arrangements whatever he was to tell her. But he would wait until he reached the Accademia, it was only a short walk along a wider, bar-lined calle.

Along the broad calle, voices, Italian and American, mixed discordantly over the tables outside the Bar da Gino; smells of fish and leather mixed with damp sand and plaster from work being carried out beneath the flagstones. At the end, a hardware shop with plastic watering cans led to the Accademia; discord and irony marked his arrival at the plastic hooded phones by the garishly and incongruously labelled 'W.C.' with sliding automatic doors. Was there, he asked himself, really no way to choose between one thing and another? He lifted the cold weight of the receiver and dialled as if moving through turgid water.

Familiar English ringing tones repeated hypnotically in his ear, directly and without reference to Venice. He might as well have been ringing from work. A burst of iced water froze his stomach as the rhythm was broken.

'Hello, Thelma Green.'

The voice was clear, there was no hint of the distance. It was he thought, ironically, digital technology at its best. This was a voice to which he felt an unpremeditated rush of warmth, a part of him that had found no place in his consciousness here and yet a voice that had been the background of his normal life for so long. The problem fell away.

'Hello, it's me. I was hoping I'd catch you.'

'Where have you been?'

The words hit David like an accusation and drove him back into himself.

'In Venice, we kept missing each other.'

'I phoned the hotel again, they said they didn't know where you were.'

'They must have missed me, I got back late.'

How many lies would he have to tell before he got back to where he started?

'I mean, I'm here getting ready to catch the flight tomorrow but with no idea of what's going on. You could at least have left a message.'

He had not been ready for this; he had thought it would be a simple matter of organising where to meet.

'I'm sorry I lost track of things, it's easy to do here.'

True but not true.

'Well what's happening? I got more sense out of the receptionist.'

Her voice was hard with a slight desperation that sent David's stomach into a knot. He thought of the red fingernails of the receptionist and heard the furies' avenging beat; finding his way back would not be easy.

'I've found the times of the boats at this end. They arrive at San Marco. I should think the one that connects with your plane arrives here at 12.40.'

There was a pause and a short Italian matron in a black dress arrived at the phone next to him breathing hard.

'I thought you were meeting me in the car.'

Coins fell in the next phone box and a loud and uninter- rupted flow of Italian began almost immediately. She had clearly got her breath back.

'I could but it would be better to meet in Venice. It's a long way round the lagoon.' He was finding it difficult to hear himself, let alone Thelma.

'I thought that was the point of taking the car.'

Things were getting unreasonable already. It was not going well.

'O.K., I'll bring the car if you'd rather but it's a long drive, the traffic will be bad and I thought a boat and then a drink in Venice would be better after the flight.'

'What about the luggage?'

'How much have you got? I thought I'd already brought most of it.'

'Oh, not much but it'll be a nuisance.'

'Well maybe we can put it in a locker or something.'

The stream of Italian was still battering his ear. There was a lot to be said for old fashioned phone boxes.

'How will we get to the hotel?'

Her voice had softened a little.

'It's easy, I can leave the car at Punta Sabbioni.'

The next phone had gone quiet and he turned just as the stream of Italian began again.

'You sound as if you're sharing the phone.'

In a sense he was. Francesca was there in the thoughts that accompanied his words, modifying them, checking them. He suddenly realised how hard he was gripping the receiver.

'All right,' she continued, 'Come to the airport on the

boat but don't expect me to walk much, a quick drink and then back to the hotel.'

That was not what he had in mind. He would have to leave early.

'I've got to get from the hotel, I thought I could meet you at San Marco.'

There was a cold pause, he felt her exasperation.

'If I can fly from England, I really don't see the problem.'

It was not a problem he could explain and he could offer no reasonable objections. It would at least be easier that driving.

'O.K., I'll be in the arrivals hall near the ticket office for the motoscafo.'

'Right.' Resignation, irritation and perhaps puzzlement were focused on the word. 'I'll see you tomorrow then.'

'O.K., about quarter to twelve.'

'Right, I'll see you.'

'Bye.'

The phone went dead. He had felt an unexpected flow of warmth on hearing her voice but none had returned. He felt cold and lost with no idea as to what to do next. Words echoed in his mind; whichever way he went was the same.

He sat on the Accademia steps. After the frenzied emotional heat of the last few days the cold emptiness threatened to take him over completely. His mind spread out as though boundless on a flat sheet of water; nothing held it together. His emotions sank through its surface like glowing embers after a fire, leaving black traces in his memory. His body felt limp as a ventriloquist's dummy, it seemed to have fallen out of reach of control; the links between mind and body were severed. There was no will nor anything to activate it: there was no reason for anything to ever happen again. He could not tell how long he stayed in this state.

Sensation returned to his body first: the cold discomfort of the steps, the warmth of the air as it touched his skin, soft gold of early evening sunlight on the creeper covered walls of the Caffé Belle Arte, voices from different distances and in different combinations, and the ever-changing splashing, smacking and churning of water.

Why did one have to want and to do? Why did one have to desire? Why, like a lazy animal, could one not just soak up the caressing sensations that wrapped around the body when the restless mind could be emptied?

He looked again at the profusion of creepers tumbling like a green waterfall over the wall by the café. Ivy or vine leaves they showed the natural life that flowed up and over dry walls: Dionysus redivivus. He would take wine in the café of Dionysus.

David sat on a high stool at the bar and ordered a jug of red wine. It arrived chilled and he sat and sipped at the glass. He had not eaten since the morning in the flat and the wine quickly took effect. The pressure to make urgent decisions became less sharp, he felt a sense of identity again; if the scattered, multi-layered jigsaw of his personality did not begin to come together then at least the edges of the pieces seemed less distinct. He poured a second glass and thought back: Francesca had made his lunch and last night he and Dionysus with Francesca the Bacchante had filled the world with passionate, sexual love. This afternoon he was a worthless shell incapable of decision or action; there was no fire, no dance, no music and no lightning blast: he had no vine leaves in his hair. Dionysus, twice-born god who brought both madness and inspiration, was displeased but how should he worship him? David smiled. He could walk through Venice with vine leaves in his hair. Once, certainly, he was a devoted follower, walking high on hills and abandoning everything at the touch of inspiration. That was the life he had searched for; that was what mattered then. ' Did he have vine leaves in his hair?' and he thought back to where he had heard that question asked, not Euripides but Ibsen. Did the death of the character he played then, a death without vine leaves, foreshadow his destiny?

It was not a play that anyone had thought suitable for seventeen year olds to perform. In the end, 'Hedda Gabler' was successful but, more important than its success in performance was the effect of the months of rehearsal on the small group who had worked on it. Every word, nuance, inflection had been studied, discussed, argued over. Whole days in the Easter holiday had been given over not to examination revision, but to intense rehearsal where more and more was revealed whilst they became aware of ever deeper layers of meaning yet to be found. After eight months of rehearsal they knew that Ibsen held still more. He felt the power of the inspired and creative Lövborg rise through him, the power that destroyed him, dismembered in a house of women. There were surely vine leaves for this son of Dionysus but no-one could see them. And what now? Even the dull Tesman in his old slippers followed his enthusiasm: 'the domestic crafts of Brabant in the middle ages', pedantic but his own. It seemed unlikely that Thelma would follow Hedda's example and shoot herself even if she had destroyed, his renewed creative inspiration, his reborn self, burned his and Francesca's child. He had felt himself close to being reborn from the fire, crowned with vine leaves, rising again from the dry and scattered ashes but Francesca was the only one who could help him, and she had left. He felt her body close to his, but she would have to return before they could pass through fire and water.

Exasperation shook him from his reverie. There he went again, searching for meaning, looking for significance. The truth, the ironic truth he told himself with a grimace, was in the wine and not in his rambling mythologies. He tipped the jug but it was finished and he thought about ordering a grappa. He felt in his pocket where he had pushed the change from the wine. With the assorted notes and coins, he pulled out a card: 'Enzo Bennato, Scultore e Architetto'. He could just read address and phone number beneath a wine stain. Francesca had said that she sometimes turned to Enzo for advice, perhaps she would have gone there.

It was, he knew, a foolish idea that rose unbidden. If she had wanted to be with him she would not have left; turning up, unwanted, would achieve nothing. He watched cynically as his thoughts told him he was just curious to know where the address was and where so large a personality as Enzo lived. They were thoughts that paraded their disinterest as a veil for the driving and irrational desire beneath.

He got up and left the bar. A warm haze settled on the scene before the Accademia: it was produced by more than the evening light. An easy solution, he told himself, that not only blurred the previously pressing problems but made him feel altogether more accepting; an easy, enjoyable though perhaps dangerous solution. Why should wine be able to change such important matters? But, on the other hand, who was to say that this state of consciousness, where things seemed so much more in perspective, was inferior to the former where he was paralysed into inaction and seemed to be without identity.

There was a large, framed tourist map by the busy stop for the water bus and he went over to it. He took out Enzo's card again and turned it over; on the back was a brief sketch map showing that the Rio Terra where the studio was, adjoined the Fondamenta del Frari. He checked the map and found the Campo dei Frari. He could, he thought, walk round that way; he could come back via the Rialto. It would be a last walk on his own around Venice; the next would be with Thelma. That was justification enough. Even the wine did not allow him to be unaware of the other possibilities of this walk or the probability that he might attempt to take one of them.

He went back to the Café and along by its side through the high curved-roofed arch. He found himself following a girl with long, curled dark hair and he watched with contentment as she walked smoothly and rhythmically in her short, cotton dress. This was much better, and all at the prompting of Dionysus and his veil of vine leaves. In vine leaves is the preservation of the world. What was the original of that? He thought and saw the cover picture and heard Miranda's voice. It was not vine leaves, but 'wildness' and it formed the title of a book of quotations from Thoreau that Miranda had given him at Christmas, his mother's last. She had prefaced it with some lines of her own when he was desperately seeking something that would point to life continuing, something about a flight of swans: how she had understood him and how much he had failed to realise her understanding. He felt his chest and stomach twist and tighten as he sensed the gulf that had opened between that understanding and his present isolation. She had loved him, and he had walked away. He had a remorseless drive to create for himself a deepening pit of loss. What was it that created such a force for self-destruction?

In this calle, on the walls in place of leaves, was a chaotic montage of posters, their corners curling, their exhibitions

and concerts past. The images were split and scattered.
Beneath the posters was spray-canned large and with
bravura, 'FASCI AL MURO'.

Split and scattered, another chaotic montage rendered
dangerous by swirling currents of emotion swam behind his
eyes until he could smell her skin and feel the salt tears on
his face. The wine blurred the images and curled the edges
of pain but left him vulnerable to the wash of feeling as they
passed.

He crossed the Rio de San Trovaso with its walled
garden and moorish windows. Somewhere here, Ezra Pound
had lived and created vast tracts of fragmented images in his
Cantos. The line about sitting on the Dogana's steps
remained in his head; then something about the cost of
gondolas and the face of one girl who stood out from all the
others.

Who were they, and which was the one? You could go
mad trying to record every image of your past, of the world's
history, every image, from every language until your mind
and memory were empty: perhaps that was what had
happened to Pound. But what happened if you did not
record them but simply let them rise up in such a whirlwind
that the sky turned black and all else disappeared from
sight? You went mad just the same but left no record. It was
as simple as that.

He walked faster to leave behind the whirlwind of
images and turned the corner to the walled Rio della
Toletta. It was a corner seemingly cut off, more cared for, a
tiny village. A cast iron pump spouted a wavering stream of
water. The canal turned a right angle widening at the
corner, creating a pool where a shoal of fish moved beneath
the green surface. The water threw patterns of moving light
high onto the walls above the Fondamenta del Squero,

dancing under the tidy window boxes. A small peaceful island.

He stood still to take it in and watched a cat walk with relaxed ease along the wall. This felt like home, a place he could stay. The cat dropped casually onto the steps that led into the canal and then strolled slowly, but in perfect rhythm, in front of him before disappearing through the bars of a wrought iron gate. He followed the cat and looked through into a large scented garden. He breathed deeply. What images of Francesca would float through scented gardens to torment him if he left without her, if he returned to his former life, denying the life force he felt driving him within? But what images of his former, ordered life would float, veiled in warm nostalgia if he left it and then lost Francesca? What decisions could he make to escape this life of self-recriminations. He was tied by the scented silk of future memory into inaction in the present.

The iron gate dug into his hands. Insufferable! He would break through, say 'yes' to life; he would risk this tyranny of fear, this terror of creating a past to torture him. He would not let the prospect of future ideas, that might hold the power to grip his chest, prevent him from breaking down the barriers to himself. That was what he was here for, and that was what he would do.

Beneath this increasing certainty he tried to ignore the growing realisation that without the urge to create a better past he was removing his only means of decision making. Without it, there was only chance or an uncritical acceptance of desire, abandonment to the unknown potency of the powers that lurked in unseen depths, monsters of unrestrained passion. He felt the blood and cold sea run: the rush of ardent tides and the wild plunge of whales and squalling gulls; a wild, blind and hectic journey dragged through the teeming unknown seas. From the beach and the market and from Laugharne returned the Long Legged Bait. Meaning by association with past layers of memory real and fantasised; the creation of meaning, or the illusion of meaning.

Reluctantly, and nervously, he left the scented garden and the quiet of the Rio della Toletta to walk through a soto-porteggio surmounted by high twisted chimneys. He emerged into the wide open Campo Santa Barnaba that murmured with white, umbrella shaded tables and over which hung the smell of coffee. The canal that ran along the other side of the square was wide and a barge piled with fruit lay moored to the left. He knew he had to go straight on but not by which bridge. He took the right hand one but paused again on top of the bridge, unsure. As he stood there, he watched a gondolier helping a couple from his gondola. The girl wore a pure white trouser suit with large quantities of gold jewellery and had the perfectly prepared beauty of a magazine cover; the man wore an untidy pair of shorts and ill-fitting shirt. David watched the gondolier turn to another and laugh and talk as they watched until the couple had disappeared from the square. David felt uncomfortable and thought of the borrowed shirt at the hotel and the increasingly crumpled one he wore now. He felt like an isolated and ill-fitting observer in a dream, there because he had dreamt it but otherwise not belonging.

A faint smell caught David's attention and he saw an image of Angelo's flat. He was coming down the stairs with Francesca and out onto the square that morning. He turned, and in the shade saw a shop window full of carnival masks. The smell was of glue and varnish: the glue that had made him think of spirit gum and theatrical disguise. He walked down to the shop and was stopped by momentary fear in the shaded calle next to it. A unicorn headed figure stood, its white cloak slowly moving in the light breeze; the unicorn in the field, the stag's horn ring. Even when he realised that it was a model it retained an eerie sense of life. He went quickly past.

He was less sure now that he was going the right way and particularly why he was going to Enzo's at all. The image of Francesca stayed with him since being conjured by the incense that rose from the mask shop. He pressed on into the Campiello dei Squellini with its running water and patched bark trees like London planes and then on past the University bookshop and building.

Through the calle, between close walls, on the left in a grey square hung with washing, stalked a large white cat, a dead rat in its mouth: dead for a ducat. It looked round furtively lest anyone should take it. It might be a dead rat, but it was his dead rat, and no-one was going to take it away. On the corner was a bar with a sign that announced Beck's beer and a Happy hour. From its windows pounded over and over again, 'It's my life and I'll do what I want!'. Two Americans in suits, with the jackets slung over their shoulders, walked purposefully past, one saying loudly to the other, ' No, no, he's a corporate man.'

David watched himself searching these random events for signs like an augur studying the flight of birds or the entrails of a goat. He sought desperately to find meaning in the way they fell and meaning obligingly appeared. It was self-contradictory, like horoscopes in different magazines. The dead rat was his present life that he hung onto even though he despised it; pop music recalled the self determination of his teenage life; the Americans had seen that he had merged into undifferentiated greyness. Was this meaning or illusion? Was he gaining insight into himself by the way he experienced the mirror image reflected back to him or was he merely being tossed by ill-assorted images and meaningless ideas?

Bells began ringing as he emerged from behind the Scuola di San Rocco and he viewed with ironic despair the pleasure he felt at this announcement of his arrival at the Campo dei Frari. There were dark shadows now and checking his watch he saw that it was six o' clock. Even this usually busy square was empty except for one briskly walking man in a shiny, well cut suit and carrying a brief-case. His footsteps echoed against the walls.

It was close now. He checked the card. Across the campo and over the Rio del Frari. He felt a constriction of the stom-ach, nerves, butterflies, as though his body anticipated more than his intended look at the exterior of Enzo's studio. There was an excitement in his body totally out of keeping with the fact that everything was finished. He was meeting Thelma tomorrow, there was no going back, her arrival was confirmed by phone. There was no scope, no time left for anything other than a last look round and a consigning of all that had happened to the hidden transformations of memory. His body, and the emotions taking it over, were locked into another possibility, a rejected future, a reality not chosen.

He crossed the bridge. The cooler air held the smell of water and he breathed deeply, spinning his emotions on the scented flow. Deeper than the inhalation were sunken memories: water, salt, mud and a faint smell like cockles in the mud flats where he had found seaweed and crab presents for his mother. The castle and the creek, water and stone: like Venice.

Closer, and he felt the blood begin to blur his mind: he must walk on, walk past. It was down the Rio Terra near the end and then he must turn right, away and on to the Rialto leaving everything, returning to the familiar.

On the left of the Rio Terra was a covered fondamenta, out of place where there was no water. Above, on the corner, a Virgin and Child crowned with a canopy of sky and stars; beneath her heel was an infant devil, red as clay. The child looked down, away from the breast, aware that his mother had conquered evil: gentle child of gentle mother.

Now was the moment when he had to decide. A last walk around Venice, bringing this intense and turbulent week to a close or to embark upon another unknown phase. The way up and the way down ….; this would not do, there must be something more than chance. If he walked away, the forces that rose and fell, that overwhelmed and spewed him out, would fade; he would be back in control of the little that was left. If he started another phase, he was at the mercy of chance or fate and the emotions and consequences that they unleashed. There was a natural hiatus, a node, a turning point between two sets of yet unmade future paths. Only one could be formed, not just for himself but for all those who would be touched by the unforeseeable chains of possibility that would grow from his turning to the left or to the right.

He could flip a coin, he could let the shift of balance from one foot to the other decide, he could choose the direction of the next gondola to travel past the narrow outlet onto the Grand Canal. What he could not do was make a rational informed decision since he was choosing between two futures, both of which were unknown.

Not quite true. The one seemed a little more known than the other, its possibilities a little more predictable because more limited. He could trace the possible moves which, as in a game of chess, were not certain but at least probable and by tracing them gained a certain degree of control. The balance shifted towards that more predictable path, he needed to exert some measure of control again, he would take that one.

He turned to the right, away from the looming presence of the building that held an unknown future and down the narrow calle by a little alimentare.

The plaster crumbled around iron gratings; darkness imprisoned him. Footsteps echoed from directions that could not be discerned; he slowed to listen and then halted. Footsteps passed across the end of the calle, going in both directions, momentarily identifiable and then amplified again into a still sphere of sound. Meaning, direction, the existence of a future appeared to have passed away, leaving him in a hollow chamber of death. The twittering sounds of souls in the dark eternity of Hades whispered on every side. Whether this dark and echoing prison was the creation of a fervid and hypersensitive imagination or the apprehension of a deeper level of reality was not relevant; it was a firm sign that he had gone the wrong way, departed from the script, and it was clear that he had to go back.

He turned in the emptiness that blocked that path of the maze. On the way in he had seen only the forbidding iron grills; now he noticed shop windows. Before him were wooden model boats backed by photographs that showed them to be traditional Venetian craft floating forward on the still mirror of the lagoon. Again, meaning from random events. He took their floating forward to be confirmation of his decision. Back again, at the Rio Terra, it seemed that there had been no decision to make, no alternative to this, the inevitable. But, there was more and he could not leave it yet.

He checked Enzo's card. The dark doorway gave little

impression of being used apart from the faded name plates by the entryphone. Dust half covered the names, but it was clear enough which was his. He pushed the button by its side and waited.

Having come by so tortuous a route to this point, it would be a bitter irony for there to be no reply. David's stomach tensed at the thought. The silence lengthened and he began to run through a new list of possibilities, alternative inevitabilities, and to console himself with the thought that a reply could have been the start of a disastrous series of uncontrollable events. An explosive crackling in the rusted grill beneath the names broke him from his thoughts. The voice, a broken parody of Enzo's, was incomprehensible to David.

'Hello, it's David Green, Francesca's friend. We met at the party.'

There was a pause and then the voice crackled again before the door buzzed. He pushed it open and was faced with a dark, musty smelling staircase. He looked around for a light switch but before he found one a light glowed from somewhere above the stairs. With as much foreboding as expectation he began to climb.

He did not have to climb far. He turned on the first landing and saw Enzo standing against an open door above him. The first thing that David noticed was that Enzo's hands were covered in a white substance that he quickly decided must be plaster of Paris. He had arrived unannounced; it looked as though it might be an inconvenient time and he began to prepare an appropriate apology.

'David, come up.'

If it was not convenient Enzo was not giving any sign of it.

'I will not shake hands, you see, I am working.' and he waved his plaster covered hands at David.

'I should have phoned, I'm sorry, I was passing and recognised the address.'

'There is no problem, come in.' Enzo indicated the door and ushered him through it.

Like Angelo and Elena's flat, it was also a studio and lighter and more modern inside than the exterior suggested. This, however, gave the impression of being mainly a working studio where Enzo also happened to live rather than the other way round. There was a protective sheet over the centre of the floor daubed with white and in its centre a table with a plaster covered figure of a rearing horse flailing at the air with its front hooves. A rough form that David could not make out lay under it. Around the room were busts and figures, some draped with material. On the walls were oils painted with broad strong strokes of colour. Some conveyed a sense of Venice but there were others that were clearly inspired by the hills and hill villages of Tuscany and Umbria. Enzo reached for a cloth and began wiping his hands. In his old cords and shirt with the sleeves rolled, he looked older than he had when dressed for the party but the energy that radiated from him was the same. David still felt awkward about interrupting.

'I don't want to stop you working.'

'Maybe I work later, maybe I don't. Later I decide. Now I need a coffee. We will go to the kitchen.'

In contrast to the studio, the kitchen was clean and tidy with everything in its place. Enzo appeared to be alone: no sign of either Francesca or anyone else to share the flat. At the realisation that Francesca was not there, David felt both the tension and expectancy fade. This was not, after all, a dangerous road to have taken, an alternative to a return to the life he had come here to escape, the life that had come to seem a predictable and comfortable option. Enzo ground the dark Italian coffee beans and released their heavily roasted aroma; he put the jug under the filter. He seemed to be concentrating more than was strictly necessary on doing something that he had done so many times before. Perhaps, thought David, it was the same quality of attention that he remembered seeing him give to smoking. They spoke fitfully and inconsequentially whilst Enzo finished making the coffee. When it was ready, he gave a tin of biscuits from one of the cupboards to David and gestured him through into a small sitting room. He set the coffee on a long, low antique table and turned to the hi-fi system.

The two large armchairs were of soft, modern leather. The seat of one was heavily indented and the arms worn so David, assuming this to be Enzo's, sat in the other. A quiet thread of melody, played on saxophone, wound its way from the speakers. Enzo took a box of small cigars from the shelf and sat down. David sipped at the hot strong coffee whilst Enzo lit a cigar. There was a long pause as Enzo drew in the smoke and then watched its slow circling ascent to the ceiling. David felt that Enzo was waiting for him to speak but he could think of nothing that justified breaking the intense attention being paid to the smoke or, indeed, his being there at all. After several more wreaths of smoke had ascended, it was Enzo who spoke.

'You have had a bad day, yes?'

Did it show on his face? Had Enzo deduced it from the fact that he was a day early, or more significantly perhaps, that he was on his own?

'A difficult day, I think would be the best way to put it.'

The piercing blue eyes followed another plume of smoke upwards.

'And tomorrow your quest will be over.'

David tried hard to remember what he had told Enzo that morning, but it was blurred apart from the fact that he had spoken about his father. He could not remember mentioning Thelma.

'This stage of it anyway.'

Another pause whilst the smoke rose, and the notes of the saxophone circled around it.

'What stage is that?'

Things were rapidly becoming difficult, what stage indeed? There was no point in the conversation, or his presence there at all if he did not at least try to be truthful.

'A natural pause somewhere along the way. I suppose I can't be more precise.'

Enzo said nothing but continued to listen, encouraging David to continue. He overcame his reluctance by telling himself that Enzo was after all an artist and could be expected to understand.

'I have travelled a long way into my past and,' David searched for a way to say it, 'imagination; that is the images, stories that are wrapped up in the past.' He stopped, fearing that he was making little sense even though Enzo's understanding of English seemed better than his rather stilted speech would suggest. Enzo looked upwards, perhaps for the words.

'I would say mythology, the mythology of your past. Yes, I understand. These are the stories we use for sculpture, for painting, for writing and for music. Sometimes, how is it in English, the audience, in the audience it meets another mythology, sometimes not. If not, we hope there is enough for understanding, yes?'

Where this was leading David was unclear, but Enzo's words awakened an awareness that the emergent images he had disturbed and travelled amongst had not been treated with sufficient interest or respect. He had treated them as forces that enslaved him, forces to be exorcised but Enzo described them as the raw material of art, the clues to understanding. This was hardly a new idea, but he had certainly not acted on it, except, perhaps, in the brief moments that had led to poems. He said as much to Enzo who listened with an intensity that drew the thoughts from him and whose interjections demonstrated an encyclopaedic knowledge of mythology.

The conversation reached a natural pause and David felt at once calmer and more energetic. Enzo left the room to fetch wine and David settled back into the chair. This had been the right choice, it was ending the week on a positive note, free from the tension and turmoil that faced him with Francesca. At her name, even though it had only run silently through his mind he felt his heart and stomach respond; her perfume faintly appeared inside his nostrils, he heard her voice and saw the liquid brown eyes that she shared with the Byzantine Madonna. He was suddenly gripped by a longing so intense that it felt like fear but as he opened his eyes again, he was determined to let it go. He was meeting Thelma tomorrow. Francesca had enabled him to break through the hardened shell that kept him from himself but now he was returning to his wife and Francesca, would, he felt sure, return to Renato. Renato would, of course, have everything: Francesca, his wife and family, his high-powered job and the freedom to enjoy all that Italy offered. David felt his face pull into an ironic grimace; jealousy was an emotional complication he could do without.

Enzo's voice, very quietly in the background, broke him from his thoughts. He could not hear any words as they were spoken quickly in another room; perhaps another visitor had arrived. Then David thought he heard the sound of a phone receiver being replaced and decided that, if anyone had arrived, Enzo would have greeted them far more loudly than that faint and rushed conversation.

The door opened and Enzo returned with an open bottle and two glasses. He had removed the plaster from his hands and changed into a clean shirt, and trousers. There was nobody else. The phone call was not mentioned, and Enzo moved the conversation to his own past. He talked about his childhood and the vineyard, his father and the close relationship they had shared when he was very young and the way they had drifted apart later until they could barely communicate, only growing closer again as his father reached old age. He talked about playing jazz in Hamburg, Paris and Amsterdam and situations, amusing and often dangerous, that he had found himself in. When he got up to show David around the studio and talk about his work, David felt a renewed sense of dissatisfaction with his own life, the life to which he was about to return. Was this intentional on Enzo's part? Was this a calculated, if friendly, way of letting David see that life could be more and that if he tried to be content with less the problems would just resurface, probably more violently than before?

When the bottle was empty, Enzo set it down on a plinth.

'Come, we will go and eat. You are hungry and I am very hungry.' As he said this he laughed and slapped his stomach theatrically. David was indeed hungry and, having had no food since the early lunch that Francesca had prepared for him, the wine was again beginning to blur his thoughts and feelings. Once more the energy of vine leaves returned and his former passivity and indecision seemed alien, the concerns of another. Perhaps the phone call had been a restaurant booking: he could get a late boat; the hotel would have been depressing that evening; Enzo's energy and unfettered life were good for his own enthusiasm; all in all, there was little to be said against it.

As they moved to go, David paused by the unfinished sculpture of the horse and tried to make out the figure beneath it. Probably human and possibly female but Enzo showed no inclination to enlighten him and held the door open encouraging him to leave.

19

THE FIFTH DAY - PART FOUR

The entrance to the trattoria was low and arched, appearing even lower before they descended the steps at the end of a small bridge. The archway was dark with just the hint of two flickering lights. David felt himself to be entering a riverside burrow. On entering, the darkness lifted in pools around small lamps on dark wood tables. The rich smell of frying fish turned David's hunger into an ache in his stomach. He realised how long it was since he had eaten a proper meal. Enzo spoke to the waiter and appeared to have a table booked so the mystery of the telephone call seemed solved. They were shown to a table at the back of the restaurant where David faced away from the entrance and the darkness served to make the lamplight all the more intense. They inspected the menus. Enzo studied his briefly and then said,

'You understand eh? Here is soup and the fish and the meat. If you want to know you ask, yes?'

Enzo waived the waiter over and ordered wine while they went through the menu. Every item David asked about was described in sensual detail and with passionate enthusiasm. Enzo particularly recommended the black risotto of squid cooked in ink and David was persuaded to follow him in this choice of starter.

The wine arrived early, strong thick, white and buttery but with a sharp edge. The food took much longer and, by the time they began to eat, the first bottle was nearly empty. David felt a vague disorientation, a contentment and total lack of interest in any future crisis that might, or might not, be waiting for him. The rich dark risotto warmed him further, deep inside, and he commented on its restorative effect to Enzo who chuckled deeply and chewed a piece of squid before replying.

'The mind, it is a cold place to be lost. You must have the senses, they make it warm, they are what makes life. You go mad if you leave them too long.'

David nodded: thoughts, ideas, memories trickling into his mind.

'When I was fifteen, sixteen, after that too, I made a religion of the senses. Intense sensual experience: sunsets, woods at night, hills in strong winds, the sea crashing and of course, love and sex. It all seemed the substance of the soul, the breath that filled the being.'

Enzo did not answer but paused to drink the last of the wine and called the waiter to order another bottle. At last he turned back to David as if having finally thought through what he had said.

'So, you know all that. You come to Venice where everything is intense, that is right, that is good. But how many years have you forgotten? They go past, you miss them, you don't feel them. You think, you worry, you are in the future, the past, never living and then they are gone, gone as minutes not years. That is right yes?'

It was very right, and David said so. Enzo continued:

'Then what you have felt, experienced, all your stories inside, your mythologies: it all begins to go bad. There is no new breath, nothing to keep it alive and it, ah how is it, it is like the dead body decaying inside you and it makes you ill.'

As though he were responding inside to what he instinctively felt to be true, David experienced the room with a new intensity. His nose savoured the complex mixture of smells, of foods, of drink, of bodies and perfume, cigars and faint indeterminate background smells dissolved in the air. His ears, his head, filled with a single compound sound like a huge orchestra tuning up, voices, plates, cutlery, boats from the canal outside. He was aware of the feel of the wooden chair, his clothes on his skin, and in his mouth the food. Patterns of dark and light, heavy tapestries of deep colour shone in his eyes. He grew bigger as though the world were filling him.

He was disturbed by the waiter setting another bottle of wine on the table, a rich dark red that reflected the gold of the lamps. Red and gold like the sanctuary lamp. Enzo was right, that moment was longer and more complete than many weeks that he had passed in recent years. He drank from the new wine and experienced it with senses heightened by the last few minutes. But where did it leave him? He knew all this even if he had lost sight of it for years at a time, but how could he use it to make his life new?

'You are right, of course. I know, but then it's gone again and it's months or years before I wake up again.'

'How we live, it is a habit; a strong habit, like a drug. You cannot just say I will be different. You come here, you make it different and things happen. Often it hurts more because you feel the pain. You go back to your old life and you go back to how you were. You scratch the hurt, no, la ferita, the wound, that is all.' Enzo leaned back and threw his arms wide to say in a loud voice, 'You must kick the habit.'

And he laughed his deep chuckling laugh as David looked around embarrassed at what he felt the people at the other tables must be thinking. Enzo drew his attention back by raising his glass and encouraging David to do the same.

'To a new life, La Vita Nuova. Yes, Dante, you know it eh? Then to Beatrice, whatever name she is called by.' And they drank deeply.

This was the same image that had risen to David's mind several times in the past week and Beatrice was of course, had been, Francesca. Francesca, the embodiment of Venice, she had given all experience the intensity of his youth; but no more and tomorrow Thelma would arrive.

His private thought emerged as a spoken question before he could stop it.

'Can you really find salvation, life, art, through an adulterous affair?'

'Salvation? Maybe I don't know about that. Art though, that comes from the senses and the stronger the experience the deeper the art. You find the world through imagination and only il fuoco, the fire, the flame, the hot senses will get you there. David, my friend, you make a wall to protect yourself from your memories and from the world too, I think. Then you find you have lost your life as well.' He paused, 'If you try to save your life, you lose it. Maybe there is some salvation there.'

The dry wall, the crumbling but obdurate wall, the life staring through the teeth of a skull: images from the past when he was more conscious of the enemy of life, the past before he lost the battle.

High on the Malvern hills at night the wind drove over him as a raging tide. In the darkness below, the lights were smeared as if by sea-bed mud. He was high, exalted on the flood: to walk on hills is to stride with giants. He knew, even then that the life of giants was always under attack; always being sought out by a force that seeks to make all things small. That was when the image of the skull and the dry wall became embedded in his mythology, real and forceful in a way that was only intimated now. There was a tree, an old thorn, that stood alone on the hillside. He knew then that life was threatened because that tree was his and he felt that he was the tree: the tree on the mountainside shaken and tormented by invisible hands but always searching, ever higher, through images, at a veiled truth.

The trattoria was busy and there was still no sign of the next course arriving. Enzo glanced briefly at his watch and David wondered if he had another engagement later. He filled his glass and then became aware of Enzo looking over his shoulder. Enzo stood and raised the hand that held the glass. David looked over his shoulder and felt a violent sinking and tightening of his stomach accompanied by a pounding of blood in his head. Walking hesitantly towards them was the figure of Francesca. As he caught her eye she looked down and then towards Enzo. David realised then that there had been more to the phone call than a simple restaurant booking.

Enzo moved from the table to meet her. He wrapped an arm around her and gesticulated to a waiter with the other. Francesca's energy usually lit up the room but now it was dimmed, quietened and questioning.

The waiter slid between the tables and brought another chair, holding it for Francesca. As she sat down, her glance moved to David for the first time. Their eyes met, resting briefly, but the dark warmth, the openness was clouded and distant. He felt the need to reach out and touch her, but his hand stayed as if clamped to the table.

Enzo broke the spell by reaching out to the next table for a wine glass and filling it for Francesca. He raised his glass in a theatrical gesture that brought David's and Francesca's up too.

'Salute!'

And they repeated, more quietly,

'Salute.'

As she took the glass from her lips, Francesca smiled for the first time: diffidently to David and then more openly to Enzo. Her hand went out and rested on Enzo's before she looked back to David.

'You see? I said he was a good friend. Maybe sometimes a bully but if I do as he says then he looks after me.'

David felt a stab of jealousy at the closeness of their relationship. He had not realised it before, even though the signs had been there. He was watching for an indication of what lay behind her presence. Was it a move by Enzo to make sure that things ended cleanly and openly or the result of some new decision on Francesca's part? For the moment, David felt Enzo to be in control, setting the scene and ruling the actors. He had picked up the broken threads of their divided stories and would, at least for the present, weave them into patterns of his choosing: a Prospero with cloak and book who cast the spells of the island and ruled the relationships of its inhabitants and visitors.

His thoughts were interrupted by the waiter returning to set a place for Francesca and to take her order. When he left, there was a deepening silence between them, a need to speak and yet an acknowledgement that it was not the right time. Enzo seemed content to drink and survey the room, leaving them to find a natural cadence from which to begin again. At length the silence grew shallower and it was Francesca who broke it first:

'You have seen some of Enzo's work now?'

It was a non-committal opening, an avoidance of all that had led to their being there; she was right though, it was better to establish the relationship again than to land the most pertinent thoughts before their time.

'Yes, I'm afraid I interrupted work in progress.'

His words sounded strange and he tried to counter their irrelevance with his eyes. Francesca shifted her gaze to Enzo and asked,

'How is she coming on?'

Enzo began to answer in Italian but stopped himself.

'We will work more tomorrow.'

Enzo's eyes left Francesca's and met David's. They were even more intense in the candlelight.

'Francesca is my model.' He paused, 'For the woman with the horse.'

The horse rearing above a female form appeared in David's mind, large, animated, no longer plaster. It was finished, muscular, rearing and with a head and neck that spoke of fire and force. The female form was still too indistinct to convey its emotion or relationship with the horse. That would come later, moulded from white earth and drawn from Enzo's mind around Francesca's body.

'You see,' said Enzo, 'You find the meaning through the form and then the fire in the senses makes fire in the stone. You sit and think, and you make nothing.' Enzo leaned forward in a dramatic gesture, 'And then, my friend, you become nothing.'

As he said 'nothing' Enzo snapped his fingers and David felt the snap inside himself. He had grown thin, invisible, mist-like as he had retreated leaving a pale phantom to manage his everyday life. Just the thought, the realisation, made him feel excited at the prospect of reversing things. He raised his glass to Enzo.

'Then I must learn to kick the habit!'

Enzo's actor's voice rose through a laugh to an exultant 'Si, Si' that hit the other side of the restaurant. He lifted his glass.

'We drink to that, both my friends!' He looked around and still in a loud voice said, 'and maybe we eat!'

At which he waved and shouted at a waiter in Italian of such rapidity that David could catch nothing at all, but Francesca laughed and lifted her glass as well.

Francesca was still unusually quiet and far from her normal self. Despite Enzo's efforts to maintain conversation it was a relief to David, and visibly to Francesca, when the food arrived along with another bottle of the same excellent red wine. David and Enzo were both eating lamb with anchovies in a wine sauce and Francesca who had said she was not hungry had ordered pan fried scallops. They shared a huge bowl of mixed salad in the centre of the table and conversation centred around the food, the wine, and the merits of Italian food and wine in general. Enzo told them stories about life as a boy growing up in a vineyard, particularly when the grapes were picked, and the scents and juices flowed from the fruit and stained the pickers as the fruit was tumbled from great baskets into vats for crushing underfoot. He described in sensual detail the meals outside at long tables with the helpers who had come in for the harvest and the music and dancing that followed. For David it was a return to the dream of the south he had allowed himself on Murano, a great flowing beakerful of warm sensation. Throughout, for David there was the strange feeling of sitting so close to Francesca, laughing and sharing stories and yet not speaking of their own story, of what had happened and what might still be to happen between them.

Without thinking he checked his watch. It was a little after nine, he would be meeting Thelma at a quarter to twelve tomorrow, that meant he had less than fifteen hours left: fifteen hours to find out what had led Francesca to come to the restaurant and whether there might be anything beyond it; fifteen hours in which to make sense of the intense and varied experiences of the last five days; fifteen hours to distance himself far enough from the drug of old habits to have a sporting chance of staying off it for good.

As they finished with rich espresso coffee laced with grappa, David felt the strength of the bond that had developed between them. Francesca's warmth and even effervescence had returned. In spite of not having spoken directly about it, David felt that the barrier that had existed when she arrived was ready to dissolve. Enzo signalled the waiter and paid the bill, refusing all offers from David and Francesca to contribute.

He got up and as David and Francesca rose with him, he told them to sit again and 'Finish the wine'. He embraced Francesca and clasped David's hand.

'Remember, the mind, it is a cold place, live and keep warm.'

He left and David feared a shadow descending but, as they sat, the warm openness in Francesca's face told him that whatever was to happen their closeness would remain. Despite the closeness there was a silence. They each looked at the surface of the wine in their partly emptied glasses. Deep as a dark sea or the obsidian of a magic mirror. At last it was Francesca who spoke, without looking up.

'I am becoming predictable in my disappearing.'

'I suppose there's something very Venetian about that.'

'Shadows and reflections, like the wine in the glass.'

'Passing shapes between walls and over bridges.'

And he remembered the headlong chase after Eva that led him breathless to the deserted corte. 'Thoughts, decisions,' he continued, 'as insubstantial and changeable as light on the canal.'

'Voices whispering, echoes, sighs.'

'The isle is full of noises.'

'Sorry?'

'Oh, just something Enzo made me think of: a magician on an island.'

There was a pause, her eyes stayed on him not, as so often, dropping to her hands, and then a smile.

'Yes, sometimes the magician and sometimes the,' she hesitated, 'the one who does tricks on the stage, you know?'

David nodded, 'But which is which?'

'Exactly.'

Her eyes were still on him and threatened to empty his mind of all else as they drew him in. He had to break through the remaining shell, to return to their previous closeness.

'And so, the magician's assistant has reappeared!'

She held out her hands, 'Ecco!'

They laughed, and in their laughing came back the beach, the party, the good times.

Francesca looked round the room, noisy with voices and heavy with the smell of food, and then back at David, 'I should like some ice-cream, I think.'

She too shared the memory of the ice-cream on the beach and the moment that he lost when he should have kissed her returned. Ice-cream, symbol of trivial, sensual enjoyment: what transformations they had both moved through since she was the ice-cream girl? His hand went out to hers and closed, his fingers in her palm. With the other hand he gestured to the waiter.

The ice cream and sorbet were piled high in glass bowls. Sauce ran like melting glaciers down the gullies in its surface. They laughed and talked without referring to the next day's inevitable crisis that Francesca had sought to avoid by her disappearance. In the darkness behind her, David saw the shape of a magician's cape. Enzo's words filtered into the gaps in David's thoughts:

'You must have the senses to warm the mind, to keep the mythology alive; break free from the habitual that robs you of your life; live your life, don't bury it away for safety or it will be lost.'

To go back to his old, habitual way of life, that would be death in life, he must make it new or everything would be in vain. He must not try to protect himself because then he shut out life. He would, he vowed, live again.

They left the trattoria and walked, their bodies close; her hair brushed his face, weaving its scent into his breath. It was comfort against the night, the darkness, a lighted candle that showed the way. There was more, however, a blackened void within him whose reality he had begun to discover by her aid and inspiration, but which had still to give up its secrets. This was the most difficult and dangerous journey of all, she was a precious light but only he could find the way and only by not looking back.

The darkness of a light flecked canal ran beneath them as they crossed the small, arching bridge. He held her still and looked down. Images remembered, revisited his mind bringing their train of emotion with them: dark fountains pouring their water into bowls before the rose garden; the tinkling of silver bells, Jane; the moon and the light from the cottage window; a whirl of fish and the shattering of silver scales like a burst of stars. Over the dome of the sky, tears fell from the eye of the golden Madonna, she looked down on his tattered broken body; candles glowed around the coffin, and then sprang up like a host of white robed angels in the Salute, bursting through the darkness. Somewhere in the darkness of the water, in the darkness within, was the being that had set out on life, safe in the knowledge of his mother's love. This was a search not just for a week in Venice where he had lit a small candle but for an unknown time during which he must not look back. He must find the strength to go on now she, Francesca, his mother, Madonna, had shown the way. Tomorrow he must be true to all that had happened since his arrival in Venice and not betray the secrets she had unlocked. With or without Francesca he must go on, that is what she had meant by her disappearance, to tell him that without her or with her he must not give up: that was what he must be faithful to now. Enzo had brought her back to help him again: brought him Beatrice to give him faith in La Vita Nuova.

The hard marble hurt their sides as they turned, and their lips pressed together hard for comfort in the pain. Desperation, determination to find a way forward, they clung together; Francesca too, she had her own mount of Purgatory to climb and an unknown future. Now, they were together and must help each other forward wherever it would lead and whether, beyond tomorrow, they would see each other again or not.

He shivered at the thought of how the life that had centred around Thelma would fall and disintegrate like autumn leaves. He would be left naked and without support but without that going forward his life was over, and it would be the right time only to die.

Francesca's body pressed warm into his, her face buried in his neck. The hot night wet their clothes and joined them, a desperate comfort before the void, an attempt to transcend death by overcoming their own duality.

'Can we be together tonight?'

She looked up and nodded as though frightened to voice a necessity that lay deep in silence. Her arm went tightly round him, and they walked into the pillared darkness ahead. In the darkness, where fate could not see, she whispered, 'At Enzo's, he will not be there tonight, but he gave me the key.'

In the darkness, as they walked under the sotoportico, David thought he felt a cloak turn and whirl the air. It was inevitable, the elements on the table, the force in the hollow wand, destiny or fate, choice or the magician's will. Was there a difference? Why would he fight it when it was the only way forward?

They emerged from the narrow calle that had seemed to end in death when he had wavered and walked away from Enzo's studio. He recalled the emptiness, the echoing darkness he had felt inside himself as he had walked down it, the feeling that he was avoiding his true path, fleeing into Hades. He must read it so, whether he was interpreting his own sub-conscious or signs of an external plan did not matter since they said the same.

Francesca turned the key and let them in. They climbed the stairs in darkness; another key and they were in the studio. She switched on a table lamp. The sculpture on the plinth in the centre of the room cast high shadows over the ceiling; the rearing horse above a female figure he now knew to be Francesca. How was this woven into their story? Begun before they had even met, it was there and a part of them. Time had lost its linear state, in Venice it floated circular and recurrent over centuries as they turned, like the lapis lazuli of the clock tower that he pondered when he first arrived. There was a still centre here and now, from which all else radiated.

They passed through the shadows into the bedroom. Gently, and without the all devouring lust of the previous night, they undressed each other and clinging together for defence against the terror of eternity made love until they slept:

Darkness

An open coffin carrying a white, silk-bound chrysalis floated on the dark, canal, under the bridge and then dived below the green water, sinking until out of sight. The dome of the Salute rose to the surface, water running from the whirled white sea shells. Shimmering whiteness, Madonna Capitana del Mare. The bells echoed louder and louder; he became a shadow and then nothing. The great dome was all around the space where he had been. Flames leaped up until the whole of the dark space burst open in a shower of white feathers and the sky was alive with stars.

He turned and she was there; he held her tightly:

Darkness

A dark pyramid drew itself down. The apex glowed gold. The gold shimmered until it became a mask; a breeze blew through space and the pyramid became a cloak. Light seeped silver from its folds, rays turning and searching the darkness. The silver leapt and clung like a ball of lightning, a ring of light; silver and gold, spires rising from the ring. Lightning descended through infinite space.

There was a moan, and something brushed his face; a voice murmured. and he was quiet:

Darkness

The long river turned through dark banks, overhung with trees. Gold streaked its surface, catching the moon-light. The boat moved of its own accord, quickly and silently. The trees moved in a blur; clouds rose like mountains against the dark sky; the moon was extinguished. In the complete darkness he knew there was a guide but with no voice, without touch. A silent presence. A moment of fear and then he had no choice but to relinquish himself to the void:

Darkness

In the void, sounds reached him, a vibration from the circumference of darkness, putting him at the centre. Chords, choirs, chorus; he sensed his father present; the music took form, Palaestrina, a motet, the single line - pure, perfect, joined in the counterpoint of heaven. A tiny golden tear in the darkness, his heart filled with unrestrainable love, swelling and reaching out. Invisibly he felt himself engulfed as the music turned into light, shining, pouring, breaking through the night and he was held in the light above the heavens. Francesca too, he could sense, Rose of Sharon, Lily of the Valleys - sicut lilium inter spinas, sic amica mea, inter filias Adae. Weightless, formless, floating in an ever-timeless space:

Darkness.

20

THE SIXTH DAY - PART ONE

H is head was cradled, sunk, supported in the valley of a thick, luxurious pillow. Light shone between the slats in the shutters. Sleep began to seep back into his mind and his eyes closed again. His grandparents' house, the first night, waking with the image of the windows and furniture of his own room at home created by his expectation, only to find it replaced by his grandparents' dark heavily varnished wood, metal bed and old books with embossed spines; the evidence of his eyes and the projection of memory both co-existing briefly. His eyes opened again, and he lifted the weight of his head sufficiently to see over the pillow. The place beside him was empty. The slight shock and the curiosity it aroused reminded him of where he was. Not the hotel, nor Angelo and Elena's flat but Enzo's studio, with Francesca. He raised himself onto his elbows and looked around - where was she?

A door opened behind him and, relieved, he turned his head. Francesca was coming back from the bathroom. She had showered and wore a towel with another around her hair. He had slept through the movement of her leaving the bed and the sound of the shower.

Then, with a sudden moment of panic that preceded its cause in his awareness, he remembered why today was different, why this morning in particular he must try to experience to the full these last precious moments with Francesca. How many of those moments did he have? He felt a second wave of panic when he realised that he did not know the time. Francesca picked up her clothes from the back of an ornate chair and as he reached out suddenly for his watch she bent over and kissed him lightly on the forehead,

'Seven o'clock. You have plenty of time. I will make you breakfast.'

He moved to put his arm around her, but she moved away with a smile.

'Not that much time.' But her movement away implied more than just a shortage of time. Gently but firmly she was beginning to put a space between them.

In the bathroom, David observed the dark stubble beginning to resemble a beard. He would tell Thelma that he had decided to grow one. Immediately he caught himself creating stories to cover the reality of what had happened. The force of habit: had he not decided that there was only one way forward? The rest, all other possibilities were to dither, to look back, to dissipate all he had gathered together in his consciousness over the last week and to return to being a scattered victim without identity or purpose. This was the fatal crossroads at which he had arrived in full consciousness of the consequences of his actions: neither prevarication nor pretence could hide the reality from him. The urge to run away, to hide was desperately powerful but he must resist it. He could pretend that the experience of the last week was just another collection of ideas, something better ignored in the cause of a quiet life but this time he knew full well that it was not.

As he dressed, putting on with a certain distaste the same clothes he had worn the day before, he became aware of the smell of coffee. A last cup of coffee with Francesca and he felt the inevitable pull of self-pity and sentiment, of over- reaction. There was no reason why it should be their last cup of coffee; she had disappeared yesterday because she wanted to make it clear that he could not see her as an alternative to Thelma; a cup of coffee was quite another matter. There was Enzo too, and Cristina: he might even buy that painting. In a week he had begun to create a new life and he should protect that, even if in the longer term, Francesca could be seen as nothing more than a friend. He had a long way to go before he would feel that his life formed an integrated whole within him, but he should not underestimate the progress he had made.

Feeling inadequate, in creased clothes and the worst stage of stubble, he left the bedroom and entered the studio. In the centre, the sculpture and its possible significance stood, patiently waiting for Enzo to breath more fire into the earth from which he had created it. He went into the kitchen. Francesca was also wearing yesterday's clothes, but she did so with considerably more success than he did.

'There is no bread I'm afraid, it is just coffee at the moment.'

David tried to be fully conscious of every sense, to repeat the trick of yesterday in the restaurant. For once, he willed, let him experience something fully and appreciate it now rather than later.

'Coffee will be fine. I'm beginning to feel too nervous to be able to eat anyway.'

Conversation was difficult, Francesca had started to withdraw into herself, to disappear again. He looked at his watch several times.

'I think, maybe I should ring the hotel, just to see if there were any messages, revised times that sort of thing.'

Francesca smiled with slightly forced but well-meant brightness,

'The phone is by the front door.'

As he dialled, he thought about the fact that he had hardly stayed at the hotel, about how they would react and what they would say when he arrived with Thelma. Nothing of course, he knew that, but still it made him nervous. The phone bleeped three times and then a voice answered,

'Pronto'

A different voice, not the girl with red nails; not her shift, or she had the day off.

'It's David Green, ringing to see if there are any messages.'

'One moment please, I will look.'

There was a pause. David's stomach knotted. It was likely to spend much of today in that state. There was a noise as the phone was lifted,

'Just one Mr Green, yesterday, from Mrs Green.' He felt himself breath more quickly, 'The message says, I have more luggage than I thought, please meet me with the car. If there are any problems ring tonight.'

'And you're quite sure there are no others?'

'Quite sure Mr Green; that is all.'

All, and quite enough. He realised that he should have rung yesterday to check.

'Thank you,'

'Ciao.'

And the line went dead. He looked at his watch, it was

no good, she would have left; he could not phone her now. He had better try to do as she asked, to keep things civilised. He thought back from the time of the plane's arrival and realised that, if the traffic were not too bad, it would still be possible to meet her with the car. The visit to the hotel would even allow him to change his shirt and tidy the room.

Francesca was looking down at a fresh cup of coffee when he returned. As he came in, she looked up, a tired and serious expression on her face. He waited momentarily, thinking that she might speak first but then said, 'I have to go, she wants me to meet her with the car, I can still do it if I hurry.'

'Yes, you must. But David, sit down a moment.' She poured another cup of coffee for him, pausing at one point as she poured, apparently preoccupied in thought. She put the cup in front of him and then sat back on the opposite side of the table.

'You know David, you don't have to make any decisions today. I said that you must not think we can be together, I have too many problems myself. I have to answer them. Maybe I go back to Renato, maybe I go home to Treviso, maybe I go anywhere or nowhere. Nothing is possible between us now.' She hesitated, 'Don't be in too much of a hurry David to make decisions when they are not needed and make sure you are certain when you think they are.'

She stopped and looked back into the surface of her coffee. A pause, and then she looked up again with a slightly watery smile, ' There, that is that, now you must go I think.'

They kissed briefly before he left. He felt as though a play were over, a novel finished, a world disappeared. People, places thinning into air. Into air, but then, and this was the point, to return as memory, as forces acting within him, a new part of the hidden world of forces from the past that form the present and determine the future. Whatever happened or whatever he decided now, after Francesca's speech, he would take them all with him. Even now, they were moving to join up with everything that had ever happened, creating new stories and modifying old ones. There was no way to hide from experience except by shutting out one's very self.

The morning light cast a thin film of unreality over the calli and canals. A pale hint of yellow, not the bright well-ordered clarity of Canaletto but the insubstantial shimmering of Turner. Perhaps he had painted in the morning before the sun became fierce against the white marble and pink and red walls. The Piazza looked like an empty stage before a show: furniture was being arranged, awnings lowered, the set moved into place in front of a few drifting tourists who had arrived early. David hurried on, across the bridges on the Riva degli Schiavoni, scarcely noticing the Bridge of Sighs or the statue of Il Magnifico. He arrived at the pier for Punta Sabbioni and checked the timetable: ten minutes, that was not too bad. He bought a ticket.

The rush to the pier over, his head cleared of the preoccupation of the task, like hurrying water broadening into a still pool. He went over to the steps of the Chiesa di Vivaldi and sat down. The water lapping at the edge of stone threw glints of silver, like shards of glass from the dark green that moved and rippled as it broke into small dancing fountains. He was certainly nearer to a sense of self than he had been when he landed at this spot nearly a week ago; changes had occurred; he was able to apprehend, albeit obscurely, images, stories, an emotional essence from the past. This was the change he sought when he stepped off the ferry and looked around, hoping that the shock of a return to Venice might awaken the early depths of his mind.

And Francesca? Was she an essential part of this renais-sance or an important catalyst? Either way she was right, and he did not need to make final decisions today. But if he did not, if he risked again returning to the way of life that had taken him from himself, could he cope? Enzo had warned of the difficulty, like kicking heroin and then returning to the same needle infested streets and haunts of dealers. To Thelma, he would have to find a way of appearing normal, of pretending nothing had happened and acting as if he had been nowhere. The alternative was unthinkable to him in his present state and yet it was the alternative that he had constantly tried to prepare himself for, to tell the truth as he saw it, to say what had happened, to stop living a lie.

In mid channel the big ferry passed the jetty and then turned in towards him, moving ever closer until the rust streaks became visible on the white: evidence of corrosion and decay. He stood, reluctant, feeling that this journey back was more than just a ferry crossing, fighting the sensation that something was ending, the unwelcome but insistent sense of self-betrayal.

He punched the ticket and the bell rang loudly, the sliding doors crashed, the ferry threatened him with the darkness between decks. All subjective, and yet this, this imperfect mirror, was the only way of reading beyond thoughts and surfaces, distorting and unreliable though it was.

There had been a surprising number on the early ferry in, many clearly not tourists, but he had few fellow passengers with him to Punta Sabbioni. He looked at his watch: eight thirty-five. He wondered where Thelma was at this moment. Two hours, excluding the extra hour of summer time, nine forty-five the plane would leave Italian time; that meant she would be arriving at Gatwick about now.

The ferry growled and grumbled its way into the Lido. One passenger got up and disembarked: a woman who had been sitting in front of David reading the local paper. David had noticed an article dealing with some controversy involving Mestre but could not make out any more than that.

The sight of Punta Sabbioni, with its low piers and bleached mooring poles seemed reassuring, almost homely as they began the big sweep round to the white railed mooring. A bigger group of tourists stood waiting to go into Venice, many no doubt for the first time; compared to them David felt almost a local. As he stepped ashore and began thinking about the next stage, he realised that he had not used the car to get there. He looked around for a taxi but there were none waiting. It would take too long to phone for one. He would have to use the bus and at this he looked anxiously at his watch. Nine twenty, Thelma would be close to boarding the plane by now. He had left Venice behind. The bus would make the timetable tighter but still possible. He walked to the end bus in the row, parked across the turning point.

David paid the driver, who had yet to start the engine, and sat on a single seat towards the rear. He sat in the silence and fought against the cloud that blurred the feelings and events of the last week; already the drug of comfort and forgetfulness was trying to take over his mind. He had suffered from years of dissatisfaction and lack of fulfilment but set against the fear of sharp and present pain they were beginning to seem tolerable and better dealt with in the longer term.

A judder, a whine and the engine started. The folding

doors half closed and then opened again to let in a small rush of last-minute passengers. The doors slammed shut and the forward movement of the bus made him feel instantly bolder. Such was the power of external symbolism to influence the mind.

Each time the bus slowed for traffic lights or traffic, David looked at his watch. At the lights at Ca' Savio the bus stopped and he recalled slowing there with Francesca in the passenger seat, first having had difficulty replacing the image of Thelma in the seat, seeing Francesca as a butterfly against the steel and leather car, and then letting his mind conjure visions of a shared life together in London and on the coast in Sussex and Hampshire: fantastic visions, as he had told himself then.

The long straight road lined with low fields growing fruit and sweetcorn changed little and several times he moved to get up, thinking that he had reached the stop. At last the bus pulled in opposite the small change bureau and souvenir shop. He could see the hotel set back behind the high hedges of hibiscus. He alighted and walked through to the car park.

As he approached the main entrance, he became painfully conscious of his unkempt appearance: creased clothes and stubbled chin. It was just as well he had come back, he thought, as he felt vulnerable and defensive in this condition. He tried to act naturally as he picked up the key, fortunately from the girl he had spoken to on the phone that morning, the one he had not recognised; he would have found it even more difficult had it been the girl with red nails. He checked his watch again, ten o' clock, she was in the air now.

His room had a deserted atmosphere about it; the bed had been made and towels hung up in the bathroom, but his clothes were still thrown where he had left them. He threw those that he was wearing to join them and showered quickly. The electric razor complained about the length of his beard but when he had finished, he felt far more positive, free to make decisions. After dressing, he tidied cursorily, bundling the dirty clothes into the bottom of the wardrobe and putting the papers and books in a pile. He paused to scan the room and saw his car keys by the travelling alarm clock. As he picked them up, he noted that it was half past ten. Traffic could be very bad along the Via Fausta and particularly the other side of Jesolo. He would need to hurry.

He felt far happier as he handed in his keys. If the brief look the girl gave him was an indication that she wondered what was going on, then perhaps he was giving her a little added interest in her job. The sense of working against time, having an objective, discouraged too much conscious worrying about the possible consequences of Thelma's arrival. The slight but constant queasy feeling in his stomach told another story, that below the surface anxiety was waiting and working until such time as it should re-emerge.

Outside again, the sun had risen past its early morning warmth and now scorched the air into a hard, clear, white dryness that hit him all the more dramatically as he was leaving the cool of the air conditioning. He walked quickly to the car park, feeling in his pocket for the keys so that he could start the car and get it cool as quickly as possible. Once inside, the heat was stifling but the comfortable familiarity of the leather seats supported and reassured him whilst it cooled. He checked that there were no signs of Francesca that Thelma could notice, again a sign to himself that he might yet back out, give in, take the way that was easiest in the short term, betray himself to avoid the challenge of doing what he knew to be right.

As the car slid quietly and smoothly out of the car park, he felt the return of a welcome sense of control. Through Cavallino, the traffic was heavy but moving and, as he turned to leave Jesolo behind, it spread out and allowed him to speed up a little. He enjoyed driving, liked the clear objective and the known rules for achieving it; he enjoyed this car in particular and the way it listened and responded to his slightest thought and movement. There were things in his life that he enjoyed, and this was one of them. Perhaps he was being too radical in the changes he proposed to make, perhaps he simply needed a different company, an opportunity to travel in Europe, more time away from home. Perhaps it was not a matter of all or nothing.

Was this the voice of sense or the sirens taking a new tack, luring him to the rocks by degrees rather than one catastrophic crash? Was it a sign that Enzo had been right when he had said that the habits of his old life would take hold again, draw him in the minute he came within their magnetic field? He saw Enzo fling back his arms and say, 'You must kick the habit!' but was this what he meant? Indecision, hovering between one path and another, making a decision only to reverse it or have it reversed: this was becoming his defining characteristic. The difficulty was that he had nothing substantial to base a decision on. He was thrown between mutually contradictory motivations: be true to the person he had been at sixteen; create a safe, if unfulfilling, present; create a better past for the person he would become; escape self-recriminations; return to the familiar and the known; keep reaching upwards with the tree on the mountainside; allow the monsters of unknown passions to rise to the surface. He could close his eyes and ears and run away but again they would come after him to tear him to pieces.

Preoccupied, he nearly missed the green sign indicating the autostrada from Trieste to Venezia. At least in the short term he had a clearly defined objective. He felt comforted by the pressure on his back as he let the car surge forward from the slip road, across the line of heavy, trailer-pulling lorries, past the other traffic until he was winning, overcoming, leaving everything else behind.

Point made, he eased off. He had asserted his ability to move emphatically forward when he knew where he was going and the attention of the Polizia would not be welcome. Short term goals were what he needed now. His glance flicked across the clock. Eleven thirty, she would be landing in ten minutes.

As he approached Marco Polo airport, the traffic became dense. Anxiety began to take over: anxiety about lateness, about how he would deal with meeting her, about when and how things might crumble and break as he began to reveal what had happened and its consequences for the future. It was past twelve when he parked, and he prayed for delays.

Inside the arrivals hall he ran down the list of flights on the screens. The plane had landed. His eyes hunted the eddying crowd but saw no sign of Thelma. He felt as though he had been transferred to a glass tank, piped away into a clear and separate world undisturbed by past events or images from baroque layers of the mind. A world so transparent and devoid of depth that he found it impossible to rationalise the sweat that broke out beneath his shirt despite the over-cool air conditioning.

He tried to break through the glass barrier that kept him from the seething world of image and emotion in which he had spent the last few days, but his eyes held him back. He

tried to find the conflict, the problem, the insoluble problem, but it would not be roused. What was his problem
anyway? He tried to visualise himself with Francesca among
the shifting, ever moving images of Venice that defied the
partition between mind and outside world. All he could
create were pale fixed pictures like old and faded
photographs, static and dead. But a few hours and he could
not make the memories live. Somewhere they were lying
dormant inside, waiting for him, but here, now, in this
sterile container of a building, there seemed nothing to
prevent him from meeting Thelma as though the last week
had not existed.

A new wave of passengers surged through the doors.
Inconsistent with his thoughts, his heart thumped, and his
stomach tightened as he again scanned the moving surface
of the flood of faces. Again, she was not there.

He moved back to the screens in case he had misread
them. He checked: the plane had definitely landed. He read
the signs around the hall, but he was in the right place. His
eyes moved back to the doors. A girl with long dark hair
emerged with a large case. As she turned, scanning those
waiting, as he had scanned the arrivals, their eyes met for a
moment. Briefly, a ghost of Francesca draped itself over her
form. Even at this distance the deep luminescence of her
eyes, Francesca's eyes, triggered a physical response. Somewhere beneath the surface, unrecoverable though they were
at the moment, the experience and images of their relationship had been absorbed into deeper, dreaming layers of his
psyche. She moved as quickly as her case allowed and flung
her arms around a waiting man in an explosion of Italian
greeting. Again, his stomach clenched but his mind stayed
cold and disconnected.

'David!'

His name landed amongst the confusion created in his body by the Italian girl. Into his stomach, already clenched, the voice fell like a torrent of iced water. He turned to where the voice had come from.

'David! Over here!'

The voice in itself was not cold, neither did it contain annoyance.

Thelma stood on the other side, her short blonde hair pinned tightly beneath her sun glasses. She had two suitcases at her feet and as she waved, she pulled up the handles. He walked quickly towards her, she tilted her face and their lips touched briefly. His hand brushed her waist and as it did so, the new unfamiliarity of her thinness almost made him recoil but she did not appear to notice.

'You didn't mind me changing the arrangements. It seemed silly not to use the car when we've got it.'

Being reminded of the phone call to the hotel, he recalled Enzo's flat, Francesca making coffee, Francesca making love. David pulled himself away from the memory.

'No, no. I quite enjoyed the drive.'

He became aware that he was looking intently at her. He quickly looked down and took hold of the suitcases. She was always tense, and the tension radiated from her now but no more so than usual.

'It was a bit of a rush getting away. I had to send a fax to the office and then the traffic out of London was awful.'

'You haven't brought work I hope.'

'Only some reports to read.'

'No wonder it's so heavy.'

He began to walk towards the exit. It was easy, undemanding, relating on this level. General management of everyday life, no inundating tides of emotion nor even decisions that wouldn't wait.

'How are you anyway? Have you been relaxing? You still look tired.'

He felt his eyes dart to hers for signs of accusation. Something inside him responded to her concern with a pleasant surprise but he felt himself tense, hunting the words for clues. Not surprising that he should look tired, but could she discern more from his appearance, his tone of voice than he intended? Now was certainly not the moment to say what had replaced the relaxation the doctor ordered. With a cynicism born of long experience of his own vacillation he wondered whether it ever would be the moment or whether he would just allow everything to slip away into the dark pools beneath the surface. Paranoia passed; it was a simple question.

'Yes I am. I've cut down on the drugs a bit though.'

'What about relaxing?'

'I've been seeing Venice.'

Thelma indicated towards the doors, 'There's a trolley over there.'

Back to general management. Just as well, things were beginning to focus too closely on his week. It was strange that their last shared experience was the breakdown and all that surrounded it. In Venice it had blurred and then been absorbed into the experience of all that he could not mention.

They loaded the trolley. David walked more quickly, pushing towards the car park. It was not clear at all what he should do or say, and the extra speed made it easier to stop talking. At the car, David loaded the boot and watched as Thelma got in. The image of Francesca's dark hair and radiating warmth and energy was replaced again by the familiar, blonde, matter of fact presence.

He settled into the driving seat and started the engine.

No butterflies alighted on the leather, but his feelings were unpredictably mixed. Her brief note of concern had elicited a warmth he had not expected. He tried to bring back the powerful, even overwhelming, experiences of the last week only to find them shut out by the grip of the familiar. If he had to work this hard to revive them, should he even bother?

21

THE SIXTH DAY - PART TWO

In the cool of the hotel foyer, the girl with red fingernails handed him the key and then looked at Thelma.

'Enjoy your stay Mrs Green.'

David searched the words and inflection for sounds of conspiracy, disapproval, sympathy or simply amusement and as they entered the lift, he continued to search their echoes. Only by the time they had reached the corridor leading to their room did he finally accept that the words and their echoes contained nothing more than the ritual pleasantry of trained hotel staff.

As they neared the room, he felt a sweat breaking out under his shirt. Francesca had never been there, but he had thought about her there, dreamed images inspired by her and spoken to her on the phone. It was there that he had determined to forget Francesca and rang Thelma; from there that he had dashed to meet Francesca the minute that she phoned, leaving Thelma to ring an empty hotel room.

Thelma held out her hand for the key; David put it in the lock and opened the door. It was just as well that he had hurriedly tidied before going to the airport; it was still a mess. Thelma raised her eyebrows when she saw it but said nothing and walked to the window, the window that until now had been his. He was aware of an almost comic sense of ownership when he said,

'What do you think?'

'Let's get everything unpacked and put away and then go down for a swim.'

David did not disagree. It would be the least confrontational way of spending the afternoon. The tension of anticipation and the conflicting feelings within had left him drained. To lie on the sand in the sun would be welcome.

He concentrated on tidying away the things he had left out whilst Thelma unpacked and hung up her clothes, leaving her swimming costume and beach robe on the bed. The familiarity, despite the inevitable distance and tension, was taking over already, draining away his intent to reveal the progress and self-discovery of the week. Had he ever really intended to do so? Mentally perhaps, but it had always lacked conviction.

'I'll have a quick shower and then we'll go.'

She took off her watch and went to the bedside cupboard. As she opened the drawer, he remembered the scarf. She took out the brown paper bag that he had put in there, at a time that now seemed distant: before the party, before he and Francesca had slept together, before Enzo, before so much that was vital and alive and was now in danger of slipping into vague memory.

'I got it for you, in the shop opposite.'

She took it out, the receipt fluttered to the floor where he had forgotten to remove it. She picked it up and put it by the phone as she examined the design.

'Yes, it's nice, thank you.'

She screwed up the paper bag and turned to put it into the bin. As she turned David tensed and went cold: he saw by the phone, the receptionist's message with Francesca's phone number on it. He tried to remember what the message actually said. It arrived in his mental vision with disconcerting clarity: 'Please ring before 12:00. Francesca.' The message that had led him to leave before Thelma had returned his call; a certain kind of justice.

Thelma's hand went towards the receipt to throw it away with the bag and then it moved sideways to the message. She picked it up and looked at it for longer than was necessary to read it. She was still looking at it when she said,

'Who's Francesca?'

She looked up and her eyes fell directly on his.

Now! now was the moment, the point of crisis, the Delphic crossroads of truth. No hunting for a time, just a straight answer to her question and all the indecision, internal conflict and dishonesty would be at an end. His mouth opened to speak but cowardice drained away his resolve. An unearthly laugh and the mocking face of Tiresius in the mirror; Enzo's warm concern betrayed. Too soon, too difficult, he could not release such a life changing situation on the throw of a die, the fall of a piece of paper from the red fingernails of fate.

'I met some people in a bar in Venice.' Stay close to the truth. 'There was an American couple and some friends they'd made.' Put distance between himself and Francesca; she was Wagner's friend now. 'Francesca wanted to let me know where they were meeting.' Now the smoke screen, 'George Wagner, that's the American, is keen on Byron.' Complex thoughts and feelings were surging beneath the surface, feelings of self-betrayal and defeat, the deep-felt stories of the week running with their dreams through channels in his mind. He made a determined effort not to look, not to see what he sensed was rippling beneath the dark water.

'And what about Francesca?'

He hadn't expected to get away with it without some further effort.

'She's an artist, she did a portrait of George's wife and they got talking.' Not quite enough. ' It's her uncle's bar, where they agreed to meet, that's why she rang.' Any more would start to seem too much. Thelma's face still showed more questions, but she said,

'We must meet up; it would be nice to meet some other people.'

'Yes, we might be able to arrange it.'

An opportunity lost or a difficult situation rescued: which of the two, he was not prepared to discuss with himself. He looked at the still, silent phone, willing it to ring, willing it to be Francesca so that his cover would be blown and he would not have to make the decision. It stood resolutely unmoved. At last he said,

'Come on, let's get down to the beach.'

Thelma's face flickered, a suggestion of a glance towards the window, then,

'I'd rather go to the pool.'

Yes, thought David: the sand, the shells, seaweed, fish, crabs, the unknown in the depths beneath as you left the shallow water; these were too unpredictable, uncontrolled, or simply messy. Resentment rose, an irrational contrariness gripped him as it always did in these moments of confrontation.

'Oh, come on. It's a superb beach, you can use a pool anywhere.'

Why did he do it? It was so predictable, a reflex almost.

Years of buried resentment driving him to this small channel of protest.

'Another time. Let's go to the pool. We don't need to take much, it's easy, the recliners are there.'

Again, it surged.

'I don't know what's the matter with you: the beach, the Adriatic, and you want to use a chlorine filled pool, surrounded by concrete.'

He saw the red marks of anger on her neck.

'Look,' her voice had hardened and her face set, ' I've been up since six, I've driven to the airport, flown here and I want to use the pool. You go to the beach if you want to.'

He was tempted to list what he had done since he woke but drew back. This was it. This was the reality, not the warm glow that greeted the familiar voice on the phone. It was the stomach-churning clash of wills, each of them unable to comprehend the other that characterised their relationship. It was the demon that took over his mind and voice when they clashed that would reveal the events of the last week, not any considered and thought out plan or conscious decision. But not this time, the moment had receded, his thoughts had defused the anger. Maybe this time he was the one being unreasonable.

'O.K. we'll go to the pool.'

He took a perverse satisfaction in the fact that they were able to get two recliners straight away. The majority preferred the beach, the smell of the sea to that of bleach. Unreasonable, untimely thoughts rose like steam from London sewers, a smell that revealed a rottenness beneath, an indication on the surface of how the dissatisfaction of years had changed and warped his existence. Enzo had said that if you shut in your true self then it began to putrefy inside, poisoning everything else. He thought of Enzo's larger than life presence and felt like a dwarf in his ineffectual cowardice. He had been presented with the time to strike but the demon had retreated, and the fire had died.

Thelma settled on the recliner with an airport blockbuster novel. He did not ask what it was. The sun was scorchingly hot, too hot really to be lying there. He watched a group of young teenagers pushing each other into the pool. Their laughter, the play, was full of the tension of unexplored sex; permitted physical contact substituted for the forbidden. In the pool they got closer, the horseplay moving to foreplay, the laughter got louder and then they retreated. Tonight, along the front, on seats between the pools of light, they would be kissing and fumbling and the fear before the storm would get stronger as the barriers began to lose the fight against waves of passion. They would embrace awkwardly, the slatted seats digging into them, like the seats on Purbrook Heath that he had shared with Jane. At the thought, he scanned the pool anxiously and then the area around. Was Eva there? Eva who had drawn him back into his past by the chance resemblance to Jane but there was no sight of her. He thought of the frenzied hunt through the narrow calli, that ended in the little corte by a well head; he remembered the silver bells of laughter and the image of a fountain; he remembered the bridge over eternity where he had stood with Jane. He looked around. What had happened? What had redefined his life in this prosaic way?

Thelma looked up, the tension of their disagreement gone.

'Whew! It's hot. Are you coming in?'

He had swum with Francesca from the beach, excitement like that of the teenagers had filled him, excitement as their bodies had grown close in the undulations of the waves, exhilaration as they had matched each other for speed through the water and the god-like intoxication as they emerged from the sea with their arms around each other. He got up and watched as Thelma lowered herself into the pool and set off in her slightly awkward breast-stroke. He went to the edge and dived in, forgetting everything as the water closed over him.

As he came to the surface, he turned to begin swimming lengths, slowly with relaxed and relaxing strokes. The water sliding past took away any sense of urgency or need for purpose beyond the next turn. After a while the pool became busier and he found the interruptions to his rhythm caused by turning to pass playing children spoilt his enjoyment: he glided to the side to climb out.

Thelma joined him and after drying herself carefully, went back to her book. He watched the silver backed leaves of the trees beyond the pool shimmering, like tiny angel wings, in a breeze not yet detectable below. The breeze blew the smell of the sea to him, blew over the fence, the concrete, the white plastic chairs and the artificially blue, disinfected water.

He caught at the breeze, dragging it deep into his nostrils and saw the long curve of the beach at dawn, the long legged Renaissance girl, the flight of a predatory gull, worm casts in the fiery mirror of the still wet sand; St John's high hill crowned with the hooked and taloned hawk of the sun, the little birds fleeing from the mystery of his power; the blood streaked, fecund sea, teaming with the flash of fish and the touch of fish-smooth naked limbs.

He would go back in a minute, back to the room and get a book. As he readied himself to stand, she looked up.

'I'm thirsty. Shall we order drinks?'

Shall we ride naked and tormented through the waves? Shall we dive deeply through the scaled mysteries and terrible power of sea and sun? Or shall we drink? A time-honoured choice where drink throughout all ages had almost always been the winner. He considered a moment and realised that the thought of drink made him also aware of the beginnings of hunger.

'Would you like something to eat? The restaurant looks out over the sea.'

The same restaurant where he had eaten breakfast and watched the storm -raised waves crash on the wet beach; waves that invoked the memory of a wild Welsh beach where Miranda as Celtic priestess cried to the moon. That was before Francesca had said she couldn't meet him, before he had gone to the islands, before they had burst into flames of consummating passion. How long would it be before the recent memories that suffused and pervaded this place erupted to the surface and changed everything irrevocably?

'I ate on the plane. We could go out and eat later. I'd just like a drink now.'

He managed to attract the waiter's attention away from a group of teenage girls at the end of the pool and ordered two beers. The girls giggled and whispered as they watched the waiter walk back towards the hotel.

He looked at Thelma, whose eyes appeared to have lost focus on the book, an indication that she was about to fall asleep. He could not remember a time when their relation-ship had reached into the fires and energies of the soul and yet for year after year they had stayed together. Having no children would have made it easy to break up. They both had good, well paid jobs so there would have been no serious material problems. She seemed no happier in the relationship than he was. It was a convenience, a habit along with all the others.

Her eyes closed and the book dropped onto her thin and

flattened chest. If that was true, then why was it so difficult to finish? Was it true, or was there something perverse inside himself that just refused to recognise the value of what he had? There were happy memories, things they had done together that had been better because they shared them. There was the beginning of the relationship when it was the lack of overwhelming claim that he valued, the fact that their relationship did not demand he gave himself to it as he had to Miranda. Now, the detachment seemed cold, unrewarding and unexciting but then it had come as a welcome change. Now, he felt that it was this very detachment that threatened his essential being whose putrefaction he had begun to smell.

Thelma's strength was that she did not threaten him because she did not move him deeply enough to do so. Francesca had liberated his mind, reawakened old layers of consciousness, rekindled his emotions and his body. Would he, at some time in the future, revolt against this, feel that he did not want to owe his being to the influence of another, just as he had with Miranda? Perhaps he was nearing the heart of the problem: he could only be himself in a relationship where he gave himself but then resented it and turned against the person who seemed to be robbing him of independence and control of his life. A tune wove its way quietly into the back of his mind., the tune his mother sang to him at the kitchen sink. His stomach knotted and he shivered. Beneath the surface, words ran: she had left him, and he felt it was his fault, though he did not know what he had done. Cold, salt air blew across the words fluttering their torn colours until they had gone.

'Due birre signor.'

The images and sounds in his head faded to be replaced by the blue and white of water and concrete. He mumbled,

'Thank you, room number 38,' and then 'grazie.' He called to Thelma, she gave a small start and her book slid to the concrete.

The cold, pale golden, beer gave them a shared and separate focus: the illusion of joining in the same thing whilst allowing them to remain with their own thoughts. David felt the just perceptible blunting of the edge of necessity, a fall in the urgency of decisions and choices as the beer, strong in alcohol if not taste, worked quickly on his empty stomach. The bar at the Accademia bridge and the tumbling vine leaves rose in his vision. Did he want, could he still contemplate the effort needed for vine leaves? Perhaps he should just drink until fate offered him an easier set of choices.

Thelma finished her beer and lowered the back of the sun bed. She turned onto her front and placed the book on the concrete in front of her. In only a few minutes the pages closed as she fell asleep. He thought again of getting a book from the room and sat up, looking around. The group of teenagers had gone and the pool was quieter so he decided instead to swim. He lowered himself into the pool and began to do lengths quietly and steadily, until the remaining thoughts and pressures had become absorbed in the rhythm of his limbs and breath.

When he got out, he lay down to dry on the sun bed and was next aware of Thelma tapping him on the arm. He had slept and though the sun was still hot, some of the direct burning fire had left it. She looked more relaxed and smiled when she said,

'It's three o' clock, we've both been to sleep.'

He was aware of a peaceful vacancy in his mind and did not hurry to collect his thoughts. 'Your shoulders are starting to look a bit red, we should go in.'

She looked at her skin and felt it for heat. He raised himself onto his elbows. 'What do you want to do?'

She considered for a moment, tightening her face against the sun as she sat up.

'I hadn't really thought. We'll need to eat. Why don't we go into Venice? You can show me round and we can eat there.'

It was an obvious if adventurous suggestion that David had not considered. Thelma had never been to Venice; the fact that she had suggested he show her round was a statement of intent to get things off to a better start. His previously uncollected thoughts began to crowd in on him. What were the implications of this unexpected proposal? If Thelma and he went to Venice and enjoyed it and used it to help mend their hard-pressed relationship then he could forget the last week, forget the bursting tension that rose up as he tried to face telling her about Francesca. If on the other hand, her presence was an unbearable invasion of the last week's experience, an experience that had reached into long buried parts of his psyche bringing to life a self that he had thought dead, then it would be clearly apparent what he should do. He should look on it as an opportunity to decide and to act.

'Yes, that would be good. We'll have a wander round and you can get the feel of the place and then I've got a few ideas as to where we could eat.'

Thelma picked up her towel and the book from beside the sun bed.

'Come on then. I'm sorry I was a bit snappy at first, it was a tiring day yesterday, the meeting went on and on and then I had to clear my desk. It was nearly midnight before I even began packing.'

He stood, and then encouraged by her conciliatory

gesture put an arm round her waist as they walked in. Perhaps if he tried to be less self-absorbed, self-centred, and yes, selfish, they could use this break as a new start for their relationship as well as for his own sanity. It would be an altogether more satisfactory solution than the radical alternative he had been contemplating. The destruction of his home, his marriage and the remains of his career began to appear more and more an act folly; a precipitous gesture with only the most improbable chance of anything that could be termed success. He had not even considered its implications for Thelma to whom he surely must owe something.

He had been on an interesting, even revelatory journey through parts of his deeper consciousness where image and memory join to create the sub-strata of mind; a process not unlike psychotherapy which, considering the condition that had led to his coming here, may have been the most appropriate and helpful thing, better even than rest. That was over now. Francesca had made it as clear as possible that she saw things as being at an end. A solution that allowed him to benefit from the experience, whilst retaining the stability of his everyday life, was surely the most satisfactory for which he could hope.

They showered and dressed whilst Thelma recounted the details of the previous day's meeting.

'I shouldn't have put those reports in with my clothes.' She held up a dress.' Look at it. I can't wear that!'

He would usually have suggested that she wore a different one or that the creases would come out with wearing but, knowing that this was the kind of situation that lead to some of their worst rows, suggested she rang reception for an iron. She put the dress back in the wardrobe and took out another.

'This isn't too bad. Maybe the other one will be better after hanging for a while.'

She put on the dress and sat on the side of the bed to inspect and repair her make-up. David went over to the chest of drawers and checked his pockets and bag. Did he need the bag? Yes, it would help to have somewhere to put his camera and map. He looked out of the window. This must not be a retreat but a new way forward.

The long penetrating bleep of the hotel phone broke into his thoughts. He remembered his earlier wish for Francesca to phone and relieve him of the necessity of saying anything. Now he was taking a new route and the possibility filled him with fear. His stomach clenched and he felt his arm pits grow wet, cheeks burn. He moved towards the phone but Thelma, already seated on the bed, was poised to lift the receiver.

'I'll get that.'

He stood helpless to intervene as she listened for what seemed an unnaturally long time.

'Yes, that's all right, put her through.'

She would see from his face there was something wrong if he continued to stare and he forced himself to look out of the window again. Suppose it was Francesca, suppose she had rung to say that she wanted things to continue, that they could be together, what would he do, say, what would become of his new way forward?

'No, no, that's quite all right. Yes, I've got them with me. He doesn't need a response before next week, does he?'

Her words began to impinge on his thoughts, layer themselves as his straining for hints as to the identity of the caller forced itself above the running commentary of his mind.

'Yes, he's fine, looking much better. We're going in to have a look at Venice in a minute.'

Breathe slowly, steadily. It was work, probably Caroline. He would not allow himself to consider whether he was pleased or disappointed; he was out of danger and he must appear normal by the time she put the phone down. She continued talking for a few minutes and he took the map of Venice from his bag so that studying it could calm his mind.

'Yes, I will. Bye Caroline.' She paused after putting the phone down as if thinking and then looked back at the bedside table on which the phone stood. With an absent look on her face she picked up the piece of paper with Francesca's name on, screwed it up and dropped it in the bin. She stayed looking at where it had fallen for a moment before saying,

'Are you ready? It was just work.'

David forced back questions and thoughts. Who had she thought he thought it was? What had been going through her mind when she screwed up the note? Such paranoia was unhelpful at best. Ignore it and go to Venice.

As they got into the car, David was aware of the persona of the last ten years taking over. It was as strong as the sensation when, in rehearsal for a play, the character arrives and takes over the actor's body and voice. When acting, however, the effort was in using attention to create the space for the character so that it is not crushed by the actor returning; now it was the character that had the force of habit on its side and David felt the self, that he had begun to rediscover, fade. Habit was a powerful force and Enzo was right to equate it with an addiction to a drug like heroin. It took over, it comforted, it fixed on to the familiar and refused to be shaken; it made itself indispensable and then it terrorised and destroyed.

'What is it?'

He had paused motionless in front of the wheel.

'Are you all right? Do you want me to drive?'

'No, no, I'm fine; just thought I'd lost something.'

That was the truth but not as she would interpret it.

'O.K., if you're sure.'

He started the engine. When he considered the state he had been in when she had last seen him, it was hardly surprising that she was concerned.

The car-park attendants' arms still gyrated like windmills as they arrived at Punta Sabbioni. Passing the first few, he swung in to the right, having got as near to the end as he dared. The spaces were covered with woven shade as well as being protected by the aspen trees. As they got out of the car, David was aware that the trees were not whispering and although it was late afternoon the air was heavy and hot. He bought tickets for the car park and ferry at the kiosk at the end of the row and by the time he had paid for them was aware of sweat on his back. They walked out from the shade towards the short pier. Thelma put on her sunglasses and said,

'My God it's hot. Is it always like this?'

'It's usually cooled off a little by this time. At least there'll be a breeze on the ferry.'

He had another moment of paranoia as he passed the attendant at the ticket punching machine, the same one who had been there on his return that morning. Would he recognise him and say something? He put the tickets in and avoided the attendant's eye. It punched and rang successfully; they walked to the end of the covered section. Ridiculous to think he would say anything at all, still less something incriminating. The water was flat with the surface of a metal mirror. In the distance, to the left, a haze joined the lagoon to the sky. He tried to avoid the melancholy feeling that this stillness was inducing in him; it was Thelma's first visit after all and the first visit to Venice should be a memorable and special experience.

There was only a small group waiting for the ferry. Most would have gone into Venice in the morning. When it arrived, curving towards the pier in its now familiar arc, it was clear that the first wave was returning with their acquisitions of the day: gondolier hats, garish Venezia T-shirts, burned shoulders and tired legs. He looked at Thelma. A look of anticipation had taken over from her usual tense expression. What were her thoughts now, what were the frames of cultural reference that shaped them? Despite their living together for so long, he did not know.

They boarded the ferry and went up the stairs. In contrast to the morning ferries there were plenty of seats.

'If we sit on the right, we'll get the best first view of Venice.'

Thelma slid along to sit by the rail. He watched her hand on the white painted metal, the white painted metal he had gripped so urgently and excitedly when he had crossed over on that first day and again when he had gone to meet Francesca before the party. He sat next to her and they looked out over the still, leaden water. Their two worlds of thought were separated irrevocably by the past; he could not even try to span the gulf by such poor means of communication as were available. With Francesca he had wanted their inner worlds to join, to experience Venice as a single being, sharing it across two minds. With Thelma, the past made that impossible even had she any inclination to do so which he doubted. Such thoughts would have been firmly consigned to the realms of fantasy, imagination and absurdity. He would try to make do.

The movement of the ferry as it turned slowly into the lagoon created a welcome breeze between the decks. Punta Sabbioni receded, and they moved out onto the smooth, heavy water. David watched the pier grow smaller and then turned to Thelma. She appeared to be watching the long low barrier of the Lido that, on his first day, had reminded him of Chesil beach. She turned, almost absent-mindedly,

'Do you remember the Stornaway ferry?'

Stornaway: not another life, more the beginning of this particular one, their honeymoon. Was that what she had been thinking about? It was a much bigger ferry and the sea was clear and sharp, not like the lagoon today, as heavy as molten metal. The thin dark streaks of land on the water, like shadows between waves, had perhaps some similarity. Was that what had made her think of it?

'Yes, a long time ago. We must go back some time; it was beautiful.'

A vague commitment but still a reassurance to himself that he was thinking in terms of their future together.

She looked back over the rail; eyes distant. David waited for a response, but none came. Something shared together, shared but the enjoyment was mixed, found more easily in retrospect.

The small, whitewashed, hotel on Lewis was everything they had hoped for. The windows looked out over sea and moss green folds of land. There was an open fire and dark heavy wood furniture. The food, home cooked, with obvious pride, from local sea food and fresh vegetables from the hotel's garden, was a source of the greatest sensory satisfaction at every meal. The family who ran it were friendly and attentive. Away from the preoccupations of work and London turmoil, he and Thelma had found conversation difficult, but the long pauses could be filled by an absorption in the place itself.

At the end of the first week, there was an evening of Hebridean music. The singer and harpist had long dark hair and blue-green eyes. Her voice had the purity of spring water, clear but reflecting patterns and colour in its flow. The harp sprayed notes like the play of a fountain. The magical, inner otherness of the haunting melodies floating on the air like mist over the sea transfixed him, filled the empty space inside that had been left untouched by his and Thelma's attempts at communication. Thelma walked out and he followed her; she accused him of lechery. If he couldn't take his eyes off the girl, he could have her. He said it was the music and she looked at him with her withering and pitying look that he had seen so often since. They had a strained and bitter row, trying not to be heard, trying to pierce each other's incomprehension with pain.

He had gone back to the music and Thelma had stayed in their room. The thin tones, yet resonant flow, of the harp drew him and mocked him as though the Celtic mysteries had come to a wake for his soul. The twilight glimmer and promise of further light beneath the green mound of faery; the world of Yeats, suppressed since he had left University, intermingled with the hair and eyes of Miranda surged back to show what he had lost. He stayed in the bar, talking with the harpist into the night and the honeymoon was wrecked; they should perhaps have stopped then, handed back the wedding gifts, limited the damage to both of them, but they went on, patched over the differences, made the best of it.

The ferry pulled in to the Lido. A girl got off from the lower deck and walked across the landing stage, under the curved shelter. He watched her and then drew his eyes quickly away. He looked at Thelma. She had got her book from her bag and was reading. He was annoyed. What was wrong with her, why wasn't she absorbing this experience? Why was she reading a book? He tried to drive any hint of irritation from his voice.

'Not long after we leave the Lido, you'll get the first sight of Venice.'

She looked up slowly and raised her sunglasses, looking quickly in towards the shade of the deck as she did so. She paused and looked around.

'Do they sell drinks on board?'

Was she ignoring the point of what he'd said, or hadn't she heard?

'Up in the front there I think.'

'It's really hot, do you want anything?'

She rose and moved past him.

'No, I mean don't miss the first sight of Venice.'

'I'm only buying a drink. Are you sure?'

It was hot, hot and humid. If she wasn't bothered why should he be? Coffee would help dispel the lethargy of the airless afternoon.

'Hold on, I'm coming.'

They went into the small wood panelled bar. It smelt vaguely of sweat and beer and strongly of coffee. The main occupants looked like crew or workmen, not tourists anyway. Thelma asked for a cold can of Coca-cola; he had an espresso that came with a tumbler of tepid water.

'I was going to take it back to the seat to drink it.'

'Sorry, I didn't fancy Coke.'

He stood at the bar and she walked to the door. The coffee was strong, even the vapour above it seemed rich enough to deliver the necessary jolt. He finished it quickly and drank a little of the water. Its warmth made him wonder about its source and the advisability of finishing it. He did so anyway and then joined Thelma who had taken the remains of the Coke back to the seat.

'I don't know how you could stand it in there.'

'The coffee was good.'

'No, I mean the smell.'

He knew what she meant and was annoyed as though it was his boat, his bar that she was criticising.

He became aware of the low ripple of excitement amongst the small group on board. He looked out over the rail and saw, like glass pulled into delicate peaks by tongs above the water, the long spire-plumed shape of Venice. They had missed the first sight as they bickered about the smell of sweat. His feeling of anger was unreasonable. He had not missed out. If she did not mind missing an experience that had made a lasting, even critical impression on generations of writers, musicians and artists why should he care?

He pointed, not trusting himself to speak, and Thelma quickly took out her camera and leaned over the rail to capture her first sight, even if it was not the first possible. She turned back to him with an excited smile, paused to take in his face and looked away again. His irrational anger clearly showed.

He was the one who was spoiling it, who had spoiled it ever since the Hebridean harpist. Harpist to harpies, Miranda to Maenads, Eumenides into furies: they had arrived, the winged avengers flying to peck out his eyes, his brain, his liver and his heart. He shivered and heard the bat wings flapping in his brain, the flying ones that had started his descent into madness. The cold wet leather of their wings wrapped his forehead, the rush of air sang in his ears, he grabbed the rail of the seat in front and fought to stop

428

himself from slumping forward. He thought he had lost them, but they had returned. They had found him.

She still looked away. The rushing changed to a long thin note, poised, waiting, not knowing where to turn, what resolution was possible. The cold clamp around his forehead began to change to a fierce pumping, a rhythm frightening yet reassuring; the blood was returning, he would not pass out. What would she have done if he had? He did not have a definitive answer, but he was sure she would not have held him as Francesca had, his ice cream girl, or like his mother.

She looked towards him. Puzzlement and irritation on her face changed to puzzlement and concern.

'You look very white. Are you taking your tablets?'

He had all but forgotten about tablets, about medication, about doctors. He had rejected the physical explanation in his search for the repair of his psyche or, alternatively, soul.

'No, they made me feel strange. I couldn't concentrate, I stopped taking them soon after I got here.'

Her irritation returned.

'How do you think you're going to get better then?'

How did he think he was going to get better? Explore images of the past, follow young girls who reminded him of early girlfriends along beaches and through narrow alley ways, have an affair, contemplate the Virgin Mary, the crucifixion, his mother and then find them all joined together, forming patterns through his mind like the changing forms in the turn of a kaleidoscope. Discover image melting into image, Francesca as Virgin Mary, as his mother; himself as baby and crucified man, his own fate in the last judgement, winged devils crying for revenge. Try to find patterns in the story, chains of symbols formed in his past from events, poetry, music and relationships.

Drawn out into the open, dragged out for inspection, it was unbelievable, possibly blasphemous and probably insane even to him. Kept warm, dark and fluid within him it had seemed perfectly natural but exposed to light and air it congealed into an alien and revolting mess. He could not tell her what could not be explained even to himself.

'I thought,' he said weakly, 'I might make some psychological sense of it, but the drugs just reduced everything to a blur.'

To his surprise she did not treat this with contempt but showed some interest.

'Yes, that was what Venice was for, I remember.'

She looked beyond David to where Venice had drawn close, the French gardens of Napoleon, a garden alien to the rest of Venice. 'Has it worked?'

'It's done something, it's brought the past close, helped me to be aware again of a life inside, to see past that dreadful door that blocked everything out.'

He saw the distance grow between them again. He had mentioned the image of the iron door that had swung shut on his soul, barring him from the source of his life. He was speaking a language that she could not understand, that meant nothing and produced the annoyance of confrontation with the alien. The distance, though greater, was at least kinder. The anger, the irritation had gone to be replaced by incomprehension, uncertainty and fear. The warmth, even at a distance, prompted him to try to dispel the fear.

'I shall be all right. It's a sort of panic, simple really - it's only the cause that's complicated.'

To his surprise she put a hand out and pushed back the

hair from his forehead. She drew away again before he could respond but it was an unexpected gesture.

The ferry had left the tree-lined park behind and was moving slowly past the first Venetian buildings, pink and flaking, shuttered against the sun and peering tourists. Finally, it began its sweeping turn, in towards the wood and metal pier and the Chiesa di Santa Maria della Pieta, Vivaldi's church, the church where David had seen Francesca waiting on the steps when he returned after her phone call.

This was how it would be. Everywhere in Venice was steeped in the memories of the last few days, hard though he tried to shut them out. A week ago, he had arrived at this very spot, open and excited, ready to welcome transformation. He had found himself facing the total destruction of everything he had lived through in the last ten, fifteen or even twenty years. Now he was arriving again and aware of an urge to shut out the possibility of change. With Thelma beside him it seemed too threatening, too fantastic, a set of pale images against hard reality. He was aware of the crushing irony of trying to arm himself against the transforming power of Venice, to shut her out. He sought to reduce her to history and guidebooks and to stones without water. A Micky Mouse umbrella rose above the crowds on the Bridge of Sighs. That was where he belonged now, that was the safe way to see Venice.

Thelma leaned out and took a photograph along the Riva degli Schiavoni past the bridges to the columns of the Piazzetta, the columns he would now have to walk through with his mind closed against any influx of water. He felt his stomach turn and his eyes to his alarm grow wet. Water would not be held back: if it could not water his heart and soul then it would emerge in tears from his eyes. He hurriedly wiped them with his hand.

22

THE SIXTH DAY - PART THREE

They walked between the columns: they need not have done but he felt that something led him there. It was like the end of children's stories, where the child brings a parent back to see irrefutable proof of faery folk who took him on a great adventure under the hills. There is nothing there, just a vague sense of presence felt only by the child, a sense of a thinning of the protective veil between two worlds. The Piazza spread out in front of them, the enhanced perspective of its arcades sweeping away into the distance at the end. Bands from each side competed with different tunes in different keys, worrying and confusing his thoughts. Thelma gestured and ushered him in front of the Basilica and took a photograph. He looked at the corn men with pigeons and remembered Francesca's fear of winged creatures and those that had tortured him. He bought a bag of corn and took Thelma's picture with pigeons on her arm. He pointed out the hammer wielding moors and noted that the blue clock face looked solid and real, an artefact and not a sea of shifting time as it had to him at the beginning of the week.

In the Merceria, Thelma looked at the leather bags and shoes, belts, purses and the theatrical displays of clothes. He thought of Francesca's bag, the one Renato had bought her. If she wanted a middle- aged man, then Renato with his money and influential friends could do so much more for her than he ever could.

'Do you want to go in?'

'No, not really.'

'You don't want a bag or anything.'

'Not now. Maybe later in the week we'll have another look.'

Even at this time in the afternoon it was crowded in the Merceria, made almost impassable by groups of sun patched tourists who seemed more engrossed in their ice creams and conversations than in their unique surroundings.

On his first day he had seen the fire-red skin of crowds walking through the deep clefts of hell, pushing and shouting in a Babel of languages for cold ice cream held out to them; a city of desires, a city of illusion, a city of the wailing dead. He collapsed and swam in the plague-ridden waters of the Thames, floating with bodies, Richmond to Moorgate, to Margate, to Carthage and the burning fires: the waste land.

Now he saw just tourists. Had Thelma rescued him from a death by immersion in the images of madness or dragged him back just when he was about to pass through into the light?

The Merceria twisted and turned and the smell of garlic and tomato grew stronger as his hunger increased. They rounded the corner and he saw, climbing through stalls laden with sweat-shirts, belts and scarves, the crowded steps that rose to the Rialto bridge. A noise made Thelma turn.

By the entrance to the Chiesa di San Bartolomeo was a cluster of people pushing together; two raised voices could be heard from its centre, one Italian and one American. Suddenly a loud whistle and a shout came from the corner. A youth, presumably the look-out, ran off with a cry of 'Polizia!' There was a shout and a scuffle and the huddle of people moved untidily to the side. A man emerged from the centre with a wad of notes in one hand and a pack of cards in the other. He broke away. An American was shouting angrily that he had been robbed. He started to give chase and then stopped, held back by his wife. Thelma looked at David,

'What's going on?'

'Three card trick boys, 'Chase the lady', it's just the same here as Oxford Street.

Polizia arrived, guns in holsters; the crowd rushed over; the American remonstrated loudly; the police talked animatedly on radios. Tourists milled about; police spoke to the shopkeepers who were standing in doorways watching. One raised his voice furiously and gestured in the direction they had gone; he was clearly tired of their venue being outside his shop. Eventually the crowd dispersed except for the American who had lost his money. He went with the police.

Thelma spoke slowly, her voice seemed a little shocked,

'I didn't expect that. In Naples, or Rome but somehow not here.'

'The wicked pack of cards.'

'Sorry?'

'Madame Sosostris and her wicked pack of cards.'

'You're not making much sense.'

'Oh, just something I was thinking about earlier, Eliot,

The Waste Land. Death by water rather than hanging, like the Tempest.'

Pale images of death, real or metaphorical, chasing the lady along secret ways in thrall to her scarlet lips and flowing hair.

'Come on, let's get up onto the bridge.'

He laughed. Unreal laughter, flesh into stone, these are pearls that were his eyes.

'What are you laughing at?'

'Oh, just not very tactful. Death by water? The bridge.'

'Oh, right.'

Puzzlement and concern were evident on her face as she turned away. They climbed the steps onto the bridge and looked out over the Grand Canal.

Death by water. He could jump now and be covered by that famous stretch of water. A fitting end for a hero or an artist, but he was neither. There would be no choice to make, no agonising failure, die at the right time, but this was not the right time; he had not yet begun to live.

Behind them the new, young, merchants of the Rialto, in tight T-shirts and jeans or short dresses and high heels, traded in cotton and silk, leather and gold. In front and below them, gondolas made their poised and precarious way over the wash from vaporetti and motoscafi. Tables with umbrellas, pizza, pasta, beer and wine lined the banks. In the calli the heat and humidity were oppressive but here there was air and space. The activity and open curve of the canal were reassuring, they drew out the urgency, the claustrophobia of circling thoughts. He breathed in the clearer air and rested his vision on the activity below.

They leant on the heavy stone balustrade. From time to time he allowed his attention to move sideways to Thelma and noted that she too seemed relaxed and happy enough to stand and watch. Streaks and high mounds of tinted cloud were beginning to pile up in the distance and an orange glow was filtering through the clouds against the lengthening shadows. His eye and then his mind were absorbed into their colour and shape, light and darkness. At length he drew back into himself, separated from the mounds of firelit, thunder-clouds. He realised that Thelma had grown restless. She looked at her watch.

'It's nearly six, I'm hungry.'

'Come on then; let's find a pizza place.'

He felt more content now, more self-contained, less dependant on making decisions about the future.

'Which way?'

'The restaurants might be starting to close on the other side of the bridge. We should probably work our way back nearer to San Marco.'

Thelma paused.

'What about that girl, didn't you say she ran a pizza place, or bistro or something? We could go there. I'd like to meet some people who live here.'

David felt his mind seize with panic and struggled to prevent his body from doing the same. She wanted to go to Francesca's to eat, of course she did, he should have seen it coming, it was obvious. It was equally obvious that they couldn't, but how to avoid it without seeming to have something to hide, that was not obvious at all. He had to say something, but his throat would not work and he had no idea what to say. Thelma seemed to take his silence for incomprehension.

'You know, the one on the note by the phone, Francesca wasn't it?'

It was, and now Thelma had used her name the two

worlds had finally joined, become real to each other. He had to speak.

'Oh yes, yes she painted George Wagner's, the American's, wife. Yes, that's right. We could. I'm not sure if I could find it again though.'

He was aware of the hesitation, the tension in his throat, the playing for time in his words, the contrived intonation. They had been married a long time and Thelma would be at least as aware of it as he was. What interpretation she would put on it he was not sure.

'What's the matter? Don't you want me to meet her?'

He turned away from the canal towards the shops on the bridge.

'No, it's not that.'

The girl who ran the leather and jewellery shop stood and looked above them to the sky. She called something to an assistant in the darkness behind her. Dark hair and eyes, short dress, tanned legs going into high heels, a gold chain on her ankle. He saw Francesca standing to say goodbye that morning, Francesca coming from the shower, Francesca's body warm and fragrant. He tore his mind away, aware that he was losing any ability that he may have had to act rationally.

'It's just that I only went there once and that was with the Wagners, they knew the way, I just followed.'

'Well let's try and find it. It'll be fun. Where's the map?'

He rummaged in his bag, glad to turn away, glad to do anything that broke the tension. He found the map and pulled it out; it unfolded as he did so. A business card fluttered to the ground. David, entangled with the map, thought of Enzo and went to pick it up but Thelma moved faster. She looked at it and read.

'Francesca Bizzoni, Pittrice. Via Riccati 46, Treviso. It's

her card. There's no Venice address but there are two phone numbers. One might be a Venice number, that might be it.'

He remembered now the card she had given him on that first night, when she had cried and wet his shirt, her uncle's shirt, against his chest. The net was tightening, the net, the webs, the skeins drawn from the spinning women of Burano. At least there was no Venice address.

'If we pass a phone box, I could ring I suppose.'

Thelma searched deeply in her handbag and took out her mobile. She slid open the phone and passed it to him.

'Here use this. It would be nice to be able to talk to someone. Less like being a tourist.'

She handed him the card and he looked at it Bizzoni, he was not sure that he had ever noticed her second name. He should have realised Thelma would have her phone with her. He imagined ringing and hearing Francesca answer. It was impossible, he had to find an excuse not to call.

'I think I know the general direction. If I feel we're going the wrong way, I'll try then.'

He tried to sound cheerful, enthusiastic about the idea. Perhaps she would see somewhere else that caught her attention and change her mind.

At the Campo San Luca, David felt that he was not far from Francesca's, something familiar, an atmosphere but he could not be sure. If Thelma forced him to take her there, then he could not be held responsible for the consequences.

Eventually, they came out into the wide expanse of the Campo Sant Angelo and he was aware, with relief that they had come too far. It was here that he had waited in the sun until Francesca finished work; nervously he realised that he could probably find it if he started from here. Tiredness and hunger were beginning to wash over him and he was in no fit state to face a major drama. He looked around. The leaning tower that had at first been mocking and then sinister, now seemed to suggest imminent collapse, destruction. Opposite, there were two places where they could eat. Empty tables with umbrellas, waiters standing idly in the doorways.

'Look, it's getting late and I think there's going to be a thunderstorm later. Why don't we eat here, we can always find, find the – the other place later in the week.'

There was something about the look on Thelma's face that told him that her intention to eat at Francesca's was not just a whim to be put aside at the sight of an empty table. She had studied the note by the phone for longer than was necessary, she would have noticed his awkwardness, then there were the phone calls, the messages. Perhaps it was obvious, and he had no choice anyway.

'Don't give up so easily. I told you, use my phone. It can't be far, just ring and get the address.'

It was out of the question of course, he had to make a stand of some sort.

'There's a perfectly good place to eat here, I don't know why you're so obsessed with going there today. We're both tired and hungry, let's just sit down and have something to eat and drink.'

Thelma's face became tense, the red marks showed on her neck.

'Give me the card. I'll ring.'

If he refused, it would turn into a petulant and childish squabble. He felt the anger rising through him as he found himself losing control. His head tightened; the blood pumped loudly. He could do it now; he could tell her. His throat began to loosen on the words when Thelma's anger broke first.

'For God's sake just give me the bloody card!'

He did so and watched her turn and walk away as she took the phone from her bag. He hated her thin cold back, the hardness of her walk. It would be the better if she rang, better if she found out through her own actions than through his telling her.

He watched her concentrate on dialling, there was a pause whilst she waited. She began walking again and he could see that she was speaking. She stopped and passed the phone to her left hand and wrote on the card. Then she finished the call and walked back towards him. As she got nearer, he could see that she was no longer angry, she was smiling.

'There we are, easy. Sorry but you just make me so cross when you're like that. Anyway, it's done now. Let me see the map. Where are we?'

He handed over the map and pointed out Campo Sant Angelo. It was pointless resisting now. She studied the map and then said,

'There we are look, we almost passed it.'

It was odd that he had not located Francesca's on the map before and as he looked, he saw that he had been right when he felt they were near at the Campo San Luca.

'Come on, it's not far and then we can sit down.'

No argument was possible, he could only go over the various consequences in his mind. The best that could happen would be a tense and difficult meal, Francesca would be out and the barman would either not recognise him or not say anything. The worst might be that Francesca, and perhaps Cristina and Enzo as well, would be sitting there as they walked in, her uncle would appear and lay him out for messing around with his niece. Or maybe Francesca and Enzo would come over to their table and tell him what they thought of him, in front of Thelma. Death by water began to seem extremely attractive.

As they retraced their steps, the route was painfully familiar to David. A route filled with memories of hope and excitement now overlaid with fear and foreboding. At the beginning of the week, the memories that drove him and formed the emotional basis of his experience reached back to his adolescence, enriched no doubt each time they had been replayed in his mind and set against the poverty of the present. They had gained colour and form from poetry, music and painting until they had created a world deeper and more satisfying than anything his daily life could provide. Set over that was the emotional, mental and spiritual turmoil of the last few days, changing everything that had existed before and yet gaining its power from the past as well, promising a new beginning.

Now, as he arrived with Thelma, what feelings and events would be added to this complex world of forces, of images and personal mythology built from his past, colouring his present and determining his future? What dark coils would thread their way through its promise and what black venom would seep into his veins poisoning the new life that had been held before him? What night and time would fall, to erase the words 'Incipit Vita Nuova' that, like Dante, he had seen written beneath all that had come before.

This time, at the Campo San Luco they turned and before him David saw the Calle that had led to his collapse into a river of darkness and to re-awakening in the arms of Francesca. He shivered at the memory of darkness. He felt again the warmth and smell of Francesca and, in deeper layers of memory, his mother: comforting in his illness, giving warmth and softness for his pain, soothing care when he could not breath, reassurance that if he slept he would wake again.

'There it is look, on the left.'

Thelma's voice burst through with the clarity of things: tangible, material. Thoughts gave way to present reality and his head echoed with the quickening rhythm of his blood, the river rising in his ears. The thought passed through his mind that perhaps he would collapse and sink through darkness into the void that waited under his feet but his legs felt stubbornly strong and upright. He knew that he would have to face whatever waited.

23

THE SIXTH DAY - PART FOUR

Thelma turned to go in. With a sense of unreality, floating, detachment from self, David followed. Desperately he searched the tables, trying to take in all at once. Most were empty. A small group, unknown, sat by the window. Behind the bar there was a solitary girl, not Francesca, perhaps the pregnant Maria. Three men sat at stools by the bar, again unknown.

'Is that Francesca?'

Thelma's question hit his raw and over sensitised mind; her name produced a surge of fear. He tried to focus on what she had said. There was no-one in the bar he knew or knew him; the initial panic subsided a little.

'Ah, no.' He scanned the tables as if he had not yet bothered to take in who was there. 'She's not here. Maybe she's gone home for the weekend.'

Out of immediate danger, David saw that he might have a last chance to go elsewhere.

'There was a place that looked good in the Campo San Luca. We could go there instead.'

'No, I like this, it's fine. Maybe she'll come in later but it doesn't matter, it was only an idea.'

She walked over to the side opposite the bar.

'We'll sit here.' She moved round behind the table and sat against the wall leaving David no choice but to sit with his back to the bar. He could make out vague reflections in the patterned glass on the wall but nothing else. He would not know if Francesca appeared, would have no warning. He turned to ask for the menus; the sooner they ate the sooner they could leave. The girl moved heavily across the floor; she was pregnant and almost certainly Maria.

'Buonasera.' She handed them the menus, paused and then said, 'Cosa desidera da beve?'

He scanned the menu and then said,

'What shall we have, wine?'

'Yes, we'll have red.'

'Are you sure?'

Thelma usually drank white.

'Yes, that's fine, it's probably better than the white anyway.'

'Una caraffa di vino rosso della casa.'

'Litro?'

Yes, he felt he would need more than a little help from the wine, from Dionysus, to navigate his way satisfactorily through the evening.

'Si, grazie.'

'Prego.'

She walked slowly back, lifted the flap and moved carefully through to behind the bar.

They studied the menus and he tried to stop his eyes constantly moving to the reflections in the glass on the wall. He recommended the pizzas and could not keep the scene of his first pizza there from replaying in his mind. If he had been in thrall to his early memories before, it was nothing compared with this. The last few days were pushing, bursting at his consciousness, insistent that they be let out.

Maria arrived with the wine. David took the large carafe from her and she smiled at him, a tired thankful smile. He smiled back, recognising a shared need for any considerate or comforting gesture, however small. They ordered pizza. With so few people in, he thought, it could not take long to arrive and then they could eat and escape. He filled their glasses.

'Well, salute!'

Thelma touched her glass on his

'Salute. Let's hope we can get you straightened out and have a good holiday in Venice.'

She had brought him into this now hostile environment but the warmth and concern in her voice moved him towards her.

He drank. The constant see-saw of changing emotions was becoming very difficult to manage. He finished his glass quickly and poured again, admiring the reflected light in the cherry-red moving stream and the darker red, blood-red turning in the glass. Dionysus would take care of him, one way or another, with or without vine leaves.

Only half following Thelma's blow by blow account of yesterday's meeting, David became aware of the phone ringing behind the bar. He turned in time to see the barman appear from the archway that lead from the bar to the kitchen and stairs to the flat. It was Giovanni, the first person who might recognise him. He lifted the phone and spoke, listened and spoke more quickly. He seemed annoyed and as he put down the phone, another man appeared in the archway. He was older, about David's age but balding and beginning to grow stout around the middle. David guessed that it must be Francesca's uncle, whose wardrobe he had inspected, the man whose shirt he had borrowed, a shirt he recalled that was still at the hotel.

Giovanni waved his hands into the air and shouted something as he disappeared back towards the kitchen. The older man, whom David just caught from the barman's tirade was called Alberto, followed also, speaking quickly but more quietly. The exchange was fast and heated but, as he strained to pick out words, David thought he heard Francesca's name.

'You're not listening to me, are you?'

'Sorry, I was; I was just distracted. Don't know what that was about.'

'Probably nothing, just a normal conversation. It doesn't matter. I need to get all this work stuff out of my system before I can relax. She should stick to her own side of things and not interfere.'

'Ah, yes.' David was perplexed by this and realised that he had missed most of the story that lead up to it. He was relieved when he saw Alberto appear with two pizzas but wondered if it meant that Giovanni had walked out and if so why. Alberto set the pizzas down with a flourish.

'Buon appetito'

'Grazie'

'Prego. More wine?'

David looked at the carafe which was now three quarters empty and said to Thelma,

'Shall we order some more now?'

'I don't want any more. There's plenty there and you've had a lot already.'

He felt that he would need to drink far more than that before the end of the evening.

'I shall want some more with the pizza.'

'Go on then, I'll drive back to the hotel.'

The ferry to Punta Sabbioni, the drive back, the hotel; how many as yet unknown events, dangers and crises were there to get through before then.

'Mezzo litro per favore.'

'Subito.'

He turned away, surveying the tables; moving around, inspecting, rearranging and checking everything with authority and firmness. He put some empty glasses on the counter for Maria to wash and said something quietly to her before disappearing again.

They ate and David drained the first carafe. Giovanni reappeared with more wine; whatever had upset him had been resolved temporarily at least. David remembered his muttered annoyance at Francesca when she sat talking over a pizza on that first day: perhaps she should have been working this evening; perhaps that was what the phone call had been about. The wine, drunk quickly, had pushed the sense of crisis and fear below a hazy surface. The pizza was satisfying with succulent black olives and salty anchovies. He felt better although still in danger. Thelma had returned to talking about work and he was trying to pay enough attention to be able to make intelligent sounding comments when she paused.

Whilst they had been sitting there, several more groups had come in and the tourists by the window had left. Each time, David had strained to see in the glass and then, cautiously, secretively, turned to discover who it was and what was happening. Each time he was nervous of arousing Thelma's suspicion but more so of not knowing. It was growing dark outside and Maria came and lit a candle at their table. David was aware behind him of more people arriving and tried again to make sense of the distorted images in the patterned glass.

The images remained blurred but as soon as he heard their voices there was no doubt. The words mingled with the wine mist in his mind; the haze that had helped, now became a fog where danger lurked, a fog that prevented thought and rational response. Clear and inescapable, Francesca's voice and Enzo's carried across the bar: the two most powerful and evocative sounds from his attempt to make a new life rise from the burnt-out shell of his past; Francesca, who had brought such a stream of overpowering emotion back into him, a stream that connected him to his past before his life had dried and crumbled; Enzo who had offered him help and advice, expansively shown him the possibility of overcoming weakness and failure, given him an example of artistic and practical success. What would Francesca think and feel when she saw him here of all places with Thelma? What would Enzo think after all his efforts to help him go forward and achieve what he had set out to do?

David could not turn; the images were no use. He tried to see from the corner of his eye, but they were out of sight. He heard the bar flap open and close and Francesca say something and Maria answer; then it went quiet again. He could bear it no longer and turned a little, enough to see the entrance behind the bar. They had gone, presumably to the flat upstairs. How long it would be before they came back, he could not guess. It could be a few minutes as they fetched something, or they might stay all evening. If he was still there when they came out, they would see him even if they had not done so already. There would be no escape.

He looked at Thelma, she had gone silent and was eating, concentrating unnaturally hard on the food. She had noticed something wrong, felt it from him. He filled his glass and drank. He drank and the silence continued. He could avoid the shame, the crisis, put it right, he could tell her now, he could will a new life for himself. He focused indistinctly on Thelma and tried to speak. There were no words adequate for this, no words to force the necessary crisis, to release a cataclysm. Whilst he struggled, Thelma looked up and spoke.

'That was her wasn't it? What's the matter, what is it you're not telling me?'

Still he could not speak, the alcohol paralysed the lies that otherwise might have run into his mind and yet he could not tell the truth.

'What is it?'

The irritation showed clearly now, her anger rising against his stupor. Her neck was red with blotches, he had no choice.

'She's, she's....yes it was. I, I'm not sure what...., we talked.'

'Was that her father with her?'

Thelma's voice became more precise, more insistent, more dominant as he lapsed into incoherence. It was a question he could answer.

'No, a friend, a sculptor.' He tried to breathe steadily and take advantage of this brief moment of clarity. 'He's an interesting...'

'And where was this?'

His mind reeled with alcohol and adrenaline and blurted out,

'A party, we went to a party.' And then tried to grasp control again. 'We just talked.'

He could feel her disbelief, her incredulity, her reading

of his face, the movement and sound beneath the words and said again,

'We just talked.'

He saw Francesca in the heat of their passion, he could feel her all around him, he could smell her presence. Sweat poured down his sides. Thelma would read images formed with such intensity; whether she knew it or no, they would tell her as assuredly as words.

Voices again and this time he turned, past caution; they came from behind the arch, Giovanni's voice raised, her uncle's quiet. Then the light flashed and Francesca appeared. Dark first in the arch and then golden in the bar light. His eyes met hers, clearly fixed on hers, no doubt, no possibility of mistake. Thought flooded between them, incomprehension, pleading, anger, disbelief; a roaring flow of unleashed, unspoken meeting between two minds.

A reflex action made him stand, an atavistic preparation for flight. Fiercely breaking their gaze, he turned from Francesca to Thelma who stared, fixed like stone. He stood and realised then that there was no longer a choice to make. He turned to Francesca, but she was moving fast and silently towards the door, the torrent of communication dead, a cold wall fallen between them. Enzo reached the door first and opened it for her. It closed and the darkness took them.

He stood and shook, fury at the self-accusations filling his head and the false interpretations that he had conjured into hers. The room receded into a blur; now he would bring all things down upon them.

'I danced with her and slept with her.' He heard his voice rising on a tide of its own, sounding without him, the room was shaking, her voice too was rising. He'd stop it, he'd stop it, he'd stop her shouting,

'We made love then, we made love, we slept together, sex, screwed, fucked.'

Still her voice came, still he had to drive it back.

'I came from her this morning. Is that enough? Is that enough?'

The lacerating claws dragged under screaming wings through his head. Blood would have blood, and would make the islands float on red. Such screaming and shaking and he would become the wings, the black wings, bat wings; he would exist no longer to this torment but become them, escape into the spiral winds of darkness.

His head exploded twice, and the screaming was Thelma's voice. She was hitting him. Other voices came between and colours moved, blurring across his eyes. He was caught by something hard and the movement stopped, the screaming stopped. He struggled but he was being held and when his vision began to clear he saw that she had gone. His breathing slowed and the pounding of his blood, that cracked through his head like gunfire, calmed. The hands relaxed on his arms. The room returned and he sat, aware of Giovanni and Alberto on each side.

She had gone, they had both gone. Thelma and Francesca both gone into darkness and he was alone. The words repeated and then again. They kept repeating until he had no choice. He surged to his feet and felt the chair hit hard on his leg; he felt the hands grabbing and voices shouting. It was easy now, all he had to do was run; this was what adrenaline was for. No thought, nothing but flight from the enemy and he was at the door, it caught, banged hard on his shoulder and then he was through it and running.

He ran with no idea of where he was or where he went. He beat his feet against the hard stones until he burst from the walls and stumbled up wide shallow steps. He came to the apex of a bridge, looked around, listened and heard the feet still pounding behind him. They were still coming: this time he was the pursued, they came for vengeance, to tear him apart. He dived forward again blinded with running, deafened with a howling in his head. He ran until his legs would not be dragged or forced further and, coming to a stop, he realised that at last he was alone.

There were no footfalls; he did not know when they had stopped following; his breath and his heart had drowned out the sound. Now he had stopped, his chest heaved with pain. Breath would not come, his heart could not keep up, he could not escape from the pain inside him. His legs gave way and he fell against a wall and then, still unable to breath, he rolled onto all fours, flanks heaving like a stag brought at last to bay: a stag ringed by darkness staring down into water and a reflected moon.

Before him, light floating on the water called to him and he shuffled towards it. It was still, dark, broad water. He looked up and saw the high dark curving shape of La Fenice, landing stage, wrought canopy, rising phoenix. A burst of lightning flashed across the sky, lighting the burnt shell of the opera house and breaking on the surface of the water. Still on all fours he was fixed by the rippling light that broke across the water and through his head. A deep rumble and then a triple flash. The dark tower rippled under the stroboscopic lightning. The water mirrored and then fragmented the sheet of silver fire. A splintering crash of sound shook and echoed. He moaned and drew himself closer to the water, slumped and aimed his weight against the railings by the steps that lapped beneath his eyes. His shoulder went forward onto nothing, his hands scrabbled on the cold wet marble steps. Another explosive crack and a flash of light, this time within his head. His body plunged forward. The cold and the darkness closed over him.

Nothing.

Then a chill awareness: something was happening, something was being done to him. His body was being lifted; a light flashed. His face was held down and covered and then darkness again.

Sensations: rocking in a dark tunnel, floating forward until the tunnel dissolved and the darkness grew into a limitless night. There was a surge, a pause, a figure towered over him, faceless at first and then the shadows began searching for a form, the formless became an animal head that quickly turned into the dark pointed head of a dog. Another surge and then more floating and rocking. Fear gripped him in an awareness of what was happening. The sickly smell of embalming oils advanced through his nostrils. He tried to scream but there was no sound, nothing. He had become a part of the orderly procession of the Book of the Dead. Now he knew. Soon they would begin to remove the viscera, place them in a jar; his brain would be extracted through his nose; he would be outwardly the same but inwardly empty. An explosion, a flash of light and a wail. There was a sharp pain and he felt cold liquid flowing into his veins; they were already replacing the blood.

He could sink, let it happen, finish, it would be by far the easiest. But there was so much not done; he had done nothing that he had been formed for; it would all have been a failure. He must try to fight it, to get away. A surge of will power tensed the muscles but there was no movement; he was already bound; the winding sheets were in place; even his head was fixed. It was all over; the mummification had begun. They would weigh his heart and then the last moments, or hours, time flowing into the timeless, were beyond any influence he could have. He would be carried forward by whatever process was ordained by eternity.

The dark tunnel closed round him again, he was dissolving into the darkness, indistinguishable from the night, soon duality would cease and there would be just the night.

Nothing.

Dim light returned and there was a lurching, a sudden angle. This time it was a different procession. Hoisted in a coffin they were mounting the church steps: plainsong chanting, a slow steady toll of the bell. Spicy sweetness, incense, seeped into his consciousness. Murmuring in the echoing space: requiem aeternam dona eis Domine; et lux perpetua luceat eis. The deep pipes of the organ swelled in waves: Dies irae, dies illa. Golden in the darkness, the day of judgement came to life before him: the golden wall of Santa Maria Assunta, judgement, separation, banishment and disintegration; fragments taken up and absorbed by the darkness.

The church rose above him but now he was sliding forward and moving smoothly, quickly, he was aware of trying to understand; the darkness was thinner, there was something there. White figures moving, hands or wings moving until they faded again, and all became night.

Night slid, then jolted, light filtered through. From the darkness he felt a softness beneath him, heard muttered words. He was aware of a presence and turned. His mother sat beside him, her cool hand on his forehead. The stars looked in through the window over her shoulder and he pushed his face into the rough tweed of her skirt. He cried as she sang that he was her sunshine. But she had been taken away from him and now he was alone. He had failed, he had wasted everything, it was no good, it had all gone and the promise of the future she had given him from her body and her love had been squandered, driven back into the ground through his failure. As he cried, her warmth faded. The stars grew closer until all he could see was darkness pierced by silver light.

24

THE SEVENTH DAY - PART ONE

Morning light fell softly on the wall, filtered by the translucent blinds. At first, he registered it as coming through the shutters at Angelo and Elena's but then a trolley rattled past waking him further. He looked up. Above the bed head was a screen showing the regular beat of his pulse. He struggled to sit and became aware of the contacts stuck to his chest. As he sat, a nurse in white came over to him; she smiled but did not speak. Reassured by her warmth he held out his hand and saw the canula inserted and taped to its back. She held his wrist and felt the pulse, putting more faith in her touch than the impersonal data on the screen. Another nurse arrived and they spoke together. He could not follow what they said.

The second nurse smiled and turned off the monitor.

' I will take these off now. You are well, I think. We must wait for the blood tests but I think there is no problem. Your head, it hurts?'

He felt the side of his head. There was a plastic coating on the skin.

'Not too bad, aches a bit. I can't remember much. What happened?'

Isolated images, sounds, pushed through into his mind as he asked: high walls, dark water, flashing lights, thunder, Thelma's voice screaming.

'You fell in the water and hit your head. We thought you had a heart attack, perhaps, but I think not. The first blood test was O.K. Now we wait for another.'

She unplugged the wires leaving the contacts stuck to his chest. He searched his memory trying to fill in some detail between the bare facts she had provided.

'How did I get here?'

'In the ambulance. You don't remember?'

He thought of an ambulance driving fast through the night, sirens and lights flashing. His mind was blank.

'No. What did you say happened?'

'You fell in the water.'

The water, of course, he was in Venice. In Venice it would be a water ambulance. He reformed the images and tried to find their equivalents in his memory. He tried to see a boat on the canal but found only dark water flowing in his mind with fear accompanying the image.

'Would you like something to drink?'

'Tea please, I should like a cup of tea.' and remembering where he was said, 'if that is possible.'

She smiled again, 'Yes that is possible, and some tablets for the headache I think.'

He was fully awake now and had become more aware of the dull thump in his head. He accepted the offer gratefully. She moved to go but then turned back to him.

'We could not find your name when you arrived. You had no passport or money but there was a card in your pocket from a woman. We phoned her and she came here.

She told us your name and that you were English. She said you could phone her in the morning. The card is on the cupboard by the bed. I will go now to get your tea.'

David reached for the card. Why had they not found his passport? He looked in the cupboard, it was empty, there was no sign of his bag or even his clothes. Without the bag he had nothing, no passport, no money, no credit cards, no phone numbers, no map. His camera and notebook were gone; he wore hospital pyjamas; he had nothing, only the card. He looked at it, badly stained but Francesca's name and phone number were still legible; they were all that he had left. He did not even have change for the phone call, perhaps the nurse would lend him that.

She returned with the tea and a phone on a trolley. The money was not a problem, it would be added to the cost of the treatment. Because he did not have his passport, they would have to sort that out, but he should not worry, it would not do him any good and she was sure it would be all right.

He lifted the receiver and began to dial the number on the card but stopped. His mind had turned to focus on the call, on what he would say and that had brought back more of the events from the previous night, particularly Francesca's bistro and Thelma. Thelma had gone, the events, the words that had led to her departure were blurred but he knew she had gone. Francesca's eyes penetrated the blur, she too was there. A dark opera driven by a plot he could not determine, buried as it was in his sub-conscious, was playing itself out; the opera was his life, he was the central character, and yet he had no control over it; it was written in his past, by the past buried where he could not interpret its meaning. He put down the phone. Could he rewrite the script, could he make a decision as to whether to bring Francesca back into his life?

He looked again into the empty cupboard. It was still empty, not an image or an interpretation of memory but a real, empty cupboard. Without a passport he had no identity, without money he could make nothing happen, without a map he was lost and without his camera or notebook he had no record of his experience. All that he was, existed in the unreliable darkness of his memory: the only way out was the number on the card.

He picked up the phone again and pressed the number pattern, a number lock to enable him to pass out of the darkness. The tones bleeped and the motif registered on a remembered sound pattern, bringing with it threads of feeling. Long tones resonated in his stomach stirring apprehension. At the other end the phone was lifted, and an acoustic space replaced the two-dimensional electronic sounds.

'Pronto'

The voice eclipsed all vague resonance and like a boulder thrown into a barely rippled pond, produced an explosion of emotion and image.

'Francesca?'

'David. How are you? What happened?'

'I was rather hoping you'd tell me. I'm O.K., a head-ache and a stitched scalp, nothing worse as far as I can make out. What happened is another matter; I'm not at all sure.'

There was a pause.

'Look, I'll come over, if you want me to.'

Again, a rush of fear in his stomach. He steadied his mind onto the only course of action possible, no wavering.

'Of course I do.'

'I'll be there in about an hour. Rest till then.'

He was surprised by the straight-forward singleness

about his mind now, uncluttered by tumults of cross currents; a course was set and he would not disturb it with unnecessary words or thought.

He lay back on the bed determined not to allow his mind to riot, destroying the new sense of purpose. His body felt heavy and peaceful. Sleep flooded into his thoughts: dark water running between the banks of barely emergent memories rising and covering them again.

Francesca's voice woke him, the sounds searching through the darkness to recover his consciousness. Before his eyes opened, he waited, absorbing the sense of her presence beside him. She spoke his name again and he was aware of other times when her voice had brought him from sleep or reverie, a note of return. He allowed a trickle of light between his eyelids and saw her shape dimly on the chair beside the bed.

'David.'

He opened his eyes and moved to prop himself on one elbow. The plastic tap, the canula inserted into his vein, caught the sheet and hurt. He winced.

'Are you all right?'

'Yes, fine.' He showed her the tap. 'It's just this thing.'

She smiled and he watched her smiling. He wanted to cross the space between them, to feel her warmth enter him, to feel less alone.

'I've lost my bag, passport and everything.' His eye caught sight of the strange pyjama sleeve that questioned his ownership of even his body. 'Clothes too, I don't suppose you know where they are.'

'Your clothes, the hospital is drying.' She wrinkled her nose. 'They will smell though; they will need washing. I have brought you some, my uncle's again.' She laughed a little. 'He was not so sure; you caused a big upset last night, but I told him you had many problems and were a good man really. I am not so sure it is true, but that's what I told him, so he has lent you some clothes.'

She was not so sure. Why should she be? Last time she saw him he was sitting with Thelma at a table in her bistro; it was inexplicable and perhaps unforgivable.

Events were returning to him.

'Thelma found your card and said she wanted to eat there. I couldn't stop her, she wanted to meet you; it must have looked awful.'

'Yes, awful and unbelievable. I called you some dreadful things to Enzo. Did she want to meet me because she knew about us?'

'No. Just to meet someone who lived here.' And then David thought back to the pauses and silences, the strange looks and wondered. 'At least that's what she said; I hadn't said anything but perhaps she guessed.'

'What caused the row?'

'She saw you, saw us look at each other. And after that I just told her everything, or enough anyway. I don't remember much; it's all pretty blurred; apart from everything else I think I'd drunk quite a bit.'

'I just saw you there and hated you.'

The emotion behind her words flashed through him and he felt a shiver of fear.

'I'm not surprised.' he paused, ' But you came when the hospital rang.'

'Yes, I came. Enzo said, "Let him drown with the rats." but I came.'

He could not trust words, but neither could he leave the ragged emotions hanging. He held out his hand and then grinned when he saw the plastic and tape. She smiled back and moved to sit on the bed. He tried to lean forwards to hold her, but she put her hand forward onto his forehead and he leant back. He breathed deeply and smelled her warmth, human in the antiseptic world of the hospital. She spoke quietly, only partly to him:

'I don't know why I came, but I did.'

The nurse returned with a doctor who felt his pulse again. The blood tests were fine. He would leave a letter to be given to the doctor in England and hoped he would enjoy the rest of his holiday. If he felt dizziness or sickness he was to return to the hospital. The nurse removed the contacts from his chest and the tap from his hand. He could go when the administrative details had been sorted out. Another nurse brought David's clothes in a carrier bag. Francesca had been right about the smell of dried canal water; he put the carrier bag, together with the clothes, into the waste bin.

He dressed in her uncle's things. She had chosen trousers and a shirt that were not too far from those he would have worn but it still felt odd to be dressed in another man's clothes. The shoes were the worst, he would buy some new ones but then remembered he had no money or any feasible way of getting any. He would not forget what it was like to have no clothes, no money and no means of defining his identity; this was taking new life, new birth to extreme lengths.

After phone calls to the consulate and then his bank, Francesca's guarantees and the filling in of extensive paperwork, he was able to leave. The hospital had been efficient, comfortable and friendly; he could not have asked for more.

Despite this, when they eventually stepped out from the vaulted darkness of the cathedral-like entrance hall into the brilliant sun of the morning, David felt as though he were emerging from the underworld, cheating Hades of a victim already processed for death. Shadowy memories rose and then sank, just out of sight in the inner dark and he shivered despite the heat.

They walked across the Campo Santi Giovanni e Paulo and then sat with a cappuccino. David was unsure as to whether the silence was a result of there being not enough or too much to say. He watched her dark hair fall to her shoulders and her profile as she stared across the square and hoped it was the latter. She was an extraordinary woman, girl seemed insufficient, and he did not intend to allow her to slip from his life if it was in his power to prevent it. He looked down at the borrowed clothes and determined to create a life that was not borrowed. The life that he had begun through childhood, that still flowed strongly when he first visited Venice; the life which he had then betrayed when he allowed fears and mundane demons to rend it and scatter its fragments across a desert of his own making. This had been his object in coming. Perhaps he was wrong when he felt he had no influence in the events and actions of the past week; he had arrived again at the purpose of his return to Venice with the first part fulfilled. Perhaps the influence was there but operating in a way he had yet to understand.

The waiter brought the bill and Francesca paid. This would not do; he would start by solving the immediate practical problems.

'I need to visit the consulate about my passport and then arrange for some money.'

'Of course.'

She looked down at her fingers on the table. It was a gesture he had noticed on their first meeting when they sat and talked after he had fallen in the calle, a torrent of darkness pulsing in his head.

'I'm sorry. It's always easier to talk about practical things.'

He put his hand over hers. 'I would never want to hurt you and I can't say how sorry I am about last night, about Thelma being there, about... everything.

She still looked down, now at both their hands, fingers wrapped around each other.

'I know. It's all right; I mean it wasn't all right last night but now, you've explained, you had no choice. I didn't make it easier either, saying that nothing was possible for us. I didn't want you to leave her though, thinking that I would replace her. I can't make that commitment and I wouldn't want to feel forced.' She hesitated and David guessed that his face had responded to the word, ' You know, obliged to. That wouldn't be good for either of us.'

The reality and complexity of the situation, hers and his, blew coolly through the heat of his new-found conviction. He had made a resolution that she would remain a part of his life, but he would have to accept that the terms might not be his. The crisis had brought a new realism into the dreamworld of their relationship.

'You're right, of course. We can still be together though, can't we, on that understanding?'

Her hand closed on his and she turned to look into his eyes.

'I'm here aren't I?'

He moved forward to kiss her. Their lips touched briefly with a new honesty, pretence no longer necessary, a real, not a holiday relationship.

'I'll have to ring the hotel and find out what's happening, about Thelma I mean, whether she's leaving. She must have gone off in a dreadful state. There'll be a lot to sort out but it couldn't have carried on. It was no good for her either.'

'Yes, do that, and sort out the passport and things. Do you remember where Enzo's studio is?

'I think so.'

'Meet me there when you're ready.' She felt in her bag. 'Here's one of his cards; the map's on the other side. I'll tell him the rats threw you back.'

He laughed. 'They were probably right.'

'You'd better have some money as well.'

He protested but she pointed out that it was ridiculous to walk around with nothing at all and he could pay her back when he had been to the bank.

He walked to the Rialto, passing the point where he and Thelma had seen the three-card trick played yesterday. Then he had nearly given up on his mission, had nearly accepted that there was nothing he could do to reclaim and transform his life. Now for better or worse it was decided, and nothing could ever be the same again. He had foreseen this when he had first arrived in Venice but had never really believed it would happen. He still felt weak and tired, so he caught the vaporetto, grateful for the money Francesca had loaned him.

The consulate was near the Accademia, not far from Angelo and Elena's, where the party had been. He completed the forms and was issued with a substitute passport. He rang the bank and arranged to collect money from the Banca Nazionale around the corner. He bought clothes and changed, carefully folding the borrowed ones and placing them in the carrier bags. Finally, when the practical problems had been solved, he could delay no longer the phone call to the hotel.

He went to the line of phones under plastic hoods by the front of the Accademia. They were all in use and he remembered the last time he rang Thelma from there with the loud Italian woman dinning in his ear. It was a long time ago, days only but a long time nevertheless. The wait increased the nervous apprehension in his stomach, but he was determined not to be swayed from the new certainty that filled him. Two girls who had been huddled together over one mouthpiece vacated a phone giggling. David moved quickly under the plastic canopy and lifted the receiver; it smelled of make-up and perfume. He pressed the metal numbers, not giving himself time for further thought, and waited for the tones. It was answered almost immediately.

'Hotel Europa, pronto.'

A familiar voice, the girl with red nails, an image from another dream.

'Buon giorno. David Green here. Could you put me through to Mrs. Green please.

'Momento. Room 38. The key is here but I will try.'

The phone bleeped as she rang the room but there was no reply. The receptionist came back on the line,

'There is no answer. I think perhaps she went out after breakfast.'

'Is there a message?'

'No, I don't think so. No there is nothing here.'

'O.K. I'll try later.'

'Thank you, Mr Green.'

So, she had probably been back but where had she gone now? Back to Venice, unlikely; to the airport, possible. He wanted to speak to her, to put things onto a more rational and satisfactory footing. She would have her mobile with her. He dialled again and got the answering service. He put the phone down. He could have left a message but did not know what to say. He would try again later.

He walked across to the framed map by the edge of the water and pulled Enzo's card from his pocket. He had done this before, at the same place after drinking and contemplating the vine leaves. This time he would not walk, he would stay away from the maze and use the broad clear water of the Grand Canal. He pushed aboard the packed vaporetto for San Toma. His head was starting to hurt again as the hospital painkillers began to wear off and he felt in his pocket for the small bottle they had given him when he left. He would take some more when he got to Enzo's.

He alighted at San Toma and walked quickly through the quiet calli. He found himself outside the shop window with wooden replicas of boats from the lagoon that he had seen when trying decide whether to take the risk of meeting Francesca again or not, the moment when he had nearly shut her out of his life and gone back, decisively, to Thelma. That had been a decision taken and then reversed when the undercurrents in his subconscious had taken over, had filled his body with an unwarranted excitement at odds with his thoughts. He had heard the sounds of voices in the calle as the twittering of dead souls and seen the Venetian boats as a sign that was where his new life lay.

How did it work, this world of symbolism that carried so much more weight than pure reason? It was like an underground river that received and absorbed the essence of experience and then acted on the small point of the present. It drew out the juice of the past and gave life to the present, a repository of inner meaning, inaccessible yet always acting and informing. He could influence and change it, but only if he worked through the medium of the inner river. Without the river, life reverted to a desert, a dry land of bones and red dust.

He walked to the end, past the small grocery shop and over to the doorway and entry-phone that led to Enzo's studio. He pressed the buzzer. There was a long pause and he pressed it again, wondering if they were out. This time the rusted speaker crackled and a distorted voice just recognisable as Francesca's answered.

'It's David.'

'Come on up.'

The front door buzzed. David pushed it open. Was the long wait and then Francesca's voice on the entry-phone a sign that Enzo was less inclined to forgive him. He climbed the dark staircase. Francesca was at the top.

'Where's Enzo?'

'Gone to get a shotgun.'

David felt his body stiffen and his voice caught in his throat whilst he forced his mind to weigh up his fears and Francesca's statement. Her laugh echoed in the stairwell.

'Silly! He's covered in plaster and gone to wash. He's been working all night.'

David laughed back, at his own emotional reaction that pre-empted and then paralysed rational thought. He climbed the last few stairs. At the top he put his arm around Francesca and kissed her on the cheek,

'Maybe he should have got a shotgun.'

'You'd better prove I was right to stop him.'

Die at the right time. He had to justify his second chance; show that it would not have been better if he had never been pulled from the water; make his new life count.

They entered the studio where the prancing horse looked finished. The naked female figure beneath it now looked more as though she were holding her hand out imploringly to the horse rather than fearful that she might be trampled. They went through to the kitchen and Francesca put fresh coffee in the filter machine. He remembered Enzo making coffee the morning after the party: his forceful, positive attitude so at odds with his own fearful and confused state. He had been very fortunate in the people he had met.

As the last drops of coffee fell from the filter cone, Enzo entered the room. His face looked tired but his eyes still radiated their penetrating force.

'So, the water rat returns eh?' He turned to pour the coffee. 'She is too good for you. I hang you up on a string, but she says I must be good. So, have some coffee. Ah, corretto si?'

Without waiting for a reply, he took a bottle of grappa from the shelf and poured a liberal measure into each cup.

'There, that is good. We sit down.'

He ushered them through into the small sitting room and sat down in the large worn leather chair. Francesca sat on a stitched leather footstool and leaned on Enzo's chair. Enzo gestured David to the other chair. He felt alone, isolated, on trial.

Enzo leaned forward and picked up a packet of cigars from the coffee table. He pulled one from the packet and lit it slowly, pausing to allow it time before putting it in his mouth and drawing on the richly aromatic smoke. As he released the smoke it curled lazily into rings. He watched them and as they dispersed, looked down and said,

'Have you spoken to your wife?'

David tried not to show the defensiveness that he felt.

'I rang the hotel; she wasn't there.'

'Where do you think she went?'

'I don't know, that is, she'd been back to the hotel but must have gone out again this morning.'

'What will you do now?'

'I'll ring them again later, check she's all right.'

'And then?'

He did not know. The pressure of Enzo's questions was

relentless, annoying too, but he could see no way round them without moving further away from Francesca.

'There are a lot of practical things to be sorted out.'

'And then the habits will suck you back. You will be comfortable with the person you know, in the house you know; Venice will be a long way away and you will make up the fight.'

Maybe, he thought. He could see Enzo's point; he would see how things went; what happened when he got back.

A crack, an explosion inside his head, a force sufficient to make him feel that he had rocked in his chair. What had happened to the conviction, the commitment he had made when he emerged from the hospital intent on creating a new life? Old patterns of thought and feeling were tugging at him, trying to force him to look back. Remember Orpheus who was promised everything if only he did not look behind him, back towards the underworld.

'I have come this far and I'm not going back now. I came here to discover how to create a new life and I'm not rejecting it however painful the birth pangs, and the growing pains.'

He heard himself speaking as if it were someone else. He waited for applause, for Enzo to recognise the effort of will that this had taken but he drew again on the cigar, watched, paused and then said,

'Drink your coffee.'

There was another pause while they drank and then Francesca said,

'What will you do?'

What could he do? What would he have done anyway with his sales career in ruins?

'I don't know, I really don't know. Just wandering and hoping, looking back to a time before I stopped being the person I identified with, has been effective in destroying the imposter, the usurper. Now I need a plan, something to take me forward, change everything.'

Francesca got up and went over to the hi-fi system. Enzo reached for his cigars and pushed the packet into the top pocket of his shirt. He spoke as he stood,

'If you do that, and you keep doing it then you will beat the rats. They will not let you go easily though, they will try to keep you, drag you back.'

Music began to play, a steady quiet tone followed by plaintive brass and his attention divided. He recognised it as Mahler and his mind was hunting for clues to identify it. Enzo spoke again.

'Every day you will need to fight them off, every day you will need to remember where you are going.'

He picked up his cup and left.

Francesca stood staring down at the floor. Brass in close harmony, the funeral procession towards the chancel of the church; as a motet the contralto voice came in clearly and strongly, stating, pleading:

> *'Der Mensch liegt in grösster Not!*
> *Der Mensch leigt in grösster Pein!'*

He felt the dissolving, spreading, washing away of pain and suffering in the sea of eternity. A tolling mountain bell, insistent as a funeral bell but higher, a bell demanding entry and then a folk melody of the mountains, folk dance transformed into a dance of the soul; spreading notes of the harp sounding an affirmation over death and a radiant peace.

Francesca's hand went down and turned the volume lower. As she turned towards him, David saw the glint of tears around her eyes.

'Auferstehungs-Sinfonie, Resurrection. I played that last night, not just that but all through, the happiness of the countryside, the hills and lakes, the fear of storms, the darkness and uncertainty that follow. Then that, the movement I've just played. We played that at my father's funeral. You must listen to it all, many times, it will bring you strength. It will also make you feel how you must do everything you have to do, not leave it for when the storms and darkness come. Do it while it is still summer in the fields and there is still dancing.'

David felt his own eyes begin to grow wet. A depth of pain and guilt grew into a dark chasm beneath him. She had gone in that cruel January of cold driving rain; he knew it was his fault but not what he had done. She had gone into the dark and he could never share a word or thought, find solace for pain or forgiveness for guilt; he could never make her aware of how much she had meant, the deep and unspoken, unspeakable love drawn and broken, forever closed. His breathing broke into an anguished sobbing and he cried oblivious to everything except the empty darkness within.

At length, the darkness thinned, and the sobbing grew lighter. He became aware of Francesca sitting on the arm of the chair, her hand on his shoulder. He reached up and covered it with his own. As his breathing steadied, he looked up. Francesca handed him a tissue and he wiped away the remaining tears. Her eyes fixed on his and she paused until he was about to ask her what she was thinking.

'I know what I should like to do now; it is up to you, but I think it would be a good thing for you too.'

She paused again and David prompted her,

'What?'

'There is an island, a small island where only monks live, monks and birds. They are Franciscans and the island is where St. Francis stopped when there was a storm. It is called San Francesco del Deserto, St Francis of the Desert. One of the monks is an old friend. I went there many times when I first came out of hospital and still go when I want peace. I could get Carlo's boat and we could go there. It would be good, good for both of us.'

It was not up to him; she had decided and her voice stirred him deeply into a belief that it was the right thing. His task had been to find life in the desert, the richness of fields and streams and the beauty of birdsong instead of a harsh and meaningless wilderness. San Francesco del Deserto was the right place for him to go.

'We'll go. I must try to ring Thelma again but then we'll go.'

'I'll speak to Carlo and get him to bring the boat around. He will do it for me. I'll tell Enzo what we are doing, and you can ring from here. I will go to see Carlo; he is only a few minutes away.'

When David was alone, the idea of ringing Thelma seemed much more difficult, but he had to find out what had happened, check that she was all right. His stomach sank and his head blurred as he heard the phone ringing at the other end. The receptionist answered.

'Can you put me through to room thirty-eight.'

There was a pause and then the extension rang; he had to speak to her. David felt himself willing there to be no answer, but the receiver clicked and Thelma's voice spoke,

'Hello.'

'It's David.'

'What do you want?'

Her voice was dull but challenging and he immediately felt defensive.

'I wanted to check you were all right.'

'Yes, I'm all right.'

He waited but there was silence.

'I fell in the canal, had concussion, it wasn't very clear.'

'Oh, I think it was clear enough.'

Anxiety twisted coldly in his stomach. It may have been clear then but now his mind blurred and his head hurt with the tension. He had to know what she was thinking.

'What are you going to do?'

'There's not much point in staying here.'

'You'll fly back.'

'Today if possible.'

'We'll talk when I get home.'

'Home?'

She was right, there was no home now, he had destroyed it.

'Well, we'll talk anyway.'

'I don't know, there doesn't seem much to talk about.'

'No, well practical things.'

'Look I'm tired of this, there's not much point is there? Goodbye.'

The phone went dead. Now he was knotted inside so much that it hurt; nothing was resolved. What had he hoped to get out of such a conversation? It could not have gone any other way and yet somehow, he had expected to feel better at the end of it. He felt a strong pull to go back to the hotel as fast as possible, to make it up, to explain it away as a brief moment of madness, blame his breakdown, anything to have a home and a routine again. This pain was his own doing, he had brought it all down around them. Enzo's voice came back to him, 'The habits will suck you back, you will be comfortable with the person you know.'

Yes, that was what he faced, a choice: comfort and a life unfulfilled in a meaningless desert, or pain and the possibility of a successful and fulfilled life. Which would he choose? He would choose the latter now, here with Francesca it was easy, but he knew that Enzo was right, and the challenge and the pain would come when he returned to England.

25

THE SEVENTH DAY - PART TWO

The small inlet from the Rio di San Polo, close to Enzo's apartment was in perpetual shade. Carlo's long white power boat, its engine idling, rocked gently towards the quay like a seabird.

David stood in the shadows looking out to the sun-glinting water beyond the walls. Since his arrival on the heavy ferry he had plunged through a dark maze with its incumbent images that sank and spiralled through his past and present. He had prevaricated and failed repeated trials until, when brought to an inescapable crisis, he had finally broken through and was ready to begin the next stage, the flight from darkness into light.

Francesca leaned behind Carlo and called,

'Where's Enzo?'

David looked back at the door to the apartments but there was no-one there.

'I don't know. I haven't seen him since you went.'

Carlo threw the painter over a mooring post climbed ashore and looked around impatiently. He said something to Francesca who put out a hand for him to help her out of the boat.

'Didn't he say anything about where he was going?'

David tried to remember any hint but there was nothing. They wandered back, past the Madonna with the white holy-child and the red devil-child and on towards the unicorn headed figure in a cloak that blew lightly in the slight breeze. They looked up and down the Rio del Frari but there was no sign of him.

Then from behind David but on the opposite side from the apartments there was a shout.

'Hey, io vengo, io vengo!'

Enzo was emerging from the small supermarket waving two bottles in one hand and carrying a bag in the other. David had thought that he and Francesca were going to be alone on the island, but it was beginning to look as if a party was planned. Francesca waved and Enzo waited as they quickly made their way back.

Enzo ushered David and Francesca towards the boat. They climbed aboard and sat on the bench seat across the rear of the cockpit. Enzo passed his shopping into the boat and Francesca stowed the bottles in a cool-bag under the seat whilst Carlo spoke to Enzo. David guessed that Carlo was giving some advice about looking after his precious boat. The reply did not seem to reassure him. Enzo laughed, slapped Carlo on the back and jumped quickly into the boat. He checked over the controls and then stood as he took the wheel.

'We are ready, we will have a good time - arrivederci!'

Looking over his shoulder he reversed slowly, the burble of the engines hardly increasing. Carlo watched and relaxed a little. He called something which may have been a last piece of advice, and then,

'Enjoy it, but take care eh?'

In response to the English, David waved and Carlo turned away.

Enzo took the boat gently down the Rio di San Polo and out into the main-stream of the Canale Grande. The engine note deepened a little as he joined the taxis and water buses, sliding through the choppy water of their wakes.

The vaporetti, pressed full with tourists, wallowed heavily and the taxis buzzed and droned like irritating insects on the water. Rounding the slow curve of the canal, David looked past Enzo to the Accademia bridge. Tourists crawled above them: cameras, coca-cola, guide-books. What were they seeing and what had it to do with him? Eliot, invoking Dante came to him again: a crowd flowed, London or Accademia bridge, undone by death.

Early in the week he had remembered the same lines and seen the damned stretching out their burning arms to an unknown ice-cream girl. Now she sat beside him, their bodily saviour and now his spiritual one? His guide at any rate, the girl who had led him, blind as Oedipus, through the burning desert away from the plague torn city of his past, cursed by his own unwitting actions. His wife was gone, all that constituted his life had gone and now her hand, Francesca's hand that might disappear at any moment, was all he had.

As they left the Accademia bridge behind them, he looked cautiously at Francesca. She was looking away towards the Molo and the pillars that guarded the Piazza San Marco. The breeze from the movement of the boat blew her dark hair in gentle swirls across her shoulders. A wave of love surged through him towards her: lover, mother, sister, daughter, he could not untangle the complexity of feelings and resonances of their relationship and the veils of past images that his own psyche threw over her. It was dangerous, this imbuing of another person with the collected significance of his life, an irrational act but one that seemed inevitable to the emotions. He put out a hand to her hair, half expecting her to vanish as an apparition. She turned and he leaned to kiss her, expecting a brief recognition. Her lips rested longer, not passionate but seemingly sleeping on his and then she half turned to rest on him whilst looking away towards Venice.

The canal widened and the powerful engine behind them deepened strongly, the bows rose and Enzo turned, a Hemingway figure grinning through his white beard.

'You are quiet, but now we have some fun eh?'

Francesca laughed and shouted something that was lost in the combined roar of engine, wind and water. She turned and pressed her lips to David's ear,

'We can go much faster, not here, in this part of the lagoon, later.....'

Her voice stopped abruptly as Enzo swooped to the left and she was pressed into his side. Water showered over them creating rainbows in the air and he slid into her as the boat turned back the other way. Enzo throttled back a little as they joined the main channel but still gained rapidly on the ferry in front, the ferry for the Lido and Punta Sabbioni, that had become so familiar to David from its decks. Enzo swooped again, this time across the larger vessel's wake, hitting each wave with a leap and crash of spray.

'David!' shouted Enzo, 'you hit them like that eh? No problem!'

Fast, head on, pick a course and don't turn or look back; was that what Enzo meant or was it just his own tendency to hear meanings for his own predicament in everything. He had been reborn as he left the darkness of the hospital, he had embarked on a new life but, as yet, it had no direction.

The boat wheeled closely back on itself to attack the waves again, a wall of water, like a Renaissance fountain, leaping into the air as it turned. He held Francesca tightly, laughing. They hit the waves harder this time, like the fairground as a teenager: like the Big Dipper with Jane out over the water at Southsea where it seemed as though you could reach out and touch the Isle of Wight; like hugging and laughing on the beach; like every high-speed, stomach-clenching experience of adolescence that mirrored the excitement of launching into a new life of one's own. And now, a second time, the privilege of another beginning born out of chaos, fear and pain. He could not afford to mess it up again.

They swept past the ferry and David looked up to see some children waving from its rail. He waved back and turned to see Francesca wave as well. He was happier and more relaxed than he could remember being for many years.

Now, to the right, David could see out through the entrance of the lagoon to the Adriatic. Enzo increased the speed again as they crossed the open water. The water was rippled with the remains of the sea's movement and a breeze blew. The boat planed high on its bow-wave, flying on water. The white heat of the sun's light flashed from its surface. He longed to turn out to the brilliant blue space of the open sea.

As they came into the shelter of the Jesolo peninsula he picked out the jetties of Punta Sabbioni, the magical point of departure for Venice: now and at sixteen. He felt that they should turn in towards it, but Enzo took the boat past and away along the pole marked channel towards Burano. He eased the throttle until the bows fell and the boat moved steadily again, through the water. The low drone of the engine scarcely disturbed the silence of the lagoon after its aircraft-roar at speed.

San Francesco del Deserto lay across their vision as an island of dark cypress spires, an isle of the dead, the isle of Avalon. Perhaps he had not progressed so far into new life as he had thought. Was he still, in fact, between life and death and being transported in a white swan barge to the island beyond life with Morgan le Fay at his side? What was there for him now? A twilight life among the shades, a passing into the land of spirits? He shivered as a cold rush flowed through his body.

'What's the matter?'

'It looks like a cemetery, a graveyard.'

She smiled a little, but he could see a seriousness in her eyes,

'It does, but wait, trust me.'

He did trust her, despite her disappearing, despite her reticence and her other lover in Milan, despite a constant sense that she was never what she seemed, he trusted her to guide him. The path was one that he felt might evaporate at any moment, no more substantial than the perfume of flowers, and yet it was all he had and he trusted that it was worth his following.

'I do, I'm not sure why but I do.'

'And I trust you," she paused but looked steadily at him, 'though perhaps with even less reason.'

The boat rippled quietly into the small cypress ringed basin, dark columns reflecting in its water. Enzo had grown quiet and thoughtful, or perhaps he was just being tactful.

'David, throw this when I am out on the land.'

He handed him the painter and stepped lightly from the

boat. David threw the rope and Enzo secured it to a mooring post.

'Bring the bag, the cold one with the wine and bread. We will have it here.'

David reached under the seat and got the bag whilst Enzo helped Francesca onto the path.

The small church of the monastery was directly ahead of them. From the path, the cypress columns seemed less funereal than they had from the water. They passed through them and now they saw them from the other side. He became aware of a rich scent of flowers filling the air, transforming him from within as he breathed their spirit into his blood. Without the sound of the boat engine, a ceaseless chorus of varied bird song poured through the penetrating blue of the sky echoing in his ears until all other sounds, even that of his own thought, had been banished. Francesca squeezed his arm:

'You see, we are beyond the grave trees, and there is more.'

A statue of St Francis was set into the wall of the monastery. A party of tourists was just emerging from a tour; three monks appeared, showing them out. Francesca went over to one of them and greeted him, gesturing towards Enzo and David as she spoke. The monk indicated the doorway and she beckoned them to join her.

'It is not usually possible to go round without a guide,' she explained, 'but they will make an exception for us; Brother Lorenzo is happy for me to show you round.'

Brother Lorenzo was young, in his twenties with soft brown eyes and long dark lashes. David and Enzo shook hands with him as he gestured them in.

'There is a connection with the nuns who looked after

me when I was in hospital.' Francesca explained. 'I often used to come here when I was recovering.'

David and Enzo walked behind her into the nave of the small chapel.

Nave, navy, navel: boat-like and central to all, ark of renewal above the storm enraged flood; a sanctuary from which to deal with the turbulent might of the sea. He thought of the larger ship and the green sea marble of Santa Maria Assunta on Torcello, the Crucifixion and the tear of the Madonna as she looked towards the universal drama of the Last Judgement. He remembered the dryness of the years between his teens and the present: cracked river beds, red dust, the death of flowers, drought where nothing flowed. Venice, where water and stone were balanced, reflecting each other, harmonising each other's shapes and reflections: that was how the soul should be.

They went out into the flowered cloisters and Francesca told them of the well of St Bernard that had fresh water always, even, by a miracle, when it had dried up elsewhere. There was always water, even when it could not be seen, even in the worst drought, deep within, in the well of miracles, it was there if you looked hard enough, if you were desperate enough.

Beyond the cloisters were the gardens, more magical because guarded by the funereal spires of cypress. Elysian fields of flowers and birds creating perfume, colour and a tumult of music, the perfect place for St Francis.

'His offering to God was to rebuild a small and derelict chapel outside the walls of the city on the Via Francesca.'

She had become serious and seemed to be speaking in something of a trance. David smiled when she said the name of the road, but she did not notice.

'It became the centre of his new spiritual life, from

which everything else grew, radiated like the rays of the sun. In rebuilding the church, he rebuilt himself and the world.'

David waited for Francesca to continue but she stood, silently looking back at the chapel. The bird song grew sharper and clearer, the colours brighter and the perfume from the flowers deeper and more pervasive, their life trembling more vigorously, visible through the thinning shell of their separate being. The moment flowed into a timeless vortex.

He was first aware of his breath and then the bird song. As he came back into his body, he felt cleansed, all tension gone and yet fired with new energy. As movement came back to his muscles he looked around. Francesca stood by the flowers ahead of him, but Enzo was nowhere to be seen. His legs did not respond when he first tried to walk towards her but then their weight eased, and he walked with great awareness of every step. She had acquired an ethereal quality that made him wonder if his hand would pass through her as he reached out to touch her back, but his fingers alighted on skin like a flight of butterflies.

She turned and smiled, dipping her head as she reached for his hand. They walked between the dark hedges and bright flowers serenaded always by birds.

Around the corner they found Enzo. He had opened the wine, and unpacked the crusty bread, olives, tomatoes, anchovies and goat's cheese. Even outside, their smells clustered in on David's heightened senses with a primitive pungency. Francesca went first to Enzo and kissed him and then they sat and laid out the food. Enzo poured the deep red wine and raised his glass,

'To the life, from the spirit.'

And they all drank. They then broke into the bread and ate saying little. A clarity of peace surrounded them, joined them, washed over them and through them joining them into one body.

After they had finished the meal, they sat in the sun and soaked up its golden warmth. The wine created a glow in the afternoon that spilled its secret fire into every part of David's being. He heard the cymbals of the Maenads and felt the energy of Dionysus high in the pine scented hills. If these gods and these images could stay with him, if he could dwell in the sanctuary that let him worship them and absorb their strength, then he would manage. He would create new life built in the image of the dreams that sprang up from his childhood and appeared lost for so long. He would do that which he had come to do, water would spring again in the desert and flow through the hidden paths of his imagination like the canals of Venice.

They stayed in the garden, hymned by birdsong and wreathed in the scent of flowers, until the fierceness had begun to leave the sun's heat. Enzo said that he had to meet someone on Burano; they could take him there and then take the boat back; Francesca could manage it perfectly well. They rinsed the glasses under a small fountain, collected the few remaining things together and packed away in silence.

As the boat floated out from the jetty and Francesca gently nudged the engine into life, David felt an ache within him at leaving this enchanted island, one with all the enchanted islands of stories, myth and painting; an ache too at leaving a sense of home that he had not experienced since his mother's death, a centre whose identity was at one with his own.

They crossed the short strait to Burano, the brashness of the brightly coloured houses a sharp contrast to the mystery of San Francesco. As they drew to the quay Enzo stood to leave the boat.

'Remember, David, it is when you are in England that it will be hard. The habits, they will take over if you do not stay awake to watch for them. I hope we will meet again David.'

He kissed Francesca and held David's hand. David felt he was saying goodbye to his father - the relationship he had never resolved or come to terms with. The possibility of not meeting again made him want to hold on to Enzo's hand, hold on to his father and find and mend the fractured bond that lay broken inside him, making the task of healing more difficult. He thought back to playing the piano after the party and his talk with Enzo who detected the self-effacement in his voice when he spoke of music and interpreted it as shame. He heard Enzo's voice again saying, 'It's good to be a musician.'

The force of awakened energy within him was the key but there were still blockages to the new life that needed to be worked out.

They parted and Francesca sent the boat curving away out into the stream. David watched her as she concentrated on their course, her dark hair floating in the breeze.

'Thank you for San Francesco, you were right, it is an extraordinary place.'

She turned quickly and smiled.

'It was also the right place, for you and for me. It is like returning to Eden.'

That was exactly what it was like, no wonder it had been so hard to leave again. He put his hand into her hair and kissed her cheek. They had been together in the garden of Eden, a glimpse to help them on the return journey.

She was quiet and then laughed, sensual energy dancing

486

in the laugh like Maenad bells.

'We can turn out of the lagoon after Punta Sabbioni, the boat is very fast.'

Yes, that was what he wanted. Go out to sea, let the white bird fly her fastest.

'What are we waiting for then?'

They turned across the widening expanse of water the roar of the engine broken by the rhythm of the waves. White spume left her sides like foam from a horse's flanks, the foam that bore Aphrodite from the waves. Francesca pushed the throttle forward and the boat leapt ahead riding over waves that beat at the hull like hammers.

She shouted, her voice blending with the wind, water and crescendo of the engine.'

'There is nothing now between us and Greece.'

Cithaeron, mount of Oedipus and of Dionysus, mount of music and the lyre. The dark green, pine scented resinous hills of Attica with goats poised on rocky promontories, horned gods of the mountain. The cymbal clash and the frenzied, climactic dance of the Bacchae, ungovernable vessels of the god born in a lightning blast.

David placed his hands on the wheel and there was something in his face that lead Francesca to withdraw hers. A spraying fan of water exploded into the sun, dazzling his eyes and covering the sky in a rainbow veil. He lowered one hand to the throttle and pushed it as far as it would go.

He felt an uncontrollable force rising through him, and into the engine's howl and thunderous drumming of the water a voice released itself from the bottom of his being, an ecstatic cry:

'Evohé!'

It continued until, as his breath ran out, he finally recognised its sound as his own.

26

THE SEVENTH DAY - PART THREE

The white boat touched the quay lightly, settling against the stone like a seagull. Carlo walked towards them, having descended from his vantage point on the Accademia bridge. His eyes ran quickly over the boat and he relaxed visibly as he saw that all was well with her. He tied the painter to a ring, looking contentedly along the deck as he did so.

'You have a good time, yes?'

Since he had spoken in English, David replied,

'Yes, thank you. She is a wonderful boat, very fast.'

As he spoke, he felt Francesca tense and he realised that it would not be a good idea to reveal all the details of what had happened. Carlo darted his eyes to Francesca and spoke quickly. He heard her mention Enzo's name and her reply appeared to allay any suspicions he might have had. He put out his hand and helped Francesca onto the quay and then did the same for David who said,

'Once again, thank you very much for making this afternoon possible.'

Carlo put his hand on David's shoulder,

'I do anything to help Francesca. And now I must get back.'

He untied the painter and stepped lightly into the boat as it began to drift. The boat moved back into the stream and David watched it go regretfully as if it were a living thing that had taken part in the Dionysian mysteries of the afternoon.

There was a moment of awkwardness, no longer than a breath but a moment in which they were at a loss as to what could follow the visit to the isle of the dead and the start, at least, of his resurrection. David turned and saw the rich layered green of vine leaves that mounted and spread across the wall above the little bar.

'I think we deserve to drink there.'

'Deserve?'

David paused, unsure as to whether he could explain, but then gathered his confidence and said,

'Vine leaves in our hair? For the victory we have won.'

Francesca's smile flashed vividly but then faded,

'Perhaps, but there are still many things that are unsolved.'

They sat and David ordered a carafe of red wine with which to toast Dionysus and his victory over the deadly and mundane. The sun had cooled but the corner by the wall was a warm sun trap, keeping in the fire. They sipped the cool wine and despite Francesca's reservation he felt a relaxed sense of triumph spread through him. Francesca, too, relaxed as they drank and moved towards him as she said, 'What will you do now?'

It was not something about which he wished to think at that moment but sensed it was important to the course, even the immediate course, of their relationship.

'I suppose that I should go back, deal with the mess I have created or at any rate, uncovered.'

She answered quietly,

'Yes, you should.'

'But I don't know that I am strong enough yet, that the new life is able to withstand the strength of the old one. I don't want to be dragged back into the wilderness again.'

Francesca did not answer. She paused and sipped again at the wine, resting her eyes on her fingers curled around the glass. She breathed deeply and finally drew her gaze from the glass and turned to rest it on David's eyes. He felt a momentary shudder from their force.

'I spoke to Renato yesterday.'

David felt his breathing stop.

'On the phone, after you left. He has business next week, in America, and wants me to go to New York with him. He has a friend with a gallery there. I said I didn't know and that I would get back to him.'

He breathed again, slowly. At least it was only on the phone and at least she was not sure. He wanted to tell her again that he loved her, and they should stay together but he had admitted already that he still had work to do to resolve his past. Instead he said cautiously,

'It sounds as though we both have things that are unsolved.'

'Renato has been very good to me and this week has somehow helped the guilt to go away.'

David forced a smile at the irony of this and said,

'I'm glad to have been of some use anyway.'

He immediately regretted it as Francesca stood quickly and walked to the water's edge. He paused and then went over to her and put a hand on her shoulder. She lowered her head as she turned and when she lifted it her eyes were wet. She pulled him to her and said softly,

'These are not easy things. I'm sorry if I have said it badly but there is no simple way.'

He felt the heat of their relationship receding, being pushed surely into the distance.

'I'm sorry too; I shouldn't have said that; you've always said that I should not..., should not...'

She moved away and wiped the dampness from her eyes.

'No, no. You are right. We both need time to think, to reflect; but you must go, there is Thelma.'

He thought of the last phone call to Thelma and the blank indifference in her voice.

'I don't think there is any hurry for that. I tried to speak on the phone, but she made it clear there was nothing to say.' He paused, breathing deeply before saying, 'There is no need to stay here. We could go somewhere, get away and think.'

'Together?'

'Why not?'

To his relief she smiled,

'Many reasons but perhaps not all good ones. I think I must go to New York next week; it is important to show and to sell my paintings. Otherwise, I have to sell too much ice-cream.'

David forced a smile as he held back the churning, conflicting currents of emotion that surged through him at the thought of Francesca with the confident, successful Renato. He could not let her see them. She spoke again, softly,

'- but afterwards, maybe.... Where do you suggest?'

'The mountains? Venice is a wonderful place, but it is all

inward looking. Dreams, images, reflections. The mountains might give us a clearer view.'

She paused and to his surprise drew close to him and he felt her eyelashes against his neck. When she looked up her smile had returned.

'Yes, that is possible. We must not be too serious about these things. I know a small mountain chalet above Cortina that my father and I used sometimes. I haven't been there since he died but I will ring and check with the owner, ask if it is free when I have returned from New York.'

'I may have to go to England while you are away. I could fly back the next week, or even drive again.'

'You need to sort things out with the hotel; find out what Thelma is doing. Many things, practical things need to be done; things that didn't seem to matter this afternoon. You must go back to the hotel and to England, but I will find out when the chalet will be free.

David felt a strong, singing flow of energy running through him as it had when he had finally taken the wheel of the boat at speed. There was still doubt and there was no knowing or guessing the eventual outcome, but it was riding forward and he at last had the courage to let it go.

They walked back across the bridge and along the now familiar way to St Mark's square. The warm sun of the early evening spread its gold across the emptying Piazza to meet the gold of the mosaics. Competing bands blended around them into a confusion of sound resonating with the confusion resting within.

By the pier on the Riva della Schiavoni they clung together. They had planned to meet again but knew that either of them could make this their last parting. Images of the week ran chaotically before David's vision: stories created and now plunging out of sight to join rich sea of myth below his consciousness; stories that bound him into his past woven from love and guilt, hope and fear, faith and doubt. He looked long into her eyes before their grip relaxed; they kissed softly and moved backwards and away.

'I'll ring you at the hotel tomorrow.' and in response to all their uncertainties she added, 'I'll ring, we'll speak. Till tomorrow. Ciao.'

They had moved apart, she waved with just her fingers and walked away. He called after her,

'Ciao.'

Without turning or pausing she raised her hand and waved her fingers once again. He felt his own eyes wet this time and his throat blocked. He turned and moved with the slow crowd on to the ferry.

He quickly climbed the stairs inside to reach the upper deck and reached a seat by the white painted rail. He scanned his eyes along every stone for a sight of her, she might have turned to wait, but there was no trace.

He closed his eyes and saw her dark eyes looking into his as clearly as if she had been there. He had to build his life on this new foundation that was in fact the old one. Her eyes, he knew, drew a part of their magnetic force from the long-hidden image of his mother's eyes deep in his psyche, in his mythology. If he could regain the child that she had born and tended, the child that he had been, then he could find his purpose, his mission, as San Francesco had found his mission and created new life. He must not confuse and dissipate this vision as he dealt with the everyday events that would begin to crowd in as soon as he disembarked. He must keep returning to the vision whether he went to the mountains with Francesca or no, regardless of anything and everything.

The wind on his face told him that the ferry was moving.

He opened his eyes and looked back, watching the receding image of Venice in the setting sun until she had merged with the sea.

As Venice merged with the sea, he willed his new mission, his vision, to merge into the darkness of his mind from whence it could re-emerge and guide him. As he did so he recalled a dream from earlier in the week, which night he could not say. There had been a stone egg inscribed with letters of fire. Now he held it in his pocket and in the warmth the egg that had glowed had come to life and it was hatching, a baby bird was beating its way through the shell.

Printed in Great Britain
by Amazon

28022356R00283